DAY OF
NO RETURN

(*Until That Day* published in 1942)

(*Jour sans retour,* published in French, 2002)

(*Bis zu jenem Tag,* published in German, 2002)

(*Senza Ritorno,* published in Italian, 2003)

DAY OF
NO RETURN

(Until That Day)

Kressmann Taylor

Cover art by Catherine Wright Taylor

Until That Day, Copyright, 1942, by Kressmann Taylor
"The Real 'Karl Hoffmann,'" Copyright, 2001, by Charles Douglas Taylor
Day of No Return, Copyright, 2003, by Taylor-Wright Corporation

To order additional copies of this book, contact:
Xlibris Corporation
1-888-795-4274
www.Xlibris.com
Orders@Xlibris.com
18116

ACKNOWLEDGMENTS

In order to tell again the fictional story of "Karl Hoffmann" and to bring out the very real true story that lay behind it, I have been greatly assisted by the following persons, who were friends, relatives, and associates of the author and her subject, Rev. Leopold Bernhard.

I would not have been able to present the wealth of new information, nor to verify the authenticity of the old, without the generous and unstinting aid of

Christopher Brown
Reference and Research Assistant
Concordia Historical Institute

Joel Thoreson
Assistant Archivist
Evangelical Lutheran Church in America

Helen Kressmann Taylor Crisp
daughter of Kathrine Kressmann Taylor

Thelma Bernhard Nesbitt
daughter of Thelma Kaufman Bernhard
step-daughter of Leopold Bernhard

Dr. Arnold Keller

Milton Kotler

David J. Zubke

Prof. Robert Jenson
Senior Scholar for Research
Center of Theological Inquiry

Rev. William Kirsch-Carr
Archivist, Metropolitan New York Synod

Charles Douglas Taylor
son of Kathrine Kressmann Taylor

INTRODUCTION TO THE 2003 EDITION

This new edition of Kressmann Taylor's second book, *Day of No Return*, first published in 1942 as *Until That Day*, contains the complete original text, plus several major additions: an up-to-date Introduction; a final "Afterword: The Real 'Karl Hoffmann'," revealing the long-secret true identity of the person whose story lay behind the fictional character; the beginning of an unfinished autobiography by that man, and a signed copy of his 1943 "Curriculum Vitae." The original introduction, by Kressmann Taylor, has been left intact, as has her text, so that the reader will have the advantage of the story's first impact, plus historical perspectives, insights, and references.

Author Kressmann Taylor, "the woman who jolted America," was born Kathrine Kressmann in Portland, Oregon in 1903. Her father, Charles August Kressmann, was a banker, and a first-generation American, having been born in Chicago in 1870, only days after his Alsacian/German parents had arrived in the United States. Her mother, Susan Starr Kressmann, was a tenth-generation descendant of a New England family dating back to 1634 in Massachusetts and including Revolutionary War soldiers, early manufacturers, and a doctor who was one of the founders of Harvard University.

A precocious child, Kathrine won her first writing prize at age eleven, First Prize in a contest for children up to age sixteen; with the prize money she bought herself a complete set of the *Book of Knowledge*. Graduating from high school at age seventeen, and the University of Oregon at 21 (with a double major in English literature and journalism), she then moved to San Francisco, where she worked as an advertising copy writer, in her spare time writing fiction and poetry for some small literary journals. In 1928 the editors of the *San Francisco Review*, a magazine she particularly liked, invited her to a party where she met Elliott Taylor, the dapper, successful, and engaging owner of his own advertising agency; they were married within two weeks. Three years later, when the Great Depression had put an end to both their jobs and the advertising industry, the couple bought a small farm in southern Oregon, where they literally "lived off the land," growing their own food and panning gold, taking their two small children, and adding a third (of four) in 1935.

In 1938 they moved to New York, where Elliott worked as a trade-paper editor, and Kathrine finished writing "Address Unknown" which Elliott showed to *STORY* editor Whit Burnett, who immediately wished to publish it. He and Elliott decided that the story was "too strong to appear under the name of a woman" and assigned Kathrine the literary pseudonym "Kressmann Taylor," a professional name she accepted and kept for the rest of her life, largely because of the success of "Address Unknown."

When "Address Unknown" was first published in the United States, in *STORY* magazine in September, 1938, it caused an immediate sensation. Within ten days of publication, the entire printing of that issue of *STORY* was sold out, and enthusiastic readers were mimeographing copies of the story to send to friends. National radio commentator Walter Winchell heartily recommended the story, and *Reader's Digest* magazine put aside its long-standing no-fiction rule to reprint the story for its more than three million readers.

In 1939, Simon & Schuster printed *Address Unknown* as a book and sold fifty thousand copies—a huge number in those years. *The New York Times Book Review* raved, "This modern story is perfection itself. It is the most effective indictment of Nazism to appear in fiction." The United States was at this time officially neutral, but many in America, including the Roosevelt administration, openly supported the British in their singular war against Hitler. So, when a young German cleric, who had fled religious persecution in the Fatherland to seek asylum in the New World, wished to tell his story and expose the clandestine Nazi domination of the Lutheran Church in Germany, the FBI was immediately engaged to arrange his secret meeting(s) with the most eminent anti-Nazi story-teller in the U.S., Kressmann Taylor, who took his real life story and fictionalized it into this, her next book, *Until That Day*, published in 1942.

With unofficial government backing and major private financial support, *Until That Day* would probably have had an early success to challenge that of *Address Unknown*, but before the book was off the press, the Japanese bombed Pearl Harbor, fascist-support sentiment dissolved in America, and the nation went to war. The book was well received, and sold well, but did not have a second printing or paperback edition, and was never translated or distributed beyond the U.S.

In 1942, Elliott and Kathrine moved to another farm, in Pennsylvania, near Gettysburg, where, because of her literary reputation, Kathrine was soon offered a guest lectureship at Gettysburg College, a small Lutheran-related liberal arts college. Her first course attracted such student interest that she was offered a full-time instructorship after the first year, and she continued to teach there for nineteen years, becoming the first woman ever granted professorial status, and the first ever granted tenure.

Following the war, both *Address Unknown* and *Until That Day* slipped from public notice and were largely forgotten. Elliott Taylor died in 1953, and Kathrine lived on as a widow for the next 13 years, continuing to write and to teach writing, journalism, and humanities at the college. Retiring in 1966, she sold the farm and moved to Florence, Italy, where she experienced the great flood of the Arno river in November of that year—resulting in her third book, *Diary of Florence in Flood*, published to critical acclaim in America and England (as *Ordeal By Water*) the following spring.

En route to this Italian "retirement" in 1966 on the Italian Lines' *Michelangelo*, Kathrine met the American sculptor John Rood. The two felt an immediate attraction, had a shipboard romance, and were married the following year in Minneapolis,

Minnesota, where he made his home. Thereafter, they lived part of each year in Minneapolis, part in the Val de Pesa, outside Florence. Even after Rood's death in 1974, Kathrine kept both homes for many years, living quietly in each six months a year, simply as Mrs. John Rood.

Then, in 1995, when she was 91 years old, Story Press reissued *Address Unknown*, "to commemorate the 50th anniversary of the liberation of the concentration camps," and because, as *STORY* editor Lois Rosenthal wrote, its "significant and timeless message . . . has earned it a permanent place on the bookshelves" of America. The book was well received, and Kathrine, happily signing copies and granting television and press interviews, was gratified at its re-emergence, this time with the stature of a classic of American literature.

Kathrine Kressmann Taylor Rood died the following year, in July, 1996, late in her 93rd year, sharp-witted, perceptive, and enthusiastic about life until the end. Shortly after her death, a copy of *Address Unknown* came into the hands of the French publisher of Editions Autrement, Paris. He saw at once its relevance to the entire European community, both those who had lived under the Nazi domination and those who had not. He determined that a French translation must be undertaken, and that translation hit the French best-seller list in late 1999. Since then more than 300,000 copies have sold in France, and translations have been done in sixteen (as of January 2003) other languages, around the world.

Demand from readers the world over for other works by Kathrine Kressmann Taylor has led to republication of this, her second book, published in 1942 as *Until That Day*, in French in 2002 as *Jour sans retour*. Its popular reception in that edition led to extensive research and new background materials for this new updated edition, printed in German (*Bis zu jenem Tag*, 2002), Italian (*Senza Ritorno*, 2003), and now in English: *Day of No Return*, by Kathrine Kressmann Taylor.

Charles Douglas Taylor
son of Kathrine Kressmann Taylor

INTRODUCTION
(1942)

KARL HOFFMANN'S story is told here substantially as he told it to me. If you should ask me, "Is it true?" I can only reply that it couldn't be otherwise. I know that, because I have talked to the man. He is a broad-shouldered, humorous-faced man of thirty, diffident when he speaks of himself, controlled when he tells of the violence and tragedy he has had a part in; but when he speaks of what he believes, the words, in his mouth, become strangely important and new, as if they were being discovered for the first time.

The man, like his words, is alive from the inside out. He is not naïve; he is a sophisticated man, a scholar, but his scholarship is something that he pushes aside so that the intensity within him is all you see. You begin to think that if it were possible to subtract from him the belief that fills him there would be nothing left.

If you were told that he has recently escaped from Germany, where he lived through years of persecution, you would be startled. There is something missing from him that you have become accustomed to seeing in the refugees who have poured into America, the fear, the haunted eye, the shaken spirit. This young country pastor did not learn to be afraid.

The story of what happened to him and to men like him in Germany is something of a modern miracle. The Nazis had prepared a perfect plan. By a subtle scheme that looked on the surface like co-operation they would take over the Lutheran Church and use it to serve their purposes. They would disarm the churchmen and place their own men at the head of a united Church. They would control the whole organization and it would be an easy matter to destroy any dissenters. The Church, with its great authority, would become a strong tool for the dissemination of Nazi doctrine.

The scheme was foolproof. The first steps went off with the clocklike precision the Nazis had anticipated. All the outer appurtenances of churchly power fell into their hands as they had planned. From their material viewpoint, the thing was accomplished. But gradually they became aware that something was wrong. They controlled the Lutheran Church but they did not control it. The organization they had their hands on was not the thing itself. A force was resisting them, something they could not put their hands on—a belief.

Because they were materialists the masters of Germany turned to attack this resistance with physical forces. They had all the power; they were used to seeing organizations crumple under the sort of pressure they knew how to apply. But the thing they were attacking did not lie in an organization. There was a look in men's eyes—but you could not arrest them for that. There was hope in patient faces—but how are you to prove that hope is treason? There were words sounding in the air, commands from an unseen Leader, and against them the Nazis' countercommands rang futilely down the wind. And the words were: "Thou shalt have no other Gods before Me."

The strange thing about Karl Hoffmann's story is that it is a story of the defeat of the tremendous Nazi force, inside of Germany. There is a citadel in the very heart of their power that they have not breached; there are men living in Germany who have defeated them. The men who trust to the forces of physical power can conquer but they cannot win. They have no weapon which can penetrate the reaches of the spirit.

This story emerged because young Hoffmann could no longer keep it to himself. In spite of the very real danger that lay in revealing his experiences, he was so filled with the significance of the struggle he had gone through that he felt it must be told in America. For obvious reasons fictitious names have been used in the book, except for a few well-known public figures. But the young man who today is filling a little back-country pulpit in this country refused to hold back his revelations through fear.

You can see by looking in Karl Hoffmann's tolerant and generous face that he has not learned to be afraid, although many men have grown timorous who have endured far less. He has stumbled and groped his way as all humans must, during the bitter years, but he was never enslaved. He wears a man's dignity because his strength is fed by the Source from which men first drew their dignity and learned to walk with their heads uplifted. God is the strength of man. Material forces have altered history hardly a jot, but ideas have moved it and faith has sent the men who held it to accomplish the impossible.

The story has been told in the first person because it is essentially a personal story. Karl Hoffmann lived through those dark happenings, and his reactions and his steadfastness are of more significance than are events and statistics. The choice he was forced to make between faith and complacency is one that faces all Americans, not for the duration of a war but for the duration of our democracy.

KRESSMANN TAYLOR

CHAPTER ONE

I WAS born into a time and a place where the tides of two strong beliefs were to meet and clash. One of them, the wide clear current of Christianity, has provided the smooth underlying stream of history for nineteen hundred years, and nations and dynasties, battles and armadas have been only surface excitations upon it. Most of us have supposed, have even taken for granted, that we should sail on it forever without check, so that when the black countercurrent appeared we did not recognize its strength in time. I was caught in the turmoil at the very point where the tides came together and I have fought the new force and seen its vigor and the appeal it exerts on men's imaginations. I was catapulted out of the conflict before it was decided but I know how fiercely it still goes on and I believe that the real battle of Titans is being waged not between military powers but between men's fundamental beliefs. In spite of all the catastrophes and the bitter discouragement I have seen, I do not doubt the outcome.

I made my first appearance in this world seven years before the end of the German monarchy, the year 1912, in one of the big upper bedrooms of a parsonage in the beautiful old city of Magdeburg on the river Elbe. I was christened Karl Augustus. My father, Franz Hoffmann, was pastor of the Domkirche, one of the largest Lutheran churches of the town and the spiritual fount of a substantial and prosperous suburb.

Here the avenues ran straight and wide as contrasted with the narrow and winding streets of the older part of town, and the squarish villas sat far apart, surrounded by landscaped gardens. If when I grew somewhat older and had gathered a smattering of architectural knowledge I saw that these houses had their fair share of ugliness and were far too repetitive one of another, still to the eyes of my childhood they were all fine and handsome residences and their sprouting turrets and their uniformity seemed as natural an outgrowth of the building process as the similitude of linden trees was an inevitable result of the process of nature.

I grew up through the war years without experiencing much of their bleakness, for I was only six when the peace was signed and my first recognition of a world outside the parsonage walls came after the establishment of the Weimar Republic. My parents were strongly conservative in politics, as were all our neighbors who lived in the respectable villas around us, and since neither they nor their friends liked the Republic they unanimously ignored it and continued to live their daily lives and bring up their children according to the strict old forms, as if the Monarchy were still in existence. We were shut away from the swiftly changing life of the people and the nation in a rigid little circle, constricted by class lines which no one was aware were disappearing elsewhere.

However, there were hints of disaster and disintegration which filtered in to us: the loss of family estates among our acquaintances, the suicide of one of my father's old school friends after his bankruptcy, the unavailing search of the sons, who were university graduates, for a livelihood, the sour speech and the despairing faces that we encountered in the streets and in the stores. All of this established an uneasy curiosity beneath the precise formulas of our daily life. We children were carefully brought up to follow the old-fashioned etiquette: we were kept well in the background and learned to treat our elders with dignified formality. I always kissed my mother's hand upon greeting her and this seemed to me the most natural thing in the world, as it was natural to stand erect before my father and shake his hand when I came downstairs in the morning or retired at night. Little girls were required to combine a deep curtsey with a hand kiss and spent sober hours learning to perform this gymnastic feat with poise.

It never seemed to occur to anyone that such training might prove anachronistic, that there were more vital skills we might have been learning before we entered the strange new social pattern Germany then presented. We were young gentlemen and we must learn to behave like gentlemen. Not that there was anything cold or forbidding about the lives we lived. A great deal of warm affection was showered upon me by my parents, but all children were expected to have learned graciousness and be old enough to have something worth contributing before they were admitted to the society of their elders. Good form was made a matter of course but it was intended to reflect an inner dignity, and manners too smooth were frowned upon.

This was bad enough preparation for the lightnings that were to strike us before we were fully mature, but the worst of it was that we were carefully secluded and shut away from the doings or ideas of any people outside our narrow social circle. When we began to be aware, as was inevitable during our school days, of the corruption and lack of direction that existed in our city and nation, we were fascinated but we were also totally unprepared to understand or evaluate it.

We saw emaciated faces and heard of children in our town dying of hunger, but we did not know why starvation was here. We saw much of ostentation and hectic gaiety, but we could only sense the insecurity that lay beneath it.

We were not permitted to grow up too fast. Children were never included in adult gatherings and we boys were kept in knee pants until well into our teens, usually until the day of our confirmation when we were about fifteen years old. That was a tremendous day for us, for we graduated not only into long trousers but also into the dignity of stiff collar and tie and out of the open-throated shirts of childhood. It was the custom for our fathers to recognize this occasion by tying the new ties for us, and since it is not an easy matter to reverse one's accustomed procedure and tie a tie backward, the holiness of Confirmation morning was likely to be threatened by a burst of exasperated profanity, to the boys' secret delight.

Boys and girls were kept largely segregated until late in our college days. I was fifteen when I attended my first important social functions, a series of dancing classes which were held every week at different houses and which were designed to put upon each of us the final polish demanded of a young German of good family. We were the sons and daughters of army officers and bankers, college professors and the leading doctors and lawyers of the town who lived in the neighboring suburban villas. It was in this circle of twenty-four young people that I first made the acquaintance of the tribe of youthful femininity, with their constant whisperings together, their demure or gay glances, which I found as disquieting as they were exciting.

It is not really true that I had never been well acquainted with a young woman before. Erika Menz, a fair, bright-faced girl of my own age, had been the companion of my childhood and we had practically grown up in each other's houses. I remember very vividly the day of her coming to Magdeburg. Her uncle, Werner Menz, was a retired banker and a crony of my father's, and on that day he came to our house to ask my father to accompany him to the train where he was to meet his orphaned niece, who was coming to live with him. My mother, with characteristic generosity, insisted that we must all go, that the little girl would feel less lonely on seeing a woman and another child.

I was seven years old that year, and I remember the excitement of the unfamiliar railroad station, the tremendous size and noise of the puffing monster that drew the train. My excitement was somewhat subdued by the gravity of the older persons and by the frightening ambiguity of their talk. It was all in some way related to the trouble, the uneasiness in the air that I felt whenever I left the walls of my ordered home. There were bits of Werner Menz's talk that remained deeply printed on my memory, a solemn and frightening background to the appearance of Erika.

" . . . The mother could not survive the shock of my brother's death . . .

"He had come through the war . . . was made a colonel . . . served gloriously . . . now he was back in Germany. The family was to be together again.

"A band of looters . . . broke into the house at night and started to tear down everything. My brother behaved like an officer . . . tried to defend his home . . . shot down on his own staircase . . . Ah, these looters . . . who will protect us all? They are everywhere and there is no one left to protect the citizens now. It is our army that destroys us.

" . . . Only a few months ago. Now they are both gone and only the child is left. So she comes to me."

And then the train had come to a stop and a compartment door opened and a gaunt woman in a nurse's uniform handed down a gangling, fair-haired child. I hung back as Werner Menz started toward her, but the little girl looked at me and she seemed to be all frightened gray eyes. She looked so terribly lonely that I forgot my own diffidence and stepped forward smiling and made her my best bow. My mother, with a little gasp of pity, picked the child up in her arms and the little girl's skinny hands clung to her desperately.

"Who knows," muttered my mother, "to which of us it may happen next?"

From that moment on my mother cherished little Erika as she would have cared for a daughter of her own. She spent a great part of her time at our house and she and I soon became fast comrades. I led and she followed in inventing games, in exploring books, in trying out tunes on the great dark piano in the high-ceilinged music room, in tree climbing and racing out of doors. She allowed me to be more masculinely domineering than was perhaps good for me, but if I extended this inequality too far she responded with a flare of spirit that would leave me more respectful of her for days to come. By the time our dancing classes started she had grown very pretty in a fresh, rosy-cheeked way, but because she had become so familiar to me I was too obtuse to recognize her charm and it never once occurred to me that she belonged in the category of those agitating young ladies whose acquaintance I was making for the first time.

After our dancing classes started we were occasionally invited to join the older people, perhaps for an evening of music, although until we were out of college we were never included in anything really formal. Even at these simpler affairs we found little opportunity of sitting down with the company but were kept constantly on our feet to perform any little courtesies that were called for—keeping the coffee cups filled and passing the ample platters of smoked fish, cold fowl, and jellied salads and the mountainous piles of cakes.

Our circle was in fact rigidly constricted and I approached maturity hardly aware that people existed who followed a different or even a less comfortable pattern of life than our own. Hemmed in by a narrowness of social strata, blinded to the implications of popular unrest, when the Nazi threat appeared we did not begin to understand it.

I heard a great deal of political talk at home during my childhood, for my father discoursed freely on such matters and my mother and I made him a most attentive audience. I was of course not privileged to question him or make comment, and my mother did so most infrequently. When she did interrupt the flow of his talk her ideas were such precise, although more simply stated, copies of his own that he was invariably pleased. He would nod his big head at her, smile gently, and when she was through speaking tell her she showed very good sense for a woman, which gratified her completely.

"All this lawlessness is the result of the penetration of socialism," my father would say. "The Monarchy had its faults, but such a reign of criminality as we are living in today, such widespread hunger, the breakdown of industry, such an abandonment of all morality, the depravity of officials, the looseness of the young people, could never have occurred under its strict forms. We have tried to help a bad situation by abandoning all values. Not until we return to a responsible government can we hope for a good life for Germany."

My father never refrained from these discussions because of my presence, and since he held such vigorous views I soon gained a strong but confused impression that socialism was some sort of stalking cutthroat and that the Monarchy was a being that would return to us some day, somewhat in the dignified guise of an army officer, and set our world right again.

My father, like most of his parishioners, was a conservative and a staunch monarchist. He had been appointed to the Domkirche by the Kaiser himself and was very proud of the fact. It was not the ordinary procedure for a minister of the Lutheran Church to be appointed to his post. The accepted custom was to have the bishops recommend a candidate to a vacant pulpit; then, after a trial sermon the congregation might either elect him or refuse him. However, there were some very few charges, and these of the highest importance, which were filled only upon the recommendation of the Pontifex Maximus of the Lutheran Church, who was the Kaiser himself. The Domkirche was one of these. And young Franz Hoffmann had made himself so brilliant a name as a student, his scholarship and his sincerity had both so marked him out that early in his career he had been brought to the Domkirche upon the Imperial recommendation.

He loved to tell the story of the day of his appointment. He had been invited to have dinner with the Kaiser that same evening and the young pastor possessed no formal attire. He had a towering fine frame and only his father-in-law, of all the men he knew, was built on such large lines as his own. However, he had been married too recently to feel free to go to him and ask for the loan of his tails.

"I was a very proud young man," he used to say, glancing slyly at my mother.

He had spent the whole day in frenzied search of a tail coat but was finally reduced, at a late hour, to borrowing the essential garments from his wife's father. At the last moment the tie broke and he arrived at the palace with a hurriedly purchased replacement in his hand and persuaded one of the astonished attendants to tie it for him just in time to be announced. In after years he repeated this yarn to the Kaiser, who laughed heartily over it.

My father was always a welcome guest at the Kaiser's residence and figured among the personalities of the Imperial Court. It was a source of great pride to him that after he had gone to the church at Magdeburg the Kaiser had made a journey there to attend a service at the Domkirche, when my father was to confirm a large class. The crowning point of the day had come at the end of the

service, when, while the people stood in silence waiting for the
Keiser to leave, the sovereign had himself interrupted the formality
to come forward and shake hands with my father and thank him
in hearty tones for a splendid sermon.

My father had served for three years as an army chaplain during
the war, had been under fire innumerable times, and had finally
been invalided home with a wound in the head which afterward
affected his memory. As far back as I can remember him he was
unable to trust his memory to the extent of preaching without a
prepared manuscript. He used these notes seldom, for he was a
man of great religious ardor and preferred speaking earnestly and
with considerable vigor on the themes closest to his heart rather
than making the sort of discourse he called "hairsplitting."
Occasionally, however, his memory would fail him completely and
I have seen him pause at the end of a sentence, catch his lower lip
in his teeth, look over the heads of his congregation with a frown,
and then, with the faintest sigh, turn to the beautifully spaced
pages of his handwritten sermon.

My father's devotion to the Monarchy was an inevitable result
of his background, and in his heart he continued to hope for its
restoration. He had watched with sadness and wrath the collapse
of Germany at the war's end and he followed anxiously every
indication of a strengthening of the German nation. He held the
revolution mainly responsible for the breakdown and surrender of
his countrymen. He did not absolve the Kaiser's government, but
he considered the Socialists blamable for most of our woes and he
despised the Weimar Republic.

He used to fight the war over with his cronies, particularly
with Colonel Beck and the other officers who frequented our house,
and I have heard them argue for hours as to whether the navy
should not have been risked at sea instead of keeping snugly in
port, or whether the soldiers behind the lines had not enjoyed too
great a comfort so that they were unwilling to encounter the rigors
of the trenches. These questions were discussed as if they were the
most timely matters in the world and such I confidently believed
them to be.

He believed that the Kaiser was badly advised but he blamed the ruler for surrounding himself with poor advisors. "He was never able to tolerate any man of superior quality around him," he used to say. "It was seen in him long before when he dismissed Bismarck."

There was one thing my father had never been able to accept— that was the flight of the Kaiser to Holland.

"We should never have collapsed so completely," I have often heard him say with deep sadness, "if he had stayed with his army. It is the one thing I cannot forgive him."

Nevertheless, although he criticized the Kaiser's shortcomings freely, he never questioned that the Monarchy was the only right and profitable form of government for the German people. When Hindenburg, the conservative, had been elected to the presidency his hopes bloomed again and it was a great blow to him when Hindenburg took the oath of loyalty to the Republic, as it was a blow to all monarchists. From that time on, I believe, his hopes for restoration became more passive and he learned to watch the turn of events with patience while the younger men of the Right, disappointed in Hindenburg, began to look forward to the rebuilding of Germany on some different foundation.

He looked upon the growing Nazi party with good-natured tolerance. "Youthful hotheads," he used to call them, and was amused by their arrogance and enthusiasm. But he never took them seriously and said they would "never amount to anything."

If we were all blinded to the larger implications of the events that were sweeping upon us it was not entirely due to the stubbornness with which the German mind clings to its old forms and disciplines. We were bound together by a strange sort of insularity of pride and of emotion. The German nation itself was shut away; we had been marked out and imprisoned within the walls of a caste system of nations. Good treatment, we felt, was afforded us as a sort of charity, and we were not invited to partake any longer in the great events of the world.

And with the inflation our inner system disintegrated utterly. Fortunes disappeared overnight. Money that one day would have meant lifelong security, on the next would not buy a loaf of bread. Workmen were paid daily and carried their baskets of paper marks in desperate haste to the stores, buying the first articles they could lay their hands on before the price should double. Then they began to be paid twice a day, staggering barrow-loads of bills that would be hardly enough to buy a cabbage by the time they could get to the market.

Professional men were bankrupt. Barons became paupers. Theft was a commonplace and it was unsafe for a well-dressed man to walk out at night alone. A body was found in our neighborhood with the clothes stripped from it and a knife wound in the back. Bands of discharged soldiers who could find no employment became a menace to outlying districts and many a farmer found his fields stripped or his barn broken open and his livestock gone at the hands of the hungry.

Security, the dignity we loved, were nowhere. So ugliness boiled up within us and resentment at the outer world which we were told was responsible for our catastrophes. The Germans in their pride and their despair began to make a fetish of their enforced isolation from the security of the normal world. It is a truism that the wider world a man feels himself to be a part of, the less likely he is to be seduced by notions of the superiority of some narrow group. Conversely, the walls that shut us in with our pride and our degradation turned Germany into a hothouse in whose soil the myth of Aryan supremacy flourished sadly.

None of this could I guess at the time, but I know that to my youthful mind the choice that was offered Germany seemed to lie between the old Monarchy, the impossible, and this disastrous and unwanted Republic, and that I longed as my companions did for some miracle to happen which would save and glorify our nation.

If I learned at home, during those years of unreality, any values that were later to stand me in good stead they were derived from certain qualities in the character of my father. Just as the Domkirche with its lovely spire and its bulk of richly carved stone dominated the houses on the flatland surrounding it, so did the personality of my father overtop all the varied influences of my childhood. He was an immensely hale and rugged man with a magnificent, massive head crowned by a curling shock of dark hair which even in his fifty-sixth year, at the time of my departure for the university, had very little gray in it. His strong jaw and heavy eyebrows were marks of a choleric temperament, but his full lips were gentle and humorous, and whoever looked into his deep blue eyes found only peace in them.

The fundamental root of his nature was an unquestioning faith in the love of Christ, and he drew warmth from his knowledge of the goodness of God in the same way that other men expect and accept warmth from the sunlight. His wit and youthful spirits were tempered by a heart-warming tenderness and he knew with an inward solidarity what things came first both in this world and out of it. If there was an evil to be called by its name, he was straightforward to the point of hardness.

His preaching was incisive, direct and forceful, and he used to say he knew when he had delivered a good sermon by the number of abusive letters he received on Monday. He had no patience with equivocators.

"There isn't any way to protect yourself from the truth, except to like it," he told me.

His forcefulness was kept balanced by a great human gentleness and by the quietness of his deep and unshakable belief. He walked like a man who bore a light inside him, and many who came to see him in serious trouble or bewildered by pain, told afterward that, sitting in front of him and looking into his eyes, their problems seemed solved before they had spoken them.

He had a very beautiful voice, and his reverence and sincerity were so marked that to hear the burning words of the service ring out from his lips under the dark beams of the vaulted church brought a hush that was not from habit across the crowded pews. As a child I used to sit watching the dust motes whirling and disappearing as they traversed the lean streaks of sunlight that slanted in from the recessed windows, until I felt this silence come over the congregation, and then, although I knew it was my father standing up there in his black gown by the altar and the crucifix, it seemed to me that the voice of God was speaking.

Pastor Hoffmann would tolerate no disturbance of the service. One Sunday morning the widow Goedel, one of the wealthiest and most self-important members of the congregation, came into church so late that the pastor was halfway through his sermon. Instead of slipping into a seat at the back she clumped slowly down the marble-floored aisle to her accustomed pew, her stiff brown silk rustling, her innumerable gold chains clanking, and her heels rousing a little clatter of staccato echoes from the high roof. The heads of the entire congregation turned to regard the source of so much noise. My father stopped dead in the middle of a sentence and bent his eyes upon the approaching woman.

"I do not understand," he pronounced sternly, "how one can be late for church. Still less do I understand how, if one is late, one can disturb the solemnity of worship with such an unseemly tumult."

After which he finished his sermon. Unquestionably he made a number of enemies by this sort of forthrightness, but that was the last consideration which could have caused him to change his tactics.

With the children he was always at home and full of good humor. He had a great deal of the boy in him and none at all of the bluestocking. His relationship with the younger denizens of the parish became so cordial that some of the more censorious looked askance at it. There were two youngsters of whom he was especially fond: little Gretchen, a sunny-haired girl with a delicate face and sprightly mind; and young Phillip, a quiet, almost stolid lad who took life very seriously and was continually astounding my father by the originality of his speculations.

It was the pastor's early morning habit to take a walk in the brisk air accompanied by his little dog. He managed to meet his two young friends every morning and walk with them to their respective schools, the little girl bobbing up and down at his left, shrilly reciting her small litany of games, schoolwork, and any new ideas that had come to her, while the boy walked at his right with his head cocked to the side and his big dark eyes on the man's face.

Both the children found mathematics troublesome and they often saved for their morning meeting the problems they had been unable to solve. My father would walk along, explaining and gesticulating until, seeing the two small faces still puzzled, he would ask for paper and pencil, plant himself upon a near-by stoop and, with the boy at one elbow and the girl crowding close to him on the other side, thoroughly oblivious of time and space, he would work out the problem for them. Passers-by, seeing the rapt threesome sitting there in the misty sunlight, would call out, "Good morning, Herr Pastor."

The pastor, if the words came through to his consciousness, would answer with a wave of the hand, not lifting his eyes from the paper, and sometimes he would not hear the greetings at all, so absorbed would he be in his explanation.

"Now you must explain it back to me," he would say when the solution was triumphantly laid out before his young auditors.

This harmless morning exercise became a prime topic of gossip among the more prurient-minded parishioners. They said their pastor should be reprimanded for thus "bringing the sexes together," and the more they talked about it, the more evil they saw in it, until finally, after they had spent several weeks boiling themselves into a nice stew, they prevailed upon three members of the church board to call upon the pastor and make a protest.

It was not a very impressive delegation. Simon Falk, the spokesman, was a petty politician of suspicious mind; Herr Lasher was a fleshly hulk of a man who had a reputation for lechery; and Kurt Schwartz, the shoemaker, was a big, simple fellow whose brain grasped little beyond his business dealings and who had been talked into joining the delegation by his womenfolk.

My father received them in his study where Herr Falk, with considerable mumbling, informed him that his conduct was suspect, that it would result in impropriety if not worse among the young and, in short, demanded that he discontinue his walks with the children.

As he listened the pastor's eyes began to glow with anger. He stared straight at the speaker and before that strong gaze the man's tongue began to falter and finally his speech came to a fumbling stop. There was an uneasy silence.

"So I am to take instruction from such lecherous minds as these." A light of bitter judgment gleamed in the pastor's eyes. "It would be better if you would cleanse your own minds, my friends. That is where the obscenity exists. You must be well acquainted with filth to see evil in association of your pastor with your sons and daughters." His voice became caustic. "How guiltless of ugly desires your hearts must be, that you can come here and set yourselves up as my judges!" He flung his big fist upon the table. "If one man of pure heart will come to me and repeat these shameless charges I will listen to him. And now get out! You make me want to vomit."

The scandal died silently and suddenly. Indeed, if there was narrow-mindedness among the parishioners it got scant sustenance from my father. He hated all small thinking. His people had a tremendous respect for him, but he did not want their awe, and they loved him for the way he put them at ease if some small indiscretion was committed in his company.

My mother was an intensely practical little woman, short-statured and fair, round as a butterball, and openhanded as nature. Her chief occupation was keeping my father comfortable. Her furniture shone, her windows sparkled, her curtains stood stiff as ballet skirts. But better than these, she kept all the details of a practical nature in her own capable hands, never allowing her husband to see any of the problems that underlay the smoothly functioning and thrifty household. That my father was impractical and would be hopelessly lost and confused without her care she knew, and she cherished the knowledge of her usefulness to him.

That she was his wife was the most important fact of her existence. She had a great respect for his erudition and while she shared with great dignity the respect accorded his ecclesiastical position, she was always a little humble about it. Day by day and year by year it remained to her something of a marvel that she, Hedwig, with her spiritual limitations, presided over the parsonage. She was well fitted to preside there. As a young girl she had been strictly trained in etiquette. But her chief grace and qualification was kindliness. She was a modest woman whose belief in God was simple and unquestioning; and, as with many such women, her pastor personified the nearest approach to Glory toward which her eyes dared reach. She never lost her sweet astonishment that it should be given to her to mend socks, to darn and lay out the linen, to warm the bed sheets even, of one who had his hands upon the very door latch of the Kingdom of Heaven.

These two were very deeply in love with each other. I must have felt the rich quality of that affection very early, for in the confused and sickly scene of a broken people in a broken nation which was beginning to touch and disturb my youth, and through the rushing disasters that were to sweep upon us before I had become fully a man, my father's gentleness with my mother and her adoring confidence in him made a strong rock of solidity to which I could always return for strength and for reassurance.

CHAPTER
TWO

THERE was a fetid atmosphere throughout the cities of Germany during the postwar years that laid its breath on all of the generation who grew up under the Republic. It was as if the stresses of recurrent catastrophe, the defeat, the shame of the peace, the inflation, the grinding poverty had crushed the steadfast and simple qualities of the people, so that they moved in an amazed and hectic round above the rotting body of their old, sure beliefs. There were social degeneracy and political unease; there were mental skepticism and moral profligacy.

It was impossible to walk on the streets without being accosted by pinched-faced beggars. You learned to keep your hand upon your purse when the rickety children of the poor brushed against you. The number of deaths from malnutrition was frightening. Those who still possessed means spent lavishly for the most extravagant diversions, as if they wanted a last fling while their pockets were still lined, and decency and the concern for one's fellows were lost in the frantic scramble to survive. To my schoolmates and me, who saw everywhere the effects of this demoralization but were too young to understand its causes, it appeared often that there was no sure ground to stand on, only an unhealthy ooze in which we were never sure of our footing and whose little islands of security might shift from one day to another.

I was still young when I began to find a fascination in trying this slippery ground, in stepping out from the wisdom and conservatism of my home to explore for myself what values I should cling to as a man, what place I should make for myself in the convulsive and disordered scene that was Germany in the twenties.

My parents made no effort to influence me in the choice of my profession and I wandered far from their sympathy and tried their patience for a time, but before I was nineteen I had decided to become a Lutheran minister.

When I look back upon the causes that brought about this decision I am certain that I had no conscious wish to follow in my father's footsteps. He would have scorned such a choice on my part if made from any considerations of expediency or even if I had been influenced by affection for him.

"Whoever chooses the service of God must be driven to it by an inner power that is stronger than he," he told me, to discourage me lest I might be only imitating him.

Like most boys I wanted to find my own way through the maze of ideas in books and in minds as I encountered them; I wanted to try out some of the dangers and see if they were dangerous, and so during the tumult and unsureness that is adolescence I drew away from my father and into myself, seeking what I could use as I ventured into new experiences and making rejections only according to some hidden touchstone that was my newly forming self.

My mind was set astir by a circumstance that happened while I was not far into my teens. I made a friend, a complete pagan, a boy of my own age. We formed a strange and ardent alliance, drawn together by our very differences, a friendship that continued for years, both stormy and satisfying, a piece of ground touched by bright noonday splotches of joy and shared feeling, yet increasingly overcast by shadows that were dark forebodings of tragedy.

I must have been fourteen or fifteen when he entered our class at the gymnasium, the school which for us combines high school and college training. I shall call him Orlando von Schlack (his own name was as odd and even more euphonious) and he was to be the most vividly real person in my life for many years. He was the illegitimate son of a German noblewoman and one of our great writers, now in exile, a man of considerable note in Germany although his works have been little translated. The boy was extremely talented. He had been in the school only a few days before he had fascinated us all, and by the time he was expelled toward the end of our college years he had come close to disrupting the school and had changed all of our lives.

Orlando lived with his fashionable and gifted mother and bore her name. The Countess von Schlack was herself very close to genius. She was a musician of concert rank; she wrote extraordinary pieces which were widely talked of, and had the literature of many ages at her tongue's tip, as she was a university graduate and had done extensive work in the literary field. She looked very young and she was very beautiful, with a cool, bright allurement half created by her own vanity. We found her a heady creature when we visited Orlando's home, for she liked our adulation and flirted with the young boys for the pleasure of seeing the effect she could create. One or two of them fell hopelessly in love with her and she kept them dangling for a year at a time, much longer than she should have allowed if she had been as gracious as she was lovely.

She had brought up Orlando to hate and despise his father and the boy spoke of him in the most brutal and ugly terms, strangely shocking to all of us who had learned respect and reverence for our own fathers from our very cradles.

But if Orlando shocked us he charmed us far more. Day after day you would see his dark curls in the center of a group of intent lads who hung about him listening to his brilliant spate of talk. He could weave magic around us like an ancient minnesinger, for he had an amazing talent for words and the classics of German literature and philosophy were as familiar to him as Andersen's fairy tales were to the rest of us. He was so far beyond us in the growth of his mind and in his erudition that he was almost unbelievable to us.

He had a handsome head and the same bright beauty of face as his mother, and he had, as well, her trait of using human beings as guinea pigs for the experiments of his gay vanity, and her same unconcern for the victim's fate if the experiment did not turn out well or became boring to him. His nose was small with almost no bridge to it and had a squarish, chiseled tip as if it had been exquisitely cut out of marble. His eyes were dark and sharp. His fantastic name, his romantic origin, his beauty and brilliance were a combination that immediately set him apart from us so that we never minded his manner of speaking to us, curiously, with his eyes seeming to question what sort of clay we were made from, trying out his ideas upon us with a teasing flippancy that said we were a clumsy and clod-footed lot who could never keep up with the elastic quality of his own mind. And we all felt ourselves to be clumsy and clod-footed in front of him. We could feel the difference in his quality. He was unique and startling and yet so completely warm and charming that we all of us, teachers as well as pupils, came under his spell.

When Orlando singled me out to be his friend I experienced the most glowing elation I had ever known. He would seek me out and slip his arm over my shoulder and we would walk off with our heads together, tearing off into ever new and more exciting avenues of talk. I began to read avidly works I had only dimly known the names of, for I was far behind him and felt myself at a disadvantage. He could confound me with swift arguments while I plodded along trying to find out whether and why my own beliefs were valid. I was completely fascinated by him and found no fault in him. I found myself laughing while I gaped at his outrageous behavior in the classrooms, for he had no pity and showed respect to no one.

We had a dreary old professor of Latin, who would lose himself in the middle of a lecture and sit for minutes at a time with drooping head, his mouth hanging open. Orlando thrust himself under the old man's nose and shouted, "Gone to sleep, Doctor?" his handsome head dangling and his mouth agape, imitating the ancient, fishlike lips. For anyone else it would have spelled expulsion. He kept the school in a constant ferment but somehow the teachers could never bring themselves to reprimand him, or the rest of us to do anything more than follow his flashing ways with grateful admiration.

He had no mercy on our ignorance and shamed us because of our childish admiration for Schiller, whose poems we had enthusiastically recited for years. But when he had scorned us and had us all blushing and uncomfortable he won us again, singing into our rapt ears the great cadences of Goethe until we ourselves were alive to the contrast. Everything he had to teach I absorbed eagerly and many were the shining new lanes of thought down which I plunged as he laid them open to me.

Most exciting to me of all Orlando's convictions was his complete atheism. He was violent in his unbelief, which was a possibility so new to my mind that I found myself floundering when he first sounded me out on the subject. I remember that he had gone with me to the church where I was to practice on the organ whose deep and mellow old pipes were my favorite source of music. Orlando was curious, since he was something of a virtuoso at the piano but had never before seen an organ close at hand, and I explained the various stops and keyboards to him while he leaned over me, his eyes shining.

"Let me try it," he murmured, and after a moment's feeling around upon the keys he launched into a fugue of Bach's, so that the whole vaulted emptiness of the church around us rang and caroled back to us the majesty of the sound. I am sure he faked a good bit of it, but his feeling for the essential melody and movement was so beautifully sure that I could only stare, marveling, for I knew the instrument was completely new to him. While the last chords were still humming in the pipes he turned around to me, his face curiously aglow.

"The reason I like you, Karl," he said, "is because I don't have to explain things like music and poetry to you. You understand them instinctively." He laughed ruefully. "I was going to impress you by my performance, but I can see by your face that you weren't taken in. But Bach has bewitched you just the way he bewitches me. He makes me wish I were more serious, that I had the sober patience to become a really good musician." He regarded me with that curious sharp glance of his for an instant and then waved his hand toward the vastness of the church interior, the empty pews stretching back in the gloom, washed by a faint colored light from the windows in the transept, the looming statues of Luther and the twelve Apostles half in shadow—

"About this too you *must* feel as I do. Look, Karl, at this great clumsy monument to superstition. For how many ages they have been mumbling the same dreary liturgies, the same old hocus-pocus in just this sort of crude medieval vault! It is a monument to mental darkness. Don't you feel it?"

"How do you mean?"

"Dear boy, can't you see what religion is? It is a dope for the people, stirred together out of old mythology and musty fear. It is only for weaklings. Karl, you must read Nietzsche! Everything you have been taught here was born out of a sick and feeble imagination."

"I don't believe you," I flung at him. "There wasn't anything sick or feeble about Luther. Or about Bismarck either." But he laughed at me and began to quote his favorite philosophers and I had nothing with which to answer him. Still he had stirred something new in me.

"How can you believe in a God?" he demanded of me, and for the first time I saw this was a question men might ask. Hitherto I had been dimly aware that divergences of opinion existed within the Church and I had heard my father debate points of doctrine, but that anyone might doubt the foundation of all belief, the existence of a very creator, was so completely outside my realm of speculation that Orlando's question sincerely shocked me. It was as if he had opened a dark and forbidden door whose very existence had been kept concealed from me.

His elbows on his knees, his eager face resting on his hands, he leaned towards me and began to tell me of the immense magnitudes of the far stars, of light that had been traveling through space since before our earth was born, how the earth itself was the puniest of fragments and men like microscopic worms upon it.

"If there were a God who had created all that immensity," he asked me, "can you imagine Him interesting Himself in the lives of such infinitesimal creatures on such a piddling little ball?"

"But God is a Spirit," I cried, my mind burning. "Why should He be concerned with our *size?* The very hairs of our head are numbered." It seemed to me that I was somehow fighting for my life, and my instinct was quite right. "Why should size be so important? Do you think you are not as important as Heinrich Neu because he is bigger than you are?"

Heinrich Neu was a cripple who lived in a house near the school, a man with a mind completely dulled, who was obliged to spend most of his time in a wheel chair and because of this enforced inactivity had grown to a tremendous bulk, with heavy larded jowls and great rolls of fat upon his belly.

"Do you think a popular operetta is better than that piece of Bach you just played because it is longer?"

"Brilliant, my dear Karl," said Orlando, smiling. "Your God cannot be indifferent to us merely because of our size. And it is by the same token, I dare say, that if you walk down the street you will trample both ants and horses underfoot without differentiating between them.

"But let that go. I shall even grant you there is no difference in the way you will see an ant and a horse. I want to give you an idea of how men must appear to some cosmic Being. Look then at your squabbling generations of mankind, each with an inch in time and filling it with such silly scurryings before it is hastily and brutally extinguished to make room for another lot with the same absurdities.

"How many of the millions of grubby and indistinguishable dead do we remember? Maybe a couple of dozen, and *they'll* be forgotten in another thousand years. Yet you hypothesize to me a God of the scope of all the vast universe who faithfully memorizes the structural details of these billions of vanished nobodies and concerns Himself with each of their pointless carryings-on! Get a vision of yourself, a schoolboy sitting at your desk with the Lord of the Universe leaning over your shoulder in breathless concern as to whether the digit you are about to put down on your paper will be a five or a six."

"But God is interested in us because He made us . . . ."

"Then He botched the job badly. I, even, could have made a better world than this. You, dear boy, would have made a much kinder one. Don't try to sell me your good and just God as the Creator of this brutal concoction. If He were good, why should pain and evil be the rule; why should He have arranged it so that all living things must struggle constantly to kill and devour each other in order to survive at all?" Orlando looked at me with mocking eyes. "If there is a good God, come, prove Him to me. Show Him to me."

"But He is invisible."

"Dear Karl," he laughed, "He is a fairy tale."

When I came home I selected several volumes from the library in my father's study and lugged them upstairs with me. For nights, thereafter, I would lie on my stomach in bed, with a single bulb burning beside me, reading until I grew chilled, until my arms ached and my neck was stiff. I read Luther and Nietzsche, Schopenhauer and theological works. I began to explore the philosophers and ploughed into Kant, Fichte, and Hegel, although they proved terrifically hard going for so young a scholar as I. I read many a night until the dawn came with its gray light through my unshuttered windows.

The arguments with Orlando continued for long months. I would go home with him when school was over, and while I lounged on a brocaded sofa he would sit at the piano and play the music I loved with brilliant improvisations of his own, until I was half hypnotized with melody. Then he would drop his hands from the keys, smiling his charming, enigmatic smile, and suddenly sting me with a skeptic's question.

All the familiar world I had known receded and I was alert only when I was with Orlando in his shimmering kaleidoscopic landscape, where sometimes the reality of God would appear as a great truth, rooted like a tree, and sometimes as a glittering chimera. Commonplace objects became unreal to me and I doubted, seeing the river, the slim stratified clouds, the door of my own house, that they were there at all. I had lost any measurement for reality and I was not aware of the passage of time.

But gradually through the tumultuous talk of the days and the nightlong wonderings when I sat groping for hope through the darkness, there began to form in me one deep belief, that if there were no God there was no meaning in life. Like a child with a foot rule trying to measure a mountain, I demanded of this Mystery what its attributes were, asking assurance, trying to frame a pattern for the Ultimate. Every time I turned back baffled from that hidden face I was brought up again by the beautiful symmetry of the world or by the strangeness of some everyday organism. The delicate beauty of leaves and of bare branches, the perfection with which the tiniest creatures were designed, the constant recurrence of the seasons were phenomena which tugged at my senses, saying, "Somewhere there is a Cause for us."

I grew thin with tension, straining beyond my strength. The more I tried to probe this Mystery the greater it became; the closer I attempted to approach Him to test Him the vaster and more impenetrable He appeared, until I saw I had no measure huge enough to encompass Him and began to sense why faith must accept Him without questioning.

I stood one day by the river on a dock where the ships came in, and all at once I found myself thinking, "If I can see a tree and cannot understand at all how it grows or why, how much less can I hope to understand the Cause of that tree? If I cannot understand why my mind gathers impressions and sorts and arranges them as it does, how can I hope to reach the Source from which my mind sprang?" This idea came to me with the accompaniment of a clear and sudden peace, as if someone had quietly spoken the answer to my long turmoil; and I knew that I believed in God.

I remained very ardently Orlando's friend and became increasingly his confidant. He had been baffled by his failure to convert me to his way of thinking, not quite sensing what it was in me that had refused him, but it increased his respect for me that he had been unable wholly to establish his dominance. His school career as the months and years went by became increasingly cloudy. His charm for us never abated and he wielded a power over his companions that made him unusually dangerous.

I observed a new tendency in him as he grew older that filled me with a sick disgust, but he refused to listen to my chiding and mocked at me as a moralist. I was repelled and our friendship strained, yet his volatile intelligence was still a whet that my mind needed, and our comradeship persisted, although not on so close a basis.

He would form a close friendship with a boy, taking him everywhere, spending all the eagerness of his personality upon him, almost courting him, for a period of perhaps three months, and when he had completely possessed the mind of his new disciple he would lead him subtly from one looseness to a worse until we used to say that we could see Orlando's puppets degenerate from one day to another. He had a taste for experimenting in corruption, and the whole atmosphere of the times abetted him; the fact that his pupils were adolescents, denied the wholesome company of girls, the leaping tides of their natural development plaguing and disturbing them, rendered them peculiarly receptive to the flagrancies he would induce them to toy with. When he had reduced a boy to this level Orlando would lose all interest in him and would turn upon him brutally one day, showing his derisive distaste for the fool his sycophant had allowed himself to become. The boy would be completely shattered. Many of them did not recover, these victims of Orlando's experiments. Their confidence destroyed, their spirits injured, they clung to the unhappy vices he had taught them because they could not face the fact that someone they loved had hurt them so. To this Orlando was indifferent.

"I take out their souls," he told me one day with a sort of adolescent pomposity, "absorb what is good, and then when they are empty I push them away."

"What is going to become of you, Orlando?" I demanded.

"If I live," he said, "I shall be either a criminal or a genius."

In time everyone became afraid of him in spite of his physical frailness. He once circulated a rumor that one of his discarded protégés was in danger of losing his mind because of his obsessions, and the rumor when the boy heard it very nearly had the foreboded effect. In all he must have ruined at least eight boys and I began to find myself cursing inwardly when I saw him turn his unhappy fascination toward another subject.

One of our professors, a man of about fifty named Kamps, an outstanding figure in the school, of great humanity and strong common sense, was tenderly fond of Orlando. He spoke of him sadly as his "child of sorrows," and was the only one who dared to castigate the boy, blazing at him for the havoc he was raising with this folly of playing with souls. Orlando adored Dr. Kamps and never mocked him. But the years went by and he did not change.

Toward the end of our college days, when he was nineteen years of age, Orlando befriended a very gifted youngster who had just entered the school. Young Hugo was one of those fragile, ethereal children in whom musical genius develops amazingly early, and he was at twelve years old a superb violinist. Orlando became his god. The child followed him everywhere. They would play together for hours, the youngster's violin singing above the thundering notes of the piano, and every day the beautiful face and voice of Orlando brought the boy more closely under his sway.

Then for the first time in the years he had been among us someone dared to protest in dead earnest. Rudolph Beck, an officer's son, went to his father. His story was so bitter that all our parents were aroused and came to the school authorities demanding Orlando's expulsion. His mother's position had been a protection to him but it did not avail him now. He was thrown out of the school.

Little Hugo went from one to another of us, questioning,

"Where is Orlando?"

"He has left the school," we told him.

"When is he coming back?"

"He is not coming back."

"Not *ever* coming back?"

"No. Not ever."

The boy's face turned white and he went off by himself. In a few days we heard that he was sick, and then that the doctors were unable to diagnose his illness and that he was rapidly growing worse.

"He has lost his interest in living," the doctors said to his parents and begged them if they could to discover his dearest wish and to gratify it.

"There is nothing I want," Hugo told them feverishly.

So, daily, we at the school waited for bulletins, afraid of what was happening and afraid to interfere, until at last one day we heard that the boy was dead. It was something we never talked of afterward.

All this time Orlando was being held an actual prisoner in his mother's home. He was never allowed to go out and when I called to see him at the time Hugo died, the countess told me he was confined to his room and refused to allow me to go up.

Shortly after this I received a letter from him, a long and bitter lament, so full of the pain of existence, so burdened with dejection and despair that its tone frightened me.

"What justification is there for my life," he wrote me, "or what redemption for this piece of spoilage that I know myself to be? I look into myself and see only a grotesque, a buffoon, and when I look at the world it shows no more than the shocking image of my own worst features. Why should I atone by longer suffering for the bungling of the clumsy hand that fashioned me . . . ?"

I took this letter to Rudolph Beck, the boy at whose instrumentality Orlando had been expelled. Rudolph and I had formed a working partnership on our Greek and Latin studies. He needed the work in order to enter the law school at the university but it was exceedingly difficult for him. The collaboration was at his suggestion.

"You will find Latin too easy and neglect it, while I need help, so let us work together."

Rudolph and I had long been friends and after Orlando left the school this friendship developed into a strong comradeship, perhaps because I found in Rudolph's frank honesty and continent mind both a contrast and a release from the scintillant and exotic charm of the other boy. Rudolph read Orlando's letter gravely.

"He is planning suicide," he said, and this was what I also had feared.

We decided to go to see Orlando's mother to warn her of her son's state of mind and to see if she could help him. The Countess von Schlack received us coldly, while we sat on the edges of her gilded, spindle-legged chairs uncomfortably conscious that we were not welcome, and attempted to blurt out the terror that her son's letter had evoked in our minds.

"We feel certain that he is planning to take his own life," I stammered out to her, and she smiled at us with the coolest little interrogatory smile, as if we suggested that Orlando was in danger of tripping over his bootlaces.

"I do not think so," she said lightly. "He is hardly the sort who would commit suicide. He is too vain. He would never be satisfied unless he could be here afterward to observe the effect he had created."

All of a sudden her face changed. The emotion under her mask showed cruelly through and I have never since seen on a face so thorough a hatred. "You boys are both too nice to concern yourselves with him," she said in a thin voice. "He is rotten to the innermost part of his soul."

"But he is in danger," I peeped, knowing that I was not having any effect upon her. "His letter was so despondent . . . I am afraid."

"Very well," she said with her former hard smile. "If you think it necessary I shall keep an eye on him." And we two baffled boys found ourselves being dismissed. We went down the high stone stairs of her big house in silence, filled with a sense of cold as if we had stood too long on ice and it had penetrated to our very bones.

"I shall have caused two deaths by my meddling," Rudolph said as we neared home. "Hugo's and Orlando's." And I could not comfort him.

A week later Orlando escaped from his home. His mother at once telephoned to Dr. Kamps begging him to find Orlando and persuade him to return to her. That same night Orlando appeared at the house of his beloved professor, haggard and frantic, and the good man took the sobbing boy to his heart, comforted him, gave him letters to friends of his own in Berlin and even aided him on his way with a present of money. Inside a month his mother had found him, and since he was still under age she brought him back, and this time turned him over to his father. The man, finding himself burdened with this problematical and unwanted son, placed Orlando in one of the new Socialist schools where there was a complete lack of discipline and where the theory was to allow boys to develop their normal bents without any sort of restriction. Within three months Orlando had the school in an uproar and was removed by his father and placed in a reformatory.

It did not take him long to find an opportunity to escape again. This time the person he turned to was my own father. I did not know of this until long afterward. Only once during our school days had I been able to persuade Orlando to accompany me to church and on this occasion the solemnity and beauty of the service had had a striking effect upon his poetic nature. His eyes had filled with tears and he had appeared completely rapt. The strong personality of my father and the force of the sermon had moved him.

"Now I understand you, Karl," he had said, "because you are that man's son."

My father had long forbidden me to associate with Orlando. He distrusted him and thought him a dangerous influence for me. That I had continued to know him and to spend the greater part of my time with him was a direct act of defiance and had contributed to an estrangement from my father on my part that lasted nearly through my teens.

Now in his despair, Orlando turned to my father. He gave the boy no soothing counsel but told him that the responsibility for making much or little of his life lay in his own hands, that brilliance was not enough and that he lacked much of being as wise as he thought. Orlando left him soberly and was not seen again in Magdeburg. We heard after a time that he was living in Berlin and that he had degenerated shockingly. His companions were said to be a loose and vicious circle of young roisterers and Orlando had once been jailed for theft which he had undertaken on a dare. All the promise of his genius seemed to have been forgotten.

But I did not forget him. Although we had become estranged in our sympathies as we grew older I missed immeasurably the foil he provided to my developing beliefs, the stimulating contrariety of his fine mind. It was through his atheism that I had formed my own convictions, had so early explored the philosophers and had fallen in love with the roughcast phrases of the German Bible. Luther's translation of the Bible is in the true vulgar tongue, so crude in places as to be actually coarse, and for this reason it is a peculiarly trenchant and live document. It had become the vivid companion of my nights and the reference from which I found myself drawing all the illustrations of my arguments.

With Orlando gone, our long controversy ended, I had nowhere to turn the burning force of my religious convictions. It was nearing the time when I must make my choice of a profession, and I found myself being more and more drawn to the ministry. I was not a boy who took orders easily. I was independent and because of my independence aloof. But I had begun to see, in that interplay between the lives of men on this earth which is essential to their existence in a society, that every man is of necessity a servant . . . the only choice left to him being the choice of a master.

There kept stirring in my mind an old folk tale which my mother used to tell me when I was a child: how a man had gone out into the world resolved to serve the greatest lord there was. For a time he served kings until he found that the Devil was their master, whereupon he enlisted in the Devil's service, convinced now that he had found the greatest sovereign. Then one day he observed his great overlord to cringe and flee from a wooden wayside Cross and he turned from him and went all over the earth looking for the master of the Cross, who was surely the greatest lord of all. Thus it was that he came to serve the Christ in humbleness and meekness.

This story swayed the mood of my thinking. If I could serve the greatest Power of the universe I knew I should only be unhappy in some lesser employment. I rejoiced in the thought that I might become a missionary or a great preacher who could make men cleave to the truth, and it seemed in my heart a predestined and wholly wonderful thing that I was born to be a man from whose lips the words of God might fall. I went to my father and told him my decision and as soon as he felt assured that I was sincere and that this profession was a necessity to me, the long constraint that had been between us dissolved of itself.

Our days at the gymnasium came to a close and those of us who were graduated entered upon a new dignity. Each of us was addressed as "Mulus" (the mule) and very proud we were of the title, for it signified the end of our youth and marked the brief transition period before we entered the university, at which time we would become men.

There was an elaborate celebration upon our graduation. It was our first real party. Wine flowed liberally; the professors attended; there were charades and noise, flushed faces and genial toasts and a great deal of spontaneous oratory. Everyone made a speech to robust and good-humored applause. Dr. Kamps rose to his feet and we quickly gathered around him.

"Your days as my students are over," he told us. "It is my hope for you that you will remain *students* all your lives, always learning . . . always with an open mind." He paused and a look of gravity and pain swept over his face.

"I cannot help mentioning my child of sorrows," he said.

As if his words had been a sudden antidote to alcohol the gaiety went out of us. The evening drew soberly and swiftly to a close. So the end of my school days were marked for me by a vision of the bright and mocking face of Orlando and by my apprehension of tragedy for him wherever he might go.

CHAPTER
THREE

MY decision to enter the ministry was a fateful one. It was to involve me personally in the formidable events which were to shake and reshape Germany in the years immediately ahead and it was to give me an inside view of one of the cleverest, the most subtle and measured of persecutions the Church of God has endured during the long centuries since it became a power in the world.

I had no foretaste of coming drama when in the fall of the year 1931 I stood in the Aula, the great assembly hall of the University of Berlin, one of a crowd of thousands of awkward, incoming students. My friend Rudolph Beck from Magdeburg was one of them and so, to my pleasure, was my childhood's companion, Erika Menz, who had surprised me by deciding to enter the theological school at the university at the same time I did. We were an awe-inspired lot, uneasy and feeling our provincialism as we looked up to the huge platform where stood the imposing figure of the rector, the head of that great institution of sixteen thousand students. The rector is elected yearly from among the deans of the various faculties, and with their advice, he is a sort of unlimited monarch of the university.

The rector wore voluminous robes and around his neck hung a golden chain each link of which was of about half the circumference of a saucer and from which depended a massive medal. One by one we were brought up to the platform to shake hands with this impressive individual and when he greeted us to murmur, "I thank Your Magnificence," for this was his resplendent title and he was never addressed in the first person.

The rector presented each of us with a certificate about three feet square, which was only suiting its size to its importance, inscribed all in Latin, even to our names which were translated into a Latin form, and attesting that we had each become a "citizen of the university" and were now under its walls.

This citizenship was quite literal and conveyed enormous privileges. The universities of Germany were, and I use the past tense with sorrow, powerful institutions in their own right who owed no obedience to the laws governing other civil organizations. They made and enforced their own rules. Police or even government officials were forbidden to so much as enter the university grounds except upon the invitation of the rector. To be a student in a university was to belong to a group which exercised a great formative power upon the life of the nation. Social trends were formed there and political doctrines originated.

It is difficult to compare these institutions with the American colleges because our contact with the life of the nation was so close and we exerted a strong political leadership. The German universities are the greatest professional schools and all their entrants are already college graduates. My fellow students were almost all of voting age and, as a group, exerted a very real power in national politics. The debates which raged within a university or were carried on between different universities were discussed in the newspapers throughout the whole country and sometimes rated front-page space; the editors would join sides and many of the ensuing controversies became famous.

At the time of my matriculation at Berlin political issues were in an uproar. One professor after another was attacking the Republic for its blunders. To many of them it appeared that our present leaders had misapprehended almost totally the vital potentialities of democratic government; they made direct demands upon the government for action. It required courage for the professors to enter into conflict with the powers who governed their appointments and paid their salaries. In my first year at the university a number of men were dismissed from their posts, martyrs to their convictions. Then the students rallied to the fight and twice we held such continuous and convincing demonstrations that the ousted professors were returned to their positions. In this realistic atmosphere I found myself rapidly revising my earlier political impressions. I saw that Germany was not a democracy in anything more than name, that there had been no clear vision of a new form of government nor yet a sufficient impression made upon the people of their responsibility in giving the Republic a purpose and a direction. Too many old forms had been held over from the monarchy. Too many special interests were using the new Republic to serve their own ends. But it was not easy to orient myself at once. There were as many shades of political opinion in evidence as there are colors in a line of drying wash. The Communists were extremely noisy, but the one group which was garnering large numbers of adherents among the students was the new National Socialist party, led by a remarkable orator named Adolf Hitler.

There were constant signs of our new dignity as university students. For the first time in my life I might carry a cane, and instead of hearing my surname hurled at me in class like a projectile—"Hoffmann!"—as had been the rule in college, I was addressed with great punctiliousness as "Herr Hoffmann" and treated with solemn courtesy by the professors as well as by my fellows. I found the air intensely stimulating. Great scientific discoveries and revolutionary inventions were even now being originated in the halls around me. All our work was constructive and modern and alive. In medicine, in law, in theology, new ideas emanated which were changing the face of our national life, and in all of this the students were very nearly as important as the professors.

We followed no set course of study. There were no requirements as to the number of courses we enrolled in nor the sequence in which we undertook them. I enrolled, among other projects in the theological school, in the work on a great dictionary of the New Testament which was in preparation. The professors demanded sound scholarship of the men who were allowed to share in this work and I felt it a great stroke of luck to be included. Years of research were put on a single word. All known writings for three hundred years before and three hundred years after the date of the original document would be perused and each time the word we were seeking to define was found in any work, either sacred or profane, its use, context, and meaning would be analyzed through pages of painstaking notes. All the leading universities on the continent were assisting in this vast compilation. The dictionary was not yet completed after fourteen years of work when I left Germany and whether it will now ever appear I cannot say.

We attended lectures at our own discretion. No one checked upon our attendance, save for the first and last lectures of the term when we brought our *Testatbuch* to the professor, who signed his name after the listing of his course.

While some courses were required for a degree, the student himself decided on the course of study he would follow and on when his work was concluded and he was ready to present himself for examination. The examinations were appallingly stiff, covering the whole field of the student's work over all his university years, and lasted about six months. After the long ordeal of his examinations, a candidate for a doctorate must prepare ten theses which he was obliged to defend in public debate against three appointed opponents. At the conclusion of the debate he would be attacked from the audience, usually by the professors, and the unfortunate young man had to be able to defend himself with spontaneous argument against the wiliest dialectics of these seasoned brains. And how the professors could make him sweat! When he had come off triumphantly and was greeted as "Herr Doktor," the glad congratulations of his friends could be accepted without humility, for he would be well aware how thoroughly he had earned them.

In such an atmosphere discussion filled all of our time that was not spent over our books. The professors held open house at their homes for the students who attended their seminars, which were in themselves advanced classes for discussion; a topic would be announced and the talk would continue through a blue haze of tobacco smoke into the small hours—after which we would relax for supper and for music. These evenings provided almost our sole social diversion. We were not at the university to play but to learn, and after a lecture in the classroom we would form little groups, gathering on the grounds or hunting empty seminar rooms and arguing excitedly for hours. These gatherings had a name. They were called the *Steh-Convent*, which can be translated with approximate accuracy as the "standing convention," and for them we always sought out acquaintances with whom we vigorously disagreed.

If we joined a group where we were not known to the entire company we were formally introduced to the whole circle. All our social contacts were extremely formal and we prided ourselves upon our ceremoniousness, any violation of polite manners being considered as a great insult to the entire university. To the young women students we were studiously courteous. But their place in university life was inconsequential; there were very few of them and their presence there was considered rather amusing. Most of them were earnest and not too attractive girls who were there to work as hard as they could. The few pretty ones usually took their studies lightly and carried on merry flirtations with the men students.

All the girls were to a certain degree considered out of place, and a professor who addressed his class as "Gentlemen" instead of "Ladies and Gentlemen" would be rewarded with uproarious applause.

Erika Menz was decidedly among the pretty girls but it was delightful to observe her earnestness over her work in theology, which to my eyes made her seem very charming. I saw a great deal of her during the early and difficult months of adjustment in those unfamiliar surroundings. She helped to abate my small attacks of homesickness and I found her a completely receptive audience to all the new theories I was forming. We used to take time off from the routine of the university to go sailing on the Wansee, a large lake with wooded shores not far from Berlin. Erika loved to manage the tiller or to raise the sails and fasten the ropes, handling them sailor fashion, and her fair hair blowing in the wind. I was a lazy fellow who had never seen any great value in physical effort, so I allowed her to indulge her pleasure in activity while I relaxed upon a cushioned seat. I would watch the transparency of the blue water as we slid over it or idly follow the white squares of the yacht clubs, the quaint chalets and the spiked tops of the pine trees that formed a rustic border for the lake, rousing and clambering to my feet only when a shout from her warned me that a sudden shift of the wind had made a little co-operative effort on my part necessary.

Erika with her merry smile and her big solemn gray eyes attracted a crowd of admirers, but she always had an evening to go calling with me or to join me for the wonderful spectacle of an American movie. She was entranced by each new picture from the United States and we formed what I must say was a highly exaggerated picture of the lavish luxury in which Americans of all classes habitually moved.

A good part of my free time I spent with Rudolph, who had joined a distinguished Corps, and I used to meet him at his Corps house almost daily at the hour when he had finished his fencing practice. Groups of men would meet in the elaborate clubrooms and a political debate would be sure to start. Thus I made most of my friends among the Corps members, who accepted me in spite of the fact that I was a theological student.

Most students of theology found themselves in large measure excluded from the more active life of the University. They took little part in political discussion, for they were preparing for a profession where their whole concern must be with the Kingdom of God and not with the secular interests of their fellows. The attitude of the other students toward us was likely to be rather supercilious, although they were never actually hostile. The chief cause of this discrimination was that we were forbidden by the Church to engage in dueling and were therefore ineligible as members of the Corps, and these renowned organizations set the pattern for the activities of the whole student body.

A Corps is a highly distinguished fraternity, to find an American parallel, which it is very difficult to enter and which never seeks members. An applicant must be able to prove that his family on both sides and for three generations have been professional people of high standing, and he must find at least two sponsors within the Corps itself. Even then he is only admitted on six months' probation. An approved candidate is then received into a Corps and becomes an active member for two or three semesters, during which time he is obliged to fight at least seven *Mensuren*, the traditional duels of Corps life. When he gives up his active membership he remains a life member of the Corps; and it is from the life members or *Alte Herren* that the generous financial support of these bodies is received. Every Corps has its distinctive colors and its members all wear the bright caps and the colors across their chests whenever they enter the university, a custom which contributes a great deal of vividness to the daily scene.

My friend Rudolph became an insatiable duelist shortly after he joined the Franconia Corps. He was not satisfied with the *Mensur*, which is a comparatively harmless fencing bout, but must have one duel with heavy swords every fortnight if he was to be happy. Since each provocation to a duel must be passed on by the Honor Court, a body made up of representatives of all the Corps to judge whether an insult had actually been received and to determine the gravity of the offense and the type of duel called for to satisfy honor, it required resolute contriving on Rudolph's part to involve himself in a new action as often as he wished.

Under the Republic dueling was forbidden, but it was not in the German character to forego a custom so dear to our young fire-eaters and the authorities usually closed their eyes to the affairs. I attended one of Rudolph's duels at a little beer hall near the university one evening. This was not to be a friendly *Mensur* but a duel with sabers, for Rudolph had happily managed to get himself grossly insulted. The heavy swords were ready, the opponents were just preparing to strip off their shirts when the outer door opened and in walked three stalwart members of the police. We all looked at them guiltily and Rudolph's face grew as long as a hound's, for he had been counting eagerly on this fight. The leader of the police came over to our table and bowed to us.

"Gentlemen," he observed gravely, "we have been notified that you are conducting a duel. We shall come to investigate. We shall be here in half an hour."

He bowed again and walked out with his companions. We all shouted and Rudolph and his antagonist hastily got ready for their duel. They stood facing each other, stripped to the waist with no protection of any kind to head or body, their firmly muscled torsos gleaming in the lamplight. This was by far the most dangerous duel. The *Mensur* was child's play in comparison, a brief bout of deft fencing where the participants wear heavy protection for body, throat, and eyes, and only the face and head are exposed, where the men stand with legs outspread only a sword's length apart and the danger is comparatively trivial.

Rudolph's three seconds took their places, one at his left, one at his right, and one behind him. The three judges stood, the doctor opened his bag, and suddenly the sabers were clashing and ringing through a breathless silence. The men stood far apart and lunged at each other with the brutal blades. There was only one restriction upon this type of duel. The swords must be used to slash but not to pierce; a man might be hacked but not run through. Rudolph's stocky body was as quick as it was strong but he had picked a formidable opponent, a Corps member who was a veteran of as many fights as he. They swung and ducked and swung again but only metal touched metal and they were both sweating and panting when the end of the round was called. The second at the left of his man leaped in front of him to protect him, the second at his right held his sword arm aloft so that he might rest it but still keep it in fighting position, and the second who stood in back of him disinfected the blade of the saber.

During the second round Rudolph switched to new tactics. He swung his sword high and brought it down broadside over the top of his antagonist's head. The young man staggered, recovered himself, and made a furious lunge at Rudolph, who parried it, lifted his sword, and battered him over the crown again. The boy flung his sword in front of him and Rudolph again found his head. At that moment the doctor intervened.

The blow was a legitimate blow, he declared; Herr Beck had performed no breach of form in using it, but since the young man was evidently unable to parry it he must outlaw its use in this duel since it might place the boy in danger of a fractured skull. Rudolph bowed to the doctor and the fight went on, but Rudolph's adversary had been either dizzied or frightened and his resistance was less skillful than before. In a moment or two he had received a deep cut; the blood poured down his chest; the doctor rushed in to staunch the wound and the fight was over. The duelists resumed their clothing; foaming steins of beer were brought out and when the police called, at the time they had so tactfully designated, both parties were sitting around one large table, harmlessly cooling their throats and singing old student songs.

The scars of dueling were of course worn with pride, but it is well to remember that despite the seeming cruelty of the exercise, serious wounds were very rare—they were almost impossible in duels of the *Mensur* type—and that only about one man in a century would be killed in a duel in all the universities of Germany.

I was invited, about the middle of the year, to become a member of a sort of second-rate fraternity called the *Bruederschaft*. These imitated the Corps life in so far as they could. Their duels were far more brutal than the ceremonious *Mensur* but they did not require dueling of their members and a number of theological students belonged to the *Bruederschaft*. I attended one of their social evenings, but I had seen too much of the dignified life of Rudolph's Corps to relish it very much. It seemed like a shabby and unfortunate attempt to ape the Corps and I declined their invitation to join.

At that time I am afraid I was an unconscionable young snob and even something of a prig. All my contacts had been confined to one social stratum and I had yet to learn the warmth, the quality, and the fascinating variety that humans of all kinds present to a friendly mind. I was also an intense individualist, very much absorbed in myself and holding aloof from the other students of theology, partly because I did not wish to be identified with a group that were considered somewhat déclassé and partly because I actually looked upon them as quite different beings from myself and I would not have known how to go about approaching them if I had wanted to. On the other hand, they displayed the same sort of snobbery in reverse, for most of them were sons of poor pastors

or the eldest sons of nonprofessional families who hoped to push a
brilliant boy up a notch in the social scale by placing him in the
ministry, and to them my father's position as pastor of one of the
great German churches was an eminence they could never dream
of attaining. Social lines are very sharply drawn in Germany, but
at the university there was an honest attempt to disregard them
altogether and to stress the equal citizenship of all the students. In
the campus discussions there were absolutely no distinctions made;
it was only in our social life that the patterns of German caste fell
into place again.

Otto Schmidt, a big, simple-natured man who was a theological
student, once invited me to his home in Berlin. It was not without
misgivings that I accepted. But I remembered the complete accord
with which my father was able to meet all types of men, his
understanding of situations quite foreign to me. No doubt it was
with some lofty idea that I was contributing to my high calling
that I accompanied young Schmidt to the very humble home where
his family lived. I was still too young and too well inculcated with
delicacy to carry the situation with aplomb. The house was
wretchedly small and swarming with young children in various
stages of undress, and most shocking of all to me, Otto's mother
hastened to set a chair for her son—this chosen, this select son of
hers who was preparing for the ministry. I had a momentary vision
of my own mother performing the same menial service for me
instead of waiting with her accustomed dignity for me to seat her,
and so strange was the notion that I felt a little spasm of nausea at
the spectacle of poor Frau Schmidt waiting upon her son. I could
hardly leave soon enough.

Although the majority of the theological students remained
apart from political debate, my own awakening enthusiasms led
me early into the political movements that were being constantly
fomented at the university. There was one other theological student
who was always to be found where the political talk was hottest, a
dark-haired, sallow young man, very Prussian in appearance and
manner, whose name was Heinrich Gross. I had noticed him in
my classes and I had often wondered what he was doing in the

school of theology. He was both noisy and arrogant and his views had very little in common with Christianity as I saw it. He talked of the "pride of the Nordic blood" and had none at all of the humility we usually expect in a Christian minister. He was all for the establishment of a strong German nation, however, and there most of my friends agreed with him.

There was not one of us, whatever his background, who did not resent the ignominious position that had been forced upon our fatherland after the great war, and we all hoped in our hearts for the resurgence of a new and more glorious Germany.

According to my own budding theories, as I used to expound them to the group, this coming glory was to exemplify a reborn republicanism. Every man would be free to employ his merits for the welfare of the nation. I foresaw a state where the intellectual equality of the university would spread through society, with each man's choice his own for good or evil as it was in the Kingdom of God.

Erich Doehr, a lanky blond boy who always seemed to be smiling behind his eyes, used to listen to me with a gentle detachment, as if he were listening to a strain of music that was not meant for rational consideration. One day when I had finished building my dream state he asked me quizzically, "How will you people this wonderful nation of yours, Herr Hoffmann? Will ordinary men, with their little envies and meannesses and ambitions, fit into it, or do you plan to breed a race of angels to inhabit it?"

I was indeed an incorrigible idealist, and my contact with those less privileged than myself had led me to feel convinced that only financial stringency prevented the development in others of the same sense of nobility and obligation with which I was sure my own soul was imbued. My father's dream of monarchy now seemed to me a brilliant but fading fantasy which had been lost before my day dawned, and his hopes for its restoration of feudalism. I wanted something new, something better than we had ever yet seen.

"Why," I asked in one day's discussion, "shouldn't Germany, with our wealth of philosophical and scientific minds, become a spiritual power among the nations? If we can build a society in keeping with the ideas of our greatest minds, we shall be more powerful in shaping the world than any military force."

"You are one of the cowards who want to accept Germany's shame, to refuse her the military power and glory that are her right," snapped Heinrich Gross, the young Prussian. "A day is coming that will show you what Germany can become. Watch the National Socialists. Hitler is the man who dreams the big dreams."

"What we need is a strong leader," asserted a youth named Jansen, a tight-mouthed individual whom I knew to be one of the leaders of the National Socialists among the students. "If you have ever listened to Adolf Hitler, you will know we have found one."

It was among the students who hoped for a restoration of Germany to her old military and political eminence that the growing Nazi movement was winning an increasing number of followers. It was active. It was alive. It promised to do so much!

The first visual sign of Nazi stagecraft appeared among us on a day to which I had long looked forward. It was a day we observed every year throughout the nation with the gravest of celebrations, the Memorial Festival in honor of the student battalion which had been mowed down in Flanders during the World War. I had often heard in Magdeburg of the magnificent observances with which this holiday was celebrated at the University of Berlin. This year, when I was to see them for the first time, the ceremonies were held at the Berlin Sports Palace, which seats fifty thousand people. All the Corps appeared in full *Wichs*, their splendid dress uniforms, and a special place was given to those Corps, members of which had died in the famous battle. While army bands played a dirge these students solemnly paraded onto the huge platform in glittering and colorful formation, while the assembly stood with bared heads.

There were speeches by eminent professors and by student leaders, by cabinet members and government dignitaries. Bishops of the Lutheran and Catholic churches offered prayers. The Catholic bishop raised his right hand in a powerful gesture, and I shall never forget how his voice rang as he cried, "I lift up my priestly hand and bless the ground on which the flower of Germany died."

An army general read the Communiqué for the day and the Lutheran bishop made his somber prayer. Then the drums rolled and the simple, stirring melody of the *"Gute Kamerad"* song rose up. Everyone was on his feet. The students held their caps over their hearts. The flags were dipped. The students in Corps uniform drew their swords, facing each other and beating out the rhythm of the song with their sword blades, which touched and clanged over their heads, while thousands of voices sang:

> *"Ich hatt' einen Kameraden*
> *Einen bessern find'st du nicht . . ."*

(I once had a comrade, A better one you'll never find.)

After this service came the parade homeward with the students riding in open automobiles, their flags unfurled in the wind. This year for the first time there appeared among us car after car of students in brown shirts, their huge black, white, and red swastikas held high, flapping and streaming out in the breeze. Never before had this flag mingled with the others.

"What is that street-corner political flag doing here?" asked Rudolph in disgust.

But the sight of the massed swastikas was none the less impressive, and among the students many watched the display with magnetized eyes.

After that day you could watch, as you might watch a tide rising, the upsurge of Nazi sentiment among the students. I began to fear for my republican dream and I grew impatient with the government for failing to provide a forthright democratic policy. I had made a friend, a young painter of unusual talent whose preoccupation with beauty gave him a very mature detachment from the turmoil of the day, and I took my fears to him.

"It is a natural reaction, Karl," Wolfgang told me. "Everything has broken down around us. Remember, not everyone can share your hopes in the face of what they see today. Walk around Berlin. Get under your skin the level that we have fallen to. In the best parts of town you can stand on a corner and count fifty prostitutes soliciting. What despair of a better life has driven them to it? Ludwig knows a house where he said he could take his grandmother and she would see nothing wrong, yet artful boys parade there as women.

"Is this Germany? Do you remember the Three-Penny Opera? The action laid in a bawdy house—every line so off-color that it reeked! Yet the composer had the gall to use the same music in a solemn Christmas Mass which was performed before the Pope himself. That is the sort of debauchery we see everywhere we look. None of us is free from it. No wonder the people turn to something more vigorous and understandable and wholesome in comparison to the stink they are living in. Hitler says he will give them a new Germany. Each man will work for his brother and all can believe again in their own goodness; they can be great again, a fine, a clean, a chosen people.

"I don't believe him—you don't believe him. We think he lies. We have had enough monarchs and it is obvious that the man wants to rule. But what are you going to offer the people? If you talk of a republic they think that is what they have been living in and its vices smell to heaven."

I have often wondered since if anything could have stemmed the tide at that time. The students saw in the Nazi promises a rising of Germany to her old power and glory. In Berlin, where patriotism had always been strong and the political sentiment conservative, the dream of a rejuvenated Germany turned their eyes and their hopes toward the coming movement. The professors were not so easily persuaded and tried to warn us that dangers lurked in the strong nationalistic and anti-Semitic theories of the Nazis, but great numbers refused to listen to them and there was a tremendous ferment among the student body.

When the elections drew near in the spring of 1932 great student rallies were held for the cause of the Nazi candidates. The Communists among the students set up a violent opposition to National Socialism and day after day, wherever you turned on the grounds or in the halls, all you heard were fiery speeches in favor of Nazism or opposing it. Wolfgang and I attended one of the pro-

Nazi rallies and in the flare of torches we saw the police suddenly move in, shouting for the meeting to disperse. The students roared and rushed toward them and in the half darkness the place turned into a howling shambles. Near me at the edge of the crowd I saw a policeman's heavy club send a boy sprawling senseless, and when the mob finally dissolved two students lay dead.

"So this is supposed to be the democratic process at work!" I snorted to Wolfgang. And the government's action proved to be folly, for the dead students became martyrs to the Nazi cause. The National Socialists made sweeping electoral gains.

As the year drew on the turbulence increased. Riots broke out at the university and student assemblies ended in tumult. When I came on the grounds one day in November I met Rudolph running in red-faced excitement toward a knot of Corps members who stood on one of the paths.

"There's a fight going on, up on the second floor," he shouted to me.

A few seconds later there was a crash of glass and we looked upward to see a man falling from the shattered window on the second story. Before he had turned once in the air a second body was catapulted after him through the heavy plate glass. For an endless instant they twisted downward with clutching hands and then they struck the pavement of the court and lay still. A silent crowd gathered around them instantly, but from the second floor you could still hear the shouts and hubbub of rioting.

Five minutes later a squad of police appeared and raced into the building. Great masses of students collected, waiting for news, and soon we heard that the men who had been thrown from the window were dead and that the rector, in his despair, had called the police into the university without consulting the deans or the student representatives. Then there was trouble indeed. This was a violation of "academic sanctuary," our jealously guarded right which set the university in a world apart from and above all governmental interference. Before night fell the entire student body had gone on strike.

The rector was unable to placate the outraged students. For

two weeks all our classes were suspended until peace could be
made. That winter was an unbridled nightmare. The university,
like the nation, produced one crisis after another.

Then in January, with an overwhelming suddenness, the Nazi
regime was upon us. Hindenburg in desperation appointed Hitler
to the chancellorship. The Reichstag met and granted him absolute
powers. Swastikas bloomed out all over the land and the streets
were filled with the marching feet of the brown-shirts.

The first reaction at the university was almost universal
rejoicing. Heinrich Gross, the arrogant young Nazi, strutted
through the halls in his brown shirt and even men who disliked
him personally felt inclined to congratulate him because he was
on the crest of the new tide. Brown shirts broke out among us by
the score. Even those of us who distrusted the new leader felt that
we were entering a fresh era. Whatever was coming, the old
indecision was a thing of the past. We should be going ahead—
somewhere—instead of continuing to wander in an aimless circle.

Then one morning on the bulletin board where we were
accustomed to look for university news, an unobtrusive notice
appeared. Two or three of our elected student representatives had
been "dismissed" and among the men who were named to fill their
places by appointment of the Ministry of Education and Culture
was Helmuth Jansen, the hard-mouthed leader of the Nazi students.
The others, we soon learned, were also Nazis. One by one our
elected representatives were removed and replaced by Nazis. The
university was henceforth to be governed by the "leader principle."
The country had abandoned weak democratic forms, we were told,
and we must do likewise. Nazi students were designated by the
government to lead the men of each faculty; and in the theological
school we found ourselves under the dictatorship of Heinrich Gross,
the offensive young Prussian I had long felt was not of the caliber
to make even a fourth-rate minister. Now we were all obliged to
take orders from him and he treated us much as a hard-boiled
army sergeant would handle a group of raw privates. He was quick
to report any student who failed to accord him the deference he
felt was due his new position.

Silently and subtly, the government had taken over university rule and our free citizenship was a thing of the past. The hand-picked young Nazis who controlled us were an arrogant crew. We were required to salute them, to refrain from criticizing them, and to obey them on pain of expulsion or arrest.

I was a member of a group of students who were discussing the new government one morning, when Gross strode up to us.

"All political discussion is forbidden," he snapped.

"What price our free citizenship now?" said one of the boys to me as the group broke up.

Our lively discussions had been the basis of our whole university life. Now a strange paralysis lay upon the great halls, and the aggressive thinking that had characterized our days had no more voice. This silence that had been imposed on us was something so new, so removed from all our tradition, that we hardly knew how to face it. Even the Nazi doctrines were not allowed to be debated. The supremacy of the Nordic race, anti-Semitism, the importance of the state and the unimportance of the individual were not to be discussed. They were to be learned and adopted.

It seemed ridiculous and yet somehow frightening to see a whole roomful of men leap to their feet with arms extended, simply because young Gross, whom we all disliked, had entered in his brown shirt. Whenever one of these upstart officials passed, the "Heil Hitlers" resounded from all sides, but as our disillusionment progressed they were given with more noise than enthusiasm.

New requirements were made of the applicants who wished to enter the university. Not only must the new men prove their academic standing, as of old. They were brought before a board of Nazi students, whom they must satisfy as to the purity of their political background and convictions, and to whom they were required to prove their Aryan ancestry.

Then the Labor Service appeared. This was a new branch of Nazi activity which was developed at the universities. We were asked to volunteer for six months to build roads, reservoirs, or landing fields for planes, and we were enticed into joining by the promise that time so spent would be credited as having been spent at the university.

"It's a pity men like Lietzmann and all the great graduates who put in such long years of study and research couldn't have learned in their day our new simple methods of acquiring scholarship," scoffed one of the theological students. "They might have earned their degrees with a pick and shovel."

The situation was the source of a good deal of ribaldry, and there were not many volunteers.

Then one day the entire student body was summoned to a meeting, where we were to be addressed by Bernhard Rust, the grade-school teacher who had been named Minister of Culture and Education for Prussia. We were not invited, as had always been the custom; we were commanded to appear. I had a lecture at the same hour which I very much wished to attend, the class above all that I most enjoyed, but I decided to be prudent and go to the student body meeting. My individualism did not take the form of setting myself apart from the crowd by nonconformist action; I had no taste for notoriety and I did not see any point in encountering needless trouble. Thus I argued with myself, but I was also impelled by considerable curiosity to see what would occur in the assembly.

On my way through the halls I encountered Walther Vogler, one of the shabbier theological students, hurrying in the other direction.

"Aren't you coming?" I asked him.

"Listen to those demagogues when I have a chance to hear Lietzmann?" he said scornfully. "Come along, do, Herr Hoffmann. What do you want to let those Nazis make a sheep out of you for?"

"Don't you think it might be dangerous to stay away?"

"How do I know? I haven't yet sold them my soul to the point where I am going to regulate my conduct by their wishes or spend my time wondering whether I am displeasing them. When their punishments catch up with me then I'll start worrying, but no sooner."

I felt a little twinge of conscience which hinted to me that I should have made the same decision Vogler had come to, but I was too proud to change my mind because this boy I was accustomed to look down on had done better than I had.

"I think it will be curious," I equivocated. "Besides, I want to see this Rust. I think there's something up."

"Suit yourself," said Vogler, and went his way.

The students had gathered in great throngs in the Opernplatz, and you could hear the high buzzing of voices as they speculated on the meaning of the assembly. We never knew in those days what was going to happen to us next. Again the crowd was sprinkled with uniforms, but this time they were all of one color and that was brown. As on the Memorial day there were great flags flying, but these all bore the swastika. The minister was driven up in a shining big car. He addressed the students as "sharers in the new Germany," and promised great things for the future.

Then he drew himself up stiffly and announced, "The Fuehrer is not pleased with the number of volunteers for the Labor Battalions. I have come today to proclaim that henceforth the Labor Service will be compulsory. A six-months' term of labor will be required of every student who wishes a degree."

All through the assembly students looked sidewise at their neighbors. When Minister Rust left in his gleaming car there were cheers but they were not very hearty ones, and no edict could have stemmed the roar of talk that followed.

Those of us who had classes wandered glumly back to the lecture rooms. I was one of the soberest of them, for I had begun to feel that I had been used to swell the Nazi display and to share the humiliation of having to accept the enforced Labor Service cheerfully, when I might have been listening to our famous Dr. Hans Lietzmann talking on the Epistle to the Romans. I admitted to myself that a good many of us had been just precisely the sheep that young Vogler had called us.

Of my class, about two hundred of us walked in late and found that a large group of our fellows had chosen to disregard the assembly and had come to hear their professor instead. A number of them turned around and frowned or remonstrated with us for disturbing the lecture but Dr. Lietzmann grinned at us out of his lean, ascetic face and said, "I am happy these days when my students come to class at all. Don't reprove them, gentlemen."

And he went on in his quiet voice with his eloquent interpretation of the ancient words:

"For what if some did not believe? Shall their unbelief make the faith of God without effect? God forbid. Yea, let God be true, but every man a liar."

And the familiar lecture room was about us with the sun coming through the windows and a fly batting himself happily against one of the panes. The words of a letter written centuries before rang again with a timeless importance and my world slowly righted itself. The magnitude of the Nazi assemblage paled and the years of my coming life seemed to stretch solidly before me, as undisturbed by the Nazi buzzing as Dr. Lietzmann was undisturbed by the fly, and the years as I saw them were filled with just such beautiful and timeless sentences as the ones that were falling from his firm and honest lips.

Walking across the wide square before the university, only a few days later, I heard my name shouted. Hands grasped my shoulders and I found myself looking into the merry face of Orlando von Schlack. For a moment we stood pumping each other's hands and laughing with pleasure. As I looked at him I realized that this was not the petulant young degenerate of whom I had heard rumors. His eyes were bright and his handclasp hard. I let my surprise spill out of me.

"You don't look the way I expected."

He caught the implication at once. "You have been hearing things."

"I'm sorry," I apologized. "But there were stories. You always managed to get yourself talked about, Orlando."

He grinned at me boyishly. "You didn't hear half of it." Then he became swiftly sober. "I was pretty far gone. I had muddied my life up with just about everything you can think of, and a lot that your good simple mind couldn't think of. I even tried drugs, Karl. Finally I felt that there was only one sensation left to try and that was death.

"But a man reached out to me and kept me alive, one of our highest army officers. I did not know there was such honesty and goodness in a human being." Orlando's face was alight with the first stirring and honest affection I had ever seen in him. "My mother asked him to look me up and see if he could help me and I even forgive him that." He laughed with wholehearted exuberance.

"He has changed my whole life, Karl. He has become a father to me. I don't suppose that means so much to you, but you can't imagine what it means to me. He cares for me as if I were his own son. And his wife has been as kind as he has. There is nothing I wouldn't do for him. To find a father, when you have never known a father, when nobody cared whether you went to the devil or not—you can't know what it is."

Then with one of his instantaneous changes of mood, as if he were afraid he had let me see into him too deeply, he cried, "But it is wonderful to see you again. Come along, we must have a cup of coffee and talk over old times."

When we were seated in the coffeehouse Orlando asked me at once what I was doing, and when I told him he looked at me with mock sorrow and cried, "Dear Karl! You are just the same as ever. Even that musty God you love is still the same!" Then he leaned toward me across the table and his eyes glowed with a fire that I had never seen in them. "Karl," he cried, "I believe. I am saved."

"What do you mean?" I asked him. I sensed something strange in him. Much of his old mockery seemed to have disappeared and his intensity to have sharpened.

"I am in love with a new god," he told me, clenching his fingers around mine, "and his name is Hitler."

"I don't believe you."

"It is true, Karl. You remember what I was like as a boy, how I grew sickened with the world because I was too clever and everything in it had grown old to me while I was still young?"

"Yes, I remember."

"General von Schleicher does not believe in my new faith but he does not discourage me, because I am like a son to him and because his soul is so great.—But I believe—" His eyes grew soft and his mouth trembled like a young girl's who is shy and in love at the same time.

"It is glorious, dear Karl," he said. "There is something new in the world after all. I could never have tolerated following some misty religion of the past; my blood revolted at it because I belong to the new age. What I believe in is a religion that is just beginning—it is going out into the future.

"I was dying in the old swamp. I did not know what rhythms were singing in my blood. Now I have friends. Now I have a leader. There are strong emotions left in me, that I can put my teeth in, hatred, pride—all the fierce virtues—"

"Orlando, you fool," I rapped at him, "you can't possibly believe all that Nazi claptrap."

"Dear Karl," his eyes laughed at me with a flash of their familiar mockery, "who are you to berate me for my mysticism? For how many years did you tell me that it is possible to believe without questioning? Now my leader demands it and I believe without questioning."

"But it is so stupid, so irrational, what you believe."

"Ah, yes, that is what I used to tell you when we had our arguments about religion, isn't it? But look how mysterious both our faiths are—and how much alike. Why, they're absolutely parallel. The likeness simply fascinates me. You believe in salvation by the blood of Christ and I believe in salvation by the strong red stream that flows in all Aryans. We should both be kneeling at the same altar—"

"Orlando, you blasphemous devil—"

But he was out of control, laughing and talking at the top of his voice.

"You and I, Karl," he shouted, "you and I—and who would have thought it? We shall both be saved by blood!"

His hand pounded the table and a little wave of coffee slopped out of the cup and spread in a slowly widening brown stain across the tablecloth.

CHAPTER
FOUR

ORLANDO'S words stayed with me and as the months passed they began to assume the significance of prophecy. I began to sense a new menace to all I had come to believe in most deeply. There were violent political changes in Germany, to be sure, but in many ways these followed an historical pattern wholly familiar to the national temperament. To bow to a strong central authority was almost an instinct to a German and to many it came as relief to abandon the obligation of personal responsibility that a republican government demanded. The people were promised the fulfillment of their dearest hope, the resurgence of a powerful Germany, and all they need do was acquiesce and perhaps shut their eyes to those acts of the new regime of which they did not wholly approve.

The centralization of power in Nazi hands grew stronger from month to month. The political opposition was removed by the simple expedient of jailing the outspoken leaders of opposing parties and by declaring all the traditional parties illegal with the exception of one, the National Socialists. The governments of the German provinces were either dissolved or placed under the control of a *Reichsverweser*, a representative of the central government. The suddenness of these changes, together with the Germanic instinct of obedience, caused them to be accepted passively. It was hard to say at the moment whether the new plans would turn out well or not. When systematized persecutions began to grow they were met with this same passivity, but here the desire for self-preservation played a large part. If your neighbor's house rang with cries of terror during the night, if you saw a Jew dragged from his shop and beaten, still it was not happening to you and your acquiescence might be the price of your own safety. Thus the Nazis were able without opposition to single out an isolated group for purge or oppression. No section of society which had not been touched or molested was willing to utter a word in defense of those who were suffering for fear they might thus mark themselves out for the next victims. If the voice of their brother's blood cried out to them from the ground, there were many who answered in the stony words of Cain:

"Am I my brother's keeper?"

I had been disturbed and made wretched by this growing selfishness on the part of my countrymen. I suspected it was an outgrowth of the frank materialism of Nazi philosophy; but I had never doubted the power of Christianity to overwhelm materialism after the people had tasted this new idea to the full. Now with Orlando's words haunting me, I found even this surety troubled; I began to sense a new menace in the hold this man Hitler was exercising over the people, a new threat in the air. Nazism was itself becoming a religion.

Orlando had first personified to me the form it was taking; however, I had put down Orlando's exuberance to his intensely emotional nature. But the more I saw of him the more I appreciated the strength of his fanaticism. He was like one of the ancient missionary monks in the violence of his belief. He talked of turning the people to the old Germanic gods, but his own god was Hitler. And now in my classes at the university I began to notice a strange glorification of the Fuehrer which was almost of a religious nature. I began to wonder when this new religion would come to active grips with the old.

I returned home for the Easter vacation in the spring of 1933 in a very unhappy state of mind. I had written to my father of the religious tendency I saw in Nazism but he had seemed to miss the whole point of my fears. He had replied that I seemed to be giving more attention than was needful to politics, that it was only natural in a young man to attribute undue importance to the first political upheaval he encountered, but that he himself, an older man, had been through more than one upsetting change of government and as a churchman he had found that these must not concern him directly. He urged me to devote more consideration to my studies and less to the machinations of the government.

His answer only left me more worried than before. If, as I foresaw, a shadow was creeping toward the Church, this sort of apathy would provide the very opportunity the Nazis needed, just as they had utilized the political lassitude under the Republic to gain their ends. But wherever I turned I met the same complacency, even among the students of theology, who clearly felt that to anticipate trouble from the Nazis was to get ourselves on dangerous ground.

Wolfgang Kleist, my young artist friend, was the only one who agreed with me. But his attitude toward the new government was one of remote distaste and he was not very comforting to me.

"Poor Cassandra Hoffmann," he said. "You may be right, of course. Your faith is threatened by a rival, and a very powerful one at that, but there isn't any precedent for an attack on the Church in a really civilized nation, especially a Protestant one. I am afraid nobody will believe you until something actually happens."

Of course there were many other men in Germany who sensed the coming danger, but I did not know any of them, and I never in my life have felt so alone. I wanted desperately to have a long talk with my father.

I brought Wolfgang home with me for the Easter holidays since his family were abroad at the time, and the affectionate warmth of my mother's welcome, the simple, friendly pattern of life in the big old house served to put me immediately into an easier frame of mind. My fears even seemed a little ridiculous in this terrain of my happy childhood, and their forbidding phantoms less distinct.

I did try at once on reaching home to talk with my father, but I found him busy with his Easter sermon and involved in preparations for all the various observances of the Easter season, so that he had only a few minutes to give me; there was no time for a serious conversation. He patted my shoulder as he used to do when I was much younger and told me there was a very pleasant holiday in store for me. My parents had planned to entertain twice for my young friends and we should ourselves be guests at a great dinner party at the home of the mayor, whose son Fritz, one of my oldest friends, was just home from his studies at the Sorbonne. I would be expected to make a dinner speech and my father wanted me to do myself credit.

This custom of dinner speeches was cultivated with great care and elaboration. When I was twelve years old my father began instructing me in the art of speech-making. He would give me some simple theme and I was required to compose a five-minute speech to deliver before my parents without the aid of notes. The speech must be well planned, must contain literary allusions, perhaps some lines of poetry, must draw to a rather dramatic conclusion and must be delivered with an expressive range of voice and appropriate gestures. Only after I had finished college was I allowed to speak when we had guests, but I was expected to have speeches ready for my parents on special occasions and I was well accustomed to hearing some bits of fine oratory around our own board. I remember it was on the day of my confirmation that I was myself the object of dinner speeches for the first time, and since I was so young I was obliged to listen to them standing, which made me almost unbearably self-conscious.

My father was a particularly scholarly and charming speaker and I longed to please him at the mayor's party, but I was distrait, feeling that the time for more pressing matters was passing without accomplishment. Instead of calling on the friends I had not seen for so long I remained close to the house for two days, waiting to catch my father with an hour's free time on his hands. Erika came several times to see my mother, and the first day I was at home she and Wolfgang beguiled me into the music room where the great piano waited like an old friend. Wolfgang borrowed my father's violin and Erika spread out the music for us and while we played she sang in her light and lovely voice.

She was standing, leaning against the marble mantelpiece with a troubled face when I let the last chords crash and turned from the piano fretfully.

"Karl," she said, "you are spoiling your whole vacation with your seriousness. Can't you persuade him, Herr Kleist," she turned to Wolfgang, smiling, "to take things a little more lightly just for a few days?"

"The trouble is," I responded, "that I am expected to take light matters seriously and the serious matters lightly. If I must be light, I shall be light about my dinner speech." She and Wolfgang both laughed, shaking their heads as if they despaired of me.

It was not until after the mayor's party that I managed to see my father alone. The dinner party itself was not, to me, a happy experience. I found my friend Fritz dazzled by the show of National Socialism. He was just back from France and could see in Germany only bright faces and parading and uniforms and was very much impressed, even enthusiastic over the new regime.

I usually enjoyed a formal dinner, the solemn procession into the dining room with our partners on our arms, the first speech when the soup was removed, which would be the host's speech of welcome, and the responding speeches which were given between each course while the servants stood waiting to serve until the little ceremony was over. The dinner itself was excellent. The fish was trout, of which I am very fond; the roast was venison, accompanied out of compliment to my father by his favorite red wine, St. Emilion 1927. The speeches were not so happy. It was not like former days with these old friends when there were no clouds over our heads and no constraint between us.

Now the mayor rose heavily to his feet, his red face gleaming as if it had been burnished, his rotund shirt front crossed by the ribbon of his office. He chuckled and adjusted his coat at the widest point of his plentiful girth as he looked around the generously spread table. He had the brisk, jocund temperament that seems to belong naturally to some fat men and he beamed at us not just with his face but with a joviality that came from the very innards of his capacious figure.

"My good friends," he said, "I have no welcome hearty enough to match the pleasure your company has brought to my house tonight." He went on to greet my father and the other notables, to bless heaven for the charm of the lovely ladies present and to greet and compliment the younger guests who had returned for their vacations.

"It used to be the custom," he declared, "to compliment the young upon their innocence and their happy prospects. But today we have something greater on which to congratulate youth." Here, it seemed to me, his aspect changed from that of the happy host to something more somber.

"Today, in their hands is destiny. The Germany we love will rise by their loyal hands to a new place in the sun. They are to be congratulated that they had not grown old before the Leader came. They have strength to give him; they have all their years to serve him—our Leader whom God has sent us and whom may God bless."

He sat down and a strong spatter of applause ran around the table. We all joined in it, for he was our host and whether we liked his words or not we must look pleasant and seem to approve. But the speech left a constraint on many of us.

My own speech, which I had got up with as much care as I could find heart for, dealt with the pleasures of returning home after absence and the renewal of old acquaintanceship. While I felt that on such a festive occasion I dare not mention the political stresses that had touched us all, yet I could not bring myself to make my speech all flattery without letting some hint creep in of what I felt in my heart.

"To return," I said at the last, "is always to find that one has lost something. Just as it is impossible to go back in time to an earlier year that one remembers with joy and would eagerly see again, so it is impossible ever to return entirely to the same place. The complete familiarity one has longed for is not there. There have been changes. The faces of last year are not quite the same; the feeling in the air has altered. We are never so lost as when we return eagerly to a dear place only to find it greets us with a stranger's face. The mind of the friend I hasten toward has changed. He is not the same, and to him I also seem a stranger. In our very handclasp we sense our loss, knowing that last year's home, last year's friend, last year's nation live only in our memory with last year's spring, never to be achieved again."

When I sat down I felt with a momentary pang that even in saying so much I had forgotten my obligation as a guest. The mayor's smile now seemed to me to be wholly in his facial muscles, and it may have been through oversensitiveness that I felt a little uneasiness in some of the guests. I kept my eyes up, and under the cover of the table Erika, who was my dinner partner, reached over and gave my fingers a short, quick squeeze which buoyed me immensely, for it assured me that I had one ally even if she was only a girl.

I was even more reassured when after dinner my father complimented me on the arrangement of my little oral effort, with a sort of shrewd amusement in his eyes which seemed to say that although he had caught the undertones of the speech he had not disagreed with them.

So much encouraged, since I had half expected a reprimand, I dared the next morning to break in on him in his study where he was very early at work. The big, book-lined room was blue with tobacco smoke as it always was when he was at his desk, for he smoked incessantly although my mother deplored the habit. He looked up a little sharply as I entered from the secretaries' room. He never liked to be disturbed.

"Father," I said, "if you please, I must talk to you."

He flung himself around, his elbows over the back of his chair.

"It is something important, of course?"

"It is so important that I can't wait any longer. I wouldn't have interrupted you . . ."

"Very well," he said shortly. "Sit down." He put his manuscript aside regretfully and I pulled up one of the leather easy chairs that he kept for visitors.

"Father," I said, "I have been watching the Nazis . . ."

"So!" He interrupted me. "You are not taking my advice not to disturb yourself with politics, after all."

"If it were only politics," I interjected, "I would let them stew in it. I am beginning to be afraid for the Church, for Christianity.

I think they are being threatened and that we may not wake up in time."

"My dear son," he said gravely, "I do not like your concerning yourself with such matters. What you said last night did not displease me, but I should prefer you to take a more neutral course in the future. The Church's great protection is that she does not interfere in politics or takes sides in political controversies. She stands aloof, separated from secular affairs. The government directs one side of the people's lives, the Church the other. Each recognizes the other and allows the other complete freedom to serve its own ends. That is the Church's great traditional position, and by maintaining it she protects herself."

"Father," I said, "please allow me to disagree with you. I have been watching the way things are going in Berlin, and I am very much disturbed. I don't think we are dealing with a government that will allow us that historic protection. Look at the way they have concentrated power in their own hands in these brief months. They have destroyed a lot of ancient privileges. Who knows whether ours won't be the next? Suppose they combine the churches, set up a central control for all of them, the way they have for the provinces?"

My father leaned back and laughed.

"My boy," he said, "the Church is founded on a very ancient tradition. What could the government hope to gain by trying to change it? Even if they did entertain such an idea the Church would never consent."

"I am afraid of them," I insisted. "They do not like any strong organization whose ideas don't agree with their own. The Church is in danger because it is a strong spiritual power, and the thing about Nazism, the thing I tried to tell you of in my letters, is that it isn't gaining force now as a political power; it is becoming a religion. And it isn't going to want any rival religion."

"Now wait a minute, Karl. I'm afraid you're letting your fears run away with your judgment. There is a very deep cleavage between religious ends and political ends. So far as I can see, the ends of National Socialism are expressly political. It wants to break the

chains of the Versailles Treaty, to build Germany up to a first-
ranking nation, and to build a strong army to protect that rank.
Connected with these political aims are purely socialistic goals
such as raising the standard of the working class, equal distribution
of wealth, and so on. Even the methods they want to use to
accomplish these things come from the socialist pattern. They are
working toward a government-controlled economy.

"Now you may have your doubts as to the advisability of such
a program; you may have your doubts, as I have, about the benefits
a socialistic order will bring; you can argue, for instance, that a
government-controlled economy will kill private initiative and
therefore hurt economic development rather than further it; but I
can't see that all these things have anything to do with religion or
conceal even latent threats to the Church."

"All right, Father. Those are their aims, of course. But can't
you see that the Nazis are not promoting them in any such rational
way? They talk about their new form of government as divinely
appointed, as if it had come into existence as an act of God. They
aren't pushing the political program of a party. Their acts are all
cloaked in a religious fervor—the people must accept them as they
accept religious laws, without doubt . . . Nothing else can be right.

"It isn't enough to accept their results. Everyone has to accept
their philosophy. In Berlin you can begin to see the shape of a
religious persecution that strikes at anybody brave enough to
question their doctrine. I know personally of instances where men
went to jail merely because they spoke out against the Nazi theory
of the divine quality of the state. Even the divine inspiration of
Hitler is becoming something that must not be questioned. The
state is God. That is the religion they are preaching."

"My dear Karl—" My father paused to stuff and light his pipe.
"The desire for a strong central government, for a strong state, has
been a great force in Germany for a long time. It is a purely political
tendency and in accord with a powerful German tradition. Now a
strong state has been instituted and is in the process of
consolidating itself. I do not like some of the methods they are
employing. I have been shocked at some of the cruelties I have

heard of. But I question whether these brutalities are as widespread as they are reported to be. They are an unfortunate means of establishing the position of the government. And so is this tendency to reverence the state to which you attach so much significance. But you are mistaken in thinking that reverence for the state could ever replace religion. Christianity lives because it satisfies the human need for worship, for bringing men into contact with the great Unknowable, the final mystery of God."

"I am afraid," I said slowly, "that the danger is greater than you think. There *is* a natural human need for religion, but this need is always coupled with the hope for a better, a more perfect way of life. There has always been the dream of a Golden Age. I have sometimes thought that in the beginning of Christianity the preaching of the 'Kingdom of God' as a new and perfect world in which there should be no pain and no tears was its greatest lure. Today how many thousands of our people, broken, impoverished, and disheartened, pray and yearn for a better and happier life? And National Socialism promises them just that—a better life, a happier life, if and when we follow the Fuehrer *with a believing heart.*

"Hitler is the one who knows how much of a religion he is preaching. Do you remember his great speech in January, the one that marked him as the man of the hour, the one that made him Chancellor?

"And do you remember how he ended it? With the doxology from the Lord's Prayer? After his oratory had rushed to such sweeping heights, how his voice rang on the old words, 'the kingdom and the power and the glory,' and how in his mouth they somehow took on a new meaning as if he were a Moses standing on a mountaintop and pointing out to us a promised land? And it was *not* the Kingdom of God, not the *Gottes Reich* we murmur of in our prayers that he meant; it was *his own* promised land that he showed us with those great words rolling from his tongue: 'The *Reich* and the power and the glory forever, Amen.' He was posing as a prophet, not as a political leader. Or can you tell me that *that* one was only a political speech?"

My father shook his head.

"I think," he said, "that all new and especially all radical movements will present themselves to the people with a great zeal. This Hitler is a fine orator. He knows how to move the emotions, how to embroider with words; he understands the stirring quality of a Biblical phrase. But the wise, the proven position of the church toward governmental authority is to uphold it, to take a stand only when the free course of the Word of God is endangered. Such a danger I have not seen.

"Do not forget, my son," he warned me, "that we are churchmen, that our concern is not with a happier economic lot for the people, or with their choice of governments. Many of us have made that mistake in the past years, and I among them. We were caught up in the dream of an evolution of human society, following the divine laws of justice and mercy, to a point nearing God's perfection. It was a beautiful dream but the wretched years after the war shocked us out of it. We were wrong. We were not content with faith in the unfolding of a supreme plan. We were trying to work out a better one for ourselves. We heard ourselves reproached that our religion had become a sociology and the reproach was just. If the Church has erred, it has been in failing to provide enough guidance to satisfy the religious longing of the people. If the Church is so feeble that it can be attacked, if our influence has been weakened and some of the people have become disinterested and fallen away, it is because of our own laxity during the years of materialism. The only strength of the Church is to hold the light of God before the people's eyes. Now, sadly because of our short-sightedness, we have returned to faith, learning to say again the most difficult words in the world, 'Thy will, O Lord, not mine be done.'"

"I know you are right," I said, for I was moved. "But all that I am asking is: how long will we be allowed to follow that will, to teach at all? The Nazis have a new Bible and a new revelation. When you read Rosenberg's *Myth of the 20th Century* you will see what supernatural justification they have concocted for themselves. The Aryan blood is divine! The salvation of the world shall come through the Aryan blood! That is a religious doctrine and the men who teach it are pagan priests rather than political leaders. They make the claim themselves.

"Look back through Church history, if you will, and see how two religions with conflicting doctrines will inevitably clash. Now the Nazis claim they will be saved by the Aryan blood. How much longer, I wonder, will they let us say that the only blood which can save us is the Blood of Christ?"

"You are giving the controversy too much significance, I am afraid," my father said, picking up from his desk the heavy silver crucifix which was the only ornament of the room, and weighing it in his hands. "You are young, and you are impressionable. Christianity is very old and very deeply rooted. I doubt that the government would try to teach a religious doctrine, that they would dare to deprive the people of a religious tradition which has grown in them for hundreds of years. If you will permit me in my turn to refer you to the history of the Church, it will teach you that the people are willing to be deprived of many things, but not of their belief. They will suffer many outrages, but not the destruction of their religion. I do not recall that Hitler has ever attacked the Church and I don't believe he will now."

"I wish I could feel you were right," I said, the old feeling of loneliness engulfing me. "But I am afraid it isn't so simple even as that. The Nazi doctrine doesn't intend to deprive people of their faith, but to substitute a new religion for an old one. I am afraid there are many people ready to accept a new faith. I have talked to numbers of them. Life had lost all hope to them; everything they knew, everything old was a sickness and its ideals a sham. Now comes a new and shining promise, and I am afraid that many will follow it, especially since it promises more food on the table, more money in their pockets, and more power for their country."

"It will never be strong enough," said my father. He set the crucifix back in its place and regarded it. I got to my feet.

"Thank you, Father," I said, miserably.

As I went out the door he sent after me a slow smile that was meant for my reassurance. But I was not reassured.

CHAPTER
FIVE

THE first blow fell on the day of my return to the university. I had escorted Erika with her luggage from the railway station to her rooms in the town, had gone to my own quarters and unpacked, feeling the contentment that always returned to me among my own books and belongings and the few trophies of my boyhood. I then hastened to the university to find the place in a turmoil. The courtyard was crowded with milling students, their voices loud with excitement. Customary decorum was forgotten; two or three men of a group would start to speak at once or interrupt each other, a quite unheard-of performance.

The flushed faces, the gesturing hands, I saw at once belonged almost wholly to the theological students and I knew that something had happened in my own faculty. I joined the first group with whom I was acquainted and noticed that they were too excited for formal greetings. The work student, Walther Vogler, was speaking. He welcomed me gladly.

"Herr Hoffmann may know whether it is true or not," he said. "Have you heard the rumors?"

"What has happened?" I asked. "I don't know anything."

"We have just heard that the government has ordered all the Lutheran churches to unite."

Here it comes, I thought to myself; aloud I said, "I am not surprised. It is the first step."

"It doesn't seem very ominous to me," another student broke in. "Certainly it will not weaken the Church to be unified."

"I don't like the implication," I answered. "It is enough to know that the Nazis have begun to interfere in Church affairs at all. If they can force one step on us they will try another."

"We can't be sure," said a big, cautious blond boy. "The report has not been verified."

"It seems to me," said the second boy who had spoken, "that if the government wants to bring all the churches into one body they will be making us a present. The Church will become stronger. It can hardly hurt us."

"I fear the Greeks," said young Vogler fiercely, "when they bring gifts."

I left the gathering and hurried from one group to another. There were nearly a thousand students of theology at the university and they formed a great throng. I noticed that men from other faculties had joined them, that there was a wide cross section from all the student body represented. Large numbers of work students as well as members of the various Corps were among the clamorous crowd.

The work student was a new type at the university; they had appeared after the World War, when money values and social values had alike become disrupted. Before that time it was unknown for a student to work to pay part of his tuition, but after the inflation this expedient became common. A university degree in Germany was always a distinction and jobs had become so scarce the only hope a man could have of finding work was to present himself as a graduate. Not that he could find room in the overcrowded profession for which he had studied. There was little hope there; but if he wished to become a clerk in a store and sell socks he had a chance if he was a graduate of a university. The professors took a great deal of interest in the work students and used their own social eminence and prestige to push these young men on their way. We were always careful never to let an individual feel that his shabby clothes in any way debased him. The intelligence and liveliness of the work students became a valuable factor in university life, and acquaintance with them was highly enlightening to many of us, myself included, whose snobbery had been so much a part of our background that it had been an instinct rather than a product of thought. The work students did not ordinarily take much part in the *Steh-Convent*. They gave less time to discussion than those of us who had more leisure.

Today, however, they were out in force, taking an active part in almost every debate I listened to. It seemed as if students of all ranks felt drawn together into a closer group by this new threat in the air. I walked around in agitation, my hands knotted in my pockets, poking my nose into one hot discussion after another.

The chief rumor proved to be that Hitler had issued an ultimatum to the churches, requesting them to unite in one body and warning that the government would do it for them if they failed to comply. The students were all filled with a gloomy excitement, most of them with dark premonitions of an attack on our religious freedom. For me, even though my fears seemed about to be realized, there was relief in seeing that my companions were now also aware of the danger I had been dreading, that they too were awake to it at last.

Time after time I heard someone asking, "What will Lietzmann say?"

"He will be for it. Lietzmann was active in trying to unite the churches twelve years ago."

"Don't you think it! Lietzmann is an independent. He isn't going to see the Church taking orders from the Nazis."

When the bell rang for classes we poured inside and the majority of the students of my faculty turned to the great lecture hall where Dr. Lietzmann was to speak. He was one man whose knowledge and integrity we felt we could trust, and we were sure he would make a statement either confirming or denying the buzzing rumors. When the gray-haired doctor ascended the rostrum he was greeted, as was the custom, by the stamping of hundreds of feet upon the floor boards. Today, so great was our excitement, the noise was deafening.

When the pounding died away Lietzmann began at once his prepared lecture on the New Testament, but the first words were hardly out of his mouth before his voice was drowned in a renewed stamping of feet. The doctor firmly attempted to go on with his lecture, ignoring the unspoken demand that he relieve our minds on another subject. He lifted his manuscript in his hand and tried to raise his usually quiet voice above the din. The reverberations only grew louder. Finally he laid the manuscript aside and stepped to the front of the platform. There was immediate silence. His cool, blue-gray eyes studied us for a moment. Then he said:

"It appears, gentlemen, that my usual lecture would be wasted on you in the present condition of your minds. Perhaps the best thing will be for me to explain to you what has happened, so that you need not excite yourselves with unfounded speculations.

"The government has expressed its desire to make an agreement, a concordat with the Church. However, to simplify such a proceeding it wishes to deal with one body rather than twenty-eight different churches, and for this reason Herr Hitler has requested that a *Reichskirche*, a united Church, be formed."

There was a little hum of excitement through the lecture hall as we realized that the report was true.

"What I wish for you," the scholarly voice continued, "is that as future pastors, as future leaders of the Church, you will consider this matter with calm minds, evaluating it historically and dispassionately. There are forty millions of Lutherans in Germany and you are among those to whom they will look for understanding. Therefore you must be well acquainted with the historical background of the churches' present decision.

"When Martin Luther founded Protestantism in Germany, he had no intention of setting up separate churches. He envisioned one Church, whose creed he laid down, a single organization headed by the bishops as leaders and directors. He believed in the efficacy of such a structure and he fully expected the Roman bishops to come over to the reformed Church and serve as its heads. However, these men did not leave the mother Church and he was obliged to change his plans. Rome was putting great pressure on the people to return from Protestantism and he faced an urgent situation without leaders.

"So Luther turned to the princes of the German states and

appointed them 'emergency bishops,' cannily seeing that their pleasure in the religious power would greatly strengthen their attachment to the cause of the Reformation and would serve to bind the people, who already looked to their princes for all authority in civil matters, closer to the new order.

"The princes took eagerly to their new positions and each organized a separate Church for his state. Since there were twenty-eight states there became twenty-eight churches. But they were still *one Lutheran Church*, holding firmly to the single great creed outlined by Luther, which we call our 'Confessions.' Luther expected the princes to relinquish their bishoprics as soon as the new Church was set solidly on its foundations. But here he was mistaken.

"The princes, once having exercised this religious authority, declined to relinquish it and held on to their offices through succeeding generations until they were relieved of them in the revolution of 1918. Nevertheless *the Church*, in Germany, has always meant *one* Lutheran Church. Any differences in thinking, even those which established opposing branches of doctrine, have always been held to be 'within the Church.' It was a state Church, and when the German provinces united the churches' unity was further marked by the Kaiser's assuming the position of Pontifex Maximus of all the Lutheran bodies. The nation has always collected the church taxes from the people and paid for the churches' support.

"With the revolution of 1918 the state churches were placed on a free basis, modeled after that of the United States of America except that the state continued to collect the church taxes. At that time many churchmen felt that the hour had struck to form a united body, as had been the intention of our great founder. I myself, as you know, was a member of the commission which attempted to draft a constitution for a united Church.

"This undertaking failed or at least it did not bring forth immediate fruit, because all growth in the Church is an extremely slow process. There were difficulties to be overcome. There were differences in orthodoxy among the churches and many of the most orthodox churches felt that the Prussian Union was too liberal in attitude to fit into the proposed unity. There was an attempt at the meeting to impose a new liturgy which all the churches must accept, and this met bitter resistance. Some of the difficulties seemed petty but they were none-the-less real. Those churches whose heads bore the title of bishop wished this title retained; those who called their chief dignitary the superintendent claimed that bishops belonged only in the Roman Church. Unhappily, so many of us felt, these differences prevailed.

"But let me remind you that a development along the line of unity has always been considered desirable among the churches. It is not unity itself but the method of its inception to which objections have been made. Now the government requests that we bring to completion an attempt which the Church itself originated."

Here Dr. Lietzmann was silent for a full minute, looking us over with his lips compressed as if he were weighing our temper.

"The Church," he said, "has decided to comply with the request of the government."

There was a noisy murmur throughout the room, half of astonishment and half of protest, while each of us looked at our neighbor with questioning eyes. In a couple of seconds it had grown to an uproar, but the tall gray man on the platform silenced it with an imperative gesture.

"Pray permit me to finish, gentlemen," he said. "The Church, in agreeing to the government's request, has appointed a most distinguished churchman to the leadership of our united body, an office that will bear the title of *Reichsbishop*. His name you know well as that of an upright individual, a man of great strength and dignity, an upholder of all our faith holds most dear—Dr. Friedrich von Bodelschwingh, Director of the Institutes of Mercy in Bethel, Saxony."

There was a wide sigh of relief in the assembly, for this was a name we revered. If the Nazis had consented to von Bodelschwingh as the new "Reichsbishop," perhaps there was not so much to fear as we had thought. To me, however, the appointment of such a distinguished man did not mitigate the calamity of the Church's loss of independence.

We surged out into the halls and were rapidly joined by new waves of waiting students to whom we told the news. I caught up with Vogler and we circulated through the crowd, trying to discover how the feeling among the students was tending.

The name of von Bodelschwingh was on everyone's tongue but the agitation seemed less intense than it had been before the lecture. General sentiment was that the Church had not done so badly in striking a bargain with the government and that things were not so black as had been feared.

In the courtyard Vogler and I ran into Erika Menz and we all three went together to get a cup of coffee.

"It is not so bad, is it, Karl?" Erika asked me. "You don't think the Church has really been hurt, do you?"

"It is only the beginning," I told her.

"He is completely right, Fraeulein Menz," said Vogler. "The first step has been taken. And there was no resistance. Next time it will be still harder to resist, and who knows what we are to look for, the next time?"

"At least," said I, "our eyes have been opened. This fight has been lost—perhaps now we can win the next one."

"But Karl," protested Erika, "wouldn't the Church have got into worse trouble by fighting this time? The bishops are more experienced than we are; they must have considered very carefully what they are doing. Wouldn't it have been worse to refuse the Nazis and put the Church in a position where it had made an enemy of the government? After all, this unity had been a plan of the Church for a long time."

"Then the Church should have determined its own time to unite," I insisted. "The Nazis have dictated to the Church and the Church has buckled under. That is the important thing that has happened. The Church has handed its authority over to the government on the first point at issue. It had power but it did not use it. Now it will not have so much power. Frankly, I am apprehensive about the future and I don't mind saying so."

Vogler turned to me with honest regret on his hard young face.

"I am sorry, Herr Hoffmann, that I did not listen to you sooner. I am afraid I thought you a sort of Jeremiah. But there are a lot of us who have waked up today. They won't catch us off guard again."

Erika shook her soft hair back from her shoulders and smiled at us both.

"Don't you two become pessimists," she coaxed us in her pretty feminine way. "Perhaps the Nazis have made a mistake. Perhaps by uniting the Church they will only have made us stronger. Let's hope it will prove to be that way."

"Let us hope so," I said.

The following week-end I took the train for the ninety-mile trip back to Magdeburg. I got in early on Friday afternoon and found my mother in garden gloves and wide straw hat, setting out one of her precious flower beds.

"Go in at once to your father, Karl. I am very glad that you have come home. He has received a letter and it has upset him."

I found my father in his study, walking heavily up and down the wide room and puffing furiously on his pipe. He took a paper from his desk and handed it to me.

"What do you think of this?"

The letterhead was that of the new United Church. The letter advised the pastor that under gentle government pressure the Church Senate had consented to have the nomination of von Bodelschwingh to the post of Reichsbishop confirmed by a general election of the entire membership. The election would be held late in July. It was now the first of May.

We looked at each other.

"I do not like it," said my father angrily. "But if the Church has consented what can I do?"

"Why does the government want the election put off until July?" I demanded. "Why don't they hold it now?"

"They do not say." My father reached for the letter and looked over it for probably the twentieth time. "It seems like a simple enough request from the government, but why is such an election necessary? The people have been sufficiently stirred up over this business of uniting the churches. The papers are full of it. Now it seems to me the authority of the bishops, the general superintendents, and the distinguished laymen who make up the Church leadership is being interfered with. It is as if their ability to select a suitable Reichsbishop for the people were open to question."

"Couldn't the election be refused?"

"If the Church Senate has consented, I do not see what we can do."

My father laid aside his pipe.

"I have called a meeting of the board for tonight," he told me. "I think you might come with me."

That evening the church board appeared in full numbers. The events of the past week had greatly excited the congregation and not a board member was absent. Herr Oldorf, the lawyer, sat with our friend Mayor Weller. Colonel Beck, Rudolph's father, was talking to the eminent surgeon, Dr. Braun. Herr Schenk, the schoolmaster, who always seemed to be having a chill, sat huddled in his fur-collared coat even though it was May. Herr Falk, the politician, Herr Rosenthal, the tailor, Herr Schmidt, the shoemaker, Herr Wegner, the steel-mill foreman—not a one was missing.

When my father rose to speak he was met by a silent intentness in every face before him. He told them of the election that was to be held, that Dr. von Bodelschwingh's nomination must be confirmed by a vote of the Church members.

"It seems desirable," he said, "that such an election should take place in order to convince the government by a very large vote how great the confidence of the people is in their Church leaders." But as he was speaking I missed the customary tone of assurance in his voice. He seemed to be trying to convince himself, and not only the members of the board.

"Many of us," he declared, "have been made uneasy by the government's interference in matters that pertain to the Church. However, the character of Dr. von Bodelschwingh is guarantee enough that the Church has not faltered from its principles. The election of a man of such thoroughly Christian and churchly background, whose earnestness and scholarship have impressed the whole nation, will be our insurance of the continuance of a conservative and Christian Church government."

There was a general murmur of assent. Colonel Beck suggested that a campaign be mapped out to ensure full representation in the voting.

Suddenly the mayor lumbered to his feet.

"Dr. Hoffmann!" he called in a loud voice. "Members of the board! There is one great fact in the life of every German today and that is the glorious union of our people under one sublime leader, Adolf Hitler. Where there was once indecision there is now a united nation, which follows and rejoices in the glory that is coming to it. We have all one obligation: support it, support the Leader, support the new principles.

"But does everyone support it? Who are those who would deny Germany her place in the sun? I could mark them among you, but you know them—the conservatives—and we have just heard the man who wants to be the new Reichsbishop described as a conservative! Who is it who have done nothing to support the great ideal of National Socialism? The conservative churchmen. There are thousands of Germans who are church members who know that our beloved Hitler will bring new life, new strength to the German nation. You will see that they are in the majority."

The mayor's face was damp with perspiration, and his oratory became more vehement as it became more confused.

"There is a new movement in the Church," he cried. "The German Christians. The Church has ignored them, but you will soon see how strong they are. The German Christians demand recognition. They speak for the biggest part of the membership. They do not approve of this conservative, this von Bodelschwingh. For the German Christian party I nominate for Reichsbishop the Reverend *Hermann Mueller*."

He sat down amid consternation, and then three or four voices broke out at once. What did it mean? Who was this Mueller?

Mayor Weller admitted that Mueller was an obscure chaplain in some regiment in East Prussia. The talk grew to tumult. My father took the floor.

"Will the mayor be so good as to explain to me," he asked, "who are these 'German Christians'? It is a term that I do not understand. We are all Germans and I am sure we are all Christians. What special sense, then, are we to read into the name 'German Christians'? Who are this group that you claim is so large yet of which we have not heard? What is their place in the Church?"

The mayor's tongue fumbled under my father's burning glance.

"Well, it is for the new Germany," he explained. "It is a big group that wants to follow the ideals of our Leader even within the Church. We think the Church has hung back from the new march of things and we want a different attitude. We demand full representation in the Church government."

"I have never heard of such a group," insisted my father. "If the first act of this German Christian party is to nominate some totally unknown army chaplain to be the head of the great Lutheran Church, then I can only say that its leaders are mad and irresponsible men."

Several men cried, "Good!" "You are right there."

"It is an insolence," boomed Colonel Beck, "to suggest that the Church might consider a man with such a background."

Schoolmaster Schenk rubbed his blue hands together.

"We must form an organization to acquaint the people with this difficulty," he said.

"Let us listen to our pastor," said Herr Schmidt, the shoemaker, in his simple way. "He will tell us the right thing to do."

"The board *must* go on record as repudiating the nomination of this Mueller," cried Colonel Beck.

The mayor interposed again, "It might not be judicious for the board to take such action," he suggested softly. "The government looks very favorably upon the candidate of the German Christians."

Three or four men began to talk at once and there was a blistering argument. Herr Wegner, who had applauded the pastor, cooled off at once on the hint of Nazi disapproval. Thin-faced Herr Falk, who held a political appointment, supported the mayor. Lawyer Oldorf suggested that since the nomination had been legally made there was nothing to do but leave the question to the people at the election and allow electioneering for both candidates. Colonel Beck denounced the German Christians and demanded that they be officially censured. The meeting broke up in complete discord with no action taken.

As we walked slowly homeward one question occupied all our minds. Who were these German Christians and what did their new movement mean? We were soon to find out who they were.

It was commonplace in the vast Lutheran organization that different parties existed in the Church, just as in political life, each adhering to its own interpretation of religious doctrine. The two main parties were the orthodox, who held strictly to the teaching of the Word, and the liberals, who believed the social evolution was one of the Church's great concerns. The different universities produced varying schools of theological thought, some purely local, yet all tolerated as representing the right of men to choose their own belief. The followers of Schleiermacher, an outstanding theologian, went so far as to doubt the divinity of Christ, yet were included within the Church.

The German Christian party was a small and obscure group which had risen in the twenties at the time of Ludendorff's nationalist activities. Ludendorff had organized the violent anti-Christian Tannenberg bund, which later merged with the Nazi movement and which had attacked the Church's liberal doctrines as being responsible for Communism. Some of their members formed a nationalist party in the Church and the German Christians thus originated as a sort of anti-Communist Church group. They were little noticed, for nationalist sentiment in the Church was nothing new. At the time of Bismarck there had been a nationalist flare-up and the chief pastor of the great Domkirche in Berlin, Dr. Stoeckel, lost his position because of his outspoken nationalist and anti-Semitic views. The German Christian movement contained no outstanding men and remained so petty that until the Nazis came into power, the greater portion of the people had never even heard of it.

Now it leaped into prominence overnight. The papers the next day carried long stories, declaring that all over Germany, members of the "vast German Christian party" had risen in the churches to acclaim the Reverend Mueller as their candidate for Reichsbishop.

"It has been planned," my father said at breakfast. "Someone has done a very clever job of timing this announcement so that this movement for Mueller would appear to be a big popular measure, something spontaneous, arising all over Germany at the same moment. 'The vast German Christian party'!" he snorted, slapping the open newspaper. "I remember them now, vaguely, a little handful of Ludendorff's men, and not a man of sense in the lot. They must have had to hunt pretty far to find any sort of churchman who would be willing to be a candidate for them. How has the press been hoodwinked into dignifying such an unknown organization in terms like these?"

"I don't think the press has been fooled, Father," I ventured. "I believe it was well prepared for this. It must have had its orders. This attempt to make the German Christians sound like a big organization is very well done."

"Then the government is behind them?"

"I think the government has engineered the whole thing. It's plain on the face of it. The government insisted on the election. And you remember how the mayor hinted that Mueller had the government's backing. You can see that the mayor knew the election was coming before he ever came to the board meeting. You didn't surprise him when you made the announcement. He probably knew about it long before you did. He had been instructed to nominate Mueller and had been told just what to say."

"But the government has no right to interfere in Church matters."

"That's why they are using this German Christian party— puffing it up to look like a big Church party—so that no one can say the government has intervened directly."

"You may be right." My father pulled at his chin. "If that is what they have done, it was clever. It was diabolically clever. They have kept their skirts clean. They have maneuvered it to look as if this stroke for Mueller originated within the Church itself."

"But what are you going to do?"

My father struck both hands upon the table so that the breakfast china rattled.

"I am going to campaign for von Bodelschwingh! The government has made a mistake if they think they can push the Church this far. They can nominate a man. Yes! By a trick and only a trick. But they will see where the loyalty of the Church members lies if they imagine they can elect him."

Evidently the government did imagine so. When the Sunday morning service was over my mother and I came out of church to find several men standing at the outer door, distributing pamphlets and leaflets. They were handsomely printed pieces, decorated with the cross and the swastika, in which the text stood out boldly. I took several from the nearest distributor.

> EVERY TRUE GERMAN DESIRES MUELLER FOR
> REICHSBISHOP.
> MUELLER IS THE CHURCH'S MAN OF THE HOUR.
> A VOTE FOR MUELLER IS A VOTE FOR THE NEW
> GERMANY.

"I wonder how long they have had these ready," I said to my mother.

When I left to take the train back to Berlin that afternoon the anteroom to my father's study was crowded with men and women with bewildered faces, holding the government's splendid pamphlets in their hands.

CHAPTER SIX

DURING the next few weeks I spent as much time as I could spare with my father in Magdeburg, helping him to launch his own campaign. Fortunately it was only a short trip home and at the university there was little opportunity for regular work. All the talk in school and city was of the *Kirchenkampf*, the Church fight. The papers were full of it; the student discussions boiled with it and classes were only half attended. In every church in the land there was the same disturbance and uncertainty that prevailed among us at the Dom. No plans had been laid for any electioneering for von Bodelschwingh. It had not been thought necessary, for the Church leaders had not considered the possibility that a rival candidate might arise.

The electioneering for Mueller got off to a spectacular head start. The radio blared his name whenever you turned it on. The newspapers carried flaming statements from vociferous German Christians who seemed to spring up like mushrooms all over the land prophesying an overwhelming victory for their man. Their statements were so alike that the discerning eye could immediately detect the fine hand of the Ministry of Propaganda, but to the general public this apparent popular urgency for Mueller's election was very confusing.

Now statements by outstanding divines began to appear, denouncing the German Christians and their pretensions. The papers were sold out every day almost as soon as they appeared. My father had prepared two vigorous brochures for distribution to the thousands of Church members in the province of the Dom.

In order to understand how widespread the repercussions of

this Church fight were, it is necessary to realize that in Germany every citizen was a church member. The Lutheran Church was a *Volkskirche*, a folk church. Germany in its entirety was divided into parishes; each house in city or county, each living soul in any place in Germany fell automatically into a particular parish of the Church. You were accounted a Church member at baptism, an adult member upon your confirmation, and a voting member at the age of twenty-four. You began to pay Church taxes from the moment you had an income. Thus the forty million Lutherans in Germany were to the last man supporting Church members. The Catholic Church operated on a similar arrangement for its twenty million members.

It was very rare and no light thing for a man not to be a Church member. In order to leave the Church he had to file a declaration with a notary public. This declaration became effective only after three weeks and every Sunday of those weeks the pastor would read the separatist's name in the public service as one who was in danger of falling away from the Church and intercession would be made for him in public prayer.

The third Sunday he would be formally excommunicated, his name read out from the pulpit as that of a heretic who had fallen away, and in a long and solemn prayer his soul would be commended to the mercy of God. From that moment on he had no rights in the Church. No minister would either marry him or bury him nor was he allowed to partake of the sacraments.

It is true that during the long period of rationalism and materialism from about 1870 to 1910 the Church lost some of its influence and the relationship of many members became highly perfunctory, but the World War served to increase the religious interest of the German people and the great majority of them came again to look to the Church for guidance.

So it was that two-thirds of the entire population of Germany felt anything that touched the Lutheran Church as an intimate and personal shock. And so it was in my father's parish that thousands of people were members of the great Domkirche whom my father could not reach personally and did not even know.

He made a great number of calls on influential members in the first few days after the board meeting and everywhere he discovered that propaganda sheets for the election of Mueller were reaching his people in floods through the mails. He began to work on counter-propaganda. He wrote a stinging pamphlet, crying to the people that they must hold the service of God first in their lives, that to make the Church a political puppet was to betray their Lord, demanding that the Church must have a spiritual head to direct spiritual things and not a political tool whose very program was to serve a man first and God afterward.

He had taken the pamphlet to a printer and the text was set up in type when the mail brought another letter from the Senate of the United Church.

All campaigning for von Bodelschwingh had been prohibited by government order. My father was shocked but he was also aroused. You could hear his great voice thundering throughout the house.

"They have asked for a real fight now and we shall make it a bitter one," he shouted.

"How is it that we did not see this danger from the first?" he asked with self-reproach. "I was at fault. I was too sure the Church's position was so strong the Nazis dared not make an attempt on her; now it will take all her strength to save herself. I shall speak the truth and so will the pastors everywhere. We shall tell where this underhanded attempt to knife the Church originated and the people will be with us."

The people were in fact thronging to their pastors for direction in larger and larger numbers. Every day my father's study was filled with a greater and more disturbed crowd.

However, to start an active campaign against the Nazi candidate was not an easy matter. My father knew how timid the great bulk of his people would be if they were asked to make any public display against a government order. Already there had been arrests among the political figures in our town. There had followed imprisonment without trial and without appeal and the people were frightened at the loss of any recourse to justice. Houses of persons against whom some Nazi had a grudge had been looted, and people had been beaten on the street for some trifling or imagined offense by the swaggering brown-shirts, and we had learned that these outrages too were without redress. The thrifty, common-sense, upper-middle-class burghers who attended the Domkirche were not supporters of Hitler. But their position in the community was very important to them. Their clean, meticulously kept homes, their abundantly stocked tables were a mark of caste, and besides, they were used to their comforts. They kept pretty quiet about the Nazis because they were afraid of losing privileges so dear to them.

"They are good people," my father said. "They could be martyrs if they were sufficiently stirred. They would take the stroke of a whip on their backs without whining; but it is another matter to ask them to endanger their silver teapots."

My father had counted on his pamphlets to consolidate the feeling of the congregation. Now he countermanded the order for their printing, for it was too dangerous to have them printed in such a large establishment.

After careful hand picking he selected a group of fifteen to eighteen of his most faithful Church members and invited them to meet with him at the parsonage to organize a secret campaign. Colonel Beck was the first to accept; Werner Menz, Erika's uncle and my father's crony, came, looking very determined, a thin little knot of a man, rather foppishly dressed, quiet-voiced but stubborn as a mule when he was crossed. Schoolmaster Schenk, huddled in his coat, and our beloved Dr. Kamps from the gymnasium were among the strained but familiar faces. Surgeon Dr. Braun had regretfully declined to attend the meeting, saying that as he was of Jewish blood he dared not be associated with anything irregular. Four of the number were young men in their early twenties whom I had picked as rattling good rebels against the Mueller movement. With them we expected to accomplish a lot of the necessary leg work of a secret mobilization. Their leader would be Johann Keller, a close friend of mine and of Rudolph Beck's through school days and the university. Johann had come home from Berlin when his irrepressible and vigorous father, the manager of a large number firm, had been taken ill. The wiry, sharp-tongued boy had a fire in him that came to a blaze as he watched my father speak.

"No more is needed now to show us how far the government is meddling in the affairs of the Church," their pastor told these trusted ones. "We are now forbidden by edict to campaign for Dr. von Bodelschwingh. It has always been the position of the Church to uphold the authority of the government except in the direction of purely spiritual affairs which was our own province. But when we see an anti-religious government attempting to gain control of the Church of Christ, it is time for us to act. This Mueller must be overwhelmed."

Copies of his pamphlets, which had been printed in a small trustworthy shop, were handed out and each member of the secret committee took over a territory in which to distribute them. Hecklers, of whom Johann proved one of the best, were sent to attend the big open meetings the German Christians were holding in the town and to shout embarrassing questions from the anonymity of the crowd.

When I was in Berlin I visited several pastors whom my father knew well and discovered they were doing the same sort of work he was. From one day to another the radio speakers and newspapers became more confident in predicting Mueller's victory, but the opposition had become bold and for the last time in Germany there was vigorous and outspoken resistance to a policy of the government.

One day in June a delegation of the local Nazis called upon my father.

"We wish to have the use of your church for the next Sunday afternoon," said their spokesman. "A pastor of the German Christian party will arrive in Magdeburg to conduct a service and we feel it should be held at the Domkirche."

My father hesitated.

"Who is making this request?"

"It is made by the National Socialist Party."

"I am afraid I must decline, gentlemen," said my father,

standing very erect. "As pastor of the Dom, I am not in favor of such a service."

The Nazi spokesman thrust his nose into my father's face.

"The Herr Pastor is perhaps a little stupid? Does the Herr Pastor believe that we are waiting for him to consent to the meeting?" He stepped closer to my father, forcing him back a step. "We are making a demand. The German Christians will take over the Sunday afternoon service." His voice changed to a sneer. "We thank the Herr Pastor for agreeing so amiably."

The delegation turned on their heels and left the house.

On Sunday afternoon my father sat among the congregation. At the hour of the service storm troopers appeared at the doors and swastikas were borne into the church. There was consternation among the people, but they were forced by their own timidity to stand as the procession of flags swept down the center aisle.

The sermon of the German Christian pastor, a bumptious, pug-faced young man, was a purely political harangue. Openly and fervently he campaigned for Mueller from the high pulpit, and I watched my father where he sat, biting his lip, storm gathering within him. When the service was over he started toward the door with a dark face, and as he neared the exit he found himself in the midst of a group of uniformed Nazis. These men were the *Schutz Staffeln*, the elite group of the armed Nazis who constituted the main force of the feared and famous Gestapo. They could always be recognized by their black uniforms and the white skull and crossbones on their military caps.

These S.S. men were talking in loud voices and laughing, and from my position near him in the throng I could see the muscles of my father's face contort with anger at their lack of reverence. All at once, when they had nearly reached the door, one of the men produced a cigar, bit off one end, and started to light it.

This was too much for the pastor of the Dom. With one forceful blow of his big hand he slapped the cigar from the man's mouth.

"Remember that you are in God's House!" he said.

There was immediate tumult. The uniformed men pushed this way and that through the crowd, trying to locate the man who had struck one of their members. But Colonel Beck, in his army uniform, had been on the spot and had swung my father quickly about and started walking slowly toward the door with him, pressing his arm for silence. Dr. Braun moved in and took his other arm and a little press of his friends moved forward between him and the S.S. men, separating them and allowing the colonel and the doctor to walk him quietly out of the church. Fortunately the man with the cigar was not of our church and did not know the pastor, and he had been too surprised to get a good look at his face.

My father's friends brought him home and three or four of them stayed with him for a while to calm him.

"My dear friend, it is absolutely necessary that you be more cautious," declared Werner Menz.

"Nobody can blame you," said Colonel Beck, "but hereafter, for the love of heaven, be careful."

"That such men should dare to act so loosely in the very church!" spluttered schoolmaster Schenk.

"It is a sign that they feel confident about the election," said the colonel. "But they are in for a surprise. The Church is deep in the people's hearts. I have talked with hundreds in the past weeks. The sentiment is overwhelmingly in favor of von Bodelschwingh. This little incident means nothing, my good Franz, and you must forget it. The important thing is our secret propaganda and what it is leading to. We shall win the election hands down."

But my father sat slackly in his chair, speechless, his face empty, like a man who had been broken.

*   *   *

In Berlin as in Magdeburg, there was a seething undercurrent of rebellion. Yet if you read the papers or listened to the radio you would never realize that such a man as von Bodelschwingh existed or that there was any candidate for Reichsbishop except Mueller. Nowhere was the hand of the government seen directly; it could be read only in the amount of money being lavished on the German Christian campaign, the floods of expensive printing, the great halls hired for almost nightly rallies, the tenor of the radio speeches, and the enforced silence of the men of the Church. Officially, however, the government was sitting on the fence.

At the university the whole student body was constantly questioning the theological students to find out exactly what was going on. It was part of our training that we worked with the Berlin churches, teaching at the children's services and helping the pastors, so we were well acquainted with the valiant effort they were making. We became active workers ourselves almost to a man, making calls in the protective dusk of evening, carrying the dangerous bales of forbidden literature for von Bodelschwingh. The students of law, medicine, or economics would seize upon us and excitedly demand to hear the status of the fight.

It was a curious thing to note how our position at the university changed. Once we had been on the fringe of university life, the men who were not allowed to fight, who had no part in the beloved duels of the students; now that we had entered a fight of our own, risking arrest to spread propaganda for our belief, we found ourselves become almost heroes. The other students would come to us, volunteering their help in the fight, asking our advice, giving us encouragement. We began to be more and more confident as we saw group after group rally to the Church's side.

I could hardly enter the University's doors before I would be seized and almost bodily bundled over to be introduced to a waiting group of eager-faced young men. Rudolph Beck and some of the fellows of his Corps were the first to seek me out.

"How are the people reacting, Herr Hoffmann?" they pressed me. "Are they being taken in by all this blasting on the radio?"

"They are more resentful than anything else. They don't say much but the great majority will stand by the Church if we can reach them."

"Can we help?" they would ask. "Can you give us something to do? We'd like to get into it ourselves." And I would set them to copying propaganda sheets or sounding out new groups of their university comrades, for I was beginning to have hopes of an outspoken protest from the great body of students.

"The most heartening thing," said Walther Vogler one evening as we were walking homeward after scattering our pamphlets, "is that the Nazis do not dare attack the Church directly. If they dared to come out in the open they would do so in a minute. They are afraid to. They have braced too big a bear this time, and all the frenzy of the campaign they are putting on merely shows how much they respect the Church's strength."

I had come to know the men of my faculty much more intimately in the past weeks. I was no longer the rather lofty individualist on the side lines. Poor boys or work students, they were working hand in hand with me. Otto Schmidt, the same young man whose poverty-stricken home had once revolted me, proved in his simple and dogged way an invaluable help. He never complained and he never got tired. Young Vogler, I found, I admired for his intelligence and his bitter directness of speech. As I trudged out into the suburbs with him I remembered the day he had preferred Lietzmann's lecture while I had gone to the rally for Nazi Minister Rust, and I reproached myself that for all my proud mental isolation I had gone along with the crowd while he had acted independently. I told him so but he declined to be praised.

"I had an advantage you were denied," he said candidly. "To you the privilege of hearing a university lecture is a commonplace. To me it is still something to wonder at that I am able to be at the university at all. The bait of politics was not big enough for me to afford to miss a lecture."

"You are missing lectures today!"

"This work is something bigger than politics; we both have a good reason to miss lectures now."

Day after day the excitement at the university mounted. Daily Lietzmann's lectures were more crowded. Again he had become our special guide. Before every lecture the incessant trampling on the floor boards asked him for advice and reassurance on our campaign, and fervently he urged us on.

He spoke boldly in the classroom in favor of von Bodelschwingh. His brilliant tongue made a laughingstock of the German Christians.

"A Church party," he would say drily, "rises from the great

brains of some Biblical scholar. He sees a new religious light and his followers create a party. But what light, will you tell me, have these so-called German Christians seen? Their acquaintance with religious doctrine is so scant that it is doubtful if they would recognize a difference in creed if they encountered one. They have no justification to exist as a Church party, for they have no distinctive theological doctrine to make them a party. They are a purely political group and the Church must not recognize them."

"We are going to win," I told Rudolph Beck. "The Church is the stronger force. The Nazis are obliged to try trickery, to start what looks like an inside Church quarrel and then to take sides with the German Christians. They are trying to create the impression that their German Christians are the biggest party in the Church and so scare the people into following them. But anyone can see how absurd that is. The people are not fooled. Instead they are furious, and they will show it in their votes."

"My father says the same thing," declared Rudolph. "He feels sure the army will support the Church." He clapped me on the shoulder. "We're all behind you, my lad. I think your election is won."

Then one morning the sycophant press hit a new note. An official announcement had been made by the government. Hitler himself had declared for Reverend Mueller to be Reichsbishop. Of course such a pronouncement carried tremendous weight not only with the Nazis but with all those who were afraid of them—as which of us was not!

This happened on *Frohnleichnam* morning, the great holiday of the Catholic Church. Filled with the new indignation mixed with fear that the announcement had brought us, we pushed into Lietzmann's lecture hall. As we entered we became aware that something was happening in the square below. The windows of the lecture room looked down upon the Opernplatz, and into the square, in a blaze of color, was proceeding the majestic *Frohnleichnam* procession of the Catholics. The right to hold these parades in our predominantly Protestant nation was a very recent privilege, granted the Catholics during the late years of the

Republic, and we all pushed to the windows to regard the unusual spectacle.

The procession was led by hundreds of chanting priests in full clerical attire. The Archbishop of Berlin followed under the canopy, carrying the Host. After him came long files of priests and nuns who all held burning candles, then the ranks of the Catholic dignitaries, the men in full evening dress carrying their top hats in one hand and holding a lighted candle in the other.

"There is von Papen," said one of the students, and we recognized the figure of the former chancellor, now Vice-Chancellor of the German Reich, among the bareheaded throng.

Behind this group companies of infantry marched with slow and reverent tread. An endless crowd of believers followed solemnly after them. The chants, the burning incense, the flicker of thousands of candles excited us deeply.

We were aware that the Catholics were suffering persecution. Dr. Rosenberg, the powerful Nazi propagandist, had openly called the Catholic Church the "Anti-Christ," and while there was no attempt to impose Nazi leaders upon the Catholics as they were trying to do in the Lutherans' case, they were restrained not by any religious compunctions but rather by the strong international position of the Roman Church. The attacks were being made upon individual Catholic leaders, upon priests and nuns who were arrested in great numbers upon trumped-up civil charges, many of them being accused of the grossest immoralities in order to weaken their followers' confidence in them. These unhappy men and women had disappeared into the dark silence of the concentration camps. Leaders of the Catholic Youth organizations were arrested and many of them brutally beaten.

So today this great procession moved us not only by its color and pageantry but by the stoutness of faith which it represented to our agitated minds.

"If they can still parade, we can still campaign," said one tall splinter of a boy, and the faces around him brightened. I looked at him quickly and recognized Erich Doehr, who had twitted me for my dreams of rebuilding the German Republic.

When Lietzmann entered the room we scrambled to our seats and, excited as never before, stamped thunderously upon the floor until the walls of the heavy stone building seemed to shake. Lietzmann's face was drawn and he seemed in no mood to make a statement. He ignored the stamping persistently and waited coldly, with his lecture papers in his hand, for it to stop. But the students were too much wrought up. The rhythm of their pounding feet rose and diminished and rose again for ten long minutes of pandemonium.

Lietzmann finally gave in. He spoke very quietly and without enthusiasm.

"Today's announcement," he said, "which you have all unquestionably read, seems to me to alter the situation. First of all, we must be realistic. The government, as we can see, insists upon the election of Mueller. You students, as well as the members of the churches, will have to follow the trend of the times."

His words hit against my ears like little stones; they made a stinging impression; I could understand them with the surface of my mind but I could not quite believe that I was hearing them. *Not Lietzmann*, something inside of me pounded out, refusing to listen—*not this from Lietzmann!*

"If the conservative element should take a stand in opposition to the government now," the cool, carefully weighed sentences continued to knock against my rebellious mind, "it is my fear that we will be pushed out of the leadership of the Church for all time. The new movement, whose leaders have a very thin knowledge of theology, will need the guidance and help of the conservatives.

"To my mind, the wise, the judicious thing for us to do is to vote for Mueller and thus step into the new movement. Once within it, we can exert our very great influence, safeguard against extremist moves, and save what can be saved. That is the best advice I can give you."

There was a complete silence. Dr. Lietzmann turned to his lecture notes and began to read rapidly in Latin.

A wave of sickness rose in me as if I had been kicked in the pit of the stomach. It couldn't be true, but it was! Lietzmann had

abandoned us. He had told us to vote for Mueller. I sat staring at
the cropped red neck of the man in front of me while my mind
kept choking on the miserable fact I was being forced to swallow. I
did not hear a word of the lecture.

When the period was over I slipped out alone, avoiding the
students I knew, and in the great mob that waited at the coat
room I stood wretchedly by myself, catching bits of the chatter of
the impatient crowd.

"A compromise is the Church's best way out, with things in
the shape they are."

"After all, Lietzmann is right. We have to be realistic. This is a
new age and the Nazis are on top."

"Don't you think he gave in a little precipitously?"

"What would you have the man do? Risk his neck? If we vote
for Mueller perhaps we can salvage something in the end."

I received my hat and light overcoat and turned away, burning.
A bitter hatred swept me for the teacher we had looked to to lead
us, the man who had not had enough character to stick under
pressure to what, so evidently, had been his convictions. And disgust
filled me for my comrades, so easily swayed, so easily led in any
direction. Lord Christ whose faith I serve, send us a leader!

I felt a light pressure on my arm. It was Erika.

"You must not go off alone now, Karl," said she. "Let us go
and see Herr Kleist and tell him what has happened."

I understood that she was trying to save me from brooding,
and since there was nowhere I could look for peace from myself I
let her have her way and we turned our footsteps toward Wolfgang's
lodgings.

Wolfgang had just put the finishing touches to a new picture
and was in high spirits. He was making a real name for himself, for
his talent was startling, and young as he was, he had been made a
member of the *Volkskulturkammer*, the Official Chamber of People's
Art. Now he brought out a bottle of a fine light wine that had
been given him and insisted that we help him celebrate the
completion of his painting. I did not feel like celebrating. Instead
I walked over to his picture and stood in front of it.

It was painted in oils and depicted a bald, snow-covered hill. A ragged tree stretched its bare branches into a nearly black sky but beyond the hill and silhouetting the tree gleamed shafts of light.

"Come, interpret it for me, Karl," called Wolfgang, gaily. "I always enjoy hearing this young Hoffmann read philosophical and religious meanings into my canvases," he told Erika, and turning to me again, "What does it say to you?"

"It has all the bleakness of life in it," I ruminated. "You have got here Luther's 'dark vale of tears' in all its misery, and that tree might be the famous tree that grew on the Hill of Skulls. But if those bright rays are hope," I stared at him fiercely, "in a picture for these days you have put too much light in it!"

"Karl has reason to be despondent," Erika told him. "Lietzmann has given up the fight. He thinks we should do what the Nazis want; he came out in today's lecture for Mueller."

Wolfgang looked at us soberly.

"One thing after another goes down. It is hard to see it. But I never thought the Church would knuckle under."

"They are betraying the people," I said with tight lips. "The whole filthy, treacherous Nazi crowd. All Germany will be lost if we don't get rid of them."

"Karl, Karl, be careful!" cried Erika, trembling. "You must not say such things. Don't you know what will happen to you? You must not be so reckless. You have already worked against the government at Magdeburg and with the churches here in Berlin."

"You wouldn't have asked me to keep out of the Church fight, would you?"

"Karl, I am only begging you to be a little more cautious. You must not act so openly. You are too daring in the things you say— you will bring yourself trouble. And now, when you are just at the beginning of your career . . ."

"What career will there be for me," I interrupted her bitterly, "when the Church is gone?"

Wolfgang looked at us thoughtfully.

"There's no use your crying about Lietzmann's betraying you," he said, "although it probably means that a good many of the big boys will be taking the same attitude. No disaster ever turns out to be final. Things will get still worse, or else they will get better. Whatever happens, you will continue to be involved in it."

He stripped off his paint-covered canvas jacket and threw it over a chair, walked to the cupboard and brought out a more presentable coat.

"Come along, you two. I want to take you somewhere," he urged. "What Karl needs is a counterirritant. I'm going to take you to see the surrealists. If you think now the world is a bad dream, wait till you see the way those boys paint it."

Erika looked pleased and I was not averse to looking at more paintings, so we three proceeded to the Kaiser Friedrich Museum. Wolfgang led the way through the corridors, his long legs swinging him ahead of us, and Erika and I followed like a couple of children on a school outing.

"Here we are!" cried Wolfgang, turning into a long gallery and flinging out his arm like a professional guide. "Ladies and gentlemen, you will see on these walls . . ."

He stopped, looking startled and a little bit sheepish. He glanced back to the corridor as if to make sure of his bearings.

"Where in blazes have they got to?" he demanded, scratching his head.

The walls of the gallery were lined with a series of placid-looking landscapes distinguished here and there by a milkmaid or a mild-featured cow. There was no sign of a futurist or sur-realist painting anywhere.

Back we went to hunt an attendant and found a thin-haired little man in a musty black coat, whose peering eyes looked as if they had never been out in the sunshine.

"We are looking for the surrealist exhibit," Wolfgang told him.

"Oh, *mein Herr,*" muttered the little man, rubbing his hands together and speaking almost in a whisper, "those are not to be seen. They are not to be seen at all. The *Kulturkammer* has declared them to be decadent and demoralizing. They have been placed on a special floor of the building where the public is not admitted."

Wolfgang was not easily downed. He drew out his card and handed it peremptorily to the attendant.

"I am a member of the *Kulturkammer*. You will please issue a special permit for me and my two friends to view the decadent art."

The musty little man fluttered his hands indecisively, but my tall friend looked so self-assured that after a moment's hesitation he led us to the desk, shaking his head and murmuring to himself unhappily while he filled out a form admitting us to the forbidden floor. He led us up the long staircases to a door which he unlocked, standing as far back from it as he could, as if it were contaminated, and when it opened he scurried off with a haste that suggested he was afraid we might invite him to enter with us.

And there we were alone in the midst of a vast array of the censored art. The paintings were not arranged for display but were hung thickly on the walls; there were so many of them even for that great space. And they were not all modern paintings by any means. Wolfgang stopped suddenly before the portrait head of an old woman which stood out like something alive among the other canvases. You could almost feel the papery texture of the ancient skin that clung to the shrunken bones. The head was covered with a yellow shawl and the shrewd old eyes glanced from their caves with a bright audacity, like the eyes of a mouse.

"How has this come here?" shouted Wolfgang. Then his head went up and his wide nostrils snorted. "The painter is a Jew!" he said, "which makes this masterpiece decadent and demoralizing, naturally."

He gave a short bitter laugh and led me along by the arm.

"That old woman has not died, has she, because they have put her away up here out of sight?" he asked me. "She is more alive than those milk-and-water landscapes downstairs that fit in with their ideas of nationalistic culture, isn't she?

"I will tell you what I believe," he said with simplicity. "I am an artist, and I believe that art is something that comes alive in the eyes that look and in the hearts that feel of people everywhere. It is like religion, my friend. It is not killed by being shut up or put away. The ones who think they have got rid of something by covering it up are the ones who are mistaken. They can destroy neither your belief nor mine by shutting them away in their nationalist attics, and some day, to their dismay, they will find that out."

Then, as if a little ashamed of the feeling he had shown, he became gay again.

"Look. Here are our most fantastic moderns," he called, marching along. "Come, look at this, Fraeulein Menz, and tell me what you think of it."

He stopped before a highly enameled painting in which a broken chair-spring seemed to be growing out of a rosebush.

"No, wait. I am going to interpret this one for Karl in his own style. I shall philosophize for him. What do we have here?" He cocked his head on one side and his eyes sparkled. "Why, it's plain as the nose on your face. Here, drawn from the very life, we see your friend, the Reverend Mueller, trying to grow himself onto the Church."

In spite of myself I had to laugh with him and Erika.

"Then it is a very moral picture and the Nazis were mistaken in hiding it," said Erika, still laughing. She turned her head. "But I still like that old woman best."

"There I agree with you," said Wolfgang. "The old woman is something that transcends their morality."

And we all went back to stand again in front of that full-flavored portrait. Probably we were the last young people in Berlin to see her to this day.

CHAPTER
SEVEN

FOR the next few days after the capitulation of Lietzmann I wandered about the great block of the university without strength of mind enough to rebel any further. One year in my teens I had spent a vacation at the seashore and I had gone out one morning for a swim in the harsh salt water, although I had been warned that a strong cross tide would be running. I found myself moving easily with a swift current, breathing great mouthfuls of stinging air and plunging my face into the bright water while I sailed powerfully along. Then all at once the waves became choppy; two forces in the water were struggling and beating against each other; the waves churned and slapped into each other with a furious sucking and I began to swim strongly with my own current, beating against the counter force and enjoying the tussle, the push and backslap the tide was giving me. I battered against the moving water until it began to seem a solid body I was struggling with, when all of a sudden I was caught as if by fierce arms, muscles immobilized. I was dragged under; the dark green of the water whirled and mocked my open eyes; my mouth stung with brine; my nose was choked and I felt myself sliding rapidly down and down into the violent coldness. The force of the water was so much stronger than I had thought possible, I was so chilled and paralyzed by the shock of the onslaught that I could not move. Darkness swept across my eyes in little waves and I watched curiously a piece of seaweed that tangled and untangled itself as it washed through the dimness in front of my face. I was drowning; and suddenly I could feel that thought burn from my brain down into my tensed muscles and loosen them, and I was fighting toward the surface, gulping a bowlful of salt but struggling again through the smother into the clear air. Somehow I managed to beat my way to the edge of the current and swim slowly and doggedly through the easier water to the shore where I lay cold and shaking.

The nightmare of that period of frozen immobility when the rip tide caught me came back upon me sometimes in moments of shock. I would experience the same stiff paralysis, the same numbing of will that had struck me helpless when I was sucked down into the underworld of the moving water. Now the blow of what seemed to me treachery and cowardice on the part of the man we had trusted as a leader, the relief and the promptness with which the students dropped their efforts as soon as a way out was shown them, left me after the first flash of rage in a state of stupefaction and dullness. For days I felt only a complete mental apathy, colder than despair. My brain was without hope, without will, without animation.

I could feel, almost as if it were being dramatized for me, the parallel between this present calamity and the remembered physical disaster. I had been moving with the strong current of the Church, buoyed up by my fellows, proud of my faith, fighting confidently against a tide I despised, and then in a breath, the Nazi current had proved the stronger; the tide supporting me had dissolved and disappeared and the black waves surged up and engulfed me so that I hung, choking and helpless, not knowing how to protest further, unable to put out a hand in any direction.

I sat one morning on a bench in the university gardens where the nodding leaves of the lilac bush above my head made a flickering design of shadow in the sunlight on the path and protected me from the growing summer warmth. My whole body still felt numb and lifeless; I did not have enough will to resent or to welcome the glowing touch of the sunlight. I watched the live faces of the students passing, the color of the Corps ribbons, the brisk movement of feet with an incurious passivity. Somewhere within me resided a neuralgic core of misery which I would eventually bring up and examine, but for this hour my aching head refused to function and the figures passing in front of my eyes seemed to be performing the sort of meaningless antics that you recognize in the persons of a dream, with no relation to my own life at all.

Without interest I saw one of the figures detach itself from a group and move toward me, growing larger and larger as it approached, expanding as a toy balloon expands when you start blowing into it, blotting out first a little patch of path, swelling out to cover the bushes behind it, spreading up and out to hide trees and people, waxing into a monstrous covering behind which the wide wings of the university disappeared, distending until it blanketed the whole landscape and stopped in front of me, filling all my vision.

I saw a hand go up and doff a hat. A shutter jerked in my mind and I recognized, looming before me, the same splinterlike young man who had stood in the window of the lecture room watching the Catholic procession and who had said, "If they can still parade, we can still campaign."

I pulled myself to my feet apologetically, took off my own hat, and looked into a serious freckled face.

"Herr Hoffmann," the young man said, "perhaps you will remember me. I am Erich Doehr. I offer an apology for breaking in on your thoughts, but I am curious to know if you are one of us who believe that the fight for the Church's freedom must not be allowed to stop now. Would you be willing to take a further risk in order to fight this election to the bitter end?"

His words trickled into my wretched mind with a delicious coolness and clarity, and I became in that instant aware that the day was filled with the fragrant greenness of early summer and that sparrows were hopping and chuckling to each other on the grass.

"Would I be willing?" I stammered.

"You are not going to vote for Mueller?"

"Of course not." A resurgence of energy swept into me. "You mean there are others?—Some of you are going on working?"

"Come along and meet them," he said smiling, and led me to a little group that was gathered in a circle in the garden.

"Herr Karl Hoffmann, of the theological school," he introduced me. "I know the sort of work he has been doing up to now, and he is not one of those who resigned themselves to following Lietzmann into the German Christian camp."

He made the round of introductions. It seemed a curious little assemblage. There were students of medicine, of law, of theology, of national economy, of history, a completely heterogeneous group. A stocky, pugnacious-appearing medical student, named Eugen Ostwald, who carried the long scar of a saber cut on his cheek, began to question me, speaking very quietly, for other students were passing near this little circle.

"You are willing to continue to work for the election of Dr. von Bodelschwingh even after the government has openly opposed him?"

"It is an opportunity I have been hoping for but I could not see any way to do it."

"You will be sending out propaganda attacking the government. You might be caught, and then you would be treated like a traitor."

"That is a chance I am quite willing to take. I have believed all along that this election is more important than most people realize."

"We feel the same way about it. There is more to this than naming a Church government. It is an attack on our right to our belief and it must be opposed by everybody, not just the pastors."

"That is the most hopeful thing I've heard said since Mueller's name was first mentioned," I told him. "You seem to be a pretty good cross section of the professions. Are there many of you? Who is directing you?"

"One man is the brains behind the organization," answered Ostwald in the same subdued voice. "We are organizing in small groups in order to escape notice. We call ourselves the *Christliche Kampffront*, the Christian Fighting Front. We are just getting started and we look only for men we are sure we can trust. As many as there are of us work every day in secluded locations, sending out as much propaganda as we can handle because the time before the election is short."

"Your leader is intelligent," I agreed. "It sounds like a good set-up."

"He's a bulldog of a man," said Ostwald, his face gleaming with enthusiasm. "Once he gets his teeth into a fight he never lets go. He's as big a man as Lietzmann, only this one didn't get weak-kneed and timid the minute the Nazis started pushing the Church around. He put on his fighting togs."

"Who is he?"

"His name is Niemoeller," Ostwald told me. "He is pastor of the church at Dahlem."

I agreed to join the *Christliche Kampffront* at once. I told them I would sound out two or three of my acquaintances whose loyalty I was sure of and who would certainly be as ready for further fight as I was. We all shook hands heartily and they gave me a square white card on which was written an address in a suburb of Berlin.

"We shall expect to see you there early this afternoon," Erich Doehr, my energetic sponsor, instructed me. "Our work is carried on in the basement at this street number. If you are sure your friends can be absolutely trusted and if they are willing to help, they can meet us here the first thing in the morning. The time is getting short, so we shall have to work fast."

With springing feet I hurried to Rudolph's Corps house, knowing that it was his hour for fencing practice. I sent up my name and waited in one of the dark carved chairs of the clubroom for him to change, while I mused on the promising aspect of the future that this morning had looked so black.

Rudolph came down promptly, his face ruddy and his hair damp with sweat, and as I told him in a low voice of the new Fighting Front for Christians he caught fire at once. He clapped me on the knee.

"Good!" he cried. "We shall win this round yet. Do you know, Karl," he went on with a hint of mockery in his voice, "since the mighty Fuehrer has declared dueling to be legal once more, I have lost half my taste for it. The new rule is that any student must give satisfaction if he gets into a tangle with a Corps member, and if he doesn't know how to fight the army must train him and furnish him with seconds. So now I can have a duel as often as I please, and, by thunder, the zest has gone out of it. Get me into your

Christliche Kampffront, then. That promises something better. I
have to be away on Corps business for three days next week, but
outside of that I'll give them every minute of my time."

Through the vast block of the university building I hunted
out Walther Vogler, the work student. His hard young face
lightened and his eyes gleamed as I talked.

"I've heard of this Niemoeller," he said. "He must be a tough-
fibred sort if he's willing to stir up a fight now after the rest have
quit."

"We've never needed a leader more."

"It looks as if we might have found one."

The last call I had time for was at the home of Otto Schmidt.
The little house looked smaller and darker than ever and a damp
odor of clothes drying and of stale cabbage met me as Frau Schmidt
opened the door, wiping her wet hands on her apron. Otto looked
up from the living-room table where he was sitting buried in his
books as I came in, and his big moon face beamed with pleasure
because I had sought him out. But when I had taken him aside
and started to question him, his mouth grew heavy and stubborn.

"You are not willing to work any more for von Bodelschwingh?"
I asked him.

"Herr Hoffmann," he replied, gazing at me with simple and
genuine sorrow, "it is no longer whether I want to. I cannot. Every
Pfennig my mother and father possess has gone to make a university
student of me. I see them toiling from the first light to the last
light and it is all for me, so their son can take a step up in the
world.

"You do not understand what that means. How could you?
But they are glad to work, they are contented to slave so that in
future years my mother can look up proudly and speak of 'my son,
the minister.' If I should get into trouble, if I should have to leave
the university I would be throwing away their life savings, and I
would be throwing away their hopes. I cannot risk it."

"It's all right, Otto," I said. "I don't blame you." He stood at
the door as I left, a great plodding lump of a youth who followed
my progress up the street with unhappy eyes.

The way out into the suburb I must reach was long and circuitous. I made inquiry after inquiry. I took a subway, two busses, a trolley-car, and finally found myself in an unpretentious street in front of a dingy old house which seemed to be a private dwelling. I remembered that young Doehr had told me they worked in the basement, so I made my way into a hall-like basement room with many doors. There was no sign to indicate where I should go next and I walked gingerly from one door to another until I found one door with a bell button on it. This I pushed; a ring sounded off somewhere and I stood waiting. A door across the hall behind me opened unexpectedly and a voice called, "Here you are. Come on in."

I turned, startled, and saw one of the men from this morning's group standing with outstretched hand.

"Hello," I said, answering his welcoming grip. "This is a strange door arrangement you have here. What's the idea?"

"It is a safety device," he answered proudly, and a little naïvely. "It makes it possible for those of us who are working inside to look over a caller before he gets his bearings or knows where he is supposed to go." And I noticed, then, a little slit in the door I was entering which might very easily serve as a peephole.

We entered a room humming with activity. Eighteen students were busily at work at three large tables, two of them running sheets through mimeographing machines and half a dozen of them folding the sheets and passing them on. At another table six typewriters were clanging as the students who were seated there addressed envelopes from long lists of names which each one had at his elbow. At a third table a crew stuffed the sheets into envelopes, sealed and stamped them, and dropped them into large baskets at their feet.

"Can you run a mimeographing machine?" my guide asked me.

"I have done it often for my father."

"All right, Ludwig, here's relief for you," he called to one of the students at the first table.

"It's fine that you know something about it," he said to me.

"Ludwig has been helping, but it's all new to him and the machine gets balky. He'll be glad of a change."

"If only the stencil wouldn't slip and I could get the ink to come out evenly, I wouldn't mind it so much," laughed Ludwig. "As it is, I resign to you, gladly."

"Ludwig can come over here and help stuff envelopes," spoke another voice which I recognized as Erich Doehr's. "They're piling up on us." I hung up my coat and hat and rolled up my shirtsleeves. A couple of adjustments had the mimeographing machine performing smoothly and in a minute or two the sheets were dropping with a steady rhythm. My neighbor looked on me with approbation.

"Now we'll make better time," he said, and I felt unreasonably pleased with myself.

I began to read snatches of the letters as I laid them aside, and my excitement mounted, for they were written with a biting pen.

If the Nazis are allowed to dictate the Church's leadership, the next attack will be upon our faith. "He is right," I thought.

We will never allow such an intrusion. It must be stopped now.

Our first obligation is to God and to the Word of God.

If we are deprived of spiritual food, we can blame our own laxity.

Resist the unjustified demands of the government!

"Good," I applauded the writer. "That is the stand we should all have taken at the beginning."

Mueller must never be elected.

The entire Church membership must vote as a body for von Bodelschwingh.

"Who writes the letters?" I asked of Erich Doehr, when he came to my table to get a bundle of folded sheets.

"Niemoeller writes them."

"Does he come here often?"

"He doesn't come here at all. If the Nazis smelled out what we are doing the first person they'd want to pounce on would be the ringleader. We've needed a leader like this one. We have to protect him with every precaution."

"How do you get the letters?"

"We don't know for sure how they are brought here. But all our supplies, paper, envelopes, stamps, everything is waiting for us here when we come in the morning."

"What about the lists of names? How do you get all the names and addresses to send the letters to?"

"Niemoeller supplies them, too," Erich informed me. "He's an amazing man. He saw through this Nazi trickery from the start and he got to work. He wrote to hundreds of pastors all over the country and they've sent him list after list of names of Church members to appeal to, and names of other pastors as well. I can't tell you how many thousands we've sent out already and we've only been working about ten days."

The work went on at the same rapid tempo, broken only occasionally when the mimeographing machines needed a new stencil. It began to grow dark outside and the lights were switched on. Our regular supper hour passed without notice and still we kept on at it. Finally Eugen Ostwald, who seemed to be more or less directing the activities of the basement crew, stood back from his table and held his watch up to the light.

"We'll have to stop if we're going to get these to the post office," he announced.

The last envelopes were sealed and the stamps affixed. Suitcases were brought out from a corner and filled with letters until they were crammed. The overflow was piled into two of the big baskets which a pair of us could lift between us, and off we went into the balmy night with our precious cargo. Papers make a heavy weight and both suitcases and baskets proved a cumbersome load, but we were young, the stars were bright, and our hearts were exultant at the completion of a day's work. There was much joking and light-hearted calling back and forth as we trudged the few blocks to the local post office. There we took turns crowding the envelopes down the mail chutes and when the containers were empty three boys were delegated to carry them back to the hideout and the rest of us turned our faces to the city, full of a warm sense of accomplishment.

I hurried to my rooms to clean up, ate a cold bite at a nearby restaurant, and then, since it was already ten o'clock, hastened on to Erika's apartment, for I was bursting with the import of the news I would have to tell her. It was too late by this time for her to receive a caller, so she slipped into a coat and we took a stroll through the brightly lighted streets.

"We shall oppose battle with battle and lies with truth," I exulted, squeezing her round arm in my excitement until I am sure she must have winced. "If the Nazis use tricks we shall secretly expose them. Hitler may have his storm troopers, but the Christian Fighting Front will be of far greater significance. Our fight will be to combat this storm that they have brought to the very church doors."

"Karl, oh, Karl," protested Erika. "You do frighten me. I can't help being glad that the fight is still going on, but won't you please promise me to be most careful? If the Nazi students are astute enough, they can tell from the very change in your face that you have no longer given up, that you are working at something. Perhaps it is very womanish and not at all brave of me, but I am terrified that something fearful may happen to you. Think how your mother would grieve. Please be cautious."

"Do you suggest that I should continue to droop as if I were in mourning when I go to the university?" I laughed at her.

"It would be better than looking as if you were bubbling over with secrets, the way you do now," she flashed back at me.

"Very well, my dear little comrade," I told her, because I saw she was truly disturbed, "I promise you that I will take the greatest precautions." And I crossed my heart with the gesture we used to seal a promise with when we were children. She smiled up at me gratefully.

"I can't get used to it," she said slowly. "Here are the same streets and houses and the same old stones, the same streetlamps, the same people walking and hurrying and eating and talking and laughing the way we have always known them, the way they have always been, but now underneath it something dark is lurking, a menace that we can't even see when it comes near us. And yet it has the power to pick us out and harm us, to destroy us completely, and no one is even going to look up and notice if we disappear."

The streets around us were sparkling and full of life. I filled my lungs with the scented summer air.

"Tonight is good. Tomorrow I can go on working for what I believe in. I am going to take my friend Vogler's advice, Erika, and refuse to worry about this Nazi menace until it catches up with me."

The next morning I introduced Walther Vogler and Rudolph to the *Christliche Kampffront*. We were warned not to proceed to the rendezvous together, so that our movements would attract less attention, and we took our separate ways at once for the dark old house where the letters of Niemoeller were waiting for us.

Today the first letters were written in English. They were to be sent to the Churches in England and America, telling of the danger the Church in Germany faced if the Nazi-supported Mueller were allowed to take over the direction of the things that were God's. We made our stencils and the day's work began. The English letters were quickly disposed of and we turned again to the propaganda that would be pouring out in tonight's mail to all the corners of Germany, bringing a cry of hope and a call to battle to all those who loved their faith.

Day after day the work proceeded in the same uneventful rhythm.

"It's funny how prosaic this job seems," observed Rudolph. "We might as well be clerks in the dullest sort of business. I don't even get a sniff of danger."

"It's a good thing you don't," I told him. "The best thing we can hope for is to have no trouble and to get our letters turned out."

The work was completely monotonous, but it was more important than we even guessed. It was to prove the spark from which a great fire was to be lighted and a battle joined, fiercer than all our dreaming, a silent revolt that was to swell in magnitude from year to year and whose repercussions haunt the dreams of the brown-shirted rulers even now, in the midst of their war.

To ourselves, then, we were a handful engaged in fighting an election. We were attacking the first thing at hand, glad that the whole battle had not been resigned before it had begun.

On the morning of the sixth day we had settled down easily to
our swift routine. Rudolph was not there, for he had been called
away on the affairs of his Corps that he had told me of. One or two
others had been delayed but the rest of us were busily at work
when the bell rang. The nearest boy flung the door open for the
expected latecomer and before anyone grasped what was going on,
police filled the room.

"You are all under arrest," barked a harsh voice.

I felt a hard hand on my shoulder and then I was being pushed
out the door with the others and we were bundled roughly into
police cars. I watched the houses flowing past, "Just the same,"
Erika had said the other night, "just the way they have always
been." And now I was an outcast, caught and handled like a criminal
for something that among decent men should never have been a
crime. I wanted to cry out to the sleepy and indifferent city to look
and observe what was happening, to wake up, to save herself, to
save her beloved Church, to save her freedom, to protest before it
was too late.

I remembered with a little pang that I was to have taken Erika
to the theater that evening. Now I should not even be able to
telephone her that I was detained.

At police headquarters we had our names taken and were at
once led away and locked into cells. I don't believe I had realized
what my own plight might be, even when I heard the metallic
clink of the lock which closed the cell door. I walked over to the
door and gave it a little shake; and as if a light had been turned on
in my mind it came over me that it was fastened tight and I could
not unlock it, that it had irrevocably shut me in, away from summer
and open skies, away from the friendly bustle of the streets, the
stacked canvases in Wolfgang's studio, the chatter of voices around
an open fire, the spire of the beautiful old church in Magdeburg,
the faces of my father and mother. I felt the first chill of fear and
loneliness, and the strong, stale smell that was in my nostrils was
the ageless stench of jails.

The cells were overflowing. Half a dozen of us were placed in a
cell where ten men were already crowded, most of them shabby

and slouching, the routine pick-up of vagrants. The few iron cots were already filled and we could take our choice of standing or crouching on the damp floor.

"One thing with which you can credit the new government," said young Vogler cheerfully—he was keeping in far better spirits than the rest of us—"if they haven't been able to improve any other business in Germany, the police business is having a big boom."

The time passed slowly.

"When do you suppose they'll find out what has happened to us?" one of the students asked. "Will anyone inform . . ."

Eugen Ostwald cut off his sentence with a quick warning gesture and a significant look toward the other men who shared the cell with us. Since we did not know who they were, it implied, we were not free to talk or to mention names. The time passed mostly in silence. There were few topics we could think of that did not prove disquieting. The only relief I could find in my reflections was the knowledge that Rudolph had not been caught.

At the end of twenty-four hours all the students were ordered out of the cells and marched downstairs two by two into the courtyard where a truck was waiting with brown-shirted S.A. men guarding it. We piled inside and the wheels began to move.

"Where are we going?" someone asked.

Most of our guards were not inclined to answer the prisoners, but one blue-eyed young Nazi who stood at my end of the truck— he couldn't have been more than eighteen—said, pleasantly enough, "You're being taken to a concentration camp. It isn't far."

"But we haven't been charged with anything," I protested. "Aren't they going to give us a trial?"

The storm trooper shrugged his shoulders as if to indicate that he could not help me out there, but he continued to regard me with a sort of agreeable curiosity. I determined to find out as much as I could from him.

"Do you know what happened, how they came to arrest us?" I asked. Behind my question lay the fear, which must have been lurking in all our minds, that one of our comrades had given us away.

The young Nazi laughed.

"You were very careless. Did you think the postmaster would not notice the mass mailings that went on every night? He finally got suspicious and went to the police. It was no trouble, then, to trail you to your cellar."

"What a bunch of fools we were," groaned Erich Doehr, thumping his fair head with his fist, and I could see, as if the thought had been printed on all our faces, how miserably each of us was wishing, as so many men have futilely done, that we could go back in time and do over again an action we had bungled.

The concentration camp held long rows of gray buildings and was surrounded by heavy wire. The guards here were not as friendly as the young man who had brought us on the truck, but treated us with a brutal contempt.

On our arrival we were lined up for a sort of inspection. Two big S.S. men stalked down the line, looking into our faces with exaggerated frowns. Eugen Ostwald was standing a little out of line and it appeared to us that the guard deliberately ground his boot heel on the young man's toes. Ostwald flushed and the dueling scar stood out like a white welt across his cheek.

"Watch where you tread, you clumsy oaf!" he flared.

The next moment he was stretched on the ground with his mouth bleeding. We all stiffened, for this was our first lesson in concentration-camp discipline. After that we all became very discreet.

The most depressing thing about the concentration camp was the faces of the men who were prisoners. They were so resigned, so dull, so stupidly patient. To break a man's body is brutal and barbaric, but to have broken men's spirits like this was not barbarism; it was a civilized refinement of cruelty and a crime against God. One little man with gray hair whimpered constantly, like a puppy. I tried to speak to him one day out of the corner of my mouth, for conversation among the prisoners was discouraged, but he did not seem to hear me.

Every day we were worked and drilled. Every day we were lined up to hear a propaganda speech. This last was called a training in proper ideology.

Everything that impeded the triumphant march of National Socialism must be broken down, we were told. Christianity was a doctrine for weaklings, a wily concoction of Jewish minds which served to enfeeble and unman the strong type of Aryan heroes with which the Germany of the future was to abound. The true religion of nature could be discerned by one test: it would strengthen the joyous power of the Nordic blood which was our salvation.

So this, I thought, is what the Church will have to face eventually. They do not speak so boldly outside, but in here where they are safe to shout about doctrine they let us see what is really in their hearts. It is not just the Church, it is Christianity itself they are out to destroy.

In the late afternoon of my fourth day at the camp a guard came up to me. I was ordered to the commandant's office. Despite my constant determination not to fret at my imprisonment, to make the best I could of it, my mind had been unable to shake off a recurrent uneasiness about the future. I had no way of knowing whether my arrest was known to anyone outside, whether they could discover where I was or whether I had not dropped entirely out of sight and out of their reach.

Now I stood in front of the commandant's desk, my heart pounding with mixed hope and trepidation. The man ran his hand over his dark, smooth-shaven jowls.

"You are Karl Hoffmann?"

I said I was.

"You are to be taken back to Berlin to be tried there."

My heart leaped with a wild pulse of hope. At least I had not been dumped in here and forgotten. Someone knew where I was and now I was going to be allowed a trial. Two storm troopers conducted me to a car and that night I slept in a Berlin prison cell.

In the morning I was taken into a long room where a Nazi officer sat at a polished table and storm troopers guarded the doors. It was not a courtroom, but it would be at least some kind of a hearing. I was most agreeably surprised. The Nazi officer was almost pleasant with me.

"Herr Hoffmann, will you be good enough to explain to me why you were associated with sending out this propaganda against the government's express wishes?"

"I felt, sir, that I was acting in the best interests of the Church."

"Who else was concerned in this besides the men we arrested?"

"I know of no one else, sir."

"Hmm-mm." His bright eyes flashed me a sly approval. "In the future let me advise you to credit your government with keeping the Church's best interest very closely at heart." He got to his feet. "We are letting you go because of your youth. From now on you had better keep out of things you don't understand."

He nodded his head toward the door and I realized that I was free to walk out of it. I could not understand how everything had been so easy until I entered the anteroom and discovered the fine-drawn and energetic face of my father waiting for me with welcome in his eyes.

As we drove home to Magdeburg in the family car I told him how my imprisonment had come about. His eyes shone as I described the work of the Christian Fighting Front and darkened with distress at the tale of the concentration camp. I told him of the bold teaching of Aryan supremacy and the mockery with which Christianity was treated and called a doctrine for weaklings. When I had satisfied all his questions he related to me the events that had gone on outside while I had waited helplessly and without news in custody of the Nazis.

On the day of my arrest, when I failed to keep our engagement for the theater, Erika was both hurt and incensed. She felt I had simply forgotten her in the excitement of other activities and she determined to be very cool with me on the morrow. However, on the next day there was no sign of me. Erika began to be troubled and feeling, as she told my father, somewhat responsible to my parents for me, she phoned my landlady and asked if I were sick, only to discover that I had had not been home all night.

Now she began to worry in earnest and since she knew all about my connection with the *Christliche Kampffront* she began to hunt for some of the other members of the group. Not a one was to be found. She took a bus for the suburb of Dahlem and was shortly shown into the study of Pastor Niemoeller. This was the first time she had seen the doughty pastor, and his rugged face, the bright eyes, the ascetic's mouth, the air of wisdom and patience which tempered the incisive energy of his features at once inspired her with confidence.

"I have been looking for the Christian Fighting Front boys, for my old friend, Karl Hoffmann," began Erika.

"They have been arrested," Niemoeller told her gravely.

Tears sprang to the girl's eyes, but even as she felt them sting, she realized she had known all along that this was what had happened.

"Do you know where they are being held?" she asked. "I want to see Karl. I shall have to tell his parents where he is."

"I don't believe you want to see Karl more than you want to help him, do you?" Niemoeller asked her gently.

"No. Of course not."

"Let us consider what will help him most. This is a new and wily foe we are up against. I can tell you how to see Karl, of course. I know where he is, but I don't think it would avail you anything. The practical thing is for you to go at once to young Hoffmann's parents. They will have friends who can start the wheels moving for him."

"You think I should not go to the jail?"

"All you would succeed in doing would be to give the Nazis a chance to find out how much *you* know. If they put you in a cell while they attempt to extract from you the names of the boy's other associates, you will hardly be furthering their cause. I could not go to the police, myself. I wouldn't be able to persuade them to do a thing. The government has its eye on me and if I intervened directly it would hurt their case more than it would help them."

"But can't we do something?"

"Immediately I heard of their arrest," Niemoeller assured her, "I began to enlist influence in quarters where it would be most effective. I have reason to believe they can all be released before too long."

"I have been afraid," said Erika unhappily, "ever since I knew of the work they were doing."

"My child," said Niemoeller, "they have not been engaged in any personal or political fight. Their obedience has been to God. If we have all accepted the fact of physical jeopardy, it is to the end that we may remain free to tell the story of the Divine Love that did not forsake us in the darkness of Gethsemane or in the hours of torture on the Cross. It is to the end that the people may not be abandoned and disillusioned, that they may continue to realize that it is impossible for any power to oppose God, and they may hear that the only way to life is through His unbounded love and mercy, and that that way remains clear in spite of the darkness that has covered the face of our land."

The courage of the dark-eyed man seemed to flow into the girl and a sense of shame touched her for the weakness she had shown.

"I am afraid I have been very petty. I have thought only about Karl's physical danger. If this is the meaning of the fight they are engaged in," she said slowly, "then it is my fight too. I will do whatever you tell me."

"The first thing we must learn in a fight like this, my child, is not to seek any hasty martyrdom. The sort of treacherous political tactics we are suddenly faced with are a new field to us. We must learn and learn very fast how to work together in secret, how to oppose trickery with stubbornness of faith."

Erika left the study she had entered so timidly with a stout heart. She too was resolved to follow this vibrant man who combined realistic shrewdness with such devout Christian courage. That night she resolutely took the train for Magdeburg and came to my parents' home very late in the evening.

"I was already depressed and it was a severe shock to me that you had been arrested," my father said. "And it was a bad blow to your mother, Karl."

"I was afraid of that, Father. But I felt I had to do the work."

"Yes, yes, I am not blaming you. For a little while, though, I felt as if I had been stunned. The old trouble with my head.— Well, that didn't last for long. The thing to do, I could see, was to go to our friend the mayor and get him to use his influence. This, for the sake of our old friendship, he consented to do."

"Mayor Weller managed my release, then?"

"He went to work the next day. We had to file petitions. We held conferences with officials to whom we explained your youth and your impetuosity." Out of the corner of his eye my father smiled at me drily. "It took us nearly a week."

"It seems longer to me. It was a pretty full week."

"It was a very long week. Your mother was deeply worried and I gave her what comfort I could. And I was forced to listen to a great deal of advice from our friend, the mayor. He hopes that by this time I have learned which way the wind is blowing and that in the future I will be wise enough not to resist the new movement in the Church."

"You don't agree with him?"

"No," said my father. "I don't agree with him. But of course I could not tell him that at the time. However, since you are free once more and the election is over . . ."

"The election!" I shouted. "Why, it's over and I never realized it. What happened? Tell me . . ."

"I received the bundles of ballots on the same day on which Erika came to tell us you had been arrested. You have not seen them, of course. Can you imagine how they were made out?"

He fumbled for a moment in an inner pocket and then handed me a piece of paper which I unfolded. Upon it were the following words: DO YOU AGREE WITH THE FUEHRER THAT MUELLER MUST BE REICHSBISHOP?—YES ( ) NO ( )

"You mean *this* is the ballot?"

"That is the official ballot."

"But," I stammered, "there isn't any mention of von Bodelschwingh."

"Not a word. And that was what was supposed to represent an election! You can imagine how I felt. Since it would be impossible to vote for anyone but Mueller the battle was lost, and there was no possible last-minute move which a divided Church could contrive at that late hour."

"But what a trick! What an unbelievable, devilish trick!"

"I must confess," said my father somberly, "that I was pretty well dazed by it. I found it so hard to believe—that they would dare!" and I saw the flash of anger in him. "And then our little Erika arrived with her news. That was a bad day for me, Karl."

I looked at him with a strong welling of sympathy and of affection.

"And the election itself? How did that go? Is Mueller Reichsbishop? Were there many dissenting votes?"

"According to the official announcement," said my father grimly, "Dr. Mueller was elected unanimously."

The next day my friend Johann Keller, who had helped in distributing my father's leaflets to members of the Domkirche and who had done a fine job of cat-calling at the German Christian rallies, told me more about the election.

"There must have been a number of ballots marked 'no,'" he said. "But if there were, they were simply discarded. Only the 'yes' ballots counted in the official vote." His wry young face wrinkled with distress.

"There may not have been as many dissenters as we hoped for, my boy. You don't know what it is like to stand with a ballot in your hand and look at a Nazi ballot box. They took our names in order as we voted. How did we know that our ballots would be mixed in the box? It was a Nazi box and we had never seen the inside of it. We couldn't be sure the ballots weren't falling into a neatly ordered pile, so that they could be checked off later against the list of names. That's the sort of thing you think of as you stand there. You can't help it. If the people were afraid, *I* can't blame them." He spread his long-fingered hands in a gesture of disgust.

"There is one thing, however, of which I *am* sure," he said defiantly. "Their election missed being unanimous by at least one vote."

"Good for you!" I muttered, and we grinned at each other.

CHAPTER
EIGHT

IT WAS good to be home again, to have my mother fussing gratefully over me, to enjoy the easy leisure of the coffee hour, to taste again my favorite sweet cakes and the profusion of jams and fresh bread she had provided especially for me. Happy as my bustling little mother appeared at my return and despite the contented glances with which she rewarded the enthusiastic manner of my eating, my father and I began to sense that something was still troubling her. She would watch my father's face with the shadow of a frown and then would turn her head brightly and determinedly away. He soon caught her at it.

"Look here, Hedwig, my dear. You have something on your mind, haven't you? If anything is worrying you, you must acquaint me with it at once."

"It may not prove to be anything at all, Franz," said my mother apologetically, but she was obviously relieved to be telling him. "I was not going to tell you until you had your coffee. A letter is here for you from the new Reichsbishop."

"Where is it?" My father's face was dark.

"On your desk, in your study."

He went in at once to fetch it, and read it aloud to us between sips from his coffee cup. Reichsbishop Mueller proclaimed that the first Sunday in August, which was next Sunday, should be a day of national thanksgiving in honor of his election. A special thanksgiving service was to be held in all of the churches and flags were to be shown. My father ran his hand through his thick hair in agitation.

"So it has come to this!" he exploded. "We have reached the

point where the Church is honoring *men* with special celebrations! Have they forgotten entirely that our business is the worship of God?" He picked up his coffee cup and set it down again so sharply that the delicate cup cracked as it struck against the saucer. That set of Dresden china was one of my mother's treasures but she didn't say a word.

"A thanksgiving service," he mused aloud. "We shall see."

Remembering his last experience, when the German Christians had conducted their service in the church, his immediate fear was that the Nazi party would again claim a right to participate in the special service. The long hours of Saturday went past but there was no word or sign from the headquarters of the party. My father worked long and diligently upon his sermon.

When the Saturday papers arrived, however, there were published in each of them orders for S.S. and S.A. men to assemble and take part in the coming services of celebration. Places of meeting for the different companies were named, the hour at which they were to assemble, and the church to which each company was expected to march. A further order required a squad with swastikas to accompany each group.

"The swastikas will be carried first into the churches," the announcement read.

My father perused these orders with a look of profound displeasure on his fine face.

It was symptomatic that the Nazis had not bothered to inform the ministers of the churches what part the storm troopers expected to play on Sunday. By telephoning to the mayor and to others of his friends who had leanings toward the National Socialist regime he attempted to learn further details of the proposed celebration, but he could find out nothing more.

On Sunday morning, looking very calm and resolute, my father went early to the church. He personally accompanied the sacristan on his rounds to see to it that everything was prepared in the customary way. He gave the order that the Church banner was to be hung from the steeple as the Reichsbishop had commanded, and he stood watching while the great white flag with the violet cross was hoisted upward, rippling against the blue of the August sky.

Then as the deep mellow voices of the tower bells began to toll, announcing to the countryside with their bronze-toned music that the service was only half an hour away, he retired to the sacristy to collect his thoughts and to steel himself for the ordeal that was waiting for him.

About fifteen minutes before the hour of the service a knock sounded on the door of the sacristy and three uniformed S.A. men entered.

"That flag must be removed at once from the church steeple," the leader ordered. "Today the swastika is to be hung there."

The pastor's mouth dropped open and he looked at them, dumfounded. Through all the long years of German history since the Reformation no other flag had ever floated from a church spire save the great white banner with the violet cross. It was rich with tradition, the beautiful symbol of the Lord's House.

"I am sure you are mistaken," he told the storm troopers. "The Reichsbishop has ordered the flag to be flown."

"Did he state *which* flag? Today there will be only one flag displayed in the Reich and that is the emblem of the Fuehrer."

"It is impossible," said the pastor, violently. "It is contrary to all tradition. The Church does not wear a political flag. You do not understand what you are attempting . . . ."

The first storm trooper interrupted him curtly.

"Do you intend to carry out our orders or not?"

"I do not."

"Very well." The S.A. man turned to his fellows. "We'll see to it ourselves."

Left alone, the pastor stood for the space of two or three minutes, boiling with indignation. Then, gathering his gown around him, he hurried from the sacristy and his long strides carried him up the narrow stairs to the church steeple. When he reached the flagpole platform the Nazis were tying the rope which held the swastika aloft. The big church flag lay in a trampled heap on the floor.

At the sight, the violent temper of my father triumphed over his clerical garb. He seized the white and violet banner from the floor and strode savagely across the platform, knocking the surprised men aside with a lunge of his wide shoulders. A powerful pull on the ropes and the swastika was in his hands and he was furiously jerking it loose. But the Nazis had caught their balance and swung around on him. Two of them seized him by the arms, twisting them and pushing him back roughly into the wall. The third refastened the huge swastika to the ropes.

The storm troopers were young men and the big figure in the churchman's gown was nearing sixty. He could not writhe out of their grip, although he managed to pull them a step forward when he saw the black and white and red banner again flapping skyward. He was promptly slammed back against the wall.

"Take it easy, if you want to conduct your service in good health," snarled one of the men who was holding him.

"You only manage to do this," cried the pastor, "because I lack the physical strength to stop you. I protest this outrage in the name of the Church and in the name of the Lord whose symbol you have discarded."

"Protest away," one of the S.A. men laughed, and when the ropes were tied again they pushed him ahead of them down the long stairway of the steeple. Two of them walked with him to the sacristy and placed themselves on guard outside the door.

I am a prisoner, he thought incredulously. *I, Franz Hoffmann, am a prisoner in my own church.* Slowly he opened the door which led to the sanctuary. The organ was sounding a solemn prelude and that little hush of expectancy lay over the congregation which always preceded the opening of the service. Then his eyes caught something strange.

The first twenty pews on both sides of the middle aisle were completely empty. People were crowded into the back of the church and into the balcony, many of them being forced to stand. He gave the signal to the organist to begin the opening hymn.

The organist did not respond. Instead the tempo of the prelude

changed to that of a slow march. At the far end of the nave the
church doors were flung open. In flashing military rank, led by
high party officers in dress uniform, their caps held firmly on their
heads by chin straps, uniformed storm troopers came parading
down the center aisle. Over their heads waved the brazen float of
the swastikas. Down they swung through the long dim lane hedged
by the carved oak pews. Over the muted marching tune from the
organ could be heard the rustle as the congregation came uneasily
to their feet and the drumbeat clack of the marchers' boot-soles on
the marble. Up to the front they swung in steady rhythm, up to
the steps and into the chancel until they reached the high altar.
Here they stopped, formed a semi-circle, turned and faced the
congregation, standing at attention. Their heads were still unbared.
Above them the massed flags were held high like a newly sprung
forest, obscuring the depths of the sanctuary and blotting from
the view of the standing people the crucifix which stood at the rear
of the chancel, banked with candles.

After the company of flag bearers marched three hundred
uniformed men, the foremost in the black of the S.S. coats, behind
them the brown of the S.A. They reached the front of the church
and filed into the empty pews.

A groan of disbelief escaped the lips of the watching pastor. A
voice inside him seemed to whisper, "Will the folds of the swastika
hide forever the Crucifix, the symbol of our salvation?"

The storm troopers seated themselves in the front rows and
the congregation relaxed into the long pews behind them. The
flag bearers stood immobile in their place.

Now the music changed and the opening bars of the hymn
swelled out over the troubled auditorium. Courage flowed back
into the big man's heart with the ringing notes of the grand old
tune. Pride rose in him that he had been bold enough to select
this particular hymn to cry out the theme for this service. It was
Luther's old hymn, which through the centuries has been the
strident battle song of his Church. It is the only hymn for whose
singing the people stand.

The voices faltered on the first words and then, suddenly

catching their import of defiance, a thousand throats resounded, flinging the brave words like a challenge at the uniformed intruders.

> I mighty Fortress is our God,
> A trusty shield and weapon;
> He helps us free from every dread
> That hath us now o'ertaken.

Higher and higher rang the sound until you could hear the fierce beat of marching feet in it, as of a great throng pressing into battle:

> We tremble not, we fear no ill,
> They cannot overpower us.
> This world's prince may still
> Scowl fierce as he will;
> He can harm us none.

With the final verse the voices sank for a moment into a lament while the words of the hymn voiced the present dread that lay over all of our homes:

> Take they then our life,
> Goods, fame, child and wife,

And then thundered again triumphantly:

> When their worst is done,
> They yet have nothing won:
> The Kingdom ours remaineth.

While the last tones of the organ faded the pastor walked with an upright head to the altar. Over the peaks of the swastikas his deep voice rolled:

"In the Name of the Father, and of the Son, and of the Holy Ghost."

And the response poured back a rumbling echo:
"A-men."
"Beloved in the Lord! Let us draw near with a true heart . . . ."
The familiar beauty of the ancient liturgy began to soften the
tense faces of the standing people and the mood of worship
deepened. But a sense of strangeness lay upon us. The centuries-
old prayers, the poetry of the creeds, the chants so many times
reiterated sounded like words adrift in the midst of the martial
display around us, and in the singing of the Kyrie there was a
sound that was almost sobbing.

> *Lord, have mercy upon us.*
> *Christ, have mercy upon us.*
> *Lord, have mercy upon us.*

But my father's voice began to brighten with an inner boldness
as he read the beloved liturgy he had celebrated for so many years.
I could see, from where I sat with my mother, his eyes seek out the
tall statues of Luther and the Apostles which accented the church's
interior, as if looking for encouragement. But when the liturgy was
ended and he knelt in the pulpit in prayer, I could see his wide
shoulders move as if the burden upon them was too great to be
thrown off. My mother's hands were trembling and I reached over
and pressed them.

But my heart was sinking. How would it be possible for him
to rise now and to speak as he had been ordered to speak? It would
seem like an obscenity for that churchly figure to stand there, half
obscured by storm troopers, and preach a sermon of thanksgiving
for the election of their Dr. Mueller. My heart was in my throat as
he came ponderously to his feet and opened the Bible.

"The text we shall consider this morning," he said clearly and
with a cutting edge to his voice, "is found in the twenty-first chapter
of the Gospel according to St. Matthew, in the thirteenth verse.
'My house shall be called the house of prayer, but ye have made it
a den of thieves.'"

A gasp went over the auditorium as if a quick wind had stirred through dry leaves. He turned and his big hand pointed above the banks of massed flags to the shining slenderness of the Crucifix, high before the people's eyes. In a clarion tone he cried:

"Thou shalt have no other gods before Me."

Then his voice sank to solemnity.

"Let no earthly symbol hide from us," he said, "the symbol of the glorified Lord upon the Cross, which in time of pain as in the time of rejoicing, must always and forever remain first in our hearts. In these days we are hearing men say to us that new and stronger loyalties have arisen that can save us without the power of the risen Christ; but this battered Jesus," he turned his eyes upward to the Crucifix, "bruised and tortured unto death, this exalted Christ, will light the hearts of the world for long centuries after the fungus growths of pagan mythology that sicken the air today have withered and died, for these have no truth in them nor strength to withstand the sunlight.

"*He* is the King of kings; *He* is the Lord of lords and His dominion is over the whole world. It is of Him the prophet said, 'and his name shall be called Wonderful, Counselor, the mighty God, the everlasting Father, the Prince of peace—and the government shall be upon His shoulder.' The earth and the heavens are God's house, for He has made them, and the center in His house is Christ, who must be worshiped before all. Let no *man* claim a share of that reverence, for He tolerates no idol before Him."

His voice became almost conversational.

"Before the service today," he said, "an incident took place in the steeple about which I feel you should know. Upon the order of the Reichsbishop I had ordered the Church flag to be raised as if this were a day of rejoicing. Hardly had it been hung aloft when three men of the *Sturmabteilungen* appeared and substituted the swastika for the Church's emblem. I reproved these men, I pleaded with them as brothers in our faith, not to violate the symbol of the Church, but against my wish and my command, against the utmost of my physical strength, they hung their political banner from the spire, restraining me by force from interfering.

"I want you to know that the swastika is flying up there against my will. I pledge to you, as members of the Church of God, that I will remain faithful to my Lord and to His holy house and that I will protect that house with all my power against those who come against it as thieves and marauders."

A mumbling of many voices filled the great nave, but there were a number of men who sat silent, frowning, and others who sat silent in fear. The big preacher paid no attention to the disturbance of the Church's stillness. He turned to the front pews where the uniformed men were sitting.

"For you men who sit here in your brown uniforms," he began, "I have a sober warning to give you. You have separated yourselves from the people. The uniforms so bravely buckled about you have already come to symbolize a power which others fear. This separation will deepen. This separation is more than just a difference in clothing. The people do not look upon you as their protectors; you have lost contact with them. From now on, and increasingly, suspicion and fear and secrecy will govern the relationships of the people with the men in the brown shirts.

"What will be the state of a nation, where will lie the prosperity of a nation that is disrupted by such suspicion and fear? It will spread through the community, setting neighbor against neighbor. Picture to yourselves this dread, this doubt as it enters into the family circle, until love and confidence have gone out of our houses and our hearth fires no longer warm us with the warmth and beauty of friendship as they do today. Let us not destroy for any teaching the love and pity within our hearts. In distrust and hatred we shall all be lost together. Let us all, those who wear uniforms and those who wear the clothes of the civilian, harken to the words of Him who spoke to the disciples, calling them 'little children,' and saying, 'A new commandment I give unto you, that ye love one another: As I have loved you, that you also love one another.' Dearly beloved, as we have been undeserving of that Divine Love—and I know, too well, how often my own heart has been darkened by suspicion and anger—let us listen to the tender command of our Lord; let suspicion and hatred die out of our midst and love bless and nourish our community, so that we may walk together on our streets in pleasantness, knowing we are brothers, and together come thankfully and humbly and bow our heads in the house of prayer."

The sermon ended in the midst of a moving and electric silence.

"The peace of God which passeth all understanding keep your hearts and minds in Christ Jesus. Amen."

Now the congregation rose to pray, and as they intoned: "Our Father, Who art in heaven . . ." the great church bells chimed in with three melodious notes, three times repeated.

There was a serene light upon my father's face as he read the closing words of the service and intoned the benediction. The storm troopers rose at a word of command and marched stiffly out of the church as they had entered it. But by far the greater part of the people remained behind to participate in the service of Holy Communion, which customarily follows every morning service in every Protestant church in Germany.

As we sank to our knees to repeat the public confession, my mind was flooded with a choking gratitude for my father's courage, and after the Sanctus had been sung, and he took the paten in his hands, with his head uplifted, and saying, in his steady voice, "Our Lord Jesus Christ, in the night in which He was betrayed, took bread . . ." I knew that there would be many a long year of learning for me before I came as close to God as he had come.

There seemed to be a special solemnity in the way lips bent to the silver chalice, and there were more prayers than mine mingled in the Nunc Dimittis as apprehensive faces watched the big figure in the black gown:

"Lord, now lettest Thou Thy servant depart in peace."

After the communion the pastor moved through the great throng gathered about him at the altar, gripping hands and calling men by name, and on every side they clustered closer, as if to touch him were to gain some of this resoluteness, and with hesitant emotion they thanked him for his courage.

"You have not been a soldier for nothing," murmured Colonel Beck. "That was brave."

"Thank you, oh, thank you," whispered old Frau Reinsburg, dabbing at her reddened eyes.

"To speak like this in the presence of those hostile men!" croaked little Herr Rosenthal, the tailor, honest admiration coloring his sallow face.

From where I stood with my mother I could see the tears that filled my father's eyes as he gestured with a motion of his head toward the door of the sacristy. Two officers of the secret police stood before it, waiting for him, the white skull and crossbones gleaming from their caps.

When he finally turned toward the sacristy to disrobe I took my mother's elbow and we pushed out of the church as hurriedly as we were able in the crowd. We had just reached the sidewalk when we saw my father being led out of the side door of the building to a waiting police car.

Werner Menz, Erika's quiet little uncle, came up to us.

"Will you take my mother back to the house?" I asked him urgently. "I must follow him and see where they take him."

"I shall take her home with me until you can return."

With all speed I drove to the police station. But the cold-faced officers would not allow me to see him. I begged one and another of them, but I could not find out where he had gone. All I could discover, after three hours, was that he was not in Magdeburg. He was being held—somewhere—in "protective custody."

CHAPTER
NINE

CONVINCED of my own impotence to help my father—I certainly was not making any headway at the police station—I began to consider his friends to whom I might appeal for aid. The most influential of them unquestionably was Mayor Weller, and I found him at his home about three o'clock that afternoon. The mayor had just roused from a nap and received me in his dressing gown, rubbing his cheeks vigorously as we sat down, to revive the circulation in their amiable folds. But his manner with me was not at all amiable.

"You know what has happened to my father," I blurted out at once.

"I am disgusted with your father," declared the mayor. "It is all right to come running to me at once for help when some of you get into difficulties, but he was not willing to listen to the sound advice I have been giving him, which was all for his own good. Instead, he very foolishly chose to fight the government. Does he really think his position is so good that he can resist this great new movement in Germany?"

"But it has been such a shock to him, Herr Weller," I said, burning inwardly because I was not able to let him see how much I admired what my father had done. "The new situation has come on us so suddenly. It has been extremely difficult for him to adjust himself to such rapid changes."

"That is all very well, but he chose to disregard friendly advice. He was sure he knew better, and look where it has got him."

"If you could only help him—you are the most powerful friend he has."

"And what about my own position? The government knows my loyalty now but they do not take anything for granted. If I am careless I may find myself removed from office. I can't afford to become known as the friend and protector of the rebellious Hoffmanns." He scowled and struck his knees with the flat of his hands.

"A sensible pastor will conduct himself so as not to make disturbances. He will let the government run its own affairs. But no, he expects me to save him from his own folly."

"He is in great trouble," I pleaded. "We don't know how great his danger may be. You have been one of his closest friends. Surely you are not going to abandon him now."

The mayor sighed so heavily that his whole fat frame was disturbed.

"I don't like it," he snorted, but I could see that his customary good nature was getting the upper hand. Under his scowl his eyes glinted with a grudging friendliness.

"Very well," he growled. "I'll see what can be done. But this will not be so easy a matter as it was in your case, young man."

"Thank you," I exclaimed. "I know it's a great deal to ask—but I couldn't help hoping—"

"See to it, then, that he behaves himself better in the future," he snapped after me. "That is, if we can get him out at all." But I knew that, now he had committed himself, he would use every power he could command to help us.

Colonel Beck, whom I saw next, was more ready to assist; he had already made a number of inquiries by telephone, for he had seen the secret police take my father into custody at the church, but he had been unable to find out anything as yet.

"I shall use all the influence I can muster," he assured me. "You realize that a certain amount of strain exists between the army and the brown-shirts, but we still pull a good deal of weight and I shall utilize it."

Two other prominent church members promised assistance, so I was able to bring some hope with me when I called for my mother at the Menz residence. There were friends there who had called to comfort her and to offer her encouragement; but my mother was quite distrait and unable to talk with them, although she would smile at them when they came near her and pat their hands as if they were the ones who needed to be comforted.

I talked to her in my most matter-of-fact manner as we drove home, hoping that this would help to relieve the dazing effect of the shock she had had and that she might begin to make plans and thus return to her own composed and efficient self. But she hardly seemed to listen, and when we reached home she refused to sit down but wandered vaguely through the rooms like one who is brainsick.

She picked up a book my father had been looking through that morning before he had gone out and which he had left lying open, and carefully marked his place in it, laying it on the little reading table beside his armchair. She dusted his smoking jacket with a distracted flicking motion of her plump hands, started to hang it up, and then confusedly laid it back where she had found it.

Finally she looked up at me with the fear showing in her eyes; her mouth trembled but she could not speak.

"Are you afraid he is not coming back, dear Mother?" I asked her boldly, for it came to me that if she could get her terror out into the open she would recover herself.

"*Is* he coming back, Karl?" she asked timidly.

"Yes. I am sure he is." But it was not my assurance that helped her. As soon as she allowed herself to speak, her face began to resume its color and her lips stiffened into something resembling her habitual calm and competency.

"I have been very foolish," she murmured. "Now we must get to work. We must see everyone who can help him. Besides, there is the congregation to be cared for."

For two days there was no word at all. Mayor Weller informed me by telephone that the Nazis had refused to reveal to him any information regarding my father's whereabouts. Dozens of people flocked to the house bringing gifts of fruit and flowers and of little treats for my mother to eat. She made a point of seeing all of them but her face grew lined from the strain. Even so, the hours of poised courtesy and attention required by the visitors were not so hard as the times when everyone was gone and we found ourselves alone together with nothing to do.

The second night of his absence there was a thunderstorm. My mother watched the vivid striping flash and fade against the black, standing at a side window in the living room with the lace curtains pushed aside. She did not wince at the most violent bellow of the thunder but said without turning, "Do you think they will let him have aspirin for his head? The old wound is almost unbearable for him when there is thunder."

"They are sure to provide good medical attention for a man of his position," I said quickly, and then, watching her stiff back, I wondered if I had spoken too quickly, if it had not sounded forced and false.

My mother did not move. "It was always a great relief to him when I could rub his head," she said softly and she said nothing more.

The third day we had our first news. Pastor Franz Hoffmann was in concentration camp and the mayor, who had discovered this fact, was beginning to move carefully toward freeing him. Johann Keller and I circulated a petition among the church members, asking for their pastor's release, and in spite of the strong dread of Nazi reprisals there were hundreds who bravely put their names to it.

Before the week was out there was a new development. The Reichsbishop sent a pastor of the German Christian movement to fill the pulpit left vacant by my father's arrest. As soon as the new man had settled himself in the town he called a meeting of the congregation.

"Where do they dig up these German Christian pastors?" Johann Keller asked me when he heard of the man's arrival, but after we reached the meeting it was soon evident what sort of clerics were being drawn into the German Christian ranks.

Pastor Hans Kraemer was one of those energetic, excitable, small men whose ambitions are greater than their talents. He wore his hair plastered back from a high forehead and he was constantly adjusting his clothes as if he were not sure of the correctness of his appearance. He must have spent his life endeavoring to appear more respectable than he felt himself to be; he had become strident and cocksure to cover the meagerness of his mental equipment. It was plain that the promotion to a church like the Dom, which the Nazis had awarded him, was more than he could ever have hoped for in the ordinary course of his career.

The meeting was poorly attended and among those who had come out sat a large block of uniformed S.A. men. I noticed that Colonel Beck was absent, as was Dr. Kamps from the gymnasium, who was a loyal supporter of my father. I was very tired that night and would have liked to escape the meeting, except for the feeling that someone must be there to represent the absent pastor. Neither Johann nor I was old enough to be a voting member but he came along with me to back me up.

Dr. Kraemer introduced himself and began making a speech in which I recognized a strong flavor of Rosenberg and his creed of Aryan supremacy.

"Beginning now, the Lutheran Church is going to be stirred up," began Dr. Kraemer in a bristling tone, while he tugged his vest into place. "Too many reactionaries have had their say in the Church and the true German religion has been stifled. There is no true religion for Germans which offers a refuge for the decadent and poisonous doctrines of the Jews, subtly designed to weaken the people and prevent the strength of the Nordic soul from unfolding itself." He talked in a rapid, crackling style, with hardly a pause for breath.

"Our first work is to get rid of the degrading and emasculating influence of the Jews. The true German Church will work for the ideal of national honor and will exalt the Nordic hero, and all who join it must be of pure Nordic descent. We must wipe out from our midst the slimy and impure blood which yearns to pollute the noble life stream of our own blood and our ideals. We will not bow our heads to the picture of the Jewish God that His treacherous race has subtly introduced among the Aryan nations.

"Let those who wish to worship such a God withdraw and form a Church with their own kind. Let them have their own buildings; let them pray apart.

"Shall we allow our fair-haired, blue-eyed, German children to sing in their Sunday worship: 'O God of Jacob, by whose hand, Thy people still are fed?'"

Dr. Kraemer was red-faced with excitement.

"Our first business is to introduce a resolution to change this situation." He began to read from a prepared paper.

"Be it resolved by the congregation of the Domkirche in solemn meeting, that no non-Aryan Christian, which designation shall include all Christians having one Jewish grandparent, be permitted to hold any office in the church as a member of the church board or as a trustee, and that all such non-Aryan Christians shall be barred from participation in the sacrament of the altar."

For a long time no one spoke. Then a thin blue hand shot into the air.

"Do we have any right to refuse the sacrament to a fellow Christian?" piped the uncertain voice of Schoolmaster Schenk.

A number of the storm troopers turned to look at him and the shivering figure of the schoolmaster shrank back in his chair.

"So we have a Jew-lover among us!" exclaimed one of them in a loud tone, and several of the men of the church who had appeared about to speak, subsided.

"Don't you know that Jesus himself hated the Jews?" demanded Dr. Kraemer. "Have you forgotten His struggles against the Semitic treachery of the Pharisees and how when He walked in Galilee no man dared speak praise of Him, for fear of the Jews? Let me repeat to you His own words regarding this race we have so foolishly allowed to enter into our very Church. Read in the Gospel of St. John, how when they said to Him, 'We be Abraham's seed,' He said to them, 'Ye are of your father the Devil and the lusts of your father ye will do.'"

There is a certain point up to which one can entertain the fantastic acts of his fellow men. One may regard these with dislike or with compassion according to his temperament; but the capacity of one's fellow humans for cruelty or for believing the nonsensical remains a fact that must be accepted in the complexity of earthly existence. But beyond a certain point of indecency, the watching mind balks. A great outrage is harder to believe in than a small one because it is so far outside the ordinary measure of experience. An ordinary man is not capable of any great evil, so that when he observes some excessive brutality his inner mind will not accept it. He does not really believe it is possible. It may be that this is one of the reasons why there was so little protest against the early violence of the Nazi regime. Instinctively we felt that such preposterous performances could not actually be taking place in our well-ordered communities.

I had so far sat through the church meeting in a torpid state of mental fatigue and inertia, as if I were involved in an unpleasant dream. I could see the familiar church council-room and the oscillating head of the little German Christian pastor forming a grotesque substitution for my father's wide, gentle brow; I could hear the tirade against the Jews and the unpalatable resolution as it was read, but I could not quite bring myself to believe that in the place I knew so well such a burlesque was actually going on. It was only when Schoolmaster Schenk made his hesitant but courageous dissent that I realized fully that this meeting was an actual happening in which I myself was involved. When Kraemer finished calling the Jews the children of the Devil I found myself getting to my feet, not so much to disagree with him as to deny the whole farce of the meeting. Johann tugged at my coat.

"You can't do any good," he whispered, but still I had to stand up.

"The words you have just quoted, Herr Doktor, do not refer to the Jewish people but to the blindness of the Pharisees who had turned from the teachings of Moses. Jesus was himself a Jew in the flesh and he knew it well. The lost children of Israel were his sheep, and . . ."

"Enough!" shouted Dr. Kraemer. "This Jewish-apologist is very young to imagine he can teach us Scripture." And then to me he said savagely: "You will remain out of this discussion."

"All the world knows," he went on, "that Christianity, with its Jewish-Syrian origin, its primitive dogma and the ancient rites that were mistakenly retained from its Jewish past, lacked the philosophical qualities to create a great civilization. Christianity became great when it was infused with nobility of the Germanic character, and this strong character of the Northern blood is our salvation. The old Jewish superstitions which disfigure our faith must be lopped off and with them must go the Jews who are responsible for them."

"There won't be any Christianity left when those fellows get through lopping it off," muttered Johann to me under his breath.

But now Kraemer was putting the anti-Jewish resolution to a vote. Under the watchful eyes of the storm troopers, the motion to adopt it was carried with about half the attendant church members refraining from voting. But it was distressing to me to see that the "aye" voters seemed to welcome and even to relish so cruel a measure.

So ended my first acquaintance with Dr. Hans Kraemer.

The results of this amazing meeting were quickly apparent. The next afternoon Surgeon Dr. Braun called at the parsonage and showed me a letter he had just received in the mail.

"The resignations of all men of impure blood from the church board must be sent in immediately, by order of the church membership in open meeting," I read. "Failure to comply at once with this considerate request will result in public ouster."

The blue veins stood out on the doctor's forehead and his stocky body swelled with indignation. He was a fashionable physician and this was the first finger of the Jewish persecution that had touched him.

"So the *Church* is now commencing to oppress the helpless!" he said in a biting tone. "This is not how your father would have taught us to love our neighbors, Herr Hoffmann." He lifted his glasses on their black ribbon and set them to his nose and proceeded to read the whole letter through again.

"Since I have two Jewish grandparents that makes me doubly a pariah, does it not? Perhaps I had better send them two resignations, one for *Grossmutter* and one for *Grossvater,*" he said and smiled contemptuously. But the brown eyes behind the crystal lenses were bitter.

He was not the only visitor who came to protest this churchly departure from Christianity. The men who had been at the meeting had told the story widely and many a person whom the Nazis would have passed as Aryan according to their most exacting specifications came with blue eyes blazing to expostulate against the unfairness of this attack on their brothers in the faith.

"I will not set foot in a church in which this sort of thing is countenanced," declared one after another of them. Backed by this display of collective courage and rebellion, I decided to go to see Dr. Kraemer at his residence the next day.

I was not at all sure what sort of a reception to expect after the sharp manner in which I had been silenced at the meeting, but I found the German Christian pastor without the support of the storm troopers was less valiant than he had appeared the night before. I caught him sitting smoking and wearing carpet slippers, a situation which seemed to embarrass him badly, for he kept sliding his feet back under his chair to get them out of sight. When I told him who I was he became quite deferential; he had obviously not yet had time to get used to the eminence of his new position.

He pressed me to sit down and shuffled across the room to get me a cigarette, and stood and lighted it for me.

"Dr. Kraemer," I said, "I hope you will not feel I am taking too much upon myself, but a great many church members have come to me since yesterday, and since you are so new here I thought it might be of benefit to you if I acquainted you with the general feeling in the Church group concerning the present situation." I was trying to be as diplomatic as possible, for I wanted to accomplish something with this man if I could.

"It is very good of a young gentleman like yourself to—to do this," said Kraemer. I believe he had almost said "to condescend" but caught himself.

"The people do not like this resolution against the non-Aryan Christians," I told him. "You must realize that you are dealing with something different from a group of party members, Herr Doktor. They are shocked and displeased."

The little man look distressed. "The officials of the party in Magdeburg were pleased with the resolution," he said apologetically.

"But you are dealing with another group than the local party. This sort of sudden change in the church will alienate a large portion of the members. It will kill the life of the congregation. The party will not be so pleased with you if the church attendance falls off to nothing."

"Perhaps I have made a mistake," he said uncomfortably, looking at me with a wide-eyed and unhappy gaze that was not quite convincing. "It is too late for me to withdraw the resolution now, Herr Hoffmann. You can see what a position that would place me in. But I assure you," here he dropped his head almost unctuously, "I assure you that in the future, when changes must be made, I will bring them in more gradually so that the congregation may adjust themselves by degrees to the new order."

"Thank you," I said rising, glad to have achieved some concession from him and deciding that any further conversation would be useless.

"It was very good of you to come to me. I am most grateful," he murmured at the door, but as I walked away, breathing deeply to get the smell of his toadying words out of my nostrils, I reflected that I would have trusted him more if he had not agreed with me so readily.

The following Sunday my suspicions of his *bona fides* were all too thoroughly confirmed. There was a good-sized congregation, many of whom, I imagine, were drawn out by curiosity to see the Nazi pastor, but none, I am sure had anticipated the extreme contrast which the narrow-faced, tiptoeing figure with the stridulous voice made to our accustomed vision of the vast beneficence of my father in the pulpit. It would not have been compatible with my mother's piety to miss the morning service; she sat very erect beside me, but she watched the new pastor with a strange expression on her face. There were a number of storm troopers among the congregation.

Kraemer preached on the promised Kingdom of God.

"Every German heart," he declaimed, "has dreamed of that coming day of justice and of glory, 'when the tares shall be gathered and burned in the fire, and the righteous shall shine forth as the sun in the Kingdom of their Father.' Now I say to you: 'That day has come.' The Third Reich brings with it that divine justice. Now the blond head of the Nordic hero shines in his glory like the sun, and the tares, the unclean growth among us, are being burned away."

So this, I thought disgustedly, is what he calls bringing the changes in gradually.

"The people must unlearn the Jewish superstitions that have disfigured the real message of the Christian Kingdom. The Crucifix must be changed for another symbol. It is the psychology of an oriental race of slaves to worship such a broken figure, with the accompanying teachings of meekness and humbleness. We have been deluded by the Crucifix into worshiping weakness. The Nordic soul recognizes at last that the true Jesus is Jesus the hero, the strong one who laid on the lash in the temple, the Aryan Christ that our souls recognize and acclaim and whose Kingdom we are building here on earth.

"Today a new leader has been chosen and anointed," he shrilled, "just as David was chosen by God to head *His* Kingdom. Our blessed Leader, Adolf Hitler, has been sent to establish the Kingdom among us, to exercise God's final judgment, and by the strength and truth of the words that fall from his lips we know their origin is divine. When our blessed Fuehrer has completed his task and judged mankind the new heaven and the new earth of the promise will have been created."

"Therefore, Christian brethren, it is our duty, it is the religious duty of every Christian to obey our chosen government as you would obey God. The Christian who knows God's prophecies and promises will recognize the day that is dawning; he will receive the actions and laws of the Fuehrer's government as divine commands and as the fulfillment of the promise of the centuries."

I could not resist the impulse to turn my head and look over the congregation. A sadness that was like physical pain lay upon hundreds of faces; here and there a face looked complacent and pleased, but upon many of the strongest there was a wild contempt.

I found myself thanking God for the beautiful old ritual which could not be changed and twisted into a Nazi formula, but as we knelt for the final solemnity a moment after Dr. Kraemer had enjoined the first communicants, "Take and eat, this is the Body of Christ, given for thee," I felt the blood rush into my face and I was staring with unbelieving eyes at what was taking place before the altar.

Little Herr Rosenthal, the tailor, knelt with his four gentle-eyed young sons, and the minister with the paten passed them by. To Dr. Braun's handsome young Russian wife the Host was given, but it was not offered to her husband. The assured and sophisticated doctor rose to his feet with burning cheeks and turned and made his way through the crowd of communicants. The shrunken little tailor stumbled after him, openly weeping. Among us, the others who had been marked out as having "impure blood' began to rise to their feet and turn away, their faces desolate or filled with a bitter resignation, but the hardest to bear were the bewildered eyes of their children.

"He is refusing them the sacrament," whispered my mother with shocked incredulity, and a verse began to beat inside of my head with savage irony:

Ho, every one that thirsteth, come ye to the waters, and he that hath no money; come ye, buy, and eat.

And I wondered, looking with fear toward the future, how much longer we could call ourselves Christians who sat by and watched the waters of life refused to the thirsty.

The next week dragged tortuously and endlessly through one lingering hour and then another. Whatever activity my mother and I could find to put our hands to we seized on gratefully, but at the first moment of inactivity our thoughts would turn toward the man who waited without word in his unfathomable prison. I remembered with wretched vividness the chilling feeling I had experienced of being cut off from the world, and I had been held in the concentration camp only four days and with my friends for company. I thought of my father's fiery temper and remembered the sadistic enjoyment of the S.A. men when they found a man of spirit to work on. They always appeared to take more pleasure in breaking a proud man than in merely tormenting a coward. I remembered the dulled and hopeless faces I had seen by the score and I knew that most of the men who wore them must have been fighters at the beginning. They had been the dangerous ones, the rebels, the free minds, and it had not taken many months to reduce them almost below humanity.

I took two trips to Berlin to interview officials and sign applications, to see my father's friends in the city, to beg for assistance in every quarter where the least chance seemed to be offered. But I spent as much time as I could manage with my mother. Her steely courage and endurance were being drained from her drop by drop as the empty hours crawled, and for all our efforts there was no word and no result—no sign at all that we were accomplishing anything.

She would toy with her soup and make a pretense that her mincing bites at the luncheon table were really eating. Then with as much casualness as she could command she would let slip a question.

"Karl, dear, when you were in that place . . . did they feed you well?"

"Of course, Mother. There wasn't anything fancy about the meals but it was good substantial food." *Let her think so, anyway.*

"Did they—was there brutality?" *There is still that fear in her eyes.*

"It was all very matter of fact, mother, honestly. Just a lot of men eating, sleeping in a common building—doing a little work for exercise." *Looking her straight in the face and look honest, reassuring—the sort of ingenuous expression she can believe in. Don't let her guess what you're afraid of.*

"You know, Mother, what a talent Father has for getting along with all sorts and kinds of men. You can be sure he will make the best of this situation until we can get him out, and he would worry more if he thought you were grieving. We may have news any hour now and you wouldn't want him to find you looking worn and tired."

And if I had been sufficiently convincing she would brighten a little.

The following Sunday we were still without news. When I came downstairs, dressed for church, I found my mother still wearing her morning dress.

"I shall not go to hear Dr. Kraemer preach again," she said with finality. "He is not a man of God."

So I walked alone through the misty summer morning, past the square houses with their sunlit rose gardens, past the dew-dusted stretch of lawns where every tiny drop caught the light to its core as the hot August sun broke through the low ground-fog. Ahead of me the chiming bells sent up their imploratory call for God's presence to descend upon the Sabbath town and over all the streets there rested that drowsy peace which belongs only to Sunday among all the days.

The heavy church doors swung inward and admitted me to the cool and the dimness, and I stood for a minute, waiting for my eyes to lose their blinding remnant of sunlight. The long lines of pews emerged from obscurity and I saw that most of them were empty. Perhaps a hundred people sat scattered through the great nave which would comfortably hold two thousand.

Now my eyes were drawn to the altar, and so absurd a spectacle greeted them that involuntarily my throat emitted a loud echo of my insane inner hilarity. The face of the crop-moustached Fuehrer was displayed in the niche of the altar, on a sort of cheap poster. The crucifix which always stood there had been removed. I hardly know just what my emotions were in that second of time— indignation, nausea, irony were all in me, but dominating them all was an overwhelming mirth at Dr. Kraemer's appalling anachronism.

I turned back through the marble vestibule and let the church doors close silently behind me and the bright morning outside enfold me again. Dr. Kraemer had promised to replace the crucifix with the figure of the German Hero and this was the shocking, the irresistibly cheap result.

But I knew that the effect on the people would be very bad. The audacity of the Nazis, once they had got a foothold in the Church, would be likely to drive thousands of men away from any celebration of religious rites before they would continue to participate in such a mockery.

I drove straight to Berlin that morning, as fast as I could cover the ground, and hurried to the residence of the general superintendent of my father's church. I was received at once and the story of the outrages at the Dom were poured out to the accompaniment of the pained nodding of his gentle white head. Superintendent Foerster (to give his right name would bring reprisals upon him in the prison camp where he is held today) was a stout man of clear complexion with a face as mild as the pale blue sky of sping. His fine mind and quiet beauty of character had made him as loved through all the province as he was respected.

"The Nazis are trying to place these German Christian pastors as advantageously as possible," he informed me. "But there are very few men of the cloth who have stooped to join their ranks. Those who have done so are all exceedingly undistinguished men."

"The one we have is certainly an odd fish."

"There are eighteen thousand Lutheran ministers in Germany, Herr Hoffmann, and if I said two hundred of them have enrolled with the German Christians I would be making a very generous estimate. The ones who have appeared are very vocal—they are frankly preaching paganism. But the government is having its difficulties. These men are not being popularly accepted. The government is afraid to push very fast for fear of a great popular reaction against National Socialism on the part of enraged Church members."

"Can you, then, do something to relieve our situation in Magdeburg?"

"I shall put pressure on the Nazis immediately. They will not dare to refuse a demand by the body of the Church. We shall have your Dr. Kraemer removed at once."

"Dr. Foerster," I asked boldly, "why can't the Church act as a united body and expel these German Christians?"

"It is not so easy as that, my boy. I wish it were. We are denied all use of publicity. The Church's own paper has been suspended. We have no means of informing the people in one district of what is going on in another. But by far the greatest difficulty is that we have formed the habit of submission. The pressure has been very cunningly applied. We were forced to take one small backward step at a time and as we retreated, the strength of our position disappeared. The first step was hard; we were shocked that the government should insist on our uniting the Churches. But the step was so small it hardly seemed worth resisting. After that each new step was forced slowly and seemed the inevitable result of the last, until the final catastrophe of the German Christians' triumph was swallowed in miserable silence."

It seemed of great consequence to me, as I turned the nose of the car toward Magdeburg, that the Church was still strong enough to make demands upon the Nazis but I could not help wondering how long that widespread and unwieldy body, without a voice and without leaders who dared to make a stand, could retain even the strength still left to her.

The general superintendent was as good as his word. On the following Wednesday Dr. Kraemer packed his bags and disappeared from Magdeburg. He had been recalled.

Late on Friday afternoon a taxicab drew up before our door and a big, familiar figure got out of it. My mother had gone to the window at the sound of the brakes out front and she stood there frozen, the color drained from her cheeks and one plump hand clutched in the other. In another instant the front door had opened and she was lost in the folds of my father's big overcoat.

For an hour we held homecoming, the three of us, and my father ate and questioned us, keeping my mother's chair close beside him, and now and then he pinched her rosy cheek as he used to do when he would tease her. But he was not the same. His massive frame had grown lank; the color of his face was gray and the skin on it hung in folds and marked deep lines we had not seen before.

My mother ventured to ask him timidly, "What was it like? Was it bad, Franz?"

"I cannot talk about it, Hedwig." His mouth was rigid, but across his eyes an unspoken horror flared and he flinched as if a whip had lashed them.

At the end of an hour he was exhausted and we put him to bed and found he was feverish. He preached on Sunday in spite of his lingering illness, and the church was crowded to its doors to hear him. He made no reference to his imprisonment or to any matters political, but the silver Crucifix shone again before the altar and the cruel resolution barring those of our number who had Jewish blood in their veins was ignored as if it had never been.

CHAPTER
TEN

"THE election didn't settle a thing. There's a real rebellion going on here now," Erika told me the night I arrived in Berlin several weeks after the opening of the fall semester. "The Nazis expected us to truckle to them once their men held the high offices of the Church. They thought the German Christians could take over the theological school and run it. Instead, they set off a powder barrel." Her face was flushed and her eyes shining. "The students are so furious the Nazis can't handle them."

Erika had joined me for dinner on the evening of my return to the university, and I was immediately conscious of the difference in her. This was not the same girl who had warned me not to run into danger. She seemed more mature. She had laid aside her pretty coquetry and become an ardent and unsmiling young crusader.

"The German Christians are working hard on the students, but we haven't been making it easy for them," she said, and I noticed that she included herself among the rebels.

"What about the professors?" I asked, and she frowned.

"Wolff and Schickmann have been dismissed and the others have suddenly become cautious. We have some German Christian professors now, and they are almost unbelievable—bumptious, unlearned men! They aren't even Christians. They tell us that Christianity means worshiping the Germanic hero. You've never heard such bombastic rubbish."

"I've been hearing some of it in the church in the last few weeks."

"They've set up a new organization for the theological school. Our unpleasant friend Gross has the student end of it in his hands.

And the German Christian professors are changing the whole course of study. But the antagonism to them is terribly strong. And not just in our own faculty, either. The other students are as excited as we are."

The little lamp on our table made a bright ring on the white linen and Erika's earnest gray eyes looked eagerly into my own. Around us at the other tables a number of students were sitting and I began to feel the closeness of our young world where tomorrow I would be having my own say, where I would become again a part of the pulsing circle. Here among the younger men I might be more effective than I had been in the town where I had tried to carry on for my father. Or so I began to hope.

"What has happened to the boys who were arrested when I was—Walther Vogler, Erich Doehr, and Ostwald and all the rest of them? Have you heard?"

"They are all back here. They were released about two weeks after you were, most of them. A few whose parents are prominent people got out sooner. But I guess after the election the Nazis decided it wasn't worth while holding them."

My heart began to beat faster. If resistance was still going on here I would have some stout allies.

In the morning I was out early, greeting one friend after another. I had never felt so much a part of a group in my life before. Even the monument of Hermann Ludwig Ferdinand von Helmholtz, the scientist in the middle of the garden, seemed to welcome me like an old friend. In the *Steh-Convent* the talk was stinging and belligerent. It was plain that the students were not having any part of the German Christian innovations. The whole student body was alive with dissent. Erich Doehr seized upon me with eager welcome and cried, "You are back in good time. The fight is still going on."

At the ten o'clock intermission between classes, a number of brown-shirted students began to circulate among the groups in the halls and the garden.

"A compulsory meeting of all students of theology will be held at eleven o'clock in the Auditorium Maximum," they announced.

"All classes for the hour from eleven to twelve have been suspended."

"What is going on now?" Erich Doehr asked me. Nobody seemed to know what the meeting portended although we questioned men in one circle after another.

"Every time they have called a meeting like this in the last few weeks they have been up to something," Erich fretted. "I'd like to know what it is this time."

Five minutes had not passed before I observed Erika making her way through the crowd, plainly looking for someone. She caught my eye and hurried over and drew me aside.

"I have found out what the meeting is about."

"Good girl." I beckoned to Erich and he joined us.

"Heinrich Gross, our Nazi student leader, has drawn up a declaration saying that all of us, the whole theological school, have joined the German Christians. The declaration is going to be read at the meeting."

"How did you find out?"

"I asked one of the Nazi student leaders."

"She just smiled at him," said Erich, "and he told her all. It's a wonderful thing for us to have a handsome, young woman in our number, Fraeulein Menz."

"They can't pass a declaration like that," I said.

"Wait a minute," said Erika breathlessly. "There isn't going to be any vote. Gross is going to read the declaration and declare it passed. Just by being present we shall be voting for it and we'll all automatically become German Christians."

"Another slippery trick," snorted Erich. "But it's going to be hard to beat. If we miss the compulsory meeting we can be suspended from the university.

"All right." I had an inspiration. "We'll attend the meeting. But when they start to read the declaration we'll walk out."

In a few moments we had gathered together around twenty of the old *Christliche Kampffront* boys and decided that at a given signal everyone who did not wish to join the German Christians should make a united exodus from the hall. And I found myself chosen to give the signal by rising to my feet the moment the declaration seemed about to be read.

We separated among the crowd and the news of our plan began to spread like wildfire. Nearly every group one of us approached split up and its members hurried to publish the scheme.

At eleven o'clock the Auditorium Maximum was buzzing with excitement. The noise of voices was incessant and carried an angry undertone like the reverberation of breakers on a rocky coast. I was sitting near the front and on an aisle, for I carried a heavy responsibility on my shoulders and if I were to make the first move I must sit where I could be plainly seen. Walther Vogler, who had joined me as I came in, looked around and then nudged me.

"They know what we're up to," he muttered. "Look at the doors."

I turned my head and saw that the doors of the huge hall were closed and that armed storm troopers were standing in front of them. My heart sank. It looked as if they meant to hold us captive until the declaration had been read.

"What are we going to do?" asked young Vogler.

"We'll see when the time comes," I whispered, but I was not feeling any too sanguine.

Heinrich Gross, looking stern and sallow, and a young professor from another university who was prominent in the German Christian movement, came onto the platform. Gross swung up his arm and shouted, "Heil Hitler!"

"Heil Hitler," we roared back to him, surging to our feet to return the salute.

"Fellow students," began the pompous young Nazi, "I am authorized to warn you that any attempt to riot at this meeting will be suppressed by force. Only the traditional academic signs of approval or disapproval will be permitted." (It was the student custom to signify approval by stamping and disapproval by shuffling our feet on the floor boards.) Gross then introduced the young professor who was to address us.

"Our Fuehrer calls upon us for absolute unity, one mind, one voice, one heartbeat in all German breasts. This is the first duty that we owe to the newborn Reich," the professor harangued us. His voice quivered with a fanatic's ardor and rose to a shout at every mention of Germany or the Fuehrer. "You students have an overwhelming responsibility to the flowering of National Socialism. Nationalism to lift heavenward Germany's rising star; Socialism to protect the people, arm them with glory, and safeguard the purity of their bloodstream. These are the greatest goals conceived by history and to achieve them we call upon you to follow the Fuehrer blindly. He must point the way and we must follow in blind faith.

"Adolf Hitler has called upon us to support the German Christians. If you are faithful to him you will do so without questioning. Through them he will cleanse a Church that has been asleep and deaf to the deepest needs of the German people. We are a people created by God to breed and build heroes; the honor of the German fighting man must be our new creed and our new shrines shall be our heroes' stone memorials.

"How has the Church historically responded to this cry of the true German heart to show its strength? By a teaching of weakness, by a false teaching of sin that has created in the German people a complex of inferiority and has held them back from the fulfillment of their destiny. The heroic German does not need to have his sins forgiven. He carries his salvation with him in the blood that God has sent coursing through his veins."

By this time restlessness had seized upon the students. Here and there feet began to shuffle in disapproval, and with every sentence the sound grew. The young professor grew nervous and his voice more shrill as he attempted to make himself heard above the noise.

"It is not enough," he screeched, "to say that the German race is superior. The German race is divine. The German Christians will educate the people of Germany to revere the divinity of their race and to preserve its purity; they will make the Church a power in the rebuilding of the nation along noble lines." The shuffling became deafeningly louder and the speaker's voice rose to a scream as he tried to top it.

"It is your duty to free the Church . . . devilish Semitic influences . . . the corrupt Old Testament . . . the Jewish rabbi, Paul . . ." Only snatches of words came through the overwhelming uproar. He continued his effort for nearly five minutes, waving his arms and growing red in the face, but whatever there was left of his address was drowned in the terrific noise. There was no ignoring the violence of the resistance.

But when he had gone angrily back to his chair and Gross rose determinedly to his feet, a dead silence fell. The sullen young man in the brown uniform walked to the platform's edge with a long paper in his hands and I felt a chill paralysis in my bones. The eyes of hundreds of students swung to my face while, inwardly shaking, I looked toward the doors. The S.A. men still stood immovably before them, feet spread apart, left thumbs hooked over the buckles of their heavy army belts, their right hands poised over their revolvers. *It's now or never*, said something inside my head. I was deathly cold. I was afraid. For an endless clock's tick I prayed that something might relieve me of this terror of being the one to give the signal. I could not rise. And yet without knowing how I had done it, I was on my feet. I lurched into the aisle and started for the door.

With a deafening clatter the students flung back their wooden seats and pressed into the aisles. Perhaps ten per cent of the students stayed behind in their places. We surged toward the doors where the rock-faced storm troopers stood like statues blocking the way. Those who were behind began to shove and push and those in front to shout.

"Let us out!"

"We've got a right to leave."

"Open the doors!"

The storm troopers drew their revolvers. As the crowd jammed in against them their arms shot out to seize the nearest men, who were pummeled and their heads cracked together.

"Silence!" bellowed the S.A. men. "Get back to your seats."

The mob responded with angry yelling and another ramming thrust toward the doors. The tension grew uglier with every second.

In the midst of my excitement I noticed ahead of me in the mass the bright, determined face and fair hair of Erika. A quick thrill of pride ran through me that she had been brave enough to join the demonstration; and then an elbow jammed into my ribs and I stumbled and lost sight of her. A furious roar went up from the students and a fight started at one of the barred exits.

Then, unexpectedly, some one of the S.A. yelled an order and all at once the doors were opened halfway, allowing us space enough to cram through two by two. Hundreds began to stream out and some of those who were far behind, afraid of being left in the hall when the declaration was finished, started to scramble over the seats. Storm troopers moved in through the vacant rows and knocked them down. A dozen men rushed to their defense and a free-for-all started among the empty seats. At the doors, students who pushed or were jostled against the storm troopers were jerked out of the stream and arrested. Yet somehow, in spite of the melee, the auditorium was nearly emptied by the time Gross, the baffled young brown-shirt on the platform, got to the end of his long paper. It was our luck that the Nazis reveled in an expansive and flowery style of composition.

Once outside, we collected in excited knots to applaud our defeat of the Nazi scheme and to reckon the cost of our first crusade. There was no action that could be taken against us collectively without revealing to the public the strength of the resistance the government was meeting within the university. On the hundred or more students who had been arrested in the tumult we knew the brunt of punishment would fall. The Nazis would be quick to feel the shame laid on them by the meagerness of the student support given them at the meeting and it would certainly not go easily with the rebellious handful they now had in their hands.

Most of the *Christliche Kampffront* men from the other faculties had slipped into the meeting. I saw Eugen Ostwald, who thought we had given the Nazis a scare, Rudolph Beck, swaggering with pride at the success of our counterplot and waving the Corps colors on his cap, one group after another who congratulated me on starting the exodus in spite of the storm troopers and who made

me blush inwardly, remembering my reluctance to move and the
bad moment of cowardice. I began looking around for Erika but I
did not see her.

"Have you seen Fraeulein Menz?" I asked Erich Doehr, who
came squirming through the crowd, looking as tall and lean as a
willow sapling.

"Weren't you watching in the hall?" He looked surprised. "She
was arrested."

"Erika was arrested?" What a return for her fine show of spirit!
But the events in the hall had moved so swiftly and so many things
had been going on at once that I had not thought of looking out
for her, and if I had, I probably could not have reached her in the
press.

"One of the student Nazis pointed her out to the S.A. men.
He must have been the one who disclosed their scheme, and he
unquestionably connected her with its failure. But she is definitely
under arrest."

That afternoon the students who had been taken at the meeting
were brought before the senate of the university. The news, when
they came walking out at long last, was the same for all of them.
They were expelled for unacademic conduct.

Erika took it very cheerfully.

"I'm not a bit sorry," she insisted as she walked homeward
with her fingers curled tight on my arm. "It was worth doing even
if they have taken my student card. I haven't been able to study
here lately, anyway. Things have been in such an uproar and I'm
not in the least ashamed to be expelled for helping to beat the
Nazis." She shook her blonde hair back with a gesture like a young
colt flinging up its head that was characteristic of her when she
wanted to assert her independence.

"You can matriculate at another university if the degree means
so much to you," I comforted her.

"No, we have been deprived of the right ever to study at any
university in the Reich."

"As bad as that!"

"I don't mind for myself. I haven't anything of the pedant in

me and I'm not ambitious. But I was sorry for some of the men. I was
watching one of them, a big lumbering fellow. I'm sure you know
him—bristly hair and a great simple face that's big as a melon?"

"Otto Schmidt," I said.

"That's the one. He looked terrible when they told us, sort of
sick and beaten and humped over. I wonder just how much it
meant to him."

I did not have to wonder. I could see again the wretched little
house with its stale smell and the clamor of too many children and
Otto straining over his books at the living-room table. I could see
his pathetic drudge of a mother proudly setting a chair for this
favored son, and Otto standing in the doorway telling me soberly,
"Some day in the future she will look up and mention her son, the
minister." Why, I silently demanded of heaven, did Otto have to
be chosen to suffer for our revolt? I felt a hot rage at the Nazis'
imperious methods and I could have beaten them with my fists if
it would have restored to this clumsy, toiling boy his right to study
among us.

"If this fight goes on," I said with unwitting prophecy, "we
shall be sacrificing a great many more Otto Schmidts."

"It has to go on!"

I smiled down at her because of her unaccustomed ardor, and
as her eyes met mine I recognized once more a crusading defiance
in them which was undimmed by the penalty the Nazis had laid
on her for her part in this day's affair.

"I wish I knew," I told her, "of a way to beat the Nazis
permanently. They have all the power and we have only our belief.
And they have no scruples about the way they use their power. I
wish I knew what to do next. We shouldn't wait for them to take
the next step; what we are doing isn't enough. But I can't imagine
giving up the fight, however hopeless it looks."

"I have decided," she said, "to go home and see if I can help
your father at the church in Magdeburg. If he is ill, I am sure I can
make myself useful. Any of us who help to spread the resistance to
these German Christians, to see that a real fight goes on in different
parts of the country, will be accomplishing something important."

"Good enough. I'd like to think of you at home, helping him. I haven't liked to see you here in the middle of all this student violence." I realized, looking back on the morning, how badly upset I had been when I had failed to find her. "I shall miss my pretty little comrade, but I shall be happier about you."

She gave me a glance, half pleased, half demure, and I felt a new emotion welling up in me, a desire to shield her, to keep her out of this dangerous battle; there was so much courage contained in her graceful little body and in the big gray eyes that were thanking me for a protection that I had offered her only in afterthought. I should have realized before that her femininity needed my guardianship, that the merry companion of my childish exploits had been transformed into a charming and mysterious young woman, small and sensitive and therefore all the more vulnerable to the brutality against which I had so complacently allowed her to venture. I had been culpably stupid never once to open my eyes and observe how lovely she had grown. With sudden chagrin I acknowledged to myself that all my male companions had been fully aware of what she was, while I had been blind to it. I laid my hand over the fingers clinging tight to my arm and discovered how small and slender they were in contrast to my own big ones. She gave my arm a confident little pinch in return.

"Erika, my dear child, promise me that you won't take any more such risks as you did today. I don't want anything to happen to you."

"I've grown up, Karl. Don't you realize it?"

"I'm just discovering it," I told her.

That evening I was to have dinner with Orlando von Schlack, who had called me up as soon as he heard I was back in Berlin. He was leading a gay and irresponsible life in the turbulent city and had become a favorite associate of some of the high-ranking officers of the storm troopers, where his social position, his debonair bearing, and the wit of his wicked tongue paved an easy way to his becoming a spoiled favorite with these ruthless and ambitious men.

General von Schleicher, the high officer and onetime chancellor who had picked Orlando out of the gutter and straightened him up, had had a long talk with me shortly after my first meeting with Orlando in Berlin, after which he encouraged a renewal of our old friendship, and I knew that the general had no use for the Nazis.

"The boy has to believe in something," he told me. "He has a great deal of enthusiasm to spend and I am hoping that a political outlet for his intensity will not harm him. He will gradually be disillusioned. That is inevitable, considering the nature of his new gods but I am trusting that he will by that time be wise enough to take it equably. I have a feeling that the very honesty of Orlando's ardor for Hitler has served to rehabilitate the brilliant boy and is saving him from the corruption that had nearly swallowed him when I found him."

We ate that night at the celebrated restaurant at the Berlin Zoo, an immensely fashionable resort where the cream of society was accustomed to congregate, not to look at the animals but to observe each other; and surely the spectacle of that tight circle of disappearing gentility, with their delicate tastes, their exquisite manners, and their total obliviousness to the uncouth growth of the Nazi monster that was rapidly swallowing up their world, was stranger than the display of the lesser animals.

I noticed that Orlando was drinking heavily, a new habit in him and one that made me uncomfortable for his welfare. His youthful, masculine beauty was accentuated by the perfection of his evening dress; his eyes glittered as they glanced with relish around the ornate rooms and he was bubbling with a sort of hectic happiness.

"The human zoo," he said softly, staring at the sedate diners. "I love to come here and watch them because I know their secret. Beautifully groomed and curried, fat and well-fed animal exteriors— they're well trained, too—and there's not a German soul in the lot!" He laughed into my eyes. "Dear Karl doesn't like my brand of mysticism. But that's all right. I can't endure yours. I think I really come here to watch my past and to laugh over it because I used to be so like them, brilliant and bored to the edge of death."

He gave a crow of glee and then his face became rapt and ardent.

"The most perfect ecstasy that can be experienced . . . the supreme joy is to feel your own soul flutter and come alive within you, your beautiful, strong, clear Nordic soul. Did I tell you that I once nearly killed myself, Karl? It was because I was bored with my own brilliance. I was fool enough to think it something of my own creation and I had tried out all of its tricks." His moods were still as infectious to me as they had been when we were schoolboys, and as I watched his dramatic face across the table the warmth and tenseness in him brought back a wave of the youthful affection I always felt when I was with him. "I had never seen," he cried passionately, "the force of the great river of race upon which my soul is a wave. How could I know that my mind was a creation of my blood, a race mind—a thing not alone my own but shared with the most heroic of my kind? Karl, there are souls being born all around me. There are souls so strong, so daring, so heroic that I tremble before them—and yet they accept me.

"The world is so blind when it sees only a political change in Germany! It is a soul change. Millions of souls are being reborn to heroism, and a great mass soul is stirring to life, a life of nobility and honor to which we all adhere and from which we cannot be separated. Political power may be denied us for years while we bloom inwardly. It will not matter. I know a man who is a high Nazi, who tells me of the nobility and honor of our leader, Karl, and he is so strong he would frighten you. But the same power is budding within *me*."

There was something of the elation of slight intoxication in his speech, but his eyes flamed with a fanaticism that was not born of wine.

"I have discovered the secret of the new life of the world," he whispered, and his voice began to rise like song. "The ancient Norse type, the blood-created, the hero of heroes has been realized in our day—he walks among us and on human feet—at the sound of his voice we are stirred to life—our dead hearts beat—dead bodies lift their heads—dead wombs are moved to bear. His eye is the eye of the eagle, Karl, and his voice, the voice of God. I love him—the perfect Aryan of old who is made flesh today to serve us, to bind his followers into a mystic union—I love him as I have never loved—and I love the men who follow him—the *Fuehrer*, Karl—"

While he was speaking he had picked up a glass of Burgundy and as his throat throbbed "the Fuehrer," he crushed the fragile glass in his hand as if to emphasize his ecstasy. Blood and wine mingled with the shattered glass and dripped from his hand onto the white linen but he did not take his burning eyes from mine.

"He is the center—the recreated hero of old—Adolf Hitler! Now that he has been lifted above us, he will draw all men to him."

I must have shivered at the blasphemous reminiscence of the phrase as well as with dislike of Orlando's fanatic extravagance, for his blazing eyes cooled and he shrugged his shoulders.

"I suppose you think I am drunk," he said cynically.

"I think drunkenness would be safer for you," I told him. "Here, let me tie up your hand."

"Let it go!" he said angrily. "You don't try to understand me." And then, with a return of his old smiling impudence, "I don't know why I spend so much of my time trying to convert you, Karl."

"I'm a hard case for your sort of conversion, Orlando."

"The blessed old general doesn't see it either," he said with a shrug. "But he will come to it because his own soul is the soul of a hero. You do not know how much I revere him, Karl—how I want him to feel as I do. And *you* will wake up one day, too. The light I have seen will blind you as well. It is the whole hope of the future. Some day," he promised me, "I shall introduce you to some Nazi officers. Then you will see what the Nordic honor means. You cannot imagine such nobility and strength. Even so," he pouted, with a flash of boyish vanity, "if *I* can't make you understand, I don't think they could."

He pulled out a folded handkerchief, flicked it open, and tied the white cloth clumsily around his still bleeding palm. The waiter brought him another wineglass and filled it.

"To the future of the German soul!" cried Orlando, lifting the glass in his bandaged hand and laughing at me.

"To the future of the German soul," I responded. "But we are not drinking the same toast, my boy."

Erika was to remain in Berlin for a week or more, to make arrangements for her permanent removal to Magdeburg and to fulfill a number of social engagements which she had neglected because of her absorption in the religious fight at the university. She reminded me that I had promised my mother to keep up a normal social life, and I remembered with a slight qualm that I had been instructed to enter the circle of an aging baroness whose protégée my mother had been when she was a young girl. The functions I had so far attended in Berlin were huge affairs to which I was invited out of courtesy to my parents, and where I had met many of the same people time after time without ever learning their names. Introductions were always mumbled and the throngs large.

If you wanted to become better acquainted with someone you met at these balls or if it was your intention to enter a certain social circle, there was a strict procedure to be followed. You made a polite call during the formal visiting hour which followed the Sunday morning church service. If the family was not receiving you were in luck and could leave cards, but if you were ushered in you must make conversation for ten minutes, which was the correct duration of such a call. To leave earlier was a grave breach of manners and to linger longer than a precise ten minutes was unheard of, yet you must under no circumstances look at your watch or even so much as glance at any timepiece in the room. To the younger men it was an agony to gauge this interval correctly, to rise at the exact moment and make your adieus graciously, and to realize that however charmingly you might be pressed to stay, it was not intended that you should take advantage of the offer. Once you had paid your formal call, you would receive an invitation to a more intimate party in which only this family's special set would be included.

I had so far allowed my social contacts to be limited to the large balls, partly because I dreaded the ordeal of these ten-minute calls and partly because I found university life so absorbing, but now I decided to follow Erika's example and to make my call upon the baroness. I arrived at what seemed under the circumstances a forbidding old mansion, carefully counting out the members of the family so that I might leave the correct number of cards in case I should be so fortunate as to find them out. But as I came to the steps I saw another gentleman, dressed just as formally as I was, being ushered in at the door and I realized that I was in for it.

The baroness' severe and thickly fleshed face was quilted with wrinkles, and its expressionlessness so fascinated me that I could hardly make my proper greeting. I was introduced to the other caller, who turned out to be Count Wallensdorf, and was questioned courteously but drily as to my mother's health. I stammered out some sort of a reply but I was hopelessly at sea for small talk. There was no hint in the conversation carried on with bright facility between the count and the baroness that this call was not occurring in the nineteenth century.

"The baths at R—closed early this year. It quite spoiled the season."

"Ferdi had a great success with his boar hunt. His father used to be famous for them. They say young M—did not exactly distinguish himself for bravery. Everyone is smiling about it."

"So the von S—s have at last made a match for that ugly daughter. Now they can safely launch the pretty one."

Through my recent absorption in the life and death struggle of a great old faith and an envenomed young political force, I had lost all touch with this sort of brittle amenities. I had moved among arrests and mass revolt, among secret rebellion and open terrorism, and here these correct people sat chatting wittily of trivialities as if the world outside their doors had no existence. I was completely unable to get my mind to function in this forgotten groove.

Besides, the count was very much at home. It was obvious that he and the baroness were old friends, that he knew what to say and I did not. Only one brilliant light gleamed through the darkness of that seemingly endless call. I should not have to count the minutes. Since I had come in with the count, I could let him clock the time for me and leave when he did. It was with an overwhelming gratitude that I saw him get to his feet and I immediately sprang to mine and was able to recover my assurance sufficiently to thank my hostess graciously for receiving me and to promise to send her greetings to my mother.

I descended the steps with a considerably lighter heart than I had carried up them. Count Wallensdorf fell into step with me and we walked up the street together.

"You are a student here, Herr Hoffmann?" he asked politely. "For what profession are you preparing?"

"I am a student of theology." I had grown so far away from the pre-Nazi pattern of thinking in the last six months, I had so far forgotten that to the mind of the aristocrat, to enter the ministerial profession was calamitous, a ruinous false step for a young man, that I was totally unprepared for his reaction.

"My God!" the count shouted. I probably could not have startled him more if I had told him I was studying to be a janitor. But he returned at once to courtesy, and with a smile of friendly amusement playing around his mouth, he advised me, "You must never marry."

"Why not, sir?" I asked him, and he quoted an old popular verse:

> "The cows of the miller,
> The sons of the pastor,
> You always can count on
> To end in disaster."

All the way home I had a strange feeling of unreality, as if I had stepped for a few minutes into a different world. For most of the German aristocrats the inflation had brought poverty, yet here they were, living on in the afterworld of a reflected glory, adhering to their rigorous etiquette, behaving in the old grand manner as if their traditional forms were the only reality and the ground that was rapidly cracking and giving way beneath their feet would still and always support them because it was their due. It was startling to realize that these people and hundreds like them made their correct appearances at church, yet were completely ignorant that that Church was fighting for its very life and that on the other hand a rival religion had arisen, preaching a harsh and cruel paganism and that their very sons were walking the streets shouting its bombastic shibboleths.

I began to wonder, in the diverse strata of society, how far religious observance had become a mere form, to be followed because it was the correct thing to do but not to be taken otherwise than lightly. The fire that I had seen in Orlando's eyes, the wild zeal of the young German Christians and the fanatic veneration they were beginning to give the Fuehrer could only be conquered by a stronger fire, a belief that was the very life of the men who clung to it. How deep were the roots of faith?

CHAPTER
ELEVEN

WE did not expect the Nazis who now controlled the university to take their defeat at the great meeting in the auditorium easily. For the next few days we watched warily for new tactics designed to bring us into the German Christian movement. When the next move came at the end of three days, it proved one we could not combat. A new course of training was announced for the school of theology, a series of compulsory lectures on Nazi philosophy, which were made a requirement before credit would be given for any of our university work. We must attend, or resign our careers. Evidently it had been decided to abandon force and to educate us into complying with the blood-of-the-hero cultists.

That the Nazis did not trust us to co-operate with them was plain. Special cards were given out which must be presented at each lecture to be stamped, and a fully stamped card must be presented at the end of the term before our credits were issued. A further precaution against our skipping the lectures was instituted. The seals with which the cards were stamped were to be changed every week, we were warned, so that no clever student could imitate the seal and stamp his card full of attendance marks.

It was a noisy and skeptical crowd that trooped in to hear the first of these lectures. The speaker was to be an "emergency bishop" appointed by Reichsbishop Mueller, whose pompous appearances in and about Berlin were by now a source of ribald amusement among the students. The new Reichsbishop was living in state at the Adlon and rode through the streets in a veritable battleship of a car, with a liveried chauffeur and a footman and with a specially designed flag fluttering from the automotive monster to distinguish it from the cars of lesser dignitaries. Unhappily for him, nobody took him seriously and he was before long to prove useless to the Nazis, although rather than admit their mistake they allowed him to keep his title and the appurtenances of his office. Already he was being referred to with amused derision as *"Rei-bi,"* an unflattering diminutive of the resplendent title "Reichsbishop."

The new appointee of the *"Rei-bi"* who was to address us today had been the pastor of a small congregation, until he had judiciously joined the German Christians and received his reward. To bolster his new eminence at this student meeting, one of the high officials of the Ministry of Education and Culture appeared with him on the platform and introduced the "emergency bishop" to us.

We were used to hearing a very different type of man in our professors, most of whom were very much men of the world, the brilliant sons of the upper classes who could afford the years of study and travel required to attain a position at one of the universities, and who had the scholarly mind to which such work was congenial. We were accustomed to men like the bearded and impressive Deissmann, Lietzmann, or his predecessor von Harnack who had been the theologian of the Imperial Court, a little bent-over man with a brain of devastating acuteness, who bore the title of "Excellency" and who wore across his chest the wide ribbon of the decoration of the Red Eagle which had been bestowed upon him by the Kaiser.

The new "emergency bishop" proved a sort of blustering rustic, and you could feel instinctively the antagonism that rose in the crowd as he launched into an emotional speech. He began at once to expound on the sore subject of the non-Aryan Christians.

"I tell you, my desk is covered with hundreds of letters, coming to me from Christian Church members who have in their veins some of the dark blood of the Jew. They ask my advice. They ask me what they are to do.

"I tell you that our very God would have no being if it were not for the purity and honor of the Nordic blood. By the strength of that red stream, by the nobility of our souls we give to our God his existence. The fellowship of the Nordic race is strong only while it protects that blood and the purity of that soul. It is a service to our God to protect His worship from pollution, to join German with German and not to darken the nostrils of heaven with the sour, decaying breath of the Jew.

"What, then, can I say to these men who write to me as Christians and confess their polluted blood?" The speaker struck a noble attitude and turned on us an expression designed to signify benevolence.

"In Christian charity, the only advice I can give these non-Aryan Christians is to tell them to seek a heroic exit from this life."

There was a roar from all corners of the hall as if a herd of caged lions had been let loose and the whole assemblage of students sprang to their feet in fury, bellowing their disgust with this pseudo-representative of Christian charity.

A book went flying through the air toward the platform and in a second hundreds of heavy volumes were shooting toward the head of the miserable emergency bishop. It was a demonstration in violation of all our proud rules of university conduct and it was a spontaneous outbust. Gross, the student leader, in his brown shirt, leaped up at the front of the hall, his face red with fury at this defiance of the authority he represented. With contorted features he faced the rioting students, waving his arms and trying to make himself heard above the tumult. As the thick books bulleted about the cringing speaker and thudded on the platform in a crashing rain, the government official drew himself slowly to his feet, his face white with suppressed rage. He lifted his fist above his head and screamed at us:

"We have the power now and you shall feel it. We will make you crawl."

But a thousand young men continued to storm upon the floor until the Nazis finally accepted the situation and strode haughtily from the dais, with Gross walking stiffly after them.

We knew that this would not be the end, that the Nazis would push us as far as they dared—and they were not timid. The tension grew tighter from one day to the next, the student leaders threatening and the students responding with sullenness or with rebellion. There were constant clashes; disorder marked the whole life of the university until almost no one was doing any serious studying. The most heartening thing was the way the students of other faculties rallied to our defense. We were no longer a group removed from the rest; we were sought out and encouraged. We were the future leaders of German Christianity, whom the Nazis were trying to suborn to promote their vicious doctrines, and Christianity itself was at stake in the fight. In the *Steh-Convent* the religious conflict was almost the sole topic of discussion throughout the whole student body.

Two days after the book throwing had routed the "emergency bishop," Eugen Ostwald sought me out. He was full of repressed excitement and the saber scar stood out in a pale line on his ruddy face.

"I've been out to see Niemoeller."

I had often wondered how the doughty pastor of Dahlem, who had fought the election so fiercely, had taken the defeat.

"You sound as if something was doing," I said, for Ostwald's voice was elated and his tough young chin was topped with a grin of secret pleasure.

"Something is very much doing. Niemoeller is starting an underground resistance to this German Christian indoctrination, throughout the whole Reich. He and a number of other churchmen who agree with him are organizing a big movement. The German Christians have got hold of the high offices; all the outer organization of the Church is in their hands. But it's absolutely necessary for the men who follow the teaching of Christ to keep the preaching of Christianity in their own hands, not to be separated and isolated and broken down one by one the way the Nazis are trying to manage it."

"How are they going about it? I've racked my brains trying to think of some way we could work that would really count."

"They are organizing a sort of inner Church. The Nazis can keep their outer show but inside their nominal Church all the men who won't accept their blood-and-thunder doctrine will band together. The pastors will preach nothing but the Word of God and the laymen will listen only to the Christian teaching as opposed to this German Christian pap. They are calling it the 'Confessional

Church,' because it will preach only our Confessions of Faith as Luther laid them down. It is a Church within a Church. I have already joined it." He pulled out of his pocket a red card and showed it to me. It signified that Eugen Ostwald was a member of the Confessional Church of Germany.

"It's a good name," I said. That little red card in my fingers seemed to hold an ocean of promise—the Confessional Church—my mind pictured a vast and indestructible edifice of gray stone with a crowd of people standing about its doors. Perhaps at that moment I caught a foretaste of all that name was to mean to Christianity in the years ahead.

"Have many joined?" I asked. "How are they reaching people?"

"Thousands of pastors are in it already in every corner of Germany and they have brought in tens of thousands of members. You remember the lists of names we had from Niemoeller when we sent out the propaganda from the cellar? They started on those and the thing has been spreading like wildfire. Keep an eye open around here and see how many of the university students are streaming out to Dahlem these days."

"I'm going myself. Today."

Ostwald shook my hand roughly. "Of course you are. And spread the word around when you get back. I tell you this Church fight has barely started."

My irresistible first impulse was to carry the news to Erika. I was hardly aware of the extent to which I was finding it necessary to share my hopes and disappointments with her, I only knew that I must be the first to tell her and to see her gray eyes begin to shine when she heard the news. I found her quietly packing her personal things to be shipped back home, and my words stumbled and got in each other's way as I came out with the story of the forming of the secret inner Church.

Erika did not disappoint me. She clapped her hands together like a child and ran over to me, catching me by the coat lapels.

"Take me to Dahlem with you, won't you, Karl?"

"Of course I'm going to take you. What do you think I came here for, my lady? I wouldn't dream of going without you."

I caught her warm hands and we looked at each other excitedly. Her eyes offered me such a frank, affectionate happiness that the wave of tenderness I had felt for her the other evening swept through me again. I was suddenly aware that this look of unaffected fondness in her lovely eyes was something I had seen in my mother's eyes when she looked at my father. My breath caught in my throat and I knew in a flash of revelation that I should always want to turn to this girl for all the things, the tenderness, the strength, the ardor that a man looks for in a gentle woman. I was hungrily aware of her nearness to me. The thought hung like a tangible bond between us in the air, and then suddenly I read in her eyes that she also was aware of it. For a second we were allowed a glimpse into each other's minds and read the secret hidden there. Our eyes clung with a wishful daring and then Erika's eyes dropped; she gave a brief shiver and then turned on me again her frank and friendly smile. I lifted her small hands and kissed them and looked at her ruefully, but my heart was beating hard. I would not be in a position to marry for many years. I was only at the beginning of my studies and so charming a girl as Erika would be expected to choose a husband long before I would be able to offer her a home. Nevertheless it was with a light-hearted sensation of having received a gift beyond my due that I walked by her side without speaking as we covered the blocks that would take us to the bus for Dahlem.

Although I had worked for Martin Niemoeller during the days in the cellar this was the first time I had seen him, and in spite of all I had heard of him I was not prepared to find, in his compact frame, so electric a personality. Most men's faces seem only half alive; his seemed to be holding its vitality in check by an effort of will. The keen eyes reflected the brilliant brain behind them but there was quietness and temperance in his mouth. The whole face was warm with wisdom and with a strong patience, well learned.

He welcomed us gladly, gave us seats beside his desk, and told us that the young Confessional Church was expanding with amazing rapidity.

"At the university," I told him, "the indignation against the

German Christians is growing very strong. Their doctrines are so outrageous that almost everyone is revolting against them."

"That is where we must be most careful," said Niemoeller, in a tone of friendly reproof. "We are not engaged in a political fight. Our only concern is that we may continue to teach the love and the pity of Christ. The early Church, in the first hard years of Christianity, did not conquer because of indignation against its opponents but because its members walked among men with love. If the Confessional Church enters its fight with hate against those fellow humans who oppose us then our fight is already lost.

"Political ascendancy is of no importance to us; the fact that the Lutheran Church is tied to the history of the German land is no excuse for our continuance. Only in so far as we continue to teach the beautiful compassion of God and bring its hope to beat in the inmost hearts of the people are we justified in calling ourselves a Christian Church, and only while we walk with love will the hand of God work powerfully for us. If we were only trying to preserve the Church as an institution and to preserve our places within an institution we should deserve defeat.

"We may hate not the men who teach them, but the doctrines of pride and cruelty that are being taught. For these are not an attack upon an institution but upon the Lord Christ, Himself. It is because we continue to tell of the love of Jesus that they wish to render us dumb.

"Whatever happens to individuals, the Confessional Church must continue to teach that divine love and to exemplify it. To a doctrine of hate we shall oppose Luther's great Confessions of Faith which have been the standards of God's truth for us since they were first spoken. They are our creeds but they do not stultify and limit us. They were evolved in the agony and wretchedness of human life, not to shut us within a narrow belief but to set the solid ground beneath our feet. They are the essence of God's Word, the Biblical truths tested and clarified and setting a clear light before all men who strive toward God. Our only reason for being as an organization is to make that strong confession of faith, to speak that gracious Gospel of Love."

My heart was beating loudly as I hung on the words of this dark-faced, intense pastor. The doubts I had been entertaining, the fears for the strength of Christianity dwindled and I was ashamed for my own pettiness. I had cried to God for a leader, not trusting Him, not realizing that He always raised up men to lead us when our need was greatest.

"The Confessional Church," Niemoeller continued, leaning back in his chair, "will not be a new Church. It will be the old Church and continue in the old framework. But where the German Christians appoint bishops we shall secretly repudiate them and look only to men of God for direction. The government may take over the outer offices of the Church but between them and the preaching of the Word of God we shall erect an unbreakable bulwark."

Niemoeller reached across his desk and picked up a copy of the Large Catechism.

"If you want a description of what I believe the Confessional Church must mean—must become," he said, crossing his legs and opening the volume, "let me read it to you in the words of Luther. Here—this is it: 'I believe that there is upon earth a holy assembly and congregation of pure saints under one head, even Christ, collected together by the Holy Ghost in one faith, one mind and understanding, with manifold gifts yet one in love, without sects or schisms, and I also am part and member of the same, a participant and joint owner of all the good it possesses, brought to it and incorporated into it by the Holy Ghost, in that I have heard and continue to hear, the word of God, which is the means of entrance.'

"This will not be the spectacular fight which some of you young people have probably been hoping for; it will be a test of mettle, a trying of loyalty. It will be a fight," said Niemoeller with dark heat, "greater than a fight of men against men. An evil force is moving against the heart of faith, against love and pity, against the very mercy of Christ. We dare not be half-hearted or despair because of our weakness." He began to quote dramatically from the Epistle to the Ephesians:

"'For we wrestle not against flesh and blood, but against

principalities and powers, against the rulers of the darkness of this world, against spiritual wickedness in high places. Wherefore take unto you the whole armor of God, that ye may be able to withstand in the evil day . . . take the helmet of Salvation and the sword of the Spirit, which is the Word of God.'" Behind his smile you could feel the core of steel which was in the man.

When we went down to the sidewalk with our red cards of membership tucked safely away in our pockets, Erika's eyes were dewy as she smiled up at me.

"You can see now where I learned not to be afraid for you in this fight," she said.

"There is a man," I said with my fists clenched, "we can trust with everything we believe in."

The organization of the Confessional Church went on so quietly that the government failed to take notice of it. Every day more and more students slipped out to Dahlem or to one of a dozen churches in Berlin that were serving as local headquarters and came back with their little red cards. The word was seeping through underground channels all across Germany and every day thousands of new names were added to the rolls. There was no visible sign that anything was occurring, but if the Nazi leaders and their German Christian satellites could have guessed what hope was beginning to glow in the eyes of vast sections of the people they might have slept an uneasy sleep those nights. Under the outward show of their supremacy, the flapping swastikas, the parades of brown-shirted men, hidden from the eyes of their cocksure officials, a sleeping giant was stirring to life.

Two days after we had gone together to Niemoeller's, I saw Erika off to Magdeburg on the train. It was a bright, clear, winter afternoon and she wore a woolly blue coat with some sort of soft fur around her throat that made her look very fair. She was as eager and excited as if she were going home in triumph rather than as a political outcast, and she walked at my side with a skipping buoyancy in her step.

"Now I have something better to take to your father than just my own small services," she said, talking rapidly and happily.

"There won't be a church or a person in Germany who won't feel stronger and braver now that they know they aren't working alone any longer. The awful thing was that every little parish felt so separated, so cut off from the rest. It was like trying to keep afloat in a flood and not knowing whether everyone else hadn't already gone down. You might be the last one who had his head above water, and that made your struggling so useless."

"They've already had a dose of German Christian theology at home'" I said, "and from the numbers who stayed away from Herr Kraemer's second sermon, I should say that our inner Church will find its members already prepared to join."

Erika laughed with excitement. "I feel as if our real lives were just beginning. There will be so much ahead for me at home, Karl."

"I wish you weren't going." I hadn't intended to say so.

"Why, Karl!" She was both amused and perplexed. "I thought you wanted me to get out of this turmoil here in Berlin."

"It's a purely masculine selfishness on my part. I don't like losing you, Erika."

The big gray eyes looked squarely into mine.

"You won't lose me, Karl."

"All aboard," the conductor cried, and I swung her into her compartment. For a moment her face peered at me through the glass with that strange air of separateness that attaches to your friends once they are closed into a train. The wheels turned; the windows began moving past me. Strangers' faces stared briefly at me—a bit of flotsam glimpsed from the secure snugness of their moving world—and I was left alone astride the platform, hearing the vibration in the rails fade, watching the train turn toy size and disappear in the distance. Erika's last words filled me with a curious contentment and I carried it back with me as I returned to the male world of the university.

The academic air that winter was full of the noise of clashing doctrines; every effort of the Nazis to silence the raging religious discussion was in vain. There was almost no studying being done. Lectures were attended only to seek fresh fuel for the burning fight.

When the groups formed after a lecture, a student would hurl the professor's closing words like a challenge and in a moment the air would be blue with furious verbiage.

Finally the Nazis decided to recognize the opposition officially, at least so far as to allow it a hearing in public debate. A Wednesday evening in November was appointed for a public airing of both sides of the controversy and an equal number of German Christian professors and of professors who opposed them were to occupy the rostrum. Each speaker was allowed ten minutes to present his case.

When I reached the hall it was already jammed to the last seat and students were standing around the sides and at the back. There were more than seven thousand men present. The German Christians wasted no time in placating their audience. The first speaker called for the destruction of the Church if it could not accommodate itself to the great future course which was to "Germanize Christianity."

"Martin Luther's great reform has been reduced to a group of squabbling and shortsighted clergy who cling to the Judaistic Old Testament as a fit book of religious instruction for an Aryan race," he declared. "Germans will refuse to teach their children the stories of Jewish camel breeders and their loose women. They will substitute for these unhealthy tales the clean Norse legends and fairy stories to which our blood responds. In time these stories of our race will gain their true religious significance. Any Church that hopes to be the Church of the Aryan future will despise and reject the so-called Old Testament. It is not a Christian book. Its teaching has served only to allow the unclean and subtle doctrines of the Jew to dominate our thinking.

"Look back to Marcion!" he cried. "To one of the early Church fathers who was unjustly branded as a heretic. He, Marcion, was wise enough in the second century to warn us that the God who fathered our Lord, Jesus Christ, was not the God of this obscene Old Testament."

There was a low grumbling of discontent through the hall but there was no demonstration, for we desired our own men to have their say. Our venerated professor of the Old Testament rose to answer, a scholarly, white-haired man whose reputation was world-wide. His love for his subject trembled in his soft voice.

"The heart of the Old Testament, as we read it," he said, "is the pointing to the Christ. Throughout the vanity, the despair and suffering of men the promise of God begins to shine. My colleague declares the Old Testament is not a Christian book. Perhaps he has not read it with eyes that look forward to a Christian hope. Martin Luther has set the test by which we can judge it. He has said, 'Everything that drives toward Christ is apostolic and canonical.' We have lifted up our eyes with the Psalmist in the inspired beauty of his song. We have heard God exalted in many voices. We have trembled over the pages of Isaiah at the wonder of the promise. It is a book of waiting and of preparation. It is a book of the darkness of men's minds and of their hope. Without it, we should not reach in such exultation the climax of the Cross."

He sat down with tears streaming from his eyes and bowed his head. The students shouted their applause and for a moment an uproar seemed inevitable, but the crowd subsided tensely. For two hours the discussion raged back and forth.

"The rejection of the Old Testament will be as great a landmark in the advance of Christianity as the reforms of Luther," one German Christian advocate declared. "The New Testament as well must be purged of its Jewish taint."

"The German Church of the future rejects the weakling Christ," cried another. "We exalt Christ because he is the leader of an army of militant believers. His Church will be founded on confident courage in the strength that is born in the Nordic soldier. Pride, honor, and the soldier's blood will be the new battle cry of His Church.

"Christ rode into Germany as a warrior and that is why the German blood leaped to acclaim him. Now in a new era of history he appears again as the warrior King."

One of the bravest of our professors courageously named the German Christian doctrines for what they were.

"This is not Christianity that is being urged upon us," he said, "although it wears the Christian name like a false cloak. It is a brutal paganism and there is no room for it in the Church of Christ. Reconcile these doctrines if you can with the words that came out of His mouth: 'Ye have heard that it was said by them of old time, Thou shalt not kill, and whosoever shall kill shall be in danger of the judgment; but I say unto you that whosoever is angry with his brother without a cause shall be in danger of the judgment. Ye have heard that it hath been said, An eye for an eye and a tooth for a tooth; but I say unto you, that ye resist not evil; but whosoever shall smite thee on thy right cheek, turn to him the other also. Love your enemies, bless them that curse you, do good to them that hate you, and pray for them which despitefully use you and persecute you.' Reconcile these words, if you can, with the doctrines of power, unforgiveness, and vengeance that we have been hearing."

The German Christians were not abashed; they were only angered. Again and again they proclaimed feverishly:

"The Church must strengthen the nation's destiny of total power."

"There is no room in a German Church for a Jewish Messiah."

"Salvation lies in the Nordic blood and in that blood alone."

Disturbances from the audience began to interrupt the orations. The noise of feet and of irate voices smothered the speakers' words in a rising tumult of exasperation. Finally Heinrich Gross, the hard-faced Nazi student leader, leaped to his feet.

"We have had much patience with you," he said to the rebellious students, in an icy voice. "We have tried to reason with you but you have refused to follow the Fuehrer. You cling to old, outmoded Christian doctrines. This is another day. We have the power now. The Reich belongs to the National Socialists and so does the Church. The time for discussions is over. The time for reasoning is past. There is only one way to handle you. I warn you for the last time. From now on we will use force."

The next day we learned that our teacher of the Old Testament who had defended his beloved book the night before and wept to hear the attack upon it, had been forced to resign his chair at the university and had also been removed from the councils of the

Church. A brisk young German Christian came to lecture in his place.

The changes that came over the university scene were hard to accept. The Nazi student leaders, all of the stripe of Gross the overbearing, or the cold-eyed Jansen, had proved a bitter pill for us to swallow, but the gradual disappearence of our scholarly professors was stranger still. The men of strong temperament, of uncompromising intellect vanished first; the sharp stimuli these men had given to our thinking became only a memory, and mental life began to drain out of the university. More and more it resembled a political camp. The mediocre men who occupied the lost professors' platforms bombarded us with cheap political speeches, proselytizing for their myth of Aryan supremacy. There were students who made a sour game of wagering which of the eminent men who were left on the faculty would be the next to be dismissed. The Nazis were clearly determined to corrupt the university and by this means to train the students as a pagan priesthood for their pagan Church.

We waited one day for our New Testament professor to appear. He was an old and sickly man and we were used to an occasional delay in his reaching the classroom, but we liked his dry earnestness and his tolerance and we never chafed at waiting. Twenty minutes went by and there was no sign of him. Then the door opened and another professor walked quietly to the platform. He was a man we all admired and we were immediately filled with apprehension as we saw the grief and anger on his thin face.

"When Professor M—left his home today to come to this class a letter was handed to him at his door," he informed us baldly. "The letter called him a traitor to Germany. It ordered him to change his teaching methods at once to conform to those of the German Christians. If he refused he would be deprived of his professorship and sent to prison. Perhaps the shock was too much for his weak body. His neighbors saw him raise his arms excitedly above his head. Then he fell on the street and before they reached him he was dead of a heart attack. There will be no class today, gentlemen." He stared at us with his eyes burning somberly. "Heil Hitler!" he said derisively, and strode from the platform.

Our next class was presided over by a bull-necked disciple of the Aryan-blood cult. He was not sensitive enough to glimpse the menace in the fuming faces below him that morning. He commenced a loud tirade (all the German Christian teachers seemed to consider noise a satisfactory substitute for scholarship) against the "feebleness of the doctrine of Christian mercy," which the proud German race had caught "like an Oriental sickness."

"Christianity," he declaimed, "with its morose teaching of sin, is guilty of bringing immorality into the originally perfect German race."

Two seats away from me a student jerked to his feet and shouted:

> "Throw him out the window!
> Throw him out the window!"

The class rose silently to their feet. Not calling out, not scrambling or pushing, without the least confusion they moved inexorably forward in a body, like an executioner's squad marching to its fatal work, grimly intent on hurling this man to the street four stories below. The professor stared at the mob in astonishment, and then as they pressed forward implacably with still faces and savage eyes, his thick form began to tremble, he wheeled and raced for the rear door, screaming for help. His terror checked the crowd as if with disgust for the thing they had almost done.

"There goes our exponent of perfect Aryan strength and courage," drawled Walther Vogler. A couple of the foremost men shrugged their shoulders and turned back to pick up their books, and with sour faces we dispersed in silence.

"A taste of their own medicine won't hurt that crew," said young Vogler to me bitterly as we went out, but I was sickened at the whole display.

I went down to Wolfgang's studio to get the taste of the

morning out of my mouth and found my big red-headed friend painting furiously.

"It's only a natural reaction, my boy," he said when I had spilled out the whole sorry story. "Violence will breed counterviolence. The Nazis preach courage but they have not yet learned that courage and brutality aren't synonymous. You can't blame your own crowd for reacting violently when they've been pricked too far."

"It would have been a fine display of Christian fortitude if we'd thrown that fellow out of the window, wouldn't it?"

"A Church militant isn't exactly a new historical idea."

"I'm afraid," I said, "that I prefer Niemoeller's brand of Christianity."

CHAPTER
TWELVE

THE roof of the Domkirche was powdered with light snow as the taxi that was bringing me from the station for the Christmas celebration at home turned down our familiar street. Everywhere there were signs of approaching festivity, Christmas trees wherever I looked, merry red faces on the streets and delivery trucks unloading ample packages. I was weary of controversy; for the moment I had had enough of the unavailing struggle and I wanted to find Christmas, at least, unchanged from the Christmases of my childhood.

The house was full of the smell of anise-seed cookies and of evergreens; my mother beamed happily upon me as she bustled about her holiday tasks; and in my room I found an Advent calendar, exactly the same kind she used to bring me when I was a small boy. It was a large sheet of cardboard with little doors on it, one for each day; and when you received it all the doors were open. Every night during that wonderful season you closed a door to mark the passing day, until the final door was shut and Christmas was upon you in all its glory. I came downstairs filled with that wonderful sensation of having reached back into something that never changes, and I was as excited as a child of ten.

My father came out from his study to greet me with a hard handclasp, and my cheerfulness gave way to shock at the change in him. His face was so drawn and colorless. He looked so old. This was not, after all, the same as those earlier Christmases. The fight I had thought to leave behind me was still going on here and he and I were both deeply involved in it.

"There will be only one Christmas party this year," my mother said. "It's not like old times, now, Karl, with a big dinner party

every night. The Nazis watch those who entertain very much and
their taxes go up. Besides, every time you give a dinner the brown-
shirts will be around the next day to ask for a 'voluntary
contribution.' If you are rich enough to entertain like this, they
say, you can afford to be most liberal to the party."

"How do people like that?"

"They don't like it a bit, of course. They would much rather
live their lives in the old comfortable way with lots of friends around.
But even that is hard now. You have to be so careful whom you
invite together or there will be a political discussion and Frau
Holbrecht and some of the others get so upset. At some of the
evenings people have become so emotional that there were real
scenes. You can expect more tears than old-time laughter at a dinner
party now."

Before supper that night my father and I took a walk through
the snowy streets, past the bright lights in the windows and under
the pine trees with their soft white feathering. We had gone perhaps
half a block when we met Herr Wegner, a foreman from one of the
steel mills and a member of the church board, who stopped for a
minute to chat with us. In the rays of the street light his square
face looked troubled.

"Is there something wrong, Wilhelm?" my father asked him.

"It is nothing, really nothing, Herr Pastor. Nothing, at least,
to trouble you with. But it will make a big change for many men.
The *Stammtisch* is dissolving."

The *Stammtisch* was a time-honored middle-class custom,
especially in the small towns, but even in the larger ones to a wide
extent. A group of men would meet at night in their *Stammlokal*
and while they drank their beer and wine and smoked their pipes
they would discuss the events of the day, especially the political
trends, at great length, breadth, and in all directions. It was a
long-cherished custom and the men looked forward expectantly to
the evenings of good conversation with their cronies after the hard
day's work. Now, one after another, the *Stammtische* were beginning
to break up.

"So," said my father. "I am sorry to hear it, Wilhelm."

"It is very bad, Herr Pastor. But it could not go on. It had got so that nobody could talk any more. If you say what you think about politics, maybe there is somebody there listening whom you cannot trust. Here we are, friends of long years, and everybody suspects everybody else. Maybe someone is a secret police agent." He sighed gustily. "I do not know. I am very badly upset. I have been careful to keep on the Nazis' good side, but little by little the things we used to enjoy, the things that made us feel good to be together are disappearing."

Even here, I thought to myself, under the easygoing surface the life has changed. The old comfortable friendliness that made this town such a pleasant place to live in has been destroyed. Behind everyone's eyes there is a fear lurking. I remembered the sermon my father had preached before his arrest, how he had warned that the spreading suspicion would enter our very homes and destroy the old happy confidence between friends. Already there was a twisting and warping of the ties that bound the people to one another. And Magdeburg was only one town. All over Germany the same distrust, the same ugliness was hiding.

"I can't get used to seeing people grow afraid of each other," said my father sadly as we strode along the pavement.

"Is it the same—does it make them fearful of joining you in the Church fight?"

"Karl, that is becoming my greatest gratification. That is the one place where there is no timidity. By far the greater part of the congregation have already enrolled in our Confessional group. For their religion they are practically fearless—perhaps because their faith is the one thing that looms greater to them than their personal safety. It is a tremendous thing to see."

I began to sense the new solidarity in the Church early the next morning. Erika arrived at the parsonage before our breakfast was over. She was acting as a sort of liaison officer for my father, and a dozen men came in to see her in the secretaries' room on their way to work, to get their cards of membership in the Confessional Church. I talked to Herr Oldorf, who had dropped in on the way to his law office.

"The only men who are showing any courage these days are the ministers," he told me. "No other party, no other organization has dared to resist. But these men are fighting without considering first whether they may lose or not. Consequently they are not losing. Do you realize that there must have been forty organizations strong enough to put up a fight in the beginning, that have simply disappeared? The political parties melted like ice in warm water. Then there were the war veterans with their *Stahlhelm*. At the time Hindenburg was elected they numbered two million men and it was whispered that they were fully armed. They disappeared overnight, those who weren't persuaded that the better part of expediency was to join the S.A.

"We Germans are a people who admire bravery, Herr Hoffmann. It is an honor to fight under a man like your father."

I learned many things that morning. My father had written me none of the details of his work, from a fear that the Nazis were watching his mail. I learned that he had been entrusted by the heads of the Confessional Church with the organization of the surrounding parishes, and that one church after another was making brave headway in rallying their people to the defense of the faith under his leadership.

"Your father has become a very famous man around here," Erika informed me. "People in Magdeburg and in the towns all around have heard the story about the Church flag and the sermon he preached and the way he talked to the storm troopers, and how he was arrested for it. They trust him, Karl. In times like these that's a wonderful thing to say of a man—that people can trust him. He has become very powerful."

"If he is becoming powerful, then he is in danger."

"He won't even think about the danger. Your mother and I do all the worrying for him. He isn't interested in his own safety."

"What about the Nazis? Are they aware of what's going on?"

"Yes, they know. But I think they are rather baffled. Their German Christian bishops have been sending out orders to the pastors and laymen all over the country and the orders are simply disregarded. It must be maddening to them. The inner Church, our Confessional Church has set up a secret governing body of our own men, most of them the original leaders before the Nazis came, tough fighters like Gerhardt Jacobi, who put their belief ahead of their own lives. Our secret council is called the *Bruederrat* [Council of Brothers], and the only orders the churches will follow now are the ones that come from them."

"Then we are winning, Erika."

"It's a very painful sort of winning. The Nazis don't dare move directly against the Church for fear of the people. But they are making arrests. Every week in some part of the country an outspoken man disappears into a concentration camp, Some are ministers and some are laymen, but all of them are brave men who have said what they thought. Last week the office of the biggest church in Helmstedt was raided and the minister and his secretary were arrested when they found a stack of Confessional Church pamphlets—and that is only a few miles from here."

That same day my father called my mother, Erika, and me into his study and shut the door. The mail had brought the news of his election to the *Bruederrat*, the secret council by which the Confessional Church was now directed.

"They will pay for a staff of six secretaries," he said, reading the letter over. "That will mean that we can do three times as much work. Poor little Erika," he smiled at her, "has been carrying a bigger share than is right for such slender shoulders."

"It has been growing so fast that it's becoming almost too big a load to handle," said Erika with a touch of pride. "We could use a dozen more helpers."

My mother stood up and leaned the palms of her hands flat upon the desk top, bracing herself as she looked at my father with frowning determination.

"Franz, you are not going to bring six secretaries here to work in this house."

"Eh? What's that, Hedwig? What on earth do you mean?"

"Do you think such an increase of activity would go unnoticed? Now that you are one of the *Bruederrat* they will be expecting you to direct a much larger territory, and the house will be full of the

Confessional literature. Suddenly six helpers will appear in your home and the whole parish will know it in a day. The Nazis will know it too, and what will prevent them from raiding your house? Look at what happened in Helmstedt."

"Come now, Hedwig." My father gave her plump cheek a little nip with his fingers. "It isn't like you to be faint-hearted. You know there are risks that have to be run."

"That I agree to. But there is no use increasing the risks. You know that more than ever now, you will be the center of all the secret work for a very large district. It is true I have worried for your safety because all the activity has centered here at the parsonage. But you also should regard your own safety because the work depends on it. If you concentrate the work in one place you only make it easy for the Nazis to ruin the whole activity in this section by one raid directed against this house."

"There is something in what you say," my father mused. "It is not wise to render ourselves vulnerable. But we must have headquarters somewhere, and I feel that it is my responsibility to maintain it."

"I do not ask you to protect yourself, my dear husband," she urged him, "but you must protect your value to our faith. Help me to persuade him, Karl and Erika."

"Why is it necessary," suggested Erika, "to have a single headquarters? The new helpers could work in the members' homes and the literature be hidden in many places. And not the same places each time, either. We could make it almost impossible for the Nazis to discover where and how the work is going on."

"Then the members would be sharing the risks," my father said slowly.

"And so they should," answered my mother briskly. "The fight is meaningless unless all the people are concerned in it. The dangers they share will bind the people all the more strongly to the inner Church. You know that it is not possible for a group of men to save their faith *for* the people. The people must save it themselves. You do not help them if you deprive them of all the difficulties."

"You are right, Hedwig," said my father with decision. And so it was that a pattern of shifting and secrecy was adopted that was copied throughout all the offices of the Confessional Church. Weekly, sometimes even daily when the hunt was up, the whole office staff and equipment were moved from the house of one steadfast member to that of another. The literature was stored in small bundles in a dozen different homes and distributed from hand to hand.

"I dread to see him taking on the additional work," my mother said to me privately that evening. "You can see how he looks, Karl. His face is so tired and his hair has turned gray. He will not admit it, but his health has suffered badly from all that he has gone through. He has never told me a word of what happened to him when he was in the concentration camp but since he came back he has been constantly ill. He used to go to bed at night and drop off to sleep like a baby. Now he lies awake for hours and stares at the ceiling, and when he does sleep he tosses and moans. Sometimes he leaps up in his sleep and cries out terribly and clutches at the bedposts, and if I wake him he begins shaking as if he were having a chill."

"I am sure he will grow stronger as time passes, Mother." But in my heart I knew that my father had aged ten years in the last four months.

My parents seemed to have entered a happy conspiracy to make this Christmas as like the Christmases of former years as was possible in this strange new season of cruelty. The four candles burned in the Advent wreath which hung from the living-room ceiling and my mother sat at the table below it, fashioning little waxen fruits to ornament the Christmas tree, and I sat down to help her as I had done for so many times over so many years. I remembered the clumsy and lopsided pears and apples my boyish fingers had once turned out and how she had commended them with never a hint at their imperfections.

"Am I doing better this year than I used to do, *Muetterchen?*" I asked her, holding up three bright red cherries I had just finished.

"I have always thought *all* the fruits you made were beautiful." She was smiling at me but there were tears in her eyes.

"You are a dear, sentimental little woman," I said, kissing the top of her fair head.

"Why should I not be sentimental when I remember my little son who used to help me, and see my big son here with me now?" She flashed me a smile, half mischievous, half earnest. "If I cannot weep a little from happiness when it comes Christmas time, it would mean I had become a hard, bad woman."

The door of the music room remained locked and through the high fanlight above it I could see the bushy green top of the waiting Christmas tree. I remembered, laughing at the memory of my small-boy self, all the hours I had spent prowling around that forbidden portal. I could see myself toiling in my room over the gifts for my father and mother and the servants, for Christmas gifts from children were always especially valued when they were made by our own awkward fingers. I could almost shut out from this atmosphere of merry plotting, of spices and tinsel and evergreens, the darkness that waited outside the broad front door to chill us with brutal reality when our merrymaking should be over. But I could not quite shut it out. It came in upon us with the sagging of my father's wide shoulders and with the worry that lay behind my mother's eyes.

The Christmas vespers began at four in the afternoon of December 24th. Two huge Christmas trees stood in the front of the chancel, covered with lighted wax candles. On the mensa of the altar a transparency of the manger scene was made visible by a lighted candle which stood behind it. The church was filled to the doors with bright-faced and expectant people, glowing from the snowy air and the ebullition of the festive season. The glow subsided a little in the warm inner air and the excitement gave way to the hush of reverence as the service of adoration began.

Clearly and strongly from my father's lips the beautiful words of the Christmas story from St. Luke fell into the silence.

"And Joseph also went up from Galilee, out of the city of Nazareth, into Judea, unto the city of David, which is called Bethlehem; because he was of the house and lineage of David;

"To be taxed with Mary, his espoused wife, being great with child.

"And so it was that while they were there, the days were accomplished that she should be delivered.

"And she brought forth her first-born son, and wrapped him in swaddling clothes, and laid him in a manger; because there was no room for them in the inn."

He stopped speaking and the lights in the great nave were turned out. Only the candlelight gleamed fitfully in the dimness. Joyfully, from the choir loft, the carolers began to sing.

Stille Nacht,
Heilige Nacht...

You could see the people who sat ahead of you swaying softly to the beautiful old tune. When the carol ended the lights came up again and the Christmas story continued.

"And there were in the same country shepherds abiding in the field, keeping watch over their flock by night.

"And lo, the angel of the Lord came upon them and the glory of the Lord shone round about them; and they were sore afraid."

At each pause in the reading, the lights faded and in the glow of the flickering candles another of the ancient folksongs with which we celebrate Christmas was sung:

Es ist ein Reis entsprungen (Behold a branch is growing), they sang, a Rhenish ballad of the sixteenth century, and *Vom Himmel hoch* (Good news from Heaven), one of the slowmoving old *Lieder,* to which Martin Luther had written the words.

The vesper services lasted until midnight. When one service was ended the church would fill with new worshipers and the vespers would be repeated. Five times the great church emptied and filled before the bells chimed the first minutes of Christmas day.

"I have never seen so many people come as this year," my mother declared, and Colonel Beck, who was at the service with us, confirmed this.

"Two of the smaller churches in town have had German Christian pastors installed," he told me. "I understand that their vesper services tonight are nearly deserted. Most of their people are here. But even the people who have been lukewarm in their fidelity to the Church are beginning to come out, to rally to the Church since they have seen their right to their faith threatened."

It was a curious sight to see the throngs of people standing outside the church in the snow waiting their turn to take part in the festival of the Nativity. There was a different feeling in the crowd than in the multitudes that gathered for the Nazis' political displays. Those crowds were half curious, half hysterical, while these people had a friendly warmth among themselves and a quiet determination that boded well for the struggle that centered round the spired stone buildings where their allegiance lay.

It was long after midnight that night when I retired to bed, and downstairs in the music room I could hear my parents busily at work, preparing the Christmas surprises for me as if I had still been ten years old.

The Christmas morning services at the church were densely packed. We ate the customary frugal meal at midday, and after the last of the thronged evening vespers the family gathered at home for the Christmas celebration. Everything was just as it had always been in former years, with not a detail slighted. My father called my mother and me, Anna, our old servant, and her young helper, and together we stood before the closed Christmas-room door. Looking very jovial, he read a brief passage of Scripture and we all sang *Stille Nacht,* my father's voice booming strong, my mother's soft and never quite sure of the tune, and old Anna's gladdening the air with its rich contralto. In the old days I had always been required to complete this ceremony by reciting a Christmas poem, and tonight I remembered one of those verses from a long-ago Christmas and stood stiffly and piped it off to them while they leaned against the wall laughing.

Now the great moment came when my father pushed the door open and we walked in, my mother and I first, followed by Anna and the other little maid, while my father brought up the rear. There stood the great tree, covered with lighted wax candles and in all the splendor of its colored ornaments. At the foot of the tree was the same exquisite manger scene in miniature that was always there and that always took my breath with the perfect fashioning of its tiny figures, the delicate Holy Mother, the richly dressed wise men, and the drowsy camels. Right and left of the tree stood tables covered with white linens on which were placed a number of huge, brightly colored plates, each heaped with an appalling bounty of *Kuchen,* candies, nuts, and an unbelievable variety of indigestible sweetmeats. About each plate there was a pile of gifts, all unwrapped and arranged to make a fine display. Your name would be found on a small card atop the heap on your *Bunter Teller* (the colored plate) to indicate which group of gifts was yours. After we "Oh" ed and "Ah" ed to everyone's satisfaction, I asked my mother and father to leave the room and arranged my gifts for them around their plates.

Of course they returned filled with pleasure and astonishment, as if they had had no idea what I was about.

In a few minutes friends began to arrive and there was more exchanging of presents. Erika came with her uncle, and brought me a sweater of soft, fine wool which she had knitted herself. I had had a copy of Goethe's *Faust* specially bound for her in tooled leather and I was delighted to see how pleased she was with it.

"Do you remember, Karl, the wooden doll cradle you made for me when we were nine?"

"I remember that one of the rockers was uneven and that it wabbled woefully."

She laughed merrily. "It still wabbles but I wouldn't have it changed for anything. That was one of the finest Christmas presents I ever received."

"Do you remember the red and brown tie you made for me?"

"It would never hang straight, would it?" Her laughter was full of rueful amusement.

The house filled rapidly; cheerful talk overflowed the rooms and children were bobbing in and out everywhere with their shining new toys, until finally, at a very late hour, we all sat down to the Christmas dinner, before the huge, crisp and crackling brown body of the Christmas goose. Everything but the holiday was forgotten. That was the last night I remember, in the years in which I was to remain in Germany, over which no shadow fell.

After the hilarity of the Christmas holiday had faded into the calm of everyday I had a long talk with my father in his study, in which he told me of much of the work of the new Confessional Church as it was being carried on at Magdeburg.

I already knew from my close contact with Niemoeller's church how rapidly the organization was spreading. Actually it was more of a spontaneous people's movement than an organization, and the Confessional Church framework was useful only to give it a tangible form, to provide a means whereby the people could realize their own unity. The seed of the movement had been Niemoeller's work before the election. The letters that had gone out from the cellar had brought a tremendous response, but every man who answered had done so as an individual at the prompting of his own conscience. It was only afterward, when they found out with what unanimity they had responded, that a feeling of solidarity arose among millions of men who loved their faith, and they had realized they were strong enough to resist.

"The signing of the little red cards is useful," my father told me, "because it ties the people here to the others throughout the whole of Germany. But our people are ready to join the fight before we go to them. As a matter of fact they don't wait for us to seek them as members of the inner movement; they come to us.

"In every church in this territory where the ministers have refused to compromise with the sort of doctrine our friend Kraemer tried to bring in here, every place where a man is preaching the Word of God, the people are flocking in amazing numbers. In every church where a German Christian pastor has been installed, where the people are expected to listen to their brand of brash paganism, the congregations have dwindled away to nothing in spite of the fact that the government appeals to their patriotism and sends storm troopers in to fill the vacant pews. People who have attended a certain church for years are leaving it to go to hear a 'Confessional' pastor. They understand that the German Christians are trying to substitute their 'blood and honor' theories for the worship of God, trying to make the Church a branch of government, and they aren't accepting any of it.

"It sometimes startles me, the number of men who have been lax and disinterested in the Church for years who come to see me now, begging for something to do. And the army doesn't like this Nazi highhandedness with religion. Every Sunday at the Dom there are more army officers in uniform, many of them of high rank."

"At the university," I said, "it's the young men rather than the professors who are getting into the Church fight. Hitler claims that the youth of Germany support him in everything but I'd be willing to say that two-thirds of the students have joined the Confessional Church."

"The same thing holds good here. The young people are very much alive to what's going on. Your friend Johann Keller is a good example. He's got a sharp tongue in his head and he has stirred up a good-sized group of men of his own age to go around talking and get the people aroused. In spite of the fact that his father is a sick man and Johann has most of the responsibility of the business on his shoulders, he has found time to make half a dozen trips out of town for me to carry the *Bruederrat* messages to some of the outlying churches."

"How about his mother?" I asked, for I knew my father had always regarded Frau Ernst Keller as a rather silly woman who was something of a climber and longed for social prestige, in contradistinction to her husband's simple and more vigorous tastes. I wondered whether she might not oppose Johann's activities out of vanity, for fear her son might be losing caste.

"That woman has surprised me," my father smiled. "You remember how she used to dislike it and grow confused when Ernst talked about his 'peasant origin' and described the rough life he had lived when he was a young man. She has dropped all that nonsense. Both Johann and his father believe in this fight for our faith and she has joined them heartily. She has her husband to nurse and the younger children to care for but she has helped out

as far as she could. She said to me the other day, 'We are fighting
for something holy, something without which we cannot keep up
the courage of our homes or bring up our children the way we
wish.' You will see the same spirit in a great many of the women.
They feel that something vital to their homes is being threatened."

"What about the Langes?" I asked, curious about the reaction
of the sort of people who had hitherto been a thorn in the flesh of
my father. The Langes were a wealthy and arrogant family who
attended the Dom only because it was a fashionable church. They
had spells of indulgence in ostentatious charity which they called
"helping the lower classes," and which left them cordially disliked
by the recipients of their condescending bounty. Neither were
they chary of offering their minister advice, and my father had
long resented their false piety.

At my question he laughed wryly. "The Langes have become
our most enthusiastic German Christians. Herr Lange has probably
fulfilled the Nazi ideal of what a good German should be like. He
goes about making pompous pronouncements and trying to
bulldoze the congregation into the German Christian ranks. But
he is having a very different effect from what he believes. There are
any number of people who have hastened to join the Confessional
group because it puts them on the opposite side of the Church
from the Lange family. You might almost say the Langes have
become the strongest recruiting force we have for the secret
rebellion." His eyes twinkled. "God moves in a mysterious way."

I burst into laughter. "Tell me about Schoolmaster Schenk. Is
he working with you? I noticed that he was the only man who
spoke up against Dr. Kraemer when he tried to bar the non-Aryans
from the Church."

His face sobered. "Herr Schenk has been removed from his
post at the school because he opposed the Nazi doctrine in front of
the storm troopers. He was told he was not a fit person to instruct
the young in obedience to the state. He and his wife have been in
very hard straits." All at once his face lightened. "This appointment
to the *Bruederrat* will prove a good thing. I can offer Schenk a

position as one of my secretaries. He will be an ideal man for it and it will give them something to eat on."

My father carefully stuffed his round-bellied pipe and held the match over it, puffing strongly as the tobacco began to glow. I noticed that his eyes kept returning to his desk where the Crucifix stood, its shining silver alive now with little spots of fire color reflected from the burning match.

"The Nazi pressure is beginning to make itself felt," he said quietly. "There have been several arrests around here and you can feel the strain. But the people are still coming. Those who cannot stand all this cruelty and hatred in their honest lives are fleeing to the promise of God as their only remaining refuge. That is why we cannot fail them, Karl. I think we have seen only the beginnings of persecution. The long, hard years lie ahead of us. But no matter what happens to individuals, we have one task to maintain—to preserve from this upstart Caesar, the things that are God's."

Seated in the crowded church the following Sunday, I began to see how my father was succeeding in voicing the protest of the Christians against their oppressors without laying himself open to any charge of outspoken rebellion. Every word of the service breathed an air of sorrow and of defiance. The attack upon their faith was dramatized for the people in militant hymns and in the lamentation of the Psalms. With tragic voice and with his intense eyes full of meaning as he looked down into the field of faces, my father intoned:

"I will say unto God my Rock, Why hast Thou forsaken me: why go I mourning because of the oppression of the enemy?

"As with a sword in my bones, mine enemies reproach me: while they say daily unto me, Where is thy God?

"Why art thou cast down, O my soul: and why art thou disquieted within me?

"Hope thou in God: for I shall yet praise Him Who is the health of my countenance, and my God."

To hear the fullness of the massed voices that joined in the hymn was to know there was no lightness in the singing. It became, in those vigorous throats, both a prayer and a battle cry: *Erhalt uns, Herr, bei Deinem Wort . . .*

"Lord, keep us steadfast in Thy word;
Curb those who fain by craft or sword
Would wrest the Kingdom from Thy son
And set at naught all He hath done.

"Lord Jesus Christ, Thy power make known,
For Thou art Lord of lords alone;
Defend Thy Christendom, that we
May evermore sing praise to Thee."

The martial words had come down to us from Luther and their tradition made them sound the more impressively in this new battle. Without a word of direct reproach uttered against the Nazis, through all the service the defiance of their power was on the people's lips. "Despite the oppression of the enemy, I shall yet praise Him."

At the end of the long prayer there was a space provided for special intercessions, and here something new to many, and intensely moving, occurred. My father began to read a long list of names of the men who had been so far imprisoned in the Church fight.

The *Bruederrat*, knowing that nothing binds men closer together than common suffering, had prepared a roll of names of all the pastors and laymen who now lay in the concentration camps for the sake of their faith, and this was the roll my father read:

"Pastor Kurt Schaber, who was arrested November 14th, is in the concentration camp at Dachau.

"Dr. Hans Jung, arrested December 3rd, now in the Sachsenhausen concentration camp.

"Pastor Paul Wendel . . ."

As the list grew longer the faces of the people took on a terrible tension, and when a well-known or beloved name was read a low groaning sound escaped the mass and was echoed back by the vaulted roof. At the end of the long list my father cried out, with his face lifted, the prayer for those who are innocently imprisoned.

"Almighty God, Who didst bring the Apostle Peter forth out of prison, have mercy upon these men who are innocently imprisoned, having committed no crime but to serve Thee steadfastly, and set them free from their bonds that we may rejoice in their deliverance, and continually give praise to Thee; through Jesus Christ, Thy Son, our Lord."

"Amen." Two thousand voices responded in a sound that swelled with sorrow.

In every church in Germany where the Word of God was still being preached this same scene was being enacted. The lists, growing ever longer, were sent out each week to the churches, and in every church the ministers read them and offered prayer. Each week the cumulative effect was greater and in their trouble the people drew closer together.

Immediately their publication started, the government had forbidden the reading of these lists. But for once a Nazi edict was ignored. The courageous pastors placed the order of the *Bruederrat* above the command of the government. Every week, in all the churches except for the few where German Christian pastors presided, the reading continued. All over Germany, in the great stone edifices of the cities, under the lofty spires, and in the little country churches, the names of the new martyrs were repeated to the people. And the Nazis were helpless to stop it. They could seize individuals but against this mass rebellion of Christianity they did not dare to move openly.

When we came out of church that morning we found fully a thousand people standing in the street. There had been no room for them in the packed church. I turned back to the sacristy to tell my father, and a proud smile appeared on his strong mouth.

"There is more toughness in Christianity than the Nazis have counted on," he said, and he put on his robes again and prepared to hold a second service for those who had waited so patiently.

CHAPTER
THIRTEEN

FROM the southern windows of the university that look out on Unter den Linden could be seen the small dome of the monument to the Unknown Soldier. I stood with Erich Doehr one afternoon in April of 1934 at a high window, looking down upon it and upon the briskly moving traffic and the pedestrians with which the mile-wide square teemed. Everywhere your eye moved it caught sight of a uniform.

The drab spectacle the city had presented under the Republic had disappeared under a constant military pageantry. Hitler was clever. He understood the Germans' love of martial display; he knew that the absence of soldiers from the streets during the republican years had been a constant reminder to the people of the shameful defeat in the great war. As soon as he became Chancellor, Hitler began to build a lavish military show for the Reich. It was easier to believe the Nazi promises when the streets were swarming with uniforms. Their numbers and kinds were increased; the old spic and span stiffness of bearing reappeared; army officers, brown-shirts, and the trim, black-uniformed men of the S.S. turned the broad avenues into the aspect of a military camp.

Under the Republic no military exercises had been permitted at first, but popular sentiment had brought a grudging allowance of two minor parades a week on Unter den Linden. Hitler, in one inspired sweep, had restored to the people their pageantry. The army was no longer kept out of sight.

Soldiers on furlough were not permitted to wear civilian clothes. The gaudy and amazing uniforms of General Goering, which blazed with buckles and epaulets, ribbons and medals, were a source of delight to the people. Officers became most strict about the conduct of uniformed men on the street: gloves must be buttoned; smoking was not allowed; the strict formality of goosestepping and saluting as marching squads passed an officer was rigidly enforced. The older officers had been inclined to allow a little laxity, to indicate with a wave of the hand that the salute might be omitted, but the new crop of young officers who appeared under the Nazis demanded the most severe formalities. And the people loved it. These glittering signs of a forgotten glory were the strongest hold of the new regime over the popular mind.

Unquestionably the Germans loved to play soldier. During the years of the Republic when the army was cut to such small size, the people grieved for the loss of their warrior spectacles. The men who had been in the army remembered their old prestige with the greatest pride. I recall my father's questioning a plumber, who had come to fix a stopped kitchen pipe, about the days of the war, and I can see now how the man's eyes began to glow as he dropped his work and told of his regiment, his rank, and the decorations he had received. The Nazis understood this thwarted yearning of the populace. Every move a high Nazi made was accomplished to the accompaniment of fanfare. When Hitler passed through the streets to the Chancellery, to the Opera, to the Reichstag, the route he would take was announced beforehand and crowds would line the sidewalks for three hours before he appeared behind a roaring motorcycle guard, with uniformed men massed about him, flags flying and music playing as he proceeded past the saluting throngs.

Today as the noonday sun beat down upon the vast square, Erich and I watched the changing of the guard at the soldier's monument. Two sentries stood before the monument; so stiff, so immovably still were they always that I have seen children go up to them and pluck at their clothes to see if they were alive. Their guns were held vertically upright, resting in the palm of the hand and standing stiffly in the air without other support. It was not permitted that the guns should rest against the sentries' shoulders;

they must be perfectly balanced in the hand. How they managed it I do not know, but for two hours the heavy guns never wavered nor moved. A man who dropped his gun would have considered himself disgraced for life. But the guns were never dropped. The only time these rigid figures came alive was when an officer passed in front of them and then, like mechanical toys in which a button is pushed, they would present arms. Through all the crowds and the traffic of the mile-wide square they never missed the uniform of a superior. The *fraeulein* of Berlin loved nothing better than to stroll past the monument on the arm of a young lieutenant and see the sentries' presentation of arms before him. The moment their young man was home, they would be after him to take them there on a walk through the square.

Today, as every day at high noon, we could see the parade of the guard swinging down Unter den Linden. Ahead of the ranks of soldiers marched a band with brasses gleaming, led by a giant of a drum major. A great crowd of people gathered daily and walked with the band for the whole of the mile-long march, and as they approached the monument a dense assemblage collected in the square below our windows.

As the parade reached the monument the young lieutenant, who was mounted, stirred his horse to a trot and turned in sharply. He halted and whirled, coming to a rigid stop, facing outward from the monument, and cried in a crackling tone:

"Guard."

The military proceeded at a goosestep for three steps.

"Halt."

"Left face."

"Close ranks."

They wheeled into formation and in the sudden hush of the watchers only two sounds could be heard, a sharp *Spat Spat,* as if a pistol had been shot twice. It was the smack of gun against hand as the company presented arms. The precision with which it was executed was an exciting thing to watch, and you could see how the people were stirred by it.

"Advance the guard."

Twelve men detached themselves from the company and goosestepped straight ahead to the monument. The guard that had been on duty passed them, also at a goosestep, and joined the company in the square.

In America there seems to be a widespread supposition that German soldiers always goosestep. This is not only a mistake; it would be an impossibility. The goosestep is a tribute and is performed before those of higher rank, and always when troops pass in review before the head of the government. The step is not a simple lifting of the leg stiffly and high on the upswing. It is a muscular feat that takes at the least three months of practice to acquire, and it requires a great physical effort and is a tremendous strain. Two hundred feet of goosestepping are all that the best troops can do and retain their precision. The people used to watch the efforts of the storm troopers to goosestep and smile kindly upon the boys for their effort, but the shrug of their shoulders said that it would be a long time before the S.A. could equal the military. Looking down into the square, I could feel the thrill that ran through the crowd at the beautiful skill with which the little pageant at the monument was executed. It excited even me, and I realized in my heart that each of the multiple daily marchings and parades was binding the people more strongly to the new Fuehrer. The growing brutalization of life, the loss of their liberties they might resent, but if they repudiated this man now they were repudiating the newborn glory of their fatherland.

I had sensed the same thing not long before when I had stood in this same square and watched the parade for the World War dead. On that day the parade stretches for miles, the drums are muffled, and every man is on foot. As they pass the monument of the Unknown Soldier the great columns break into a goosestep and there is utter silence in the vast place. The commands of the officers sound clear and sharp in the stillness and there is no other sound except for the *shush-shush-shush* of soldiers' feet. In a band of young storm troopers who were marching along one side of the square on their way to join the parade I saw Orlando von Schlack in the trim uniform of a young officer of the S.A. He looked both handsome and distinguished in the finely tailored brown; there was joy in his face and his curly head was tilted to watch the curling and flapping folds of the great swastikas just ahead and above him. For a moment I felt a need to be identified with the spectacle in the square and with the paraders. Here with ardor in their eyes were the people of Germany, my people, turning toward their future, and my friend was among them. I felt a great wishfulness to be a part of what I was seeing. Then with a sense of deep depression I realized that I could have no part in it. The future they were entering was strange and ill-starred. And I was not going with them. As I watched Orlando's slender figure move out of sight I felt a gulf slowly widen between us that not all the memories of our boyhood could quite bridge. I was lonely, lonelier than I had ever been in my life.

Today as I watched the changing of the guard with Erich, the same depression engulfed me.

"Somehow I wish I were down there. I wish I had a part in that."

Erich was annoyed with me. "You like that Nazi show?"

"Oh, I know—that's the new Caesar, buying the people with circuses. But I wish there were some place I could feel I belonged. I realize when I think of the men in the concentration camps how ugly the thing really is—that those people down there are no more free than those who are actually in jail. But it would be so much easier if you could just accept it the way they do. I want to believe that it's valuable to be a rebel, but I feel shut in and tied down, actually, always having to be careful of what I say, of what I do, even of how I look."

"We are all in prison who live in Germany today," said Erich. "Karl, I have been waiting to tell you. I am going to America."

"To America?"

"I have an uncle in Chicago. I shall enter the United States as a student and I can live with him until I get my feet under me. For me there's no point any longer in living in this hopeless country. Everything has been arranged and I shall be leaving next week."

"I'm sorry to see you go," I said slowly, "but I can't wish to have you stay. Perhaps you may even be of more help to us when you are in the United States. If the people in other countries could only discover how the Nazis are working to destroy Christianity, we might get some support. Pressure could be put on these cocksure rulers of ours."

"Unfortunately the Nazis thought of that possibility too. A traveling theological student might be dangerous to them. Before I could get any papers they brought me in and had me sign a statement guaranteeing that I would reveal absolutely nothing of the situation of the Church in Germany. Since my father and my mother and sisters are remaining here, that is a promise I shall have to keep."

Alone in my room that evening, I could not get my mind upon my books. I kept toying with the idea of leaving Germany myself, of escaping into a freer atmosphere. There was so much discouragement in the struggle we were making here; the Nazis were so formidable a foe; their hold on the people's imagination was tightening . . . But as I remembered the resolute face of Niemoeller, the courage of my father in the face of persecution and imprisonment, the grit of the people at home, I knew that however hopeless it seemed, their fight was my fight and I could not abandon it.

Late that night, long after I had gone to sleep, there was a persistent pounding on my door. I dragged myself out of bed to answer it and found Orlando in a high state of inebriety, his curly hair rumpled and his eyes bloodshot. He had been at the Femina, a very fashionable sort of super-night-club.

"Hail, Karl, and farewell," he greeted me, grinning and staggering a little. "Put me up for the night, will you? My pockets are flat; I haven't a 'Pfennig.'" He reeled, slapping at his hips with ludicrous desperation. Then he added, as if the idea surprised him, "I must have had too much to drink."

I led him to the couch and he collapsed on it with a little whistling chuckle. He looked up at me impishly.

"Can't go home like this," he said. "The general wouldn't like it. And those two young officers like my company but they watch me. They aren't sure how much I know. They like me but they do not trust me, Karl. But I am very discreet . . . isn't that true, Karl?"

"Is it?"

"I wish I knew what they were up to," he went on as if he had not asked a question. "They are so clever . . . it was very funny." He began to laugh.

"You know the arrangements at the Femina . . . no, of course you don't. You don't go to night-clubs. Well, listen, they have pneumatic tubes going from every table that you send notes through. And there they sat, at opposite sides of the big room so nobody would think they knew each other, and sent messages all evening. I'm sure of it. And everybody thought they were sending them to the bar girls. Isn't that funny?"

"Who did?"

Orlando sat up, looking a little startled.

"What did I say?"

"Nothing that made any sense."

"All right," he said, collapsing again. "Dear Karl. Karl looks unhappy. You mustn't worry about me, Karl. I am so happy. I am saved . . ."

"I gave up worrying about you a long time ago, Orlando. If I am unhappy it is because the Church is being gravely threatened."

"Poor Karl," he echoed. "His poor Church is going to dissolve like a puff of smoke and he is unhappy. You should be saved while there is time, Karl. Saved by the beautiful Aryan blood . . . saved by honor. The Leader will save you, Karl . . . follow the Leader . . . follow our glorious Leader . . ." His voice rose ecstatically.

"Go to sleep, Orlando."

"I'm not sleepy. Did I tell you I came to say good-bye, Karl? Hail and farewell. General von Schleicher is going on a trip tomorrow and I am going with him." His tousled head burrowed into the pillows. "Mustn't forget to say good-bye to Karl. Good-bye, Karl."

He began to snore lightly through parted, childish lips, and I threw a blanket over him and left him there.

My mother had been crying during the night. I saw it as soon as I came down to the breakfast table (I had arrived at home for a visit the evening before). Her eyes were red rimmed and she looked tired, and when I bent to kiss her hand I could see from the unaccustomed frown between her brows that she was hoarding a pent-up indignation. She was not a woman who wept easily and her habitual resiliency had buoyed my father through many of the strains of these dark days, so I knew at once that something serious was in the air. My father's heavily lined face was also somber and weary this morning, and I felt uneasiness touch me as I looked at the two of them.

"What has happened? Something is wrong, isn't it, Mother?"

"Your father's salary has been stopped." She picked up a silver spoon from the table and laid it down again abruptly. "I don't know what we are going to do."

"They wouldn't dare!" I protested. But I knew that if the Nazis did dare, they had the power to cut off financial support from the pastors, for the government collected the Church taxes and paid the salaries from them.

"It is true," my father confirmed her. "We have been giving the government too much trouble. The Church fight is the first stubborn opposition they have met. Unquestionably, if they thought they could succeed, they would forbid the existence of the Confessional Church as they did with the political parties. But they do not quite dare. They have gone this far. They have published a statement that the majority of Germans now belong to the German Christians, which is of course very far indeed from the truth, but on that supposition they have decreed that the Confessional Church is operating against the will of the people. They have cut off the salaries of all the pastors who can be disclosed to be members of it. They have questioned me, and though they have not been able to prove my connection with the movement they suspect me so strongly that they refuse to give me a salary."

"How are we going to live?" asked my mother desperately.

"But they collect the money for it—can't they be forced to pay?"

"My dear boy, who is going to force them?" asked my father. "They have delivered a very telling blow this time—a blow to the belly."

"Why didn't you tell me last night? Why did you have to keep this to yourselves and pretend that everything was all right?"

"That would have been a poor sort of homecoming for you, Karl," said my mother. "It will be bad enough for you now."

"Your mother and I are not well-to-do," my father explained. "My salary has been generous but there have been many places where I felt I had to help out during these bad years, so that we have saved very little. I do not see how we can continue to send you to the university."

"I will try to find work here in Magdeburg," I said. "That will provide some income for us." But my heart was wretched.

That was a miserable day for us all. I knew that jobs were almost impossible to find; I had no training for any kind of work, and if I did manage to get some sort of place I would be earning only a pittance. It would be hard scraping for three of us.

We were figuring without the people among whom my father had worked for so many years. That evening Colonel Beck, Dr. Kamps, my old teacher from the gymnasium, and Herr Oldorf called after supper.

"A subscription is being taken up to pay your salary, Dr. Hoffmann," the colonel announced with gratification. "Johann Keller and the other young men have been out all day and the people are thoroughly angry. You will not have to worry about money."

"The members are already heavily taxed by the government and they pay a stiff Church tax besides. This will be too much for them," my father objected, but I could see the tension ease out of his mouth and my mother's rosy face was positively aglow.

"They will not hear of your being made to suffer for the work you have done for them," insisted Dr. Kamps. "Did you think all the seed you have sown had fallen on stony ground, my dear fellow?"

My father began to smile, and my mother, as if she had

suddenly remembered that the world had not stopped turning, hurried out to prepare cakes and coffee for our guests. For half an hour there was hopeful talk; then came a ring at the doorbell and Johann Keller rushed in, his dark face hot with anger and his clothes rumpled. He drew himself up before the colonel.

"They've taken the money, sir."

"What do you mean?" demanded the officer, coming half out of his chair, his mouth narrowing to a taut line.

"We all brought our collections to Werner Menz's house, the way it had been planned. But the S.A. men were there ahead of us. They didn't show themselves until we came in, and then they searched us and confiscated the money. We were warned that any further soliciting of funds for Church purposes will be treated as a crime. I don't know how they found out, sir."

"This is a bad business," declared Herr Oldorf, getting to his feet. "I shall go at once to see the other members of the church board and try to devise a new means."

The other men rose and put their coffee cups down.

"Don't imagine for a moment that this will be the end of it," said the colonel fiercely. "And do not concern yourself, Dr. Hoffmann. Your salary will be paid."

Dr. Kamps pulled a wrinkled wallet from his hip pocket, took a bill out of it and laid the money on the table.

"I cannot accept—" my father began, looking abashed.

"My dear pastor," said the gray-haired professor, "this is not a personal contribution. It is my Church tax, which my conscience requires shall be paid to the Church. What the Nazis henceforth demand from me in the name of the Church tax I shall consider a forced payment to the party."

"Good!" shouted the colonel, and Lawyer Oldorf's cautious smile assented. Both men placed money on top of Dr. Kamps' bill, shook my father heartily by the hand, and departed with determined faces.

"You are not to fret about this for a moment," insisted the colonel at the door. "This is our problem, and not yours."

I asked Johann to wait for me while I got my hat, and we went together to Werner Menz's big square house to see whether Erika had been frightened by the storm troopers. She was only furious.

"The Nazis are making a great mistake," she said, her face flushed. "The people love your father. They will never allow him to suffer. If the storm troopers behave like this in other parts of the country they will only be making the opposition stronger."

"Sometimes," said Johann bitterly, "I feel as if we were working in a squirrel cage. It goes faster and faster and we run harder and harder—and we still are getting nowhere."

"All right," replied Erika bravely, "but the Nazis aren't getting anywhere against us, either. There are forty million Lutherans in Germany. They can't put us all in jail or refuse all of us money to live on."

"A lot of them are good Nazis except in this Church affair. And the most rabid Nazis have turned German Christians," said Johann.

"There aren't so many German Christians as they'd like us to believe," I broke in. "I know from Niemoeller that with all their efforts they've only been able to inveigle around three hundred ministers into their ranks in all Germany. That leaves, in round numbers, about seventeen thousand, seven hundred good Christian pastors still on the job. It's hard to see the whole picture when you're working in a small place, but it's a big thing that we're a part of."

Johann grinned. "I'm not giving up, Karl. But this highway robbery tonight has got me feeling melancholy."

"They can't beat us," Erika said, "unless we all give up." She was standing beside me, with her round little chin thrust out belligerently, and I remembered that an hour ago this house had swarmed with storm troopers. I slipped my fingers around hers and pressed her hand, to tell her I was proud of her.

That evening with my parents was a troubled one in spite of the optimism of Colonel Beck and the encouragement he had tried to give us. It hardly seemed possible that a solution could be found to my father's problem with the Nazis on the alert to stop any collections among the church people. But early in the morning a surprising thing began to happen.

Two workmen on their way to the mill stopped at the personage and left envelopes with Anna for my father. Fifteen minutes later there were six more men at the door. My father came down to greet them in his dressing gown and they pressed upon him coins and crumpled bills and money wrapped in little twists of paper. Soon there was a steady stream of men arriving, and after the distant mill whistles began to blow and the workmen were at their jobs, the women appeared, the more affluent in their cars, the others on foot with their market baskets on their arms. The widow Goedel in her furs left a sheaf of bills; Frau Schwartz, the shoemaker's wife, counted out a handful of pennies. All day long they continued to come and in the evening the polished wooden box on my father's desk, where he was putting the money, was overflowing with marks and small coins. We laid it out and my father counted it over, exclaiming to himself as he did so:

"See what they have done for us!" he said softly, looking up at my mother, and then his expression changed quizzically, for there were tears in her eyes.

"What, my Hedwig! You surely are not crying now?"

My mother was half laughing, half weeping. "Possibly I am crying now," she whispered, "to think how foolish it was of me to have cried before."

He pulled her down on his knee and pressed his cheek against hers while he dried her eyes with his big handkerchief.

The next day we were on the lookout for a young pastor whom the *Bruederrat* had directed to our district for refuge because the police were searching for him. He arrived at the parsonage just as it was growing dark, footsore and looking very unclerical in his walking clothes. He had a bath and I provided him with fresh linen from my wardrobe, and he came down to supper with damp hair and a shining face, not at all discouraged by his plight.

"I talked too boldly," he told us, "and the German Christians in my parish reported me. The S.A. raided my office and took the *Bruederrat's* literature, but I was out making calls at that hour, fortunately, and I was warned in time to get away. My only regret is that my usefulness is ended, for the present anyway."

When he heard that I was a theological student he was enthusiastic.

"The more of you younger chaps there are to take the place of the men who are arrested, the less effective the Nazis' removal of the older men will prove."

My father had already made arrangements to have him hidden at the home of one of the members whom the Nazis were not likely to suspect of harboring a fugitive, and where there were no young children who might inadvertently let out the fact that there was a stranger staying at home. After he had eaten I took him to this house, introduced him to the family, and left him in temporary security. He was the third fugitive minister, I learned, who was now hiding in Magdeburg.

When I reached home again my father and mother had been in conference. With the financial problem seemingly settled, they wished me to return at once to my studies at the university. But I was not so sure this was the thing for me to do.

"The situation about your salary is still precarious, to say the least," I argued against my father's urging. "I would feel much better staying here and helping out as far as I can until we are sure things are settled."

"There is little promise of things growing calmer in the near future," he pointed out. "And it is my earnest wish that you continue your studies while you are able. You have a responsibility to the Christian faith which has to come first. Our guest tonight mentioned to you the importance of having a crop of young ministers ready to take over, to make up for these increasing arrests. The people must not be deprived of leaders."

"Father," I said, "I have been meaning to talk with you about the mess at the university. I'm not getting anything of any value there now. The place is in the most appalling turmoil; nobody is doing any studying and the lectures these German Christian professors are giving us are pure balderdash. I've felt lately that the whole thing was a waste of time.'

"You *must* take your degree," he insisted. "If you tried to find some sort of employment now, you would discover that to a man without a university degree all doors are shut. And if you wish to be of real use in this Church fight, which to me is more important than poverty, more important than my own life, you will see how necessary it is that you should receive your degree and be ordained."

So it was that I shortly found myself back again in the strange and tumultuous atmosphere of dissension and struggle that was the university life of that spring. It was early in June that a large group of theological students, who were all members of the Confessional Church, were invited to a meeting in Niemoeller's home at Dahlem. The lusty pastor had some very good news for us.

"You have all seen in the papers that the German Christians who are the nominal heads of the Church are holding a synod. The Nazis have been so discouraged at the impotence of their man Mueller to exert any influence at all over the Church that they are holding this synod to reaffirm his election, hoping that the people may thus take his position as Reichsbishop more seriously.

"Some of you know that the Confessional Church is also holding a synod in Westphalia in which we have repudiated Mueller and reasserted our confession of faith. This second synod has, of course, received no public notice. The government would hardly care to acquaint the people with its existence.

"But for you students, something very important has come out of it. The *Bruederrat* is aware how valueless the instruction at the universities has become. We want our new generation of Church leaders to be well taught, for your life in the Church will be a rigorous one. So we are setting up our own theological schools, and any one of you who wishes to be accepted by us as a pastor must attend seven semesters in the Confessional schools while he studies in the government-controlled universities. Some of your most eminent professors who have been dismissed from their posts will be your instructors in the new school, and we shall have our own examining board."

"Why is it necessary," someone asked, "to attend the universities at all?"

"You will have to have a recognized degree," said Niemoeller, smiling, "or you can't get a pulpit. Besides, there must be absolutely no sign that our schools are in existence. Their continuance will be precarious enough as it is. I must impress upon you that it will be terribly dangerous to talk of these schools to anyone. You must never mention the names of your new professors. To do so may send them to the concentration camp. Never let out a word about the purpose of these classes. Never divulge where one of them is to be held.

"And now that I have warned you," he smiled at us again, "here is the list of courses offered. You may enroll today."

We thronged about the table and put down our names for a more hopeful course of study than had been granted us lately. After we had registered, we were each given a membership card and advised to keep it with us. To protect the safety of the schools, no member without a card would be admitted to any of the lectures.

Thus began my participation in the strangest system of education I have ever known. There were hundreds of us enrolled but we never talked of our work even among ourselves. The whole school was constantly in flight. Every day a different house was appointed for our meetings. At the end of one lecture the place where the next one was to be held would be announced. Still we had a complete theological school with all its various departments, with the highest standards of scholarship, yet without any permanent buildings, without any certainty of existence, without any paid professors, fleeing from home to home, trying to avoid public attention and making a constant effort to escape the arm of the police.

At the end of the second week, of the new school I approached the address that had been given to me for the next lecture and saw police guarding one of the houses in the block. I walked idly past it, and sure enough, the number of the house was that to which I had been directed. I had a bad minute of fear that I should be stopped and searched and my student card found on me, but I was lucky and made it around the next corner, looking as casual as I knew how. The following day a new address was whispered to me and I learned that the professor who was to have lectured the day before had been arrested.

We learned to be wary, to make sure that all was well before turning into the appointed street, never to go more than two together and to spread out the time of our arrival so the presence of a large number of young men in the same neighborhood would not be noticed. Even so we more than once found the police waiting at the designated place.

In spite of the hazards, I found the solid course of study of the new school strongly satisfying. It was good to be doing work that had a meaning, that called for the best I could accomplish, that pointed in the direction I myself wanted to go even while it called for more years of study than I had planned. There was a difference at the university as well.

"Avoid controversy," Niemoeller advised us. "Do not point yourselves out to the police by engaging in demonstrations. This is your time for serious work and you will not help the Church by getting yourselves thrown into jail."

I think we all felt we had spent too much time in loud talking. The riotous discussions calmed down in the university halls and gardens. Life slipped into a quieter pattern and we returned to serious work. I missed the lanky figure of Erich Doehr, now safely across the Atlantic, and I found myself wishing he might have stayed in Berlin long enough to see the purpose come back into our university life.

It was during the first warm days of summer, the end of June of that year, that the nation was rocked by an event which threw all other happenings, even the Church fight, temporarily into shadow. Chancellor Hitler flew to Munich to quash an incipent revolt against the government. High Nazi officials fell before the firing squads and there were arrests everywhere. The extent of the discovered treason could only be guessed as the rumors flew from mouth to mouth. In Berlin the black-uniformed S.S. marched into the home of General von Schleicher and shot down the general in cold blood, and his beautiful young wife with him.

Rudolph Beck came to see me at my lodgings.

"What is going to happen to Orlando?" he asked. "He loved von Schleicher as if the man had been his own father."

We stood and looked at each other.

I knew Rudolph still blamed himself for the tragedy that had followed Orlando's expulsion from the gymnasium. The colonel's son seemed to feel himself in part responsible for every subsequent sorrow Orlando had encountered in his variegated career.

"I don't think Orlando had any part in the plot, whatever it was," I hurriedly assured him. "He let a hint drop that something was brewing, one night when he had had too much to drink. But he didn't know himself what was going on. I'm sure of it."

"They are certain to arrest him," said Rudolph. "If only I had known enough long ago to keep my fingers out of other men's lives, he might still be living quietly in Magdeburg."

"Poor Orlando. I am afraid he has cut out his own destiny, Rudolph."

"I am going to the general's house to see if he is there."

"You'll be arrested."

"That's no matter. He needs whatever friends he has now. Orlando's so quixotic—so mercurial; he's too sensitive to be able to meet this sort of brutality alone."

"I'll come with you."

Rudolph picked up his hat. "Dear God," he said, "I am afraid that much as I despised him, I loved the boy, Karl."

"I loved him too. And he loved Hitler. It's a sad mess, isn't it?"

I don't think we realized we were using the past tense.

We could not get near the Schleicher residence because of the crowds and we decided to try Orlando's private apartments, which he maintained on an allowance from his mother, in a fashionable section of the town. But to our long ringing of his doorbell there was no answer.

When the mail, a day later, brought me a letter in his familiar round script I had a momentary hope that all might be well with him. I read the brief message through.

"My dear, dear Karl:

"It seems an appropriate gesture that I should inscribe my farewell lines to you. What a nice irony that I should abandon my originality in the end, and adopt the prescribed formula of the suicide by explaining myself! But what can I say? If I once had a belief it ended today in a pistol shot. I loved two men. I saw a light that filled the future with honor and the marching of heroes. But is this honor, then, that butchers the noble-hearted? Heroes that slaughter gentle women? I have been made a fool of—and there is nothing left. I am so alone.

"I do not want your religious immortality. I do not want to have to live any more in any form whatsoever. Think of me and smile, Karl, but smile kindly. There is no more light for me.

"Yours—
"Orlando von Schlack."

It was Rudolph who discovered that same day and clipped for me the short newspaper notice:

"Orlando von Schlack, 22 years of age, a lieutenant of the *Sturmabteilungen,* was found dead today in his rooms at _____ Place. He had shot himself through the head with a service revolver. No suicide note was found but the young man is said by the police to have been a protégé of the late General and Frau von Schleicher. The body was discovered late this afternoon by the landlord. The dead youth was the son of the Countess von Schlack of Magdeburg."

There are times when a man weeps—and I wept that night. For the companion of my youth, for the darkness of life, for the futility of the worship he had offered to the black-hearted gods of his strange cult, for the prison house my land had become, for all the young men who were turning their eager eyes where he had turned his and found only emptiness, and perhaps partly for myself and my own loneliness.

CHAPTER
FOURTEEN

EVERY month, every day the new faith and the old came to closer grips. The Nazis were not content with obedience to their commands; they demanded belief in their mad doctrines. They would have no rival faith. They began to put on pressure.

ALL NAZI OFFICIALS JOIN
GERMAN CHRISTIAN RANKS

We read in the newspaper headlines one morning. The state had been able to force every man who held a public office to declare himself a German Christian. The means used were always subtle and devious. Any S.A. man or officeholder who wished to marry, for example, was required to renounce his Church membership first or be dismissed. It became impossible for anyone identified with the Church to gain or hold an office. The German Christian ranks perforce were swelled, until the Nazis were able to announce the complete adherence of German officialdom to their doctrines. This mass adoption of the new religion was given wide publicity in the press and on the radio. However, it was never hinted in the press, although we came to know it, that a number of well-known Nazis dropped their party connections at this time rather than forsake their belief.

In August the government took another official step. The "Aryan ministry" was announced. A decree was issued, extending the law which required pure Aryan descent from January 1, 1800, for every government employee, be he governor or street sweeper, to include the Lutheran pastors.

"All cultural matters must be in accord with the racial sentiment of the nation," declared the public pronouncement. "Religion touches the innermost feelings of the race and no alien can conceivably be allowed to instruct the German people in their belief. If any man is to be a leader of the people, his blood must be singing the same tune. We can take no orders from one of inferior blood."

Immediately there were ousters of unfortunate ministers, many of whom were generations removed from the ancestor by whom, according to Nazi theory, their blood had been tainted. But they were not abandoned this time. For the first time the persecuted had a champion. The *Bruederrat* of the Confessional Church moved to protect them. My father stood boldly in his pulpit on Sunday morning and declared, "Membership in the holy Christian family is determined not by race but by faith. Not one of our brothers in Christ shall be forsaken."

In every church in the land the same defiance was spoken. The *Bruederrat* advised the ousted pastors to disobey orders and remain in their parishes, and their people upheld them. In a few small churches where the population was preponderantly Nazi a man would be forced out of his pulpit by popular agreement with the government. The *Bruederrat* at once recommended these men to other pulpits where they were gladly, even enthusiastically accepted. The government stormed but the Church stood firm.

Then the Nazis moved against another right of the religious bodies.

Dr. Kamps from the gymnasium called one day to see my father, looking very much upset.

"You are going to be officially informed, Herr Pastor, that your services in the religious instruction of the school are no longer required. I wanted to prepare you for the news. I am certain the Nazis are behind it."

The pastor's heavy eyebrows drew down. "Are they daring to stop the religious teaching in the schools? That is one of the Church's long-standing rights, by agreement with the government."

"This government is no respecter of rights. I understand the hour is to be allotted for military drill."

My father's face grew hot. "I shall call upon the heads of the school."

He did call upon them and in such a towering rage that the men, who were obviously making the change under duress, became humbly apologetic. They told him finally that they would continue the children's religious instruction but that they would be forced to employ another man as teacher, and the pastor had to be content with that much satisfaction.

The hour for religious instruction was retained in the schedule as the school heads had promised, but the new instructor turned out to be a German Christian. Ten women of the parish arrived at the parsonage a month or so later, and some of them were crying.

"They are not teaching our boys to be Christians any more. They are teaching them to worship the state, to worship the Fuehrer instead of God. They make fun of the Bible," a woman with tear-smudged cheeks began.

"My Heinrich came home from school yesterday and tore the pages out of the Bible. He said it was an immoral book and no good German should have it in his house. Herr Pastor, can't you do something for us? We want to bring up our children the right way. We can't bear to have our homes destroyed and our children corrupted like this." The other women chimed in with the same doleful plea.

"I have already been to the school," said my father thoughtfully. "We shall have to see what we can do in some other way."

He went to the *Bruederrat*. He found the other men disquieted over the same situation. The Nazis had adopted similar tactics all over Germany. The hour for religious teaching in the schools had become no longer available. It was used for physical exercises or for the teaching of "Aryan blood" theories. The German Christians had been set to work upon the children. The mature students at the universities had the background and the judgment to refuse their new heroic myths, but the little children believed what they were told.

The *Bruederrat* decided on extreme measures. They made an official declaration and announced it to the people. The German

Christians had deserted Christianity. They were no longer to be recognized as Christians. They were outside the Church!

This was a sweeping excommunication! The government could not ignore it. The people had too much respect for such an edict by the revered heads of the Church. So the Nazis acted. The Confessional Church was declared illegal. It was made a crime for a pastor or a layman to belong to it. The Nazis did not dare give their real reason but claimed that the Confessional group, in protecting the "non-Aryan" ministers, had "interfered with the racial purification of the German nation." The Confessional Church had become "an enemy of the state."

But Sunday followed Sunday, month followed month, and the dogged resistance of the people only grew. Every Confessional Church was constantly thronged. Arrests increased. Hundreds of Church offices were raided and the men who worked there were imprisoned. Pastors began to disappear and the laymen who defended them followed them to the concentration camps. Their churches were closed. Sometimes German Christians came to take their places.

Early in 1935 a law was passed making it a crime against the state even to discuss the *Kirchenkampf* (the Church fight).

But every Sunday in the churches the long, sad lists of the imprisoned were read and the people heard them with groaning and with tears. Great throngs in the pews and in the streets outside the spired buildings prayed for them, and the government still did not dare to interfere.

But the police were on the alert for technical charges on which they might arrest individuals. Although the work was carried on with the utmost caution at the Domkirche, the search of the police became so intense that the offices were moved daily, sometimes twice in a day, from one to another of hundreds of homes in the parish. The danger became so great that my father let his secretaries go and continued his efforts with only the aid of Erika and of Schoolmaster Schenk, neither of whom would consent to stop.

One day when a big wedding ceremony was to be held at the church the pastor did not appear at the appointed time. No one knew where he was. The sacristan, who had some idea what might be delaying him, quieted the disturbed wedding party and suggested that they wait. For an hour the bride sat in her veil and her father and the groom fretted. Finally the big pastor arrived. When he had set out for the church the police had picked him up and taken him to headquarters for questioning.

This time they had been able to find nothing incriminating upon him. But wherever he moved, he knew the sword hung over him.

But now, all over the land the great Church went underground. You could have seen no sign of the massed and dogged resistance unless you had known what to look for. Visitors to Germany from 1935 onward have gone home to report that the Church was functioning normally. There was no outward sign of the persecution or the stubborn opposition. Those Germans who were motivated by expediency, those whose religion had never gone very deep turned German Christian. But the great mass of the people clung to the things that are God's.

The German Christian pastors changed their tactics. On first coming into power they had spoken plainly, trying to cram their ideas down the people's throats. They had attacked the men who believed in a higher law as "deserters from the veneration of the state and the Fuehrer." They had not hesitated to decry the teachings of Paul as "Jewish corruption" and to demand a "purification" of parts of the Gospels which "went against the bloodstream of Germans." They made some amusing compromises in an effort to retain a semblance of Christianity in their doctrine. While the Old Testament was condemned as a Jewish book, they made an exception of some of the Psalms and proclaimed that the authors of these particular songs had been Aryan.

The people would not tolerate such brazen attacks on Christianity from the pulpits of the churches. Where the cult of the Hero was taught as a religion, where the German Christian pastors promised salvation by "the noble Aryan blood," the people stayed away. Faced with empty churches, the German Christians began to tone down their speech, to hide their savage messages under the guise of Confessional language. But the people were not fooled. Some of the great churches in Berlin were so large that they had from two to four pastors. One of them might be a German Christian and the others Confessional men. The German Christian would deliver the morning sermon and there would be only a scattered attendance. In the evening a Confessional pastor would preach, calling upon the German nation to remain steadfast in its faith, and the service would have to be repeated again and again to accommodate the crowds. The people had decided by a sort of mass consent to repudiate the churchmen who were trying to remodel the Church into an organ of the state.

What was occurring was a tremendous underground opposition to Hitlerism, which involved millions of people. It became a very tender sore in the government's side because it was the one place where they had failed to conquer. The stridency of the German Christians, the increasing arrests of ministers were only symptoms of the fight. Two powerful forces had met, head on, and neither was giving ground.

"Bishop Maharens was granted a personal conference with Hitler today." A two-line item would appear on the back page of the newspapers or hidden away inside. "Bishop Meiser was given an audience by the Fuehrer at the Chancellery." "The Lutheran General Superintendent Albrecht spent an hour in discussion with the Fuehrer."

"I happen to know what the superintendent went to Berlin to demand," my father said of this last notice, folding the paper with a satisfied slap. "He represents the province of Westphalia, and he is insisting on the reopening of the churches the Nazis have closed there. The Nazis are beginning to realize what a force they are up against when the Fuehrer himself treats with the bishops. If they were faced only with rebellious individuals they could clap them into jails, but a great opposition movement has to be dealt with differently."

There was a powerful Christian block among the high-ranking officers of the army. Alfred Rosenberg, the Nazis' prime idealogist, was turned loose upon them in an effort to inculcate them with

National Socialist dogma. He requested an opportunity to address the Officer Corps in Berlin, and General von Fritsch, who was in command at the time, agreed but only on condition that Rosenberg would refrain from attacking the Church in his talk. The newspapers the next day announced that he had made an impressive address, but all Berlin was buzzing with the true story. Rosenberg had broken his promise and had flung his customary accusations against the Church. Fritsch, followed by his entire Officer Corps, had risen and walked out, leaving Dr. Rosenberg an empty auditorium in which to fulminate.

Rosenberg's book, *The Myth of the 20th Century,* had become the Nazi bible. It was the book of the Hero-cult, of state worship, of the theory that the Nordic blood is divine; its pages were full of foul invective against the Lutherans, the Catholics, and the Jews. In 1935, the *Bruederrat* published a series of papers assailing *The Myth of the 20th Century,* refuting its absurdities in clear language and opening fire on the very heart of the Nazi beliefs. These papers were widely disseminated although the government made frantic efforts to confiscate them. It is probable that no copies of any of these papers exist in the United States, since it was too dangerous— rather, it was impossible—to bring them out of Germany.

The effort to Nazify Christianity was not succeeding. Hitler and his advisors were aware that they were treading on a quicksand. The new religion had failed to win the people. But there was one thing that would win the people, many of whom had cast off their allegiance to the new government because of the Church fight. Germany must achieve a new glory. She must take a strong place among the nations.

In the early spring of 1936 Rudolph and I were making a leisurely trip through western Germany. Ostensibly on a sort of student tour, we were actually carrying on work for the *Bruederrat,* visiting the strongholds of religious rebellion in one town after another and bringing messages with us. We were in the Rhineland when on the seventh of March the voice of the Fuehrer came pouring out of the radios on every hand.

The rest of the world was no more shocked than were the

German people on that day. Hitler repudiated the Locarno pact. He declared the new Germany free of the restrictions that had been forced upon her. He announced that the German army was taking over the demilitarized Rhineland. As if it had been magically timed to synchronize with the roaring radio voice, a company of soldiers in smart formation marched past the windows of the dark little coffeehouse where Rudolph and I sat listening to the announcement. These were the first German troops to be seen in the Rhineland since the war. Everyone ran outside to get a look at them, leaving their food to grow cold on their plates.

But the faces of the people were not happy. They were aghast. They were panic-stricken. The troops were not well armed; there was not a tank or a heavy gun accompanying them; and the watchers knew that no fortifications defended the long line of the border. A short, heavy-set burgher who stood near me pulled a fat watch from his pocket, glanced at it and then lifted straining eyes toward the western sky.

"In one hour the French will be over," he said hopelessly. "In two hours the English planes will arrive."

"We are governed by a madman!" shouted a solid-faced young man with horn-rimmed glasses which enlarged his terrified eyes. "He has destroyed Germany this time! He has exposed us to the most savage reprisals—and we are helpless."

The crowd began to mutter and the women to whimper. The men held their watches in their hands, staring at the sky. There were strong voices that called down execrations upon Hitler, the fanatic, the fool, who had drawn upon us the vengeance of the armed nations, which with every tick of the watches was storming nearer, bringing our death to us through the air. The fury against Hitler's folly was so intense in Germany that day that the first sight of planes in the western sky would have been the signal for a mass revolt which would have destroyed him.

"This is the end of the Nazis," said Rudolph with harsh delight. "This is the day of the revolution. Look at the rage in those faces! He is finished when the first plane appears."

But no planes came.

An hour passed, and another. Nothing happened. Darkness fell on the little hamlet and we had neither sighted a silver wing nor heard a gun. In the fifty-mile-wide belt of the Rhineland, four thousand badly armed men had taken possession of the long-stretching border. They came lightly equipped, ready for instant flight at the first appearance of the French. There were no German armaments. Compulsory military service had been in force for only a year. Germany waited in complete helplessness for her fate, and muscular fingers itched to reach the throat of the man who had so criminally laid us open to attack. And there was no attack.

The Nazi organization was then only beginning to function efficiently. It lacked the perfect co-ordination and discipline that it later gained. Most of all it lacked the solid backing of the people. It was in the experimental stage of power, and if Hitler's bold bluff had failed it would have been ripe for overthrow.

But now, day followed day and there was no sign from France or England. On the twelfth day a note of complaint arrived from the League of Nations. The people could hardly believe there would be no reprisals. When they began to understand that they were safe they looked at each other with astonishment.

"How was Hitler able to do it?" they asked.

"There is something about this leader of ours that is more than human. He must have supernatural powers."

In swift reversal of feeling they turned to acclaim him for his spectacular success. The adoration his speeches had not won him was accorded him now. He was not only bold; he was lucky. Now in real truth he became the popular idol.

With despair in our hearts Rudolph and I returned through a rejoicing nation to Magdeburg, to the catacombs where Christianity was in hiding. There was little reason to expect now that political chance might overthrow the new order. There was more sorrow than hope in the resistance of the men of faith. The persecutions became fiercer and more determined.

"It is enough, Lord. Now take away my life," the black-gowned ministers would cry out from the high pulpits, and the Psalms that were spoken were the songs of lamentation and despair.

"Save me, O God, for the waters are come in unto my soul.

"I sink in the deep mire, where there is no standing; I am come into deep waters where the floods overflow me.

"I am weary of my crying; my throat is dried. Mine eyes fail while I wait for my God.

"They that hate me without a cause are more than the hairs of mine head.

"They that would destroy me, being mine enemies wrongfully, are mighty."

Vesper services were held in hiding and every man or woman who entered ventured his safety and freedom by coming through the doors. It was like the Christian existence of the first century, and we too hid in our catacombs and sang, and wept. Letters smuggled out of prison were read and passed around. Fugitives appeared at these meetings and were spirited away to refuges. Sometimes in spite of all precautions a spy would be among us, and the following day would bring a wave of arrests. It took the greatest quality of quiet courage to come to these secret vespers. The people knew the hazards, but they came nevertheless.

The months became years. 1935 passed, and 1936, and the secret Church grew stronger; its people grew leaner and fiercer from their sufferings. The women felt that their very home fires were endangered and they stood staunchly to defend them. Men who accepted the Nazis' political leadership refused to give them a place ahead of the God of their fathers. But the greatest number of new recruits to the *Kirchenkampf* came from the young people. Although the youths who wanted to hold a professional position in later life were forced to identify themselves with the Nazi organization, they were all young men who had grown up in a troubled world and needed a belief to cling to. They had looked upon the Nazi promise of salvation and found no light in it. The government still had a relentless inner fight on its hands. Here and there it would be faced with startling examples of the strength of the faith it was seeking to blot out.

Late in 1936 there had been a number of arrests of Church members in Magdeburg and feeling in the town was running high, when the Nazi party announced a political rally to be held in the wide square where the Domkirche stood. My father called a service of worship in the gray old church for the same hour. As the time approached the broad avenues began to fill with crowds and before the Nazis' baffled eyes, the great conflux of people streamed into the open doors of the Dom while the rally collected only a few. Louder than the oratory in the square, the triumphant ringing of the hymns filled the twilight air, and the deep notes of the church bells traveled farther and with more assurance across the city than the blaring of the brass bands at the rally. These sounds were the united defiance of the believers to the anti-religious zealots who held the power, saying "We are not intimidated. Do your worst. There is something here which you can not destroy."

You could see the same thing in the changing attitude of individuals. Johann's father had recently suffered a stroke which left his mind affected. No longer was he the gusty, free and easy raconteur who once enthralled us with the tales of his foreign adventuring and the bacchanalian festivities he had enjoyed in his youth in Russia, where he had gone to purchase woodlands from the great landowners. He became childish and sentimental and talked in a cackling voice. Alas for poor Frau Keller, whose greatest fault was pretentiousness, that she should now have this helpless simpleton on her hands and have lost her irrepressible and engaging husband! It was a hard blow to her pride. My father went often to see them and talked to poor Ernst as if he had never changed, until he sometimes struck a glimmer of light from the clouded mind. But in this crisis Frau Keller became a different character. Because of her own misfortune she could not do enough for others, and she became one of the leaders in the Church fight. She hid fugitives in her home; she secreted bales of the forbidden literature, and although she had an invalid to tend and the younger children to rear she continually found odd minutes to give to the work for her belief. The other women began coming to see her just to take courage from her undaunted cheerfulness.

Johann now had the responsibility of the lumber business to occupy him but he stood by his mother bravely and continued as one of my father's stalwarts, until any timidity that had lingered in the congregation began to be shamed out of existence by the example of the Kellers.

Dr. Braun was another who changed during the Nazi years. As a prosperous, middle-aged surgeon, he had married the vivid young daughter of a family of impoverished Russian nobles and his home had been the center of brilliant gatherings. He adored the vivacity and the stormy Russian nature of his young wife, and while he knew she was not wildly in love with him he was satisfied with his marriage. She in turn was well pleased to have position, money, a lavish wardrobe, and a host of servants after the poverty she had known as a refugee. The doctor was a man of morbid temperament. Unlike most physicians, he would brood for weeks over the death of a patient, torturing himself with the thought that he might have been at fault. He clung to his young wife the more tenderly since her lighthearted and fiery temperament was his only antidote for the blackness of these moods.

"She has a complex and beautiful nature," he once told my father. "She has relieved all my despair. She is my gift from God."

The big pastor, glancing across the room at the lovely Russian girl who was the center of a gay crowd of young people, was not so sure of the foundations of the doctor's happiness.

"There is only one relief from all despair, Herr Doktor. I am afraid that some day you may find that your wife was given to you not by God but by her father, who was a very clever man."

In the years of the Nazi persecution the doctor found himself branded as a Jew. His fashionable practice evaporated. His friends discovered other and more healthy houses in which to sparkle. His beautiful wife found herself married to an old and gloomy failure and heard the words "Jew-lover" thrown in her face. Even their wealth was fast disappearing under the constant taxation of the Jews. She left him and fled to the pity of her family.

The doctor was a broken man. After a month in which he was seen by no one, he appeared at the door of my father's study one day, his eyes hollow and darkly ringed, and his mouth sagging.

"*Is* there a relief from despair, Dr. Hoffmann?" he asked.

He remained closeted with my father for four hours and when he came out there was a look of quiet serenity on his ravaged face. From that day on, the poor and the oppressed of the community knew him. He brought to them all his old skill, together with a new and tender zeal. He never knew that he had become an exemplar to the people, but there was no wavering of faith in God where Dr. Braun walked.

In his turn the surgeon comforted the pastor on the day word reached us that gentle Dr. Foerster, the general superintendent of our Church, had fallen into the Nazis' hands.

"We shall have no leaders left before long!" the pastor cried bitterly. "We are not abandoned," the doctor told him quietly. "Neither is one man indispensable, however much we may mourn him personally. Each of us does as much as he can and when he disappears someone else finds the courage to take his place."

That same day Erika came to my father with a letter which had been delivered by a trusted messenger. It had been written in prison by Dr. Foerster and one of his people had braved the danger of smuggling it out.

"You are not to grieve yourselves or to fret about me," he wrote cheerfully. "There are hardships, even brutality, to be borne here to be sure; but even so, other men endure them. I am not permitted to have any books, not even a Bible, but fortunately my memory is excellent and I find it a heartening practice to spend my hours reciting to myself long pages of the courageous words that I have providently stored there. I picture the pages of my beloved books as if they were in print in front of me and I can see where the commas and semicolons are placed. On Sundays I hold a silent and private service that lasts longer than yours do, although no one hears it but myself.

"I have only one message to send you: Stand together; let nothing discourage you; keep the faith; continue in the Christian life. I have no doubt of Him Who will deliver us."

On Sunday my father read this letter from the high pulpit and the faces below him shone to hear the courageous words. I marveled at the very literal way in which persecution was teaching us all bravery, and I remembered the letter the Apostle Paul had sent out of prison, crying to his people to be "strengthened with all might, according to His glorious power, unto all patience and long suffering with joyfulness." The Christians of Germany were also learning joyfulness through long suffering.

All these things I saw during a long period in the spring of 1937, when I stayed in Magdeburg, helping my father, for there was increasing danger that his physical strength would soon break down under the constant labor and persecution. His hands trembled now when he wrote or ate and he could not walk far without tiring. But his great voice was as strong as ever and his tremendous spirit undimmed.

It was in June of that year that we heard through the secret channels of the Confessional Church that Martin Niemoeller was to preach at a church near by. His name had by this time become famous through all of Germany. His sermons were talked of in other provinces and so were his forthright actions. He had declined to join the *Bruederrat* because he was so well known as a fighter that he feared his notoriety might bring trouble upon the Church government if he were identified with it. He made direct demands upon the foremost men of the government for redressal of the Church's wrongs and he acquainted his people with what he had done. He was known everywhere as "the fighting pastor of Dahlem." The government had often threatened him but had hesitated to arrest him because of his close connections with England. The Bishop of Chichester had been from the beginning one of the main aids of the Confessional Church.

At this time the struggle had become so hot, with the Church reading out the German Christians and the German Christians attempting to discredit the Church, that the government had finally taken an open hand. Nominally acting as a benevolent umpire in the fracas, the government had appointed a "neutral adjuster" whose decisions were to be binding on both parties. Herr Jaeger, the adjuster, had already served the Nazis in the Church fight in Prussia, where as Church Commissioner he had furthered the appointment of German Christians to influential parishes, and the people were excited and disturbed over his appointment as official referee. The Confessional Church leaders were now placed in a position where they must defy the government's choice of an arbitrator or hand over all they had won to the direction of the German Christians.

At such a time the counsel of a man like Niemoeller would carry tremendous authority with the people. Erika and I decided to go to the neighboring town to hear the sermon of the man who had been so much of a leader to both of us. When we arrived there the church was filled. Even the church basement was jammed tight with standing men and women who followed the service and the sermon through a loudspeaker system. The streets all around were black with people unable to push their way inside. A poster on the church doors announced in large letters:

THIS SERVICE WILL BE REPEATED
IN ONE HOUR

We waited until the fourth repetition of the service before we could make our way inside and there was still a great crowd in the street when we entered. Niemoeller's glowing vigor seemed undiminished by the strain of the repeated services. His voice was warm and vibrant and his words were bold.

"Our greatest pain today is that we are being told that by serving God we have become traitors to our nation," he said. "We are called 'departers from loyalty,' 'soilers of the national honor,' and we know that our brothers who have been imprisoned suffer the opprobrium and the pain of criminals. Worse than the rigors and hardships of the concentration camps is this reproach, this grief of being held up as rogues and malefactors, as enemies of the state, as dangerous men from whom people must be protected.

"Each of us who speaks the words of the Lord Christ today must endure that shame; he must accept the bitterness of being 'numbered among the transgressors.' Dear friends, that is a reproach which I accept gladly and which we must all be willing to encounter without dismay. 'Blessed are ye when men shall revile you and persecute you and say all manner of evil against you falsely, for My sake.' So the words of our Lord come down to us with courage in this evil hour, and it is to Him that we turn for our justification and not to the words of men. It is His word we are bound to speak boldly to the people and to our children.

"Today one of our greatest sorrows is that we are refused the right to teach God's Word to our children. You know how the government has taken away from the Church the right to supervise the religious teaching in the schools. You have heard the teachers who have been brought into the schools make mock of the Bible to your sons and daughters. You have seen how the Sunday outings of the Hitler Youth are timed to take the place of the children's services in the churches, for they always come at the same hour. I ask the government in the name of the United Church to restore us the right to teach our young children to serve and love their Lord.

"Today we are being told that our first duty is to serve the state, to serve men. The Fuehrer has often promised that the service of God will not be interfered with, but he asks us to serve the state ahead of God. This, then, is the question that is posed for all of us: Shall we obey God or man? I say to you that we have no duty to obey men who repudiate God.

"The Fuehrer has appointed the Ministry of Justice as supervisor and adjudicator in the fight between the German Christians and the Church of Christ. This is the same ministry under Hans Kerrl whose appointees recently and in public called the story of the Saviour, 'an old wives' tale, invented to frighten the people.' In this case we are obliged to decide whom we shall obey—the men who have promised over and over again not to interfere with the teaching of God's Word, yet who cast His ministers and His loyal workers into prison, who scorn His salvation and mock at His sufferings and His unbounded love, who seek to deprive our children of hearing the very story of Christ?

"Dear friends, I urge you so strongly today, since none of us who dares reply publicly to the attacks on our faith knows how much longer he will be free to speak, I proclaim to you that we must obey no orders coming from the Ministry of Justice.

"One of these men of the Ministry of Justice had filed his resignation from the membership of the Church with an attorney. He was ready to proclaim himself publicly as a heretic, as an unbeliever. Then word came to him that he had been appointed as an adjudicator in the affairs of the Church. He hastened to exercise his legal right to reclaim his resignation. That, my friends, was Herr Jaeger, the sort of Christian who has been placed in authority over the Church. That authority the Church will not accept.

"I am speaking today almost wholly of our difficulties, of the obstacles that nearly overwhelm us and that drive us to our knees, for the Church must be allowed to see clearly the force against which she fights. I speak of practical things because I do not know how long it will be before my mouth will be closed. There is no one of us who can point to an outcome, who can perceive any hope for the future in the blackness which covers the fires of faith in our land. Yet even if we see no hope in this present time, it is not our task to question the efficacy of the works we do.

"It must be our sole concern to let our light still shine before men, that they may glorify our Father which is in heaven. We cannot hope to determine the outcome of this battle, but we can be certain that the light shines in each of our hearts—through trials, through persecutions and death, that the light still shines. We can make no compromise. We must remain steadfast in the faith, knowing that the light we follow is an Eternal Light. We must not trouble ourselves about the outcome. We must be content to wait His good time. That it will surely come we can not doubt, 'for neither death, nor life, nor angels, nor principalities, nor powers, nor things present, nor things to come, nor height, nor depth, nor any other creature, shall be able to separate us from the love of God, which is in Christ Jesus, our Lord.'"

How great a measure of courage such plain speaking required, the people knew only too intimately, for they had learned through the bitter years that it was not safe to whisper in the walls of their homes a word of criticism against the tyrants who ruled them. To hear such words spoken openly was fresh water to their thirst and strength to their bitter need.

"Watch the difference in the faces of the people who are coming out and those who are waiting," Erika suggested softly to me as we left the church.

"I was thinking the same thing."

That was in June of 1937. A few days later I opened a newspaper and my eye fell upon an obscure item on an inner page:

NIEMOELLER ARRESTED

A chill of cold traveled the length of my spine. The fighting pastor of Dahlem had been silenced by the enemy.

The following Sunday in the church where we had heard him preach a group of government agitators attended the service. When the minister told the story of Niemoeller's imprisonment, acclaiming him as the foremost of the new martyrs, the Nazis jumped to their feet and shouted, "They ought to hang Niemoeller!"

There was a near riot. The agitators screamed and raged and shouted imprecations until a determined group of the men of the church advanced on them, picked them up one at a time, and carried them to the doors, throwing them bodily out of the church. One brawling Nazi fought back and had to be knocked out before he could be removed. It took fifteen minutes to restore order.

"We must allow no tumult in this house," the minister warned the people. "The government is only seeking an excuse to close the church where Niemoeller spoke so bravely. We must not give them that excuse by taking part in a disturbance which they have instigated."

And the service continued calmly.

But through the length and breadth of Germany one groaning prayer went up from the hearts of the people—for the safety and for the release of the man who had taught them to fight for their faith.

CHAPTER
FIFTEEN

"THE last enemy which National Socialism has to overcome is Christianity," young Baron von Rauth said to me one evening after the day's work of the Labor Battalion was over.

Early in the summer, shortly after the arrest of Niemoeller, I was conscripted along with a large number of my fellow students into the compulsory Labor Service. I very nearly resigned from the university at the time. It seemed such folly to waste six months of my life at ditch-digging when such momentous things were afoot, when I might be so much needed either in Berlin or at home. But Walther Vogler talked me out of it.

"You've known all along that you had to go through this before you could get a degree and really get into this fight," he argued. "The Nazis have over a thousand ministers in the concentration camps now. If you are not ordained you help the Nazis by keeping another pulpit vacant."

So I found myself at the quarters of the Labor Service, forced to spend my days in military drill and in the heavy toil of road building and clearing and draining swampland, catching only echoes of the swirl of events that were going on in the world without. The camp was a Nazi hotbed. The men not only talked—they *lived* National Socialism. The pressure of their unbending belief bore in upon me until its ruthlessness and power became a weight on my mind from which I could not escape. They were so sure. They knew that the strength was theirs and that the future was theirs and that nothing lay in their way that could stop them. It was for me too close a contact with the enemy forces, the terrifying reverse side of the picture of the Church fight.

Night after night I listened to the threatening talk and from Baron von Rauth I heard thrown down the official challenge to the very existence of Christianity. On my arrival I had found the baron, whom I had known for years, established as an officer of the Labor Battalion. His people were friends of my family and I was well acquainted with the stocky young aristocrat's career. Because of the limitations imposed on the German army by the Versailles treaty, the military profession was closed to him. The von Rauths had been totally impoverished by the inflation and every branch of the family had pooled their resources to put the none too clever young baron through college and medical school. After failing twice in his examinations he was excluded from the universities. Penniless and without the resource of a degree, he started out to look for work. But the towns were filled with the desperate unemployed. He was unable to find anything to do and during the year the Hitler regime was inaugurated he was reduced to begging on the streets.

The Nazis were keenly aware at the time they came into power of their lack of social cachet. A great many of their numbers were drawn from the nation's riffraff, and the leaders were most desirous of attracting "good names" to the Nazi roster in order to increase their prestige with the people. They picked off the streets a number of impoverished young nobles like the baron and gave them officers' commissions in the S.A. and the Labor Service.

For the baron it meant an unbelievable change in the whole aspect of his life. From being a beggared outcast he was swiftly shifted to a position of authority, in which he enjoyed greater comforts and a larger income than he had ever known. Quite naturally and simply, his rather dull mind accepted the doctrines of the men who had restored his self-importance. He became a believer, in a really religious sense a convert, a disciple of the new faith. He was trusted with the direction of Nazi propaganda in the camp and was in large measure responsible for the fury of anti-Christian sentiment there. He was both puzzled and indignant at the temerity of the Christians in persisting in their belief in the face of the new revelation. Since he knew me well, he spent many long evening hours trying to wean me from my rash adherence to the doomed cause.

"We have only one savior and he is Adolf Hitler," the Baron told me over and over again. "He is saving the people now, and it is the people's duty to worship him. Why should we allow anyone to teach them that they have a different Saviour?"

"That belief has been the greatest power in the world for centuries."

Von Rauth was angry with me. "That was something for the older time. Now it is a new age. If the Christians had been willing to make a compromise, to let the people know that they must worship the state and the Fuehrer first, they could have had a certain position in the new order. But they have made that impossible."

"Hitler first and God second. Is that what you wanted?"

"Do you expect us to put Hitler second!" He was actually appalled at the idea. "The stupid Church has refused to go along with the new order. It has made itself the enemy of all progress. The party instructs us here. They tell us, 'Christianity is the last enemy that remains for National Socialism to destroy.'"

"You have had four years. You aren't progressing very rapidly in wiping it out."

"Give us time. It isn't so easy," he said angrily. "If we could only find some way for the secret police to look inside people's heads and see what they think! Then we could get rid of it in a hurry. But the Christians have no sense of honor. How are we to discover who they are? How can you tell by looking at him what a man believes? The trouble with Christianity is that it is so hard for us to get our hands on."

"You can't arrest a faith, can you?"

"If we only could!" He clenched his fingers as if they were squeezing the throat of his intangible enemy.

The days at the camp were an unrelenting ordeal in which Vogler and I each attempted to keep up the other's courage. Because we were theological students we came in for merciless ridicule from the officers as well as from our fellow servicemen. We were constantly bombarded with propaganda attacking the Church as a "corrupt and demoralizing force." Evidently the Nazis were concentrating their efforts to eliminate this "last remaining enemy" if it could be done. There were bitter attacks upon the ministers, who were called "traitors" and "renegades" and their morals and their patriotism alike impugned.

Daily we were made the butt of brutal jokes. A favorite trick, when we were working in the swamps, was for one of our companions to trip us from behind; then, as we sprawled in the sticky mud, he would cry with mock solicitude, "Where is your dignity, Herr Pastor?"

The heaviest and most offensive work was always assigned to us and we were disciplined on the slightest provocation.

After about three months of this I received a further cause for apprehension. My mother's weekly letter contained disquieting news from home.

"Dr. Braun was arrested last Monday. There was no charge made but it is unquestionably because of his work among the people. Your father at once made a protest to the party and has been trying to secure his release," she wrote. "But he has only succeeded in getting himself into serious trouble. He has been taken in for questioning three times and is now warned that he will be arrested himself if he makes any further effort on behalf of a Jew. Last night someone painted JEW LOVER on our house in big yellow letters. I have tried to persuade him to be more cautious but he insists that there are some situations in which it is only cowardice to consider one's own safety. He is right in this case of Dr. Braun and I cannot argue with him, but I tremble for him . . ."

I felt caged and helpless. What would a degree be worth to me in the face of my father's danger? I could not even get away from the camp. All I could do would be to write to him and warn him to be careful, and yet I could not make myself put the words on paper. I knew that he would have defended Dr. Braum whatever the consequences might be, and I felt as my mother did that he was right. More than any other thing the Nazis feared spiritual strength. Dr. Braun had become a shining example of quiet devotion, of the power that resides in the heart of a man. He had bolstered the people's faith and that had been his downfall. My father's courage and devotion were likewise his own peril.

It seemed an endless six months. I grew lean and hard-muscled from the long days of labor and I learned to keep a tight mouth against the taunting mockery and ostracism, which was harder work than road building.

When the period of my enforced service had nearly expired von Rauth took me aside one night. He was uneasy, which was not like him. He seemed to be fumbling for words; he lighted a cigarette and then dropped it under his boot and ground it out.

"Look here," he finally blurted out. "It's none of my business, but our families have been friends—I think you ought to be told." He glanced about us in the dusk and lowered his voice. "Your father's activities are not going unnoticed. I am in a position to hear these things. It would be wise if you could persuade him to retire. We are not going to be stopped, you know. Not anywhere."

Before I had a chance to reply he turned and marched off.

I wrote to my father and conveyed the warning without mentioning von Rauth's name. I insisted on returning to Magdeburg instead of to Berlin. But he would not have it. I *must* go back to the university and begin the final preparations for my examinations. Reluctantly I agreed.

We had hardly left the camp, freed after the months of unwilling service, when those of us who were returning together to Berlin became conscious of something new in the air. This was the outside world again but it had changed. There was a something strange in the atmosphere, something threatening and prophetic—the smell of war.

Our train was rattling through the night on its way to Berlin when we heard the sirens wailing through the countryside. At once the army officers among the passengers took control of the train. Lights were quickly extinguished; smoking was forbidden and the train raced along in complete blackness.

"What is going on?" one of us asked.

"It is the blackout," answered a voice out of the darkness of the corridor. "It is the defense practice against air raids."

"What air raids?" I asked sharply.

"Who knows?" replied the same voice. "They are for our protection. The Fuehrer has ordered drills for three nights now in Berlin. Three months ago we had two solid weeks of them."

As we approached Berlin we became aware of the sharp bark of gunfire, and overhead sounded the roaring of airplane motors. It was so realistic that I felt myself cringing. We got out of the train in a completely black city. One's first impulse was to put out one's hands like a blind man, to feel one's way in the inky blackness. The cars and the great two-story busses showed only tiny slits of light through the black paper that covered their headlights, and they traveled very slowly. We could not recognize Berlin. It reared indistinct walls around us, a ghost city of tenebrous menace, and the only familiar things were the stars overhead which blazed with an unwonted brilliance.

"I never knew before that there was such a beautiful sky or that the stars could be so bright," I heard a passing woman say with wonder.

One of our number started to light a cigarette and a warden immediately snatched it from him.

"Remember that the light of a cigarette can be seen for two miles," he snapped at us.

Now the sirens sounded again and everyone started to stream toward the shelters. We heard the rocking explosions of anti-aircraft guns start up, and caught the distant hum of planes as we followed the crowd into a huge underground shelter, deep below the street level.

"What is the idea of the gunfire and the airplanes?" I asked one of my neighbors in the shelter. "This is my first blackout. I've been away from Berlin."

"The army holds maneuvers during some of the air-raid drills," he told me. "That is so the people may become accustomed to the sounds of actual warfare, so that they will be trained for an emergency."

When the sirens sounded again we were allowed to go above ground but the blackness was still everywhere. After fumbling around for ten minutes I managed to locate the bus I wanted, and was carried through the dense midnight to my lodgings.

The next day I sensed even more keenly the changed, warlike tempo in the city. The innovations had come upon the people gradually and they were hardly aware of them, but I was seeing Berlin with fresh eyes and the feeling of impending hostilities oppressed me everywhere I turned. The city was operating on a semi-military basis. I learned that every house and every block now had its air-raid warden. There had been tremendous additions made to the great electrical plant of Siemens and Halske, by far the largest industrial buildings in Berlin. The vast new wings were now manufacturing bombing planes and guns, and 150,000 workers were at present employed there. Immense modern air-raid shelters had been built at the plant to house these workers, and the people spoke proudly of the shelters' airtight, concrete construction and how the air was pumped in to them through the ground and filtered to prevent the entrance of poison gases. The ventilators were renewed each month, and so were the medical kits with which every shelter in the city was supplied, to insure their freshness. It was boasted that with five million people in Berlin the entire population was underground in seven minutes after the first siren of an alarm was sounded.

This was in the year 1937.

There was no escaping the fast-moving trend of events. There was not even an opportunity to protest against them. You could only watch and be swept along. I found the increased taxes and the incessant demands for "donations" by the party a heavy drain on my slender purse.

The Winter-Help was the fund in whose name the Nazis did their most effective soliciting of funds. The money was supposed to be used for the relief of the poor during the cold weather, but the people were skeptical about its actual disbursal. The S.S. and S.A. sold pins on the street and everyone who walked abroad was obliged to buy one and wear it. There were weekly donations of money required as well as the "pound gift"—so many pounds of cabbages, potatoes, and other foods—to supply the big public soup kettles. Every front door in Berlin was plastered with stickers signifying the funds paid to the Winter-Help. The first Sunday in every winter month was "one-pot-Sunday" on which every man, woman, and child in Germany ate stew, even in the finest restaurants. The next day the party collected the money supposedly saved by this sort of dining for the Winter-Help. There was an occasional publication in round figures of these sums collected ostensibly for the poor, but there was no public accounting of their disbursal. The previous winter there had been a joke current in Berlin. Whenever a big squadron of bombers flew overhead you would hear someone say, "There flies our Winter-Help."

This winter the feeling was not the same. There were pride and satisfaction in the eyes that watched the flying monsters. I was one of a group who were idling on the university grounds one day when a whole fleet of planes poured across the sky above us. I could not resist saying, "The poor will have hard chewing on those this winter."

A hand struck my mouth and I looked around a circle of angry faces. Rudolph Beck, who was with me, seized my arm and began to berate me loudly for my lack of patriotism. I was so shocked that I let him lead me away, completely bewildered by his noisy anger. It was only after we were out of earshot of the group that he heaved a deep sigh of relief and I saw the solicitude in his eyes.

"You fool, Karl," he said. "Don't you know that you can't talk like that any more?"

"Have they all gone mad?" I asked in a black rage, my mouth burning from the slap I had received and my pride sorely stung.

"You can't say anything any more. They will be watching you after this. You will have to be doubly careful."

I could hardly contain myself. It was impossible for me to sit through a class and I walked blindly back to my lodgings, feeling that wherever I might turn the doors of escape were inexorably closing against me on every hand. Derision and danger were all that my homeland offered me, and I was bound here by a duty to which I owed more than my life and for which there could be only one ending waiting me. At my rooms I found a letter from my father.

"The plight of all of us who are engaged in the Church fight is growing rapidly worse," he wrote. "Like an old soldier, I sniff the approach of war and I know that in wartime we shall prove easy victims. I do not want you to be one of them. You will make my mind much easier if you will listen to my warning and begin to prepare yourself for life in another land. Christianity is not limited by geography. I suggest that you plan to go to America. You can serve your faith better in a land of peace than behind the barbed wire of a concentration camp here."

I lay on my bed for an hour with my head on my arms and my mind played with the tempting idea. But I knew I could not go. My father was asking for me a protection he would not seek for himself. I was chained to Germany by a sort of soldier's code. As long as the fight went on I could not desert it. But I felt that my father had enough griefs on his mind without adding apprehension for my safety.

I got up and wrote him a long letter, promising to consider his advice, and telling him that I would attend the American Lutheran Church in Berlin, in order to improve my English.

For two months I did attend the American services and I heard the Thanksgiving declaration of the American President read, and in the free discussions after the service I listened with amazement to excerpts from the speeches of American senators, or the editorials from some great newspaper. The freedom of language was almost shocking to me. In Germany we had so long been walled in by fear we had learned to set so close a guard upon our tongues that it was actually frightening to hear the openness of uncensored speech.

At the university there was almost no one I could talk to. Wolfgang had left Berlin and early in the spring Rudolph took his doctorate and returned to Magdeburg to begin the practice of law. Even in the brief time before he left I saw little of him. In order to enter the Nazi-dominated legal profession he had been obliged to become a nominal party member, although I knew how little he was a Nazi at heart. But I felt that in his present position I was not a safe friend for him to cultivate, and my decision not to see him left me very much alone.

The speech of my own people began to sound strange and foreign to me as the Hitler worship became more fanatical. When, in March, Austria was absorbed into the Reich without bloodshed, I walked like an outcast through the jubilant refrain of adulation for the man who had ruined my country.

"The Fuehrer was born with success in his blood!" you could hear them saying on all sides.

"He has powers that are divine. He cannot fail."

It was early on the morning of Hitler's birthday in April that my landlady knocked at my door and told me that Erika was waiting in the parlor downstairs. I ran down at once, more elated than I had been in months. Erika held out both her hands to me warmly, but her face was grave.

"Karl," she said, "I have come to persuade you to come home."

"What is it?" I was deeply disquited by her tone. "My father . . . ?"

"He would not let us write you, but your mother and I feel that you *must* be with him. He has received a number of anonymous letters, threatening him, telling him that if he persists in his work he will be stopped by force."

"I should never have come back to Berlin" I said, condemning myself bitterly.

"He wanted you to. We all felt you should finish your work. But in these last weeks . . ." Her lips quivered and I read in her gray eyes a too-close acquaintance with fear. "A terrible thing happened last Sunday."

"To him?"

"To the sacristan. Old Emil. About an hour before the time for the service some Nazis came to close the church. They brought planks to nail across the doors and old Emil tried to stop them. He—resisted them. They shot him, Karl. He died there on the church steps. And the Nazis walked across his body and nailed the church doors shut and went off and left him there."

"How could they! Didn't anybody *do* anything?"

"How can you do anything against the Nazis? Your father came at once and some of the other men, and they brought crowbars and pried the planks off the church doors and carried old Emil inside. And the people saw his body, and they prayed for him."

"And now they are threatening my father!" I was filled with a cold resolve. "Wait here a minute, Erika, will you? I'll pack a bag and we can catch a morning train."

I dashed upstairs and flung a few things in a suitcase and in ten minutes we were on our way across town. But when we reached Unter den Linden we found the sidewalks jammed with people. I had forgotten the immense celebration that was staged in honor of Hitler's birthday. The parade had not commenced and we started to squeeze through the crowd in hopes of making our way across the street before the spectacle began.

Suddenly a cordon of motorcycle troops shot up the avenue and passed us on their way to the reviewing stand. The storm troopers who were standing in formation along the edge of the sidewalk immediately locked arms, one man facing the street and the next man facing the crowd. Behind them two more rows of brown-shirts snapped to attention, with rifles ready. I set down my suitcase resignedly and stuck my hands in my pockets. The Fuehrer was coming, on his way to the stand where he would review the parade. This triple impenetrable wall of storm troopers was to protect him, to cut him off from the populace. I looked down at Erika and shrugged my shoulders despairingly.

As the Fuehrer's car approached a tremendous roar went up from the people and every hand shot up in the rigid Nazi salute. I started to pull my hand from my pocket to give the required salute when I felt something cold and hard in my ribs. A Gestapo man stood behind me with his revolver in my side.

"Stand still! As you are!" he hissed at me. And he held me there without moving until the car had passed from sight. Then he jerked me around and roughly searched me for concealed weapons. When he found nothing, he still glared at me suspiciously.

"Open that suitcase," he ordered. And when I did so, "Empty it on the sidewalk."

I was furious. "You can look through my things without spilling them in the dirt," I told him. For answer he kicked the case over so that socks and handkerchiefs disappeared under the feet of the crowd. He stirred through the rest of my belongings thoroughly until they were in a jumbled mess.

"All right. Put them back," he ordered, and I began to tumble my soiled clothing into the bag again. Then I heard him speak to Erika.

"You are with this man?"

"Yes, I am," she said quietly.

I straightened up and saw that he had taken her handbag and was poking into it. I would have struck him if some sense of caution had not hinted to me that I would be involving Erika in trouble, and as I looked at her, her eyes implored me to hold my tongue and my temper. I stood sick and silent, not even able to protect her from this public search. The Gestapo man gave me an ugly look.

"I'll let you go this time," he said. "But in the future when the Fuehrer passes, keep your hands out of your pockets."

"I'll remember," I said shortly.

Now up the street appeared the head of the military parade and it was too late for us to hope to cross Unter den Linden and reach the station. Once the military appeared in the street the public kept strictly out of their way. A pedestrian who interfered with their progress would have been shot on the spot and no questions asked. We should be blocked off for hours. There was no way of getting around the parade for the great thoroughfare bisected the entire town. Unter den Linden had been extended by Hitler's order to form a magnificent avenue for parading, straight through the heart of the city. The new street stretched north and south and was called the Axis (the origin, incidentally, of the term "Axis Powers," since the southern end of the Axis pointed toward Rome).

"We'll be held up for half the day," I told Erika. "Let's go get some coffee, somewhere where we can sit and talk."

"We can't leave now," she murmured. "That Gestapo man is watching us. If we started away he'd be sure to arrest us."

Sure enough, the man from the secret police had moved only a few steps away and was keeping a suspicious eye on us. We were forced to stand and watch the great parade for its entire length, the military band in brilliant uniform, which swept by the reviewing stand at full gallop, playing a thunderous march, the men guiding their horses only with their knees, the mounted trumpeters lifting their pennant-hung horns and emitting a spine-splintering blast that cut through your ear like a knife and ran down every nerve of your body. The field marshals and generals swung in to lead the parade past Hitler's tribune on foot, with Goering at their head, his ponderous shape glittering in a dazzling white uniform; the infantry followed, marching twelve abreast in ceaseless files, one hundred and fifty thousand of them in that day's procession. Behind the infantry came the motorized troops, mile after mile of great clattering tanks, of military trucks and armored cars until I began to think there would never be an end of them. Overhead the bombers roared and circled. And the people cheered until their throats were raw.

When it was over at last and we were once more on our way to the station, Erika was very quiet and my mind was strangely disturbed.

"They have not built all that force for nothing," I said out of my gloomy speculation. "And you saw how the people feel. They are ready to follow Hitler through the insane last folly."

Our train compartment was crowded so that we were not able to do much talking, but there would have been little encouragement either of us could have offered the other on that unhappy journey.

It was hard to believe that this old man was my father. I saw him raise himself slowly and painfully from the chair in his study and smile as he put out a hand to me. I was so shocked I could hardly move forward to take it. His hair was almost white and his face wrinkled with the deep-cut lines of sorrow and endurance of pain. His once proudly upright shoulders were bowed and he moved with difficulty.

"I am glad you have come," he said. "I would not have sent for you but I am glad you have come."

"Erika told me they have been threatening you." I still could not adjust myself to the way he had aged.

"That? I pay no attention to it." He dismissed the threats with finality. "It does not matter what they may do to me. But now you are here, there are many things I must explain to you while there is still time. I want you to know all the details of the work I am doing in case I am taken into custody."

"You must stop now. I will take over for you." I vowed to myself that he should take no more risks. I could not bear to think of the consequences to him of a second arrest and imprisonment.

"They have not intimidated me," he said in quiet denial of my fears. "While I still live I shall go on working. It would be harder than death for me, Karl, to give up this fight while I can still do anything."

"You have given enough," I cried. "Why should you risk your liberty, your life, even? I am young. I can do the work."

"What would I be preserving my life *for*, if I left in the midst of the battle?" he asked me simply. "No, Karl. We are working for something greater than our mere lives. In all the wide world there is only one profound meaning in living, and that is to serve and to love the Source from which our life springs. I would lose more than my life if I abandoned that need in the hearts of our people for the sake of my personal safety."

"They will take you and not a hand can be lifted for you!"

"We are not abandoned." The look on his face was one of deep peace and of content. "No man can ask more of his life than to use it for something greater than himself. The fruit from the seed we are sowing may not ripen in our time. But we can trust the outcome without question. The truth is never defeated. Whatever may happen to me, you must not allow it to embitter you. I am satisfied. I shall have spent my life well."

There were tears in my eyes as I clasped his lean, heavily veined hand. I could not argue with him.

For days thereafter my father spent long hours explaining to me the secret work he was doing. I learned the names of those who were to be trusted with the preparation and hiding of literature. I learned the means employed to get in touch with the Christians who were imprisoned and what could be done to make their lot easier. I learned how secret funds were solicited for families orphaned by the persecution, the work that was being done for the Confessional schools, and the inner channels of the *Bruederrat.*

He told me how the German Christians were working, for they had long since learned that only empty churches rewarded their boldly spoken doctrines. They had put on meekness and cloaked in the words of the Psalms and in Biblical phrases their subtle pressure to turn the people from the worship of God to the worship of the state, until the simpler souls among the congregations could no longer distinguish them from their honest ministers. He told me how these men were pointed out to the people and how their following fell away and they were transferred and the warnings must be given again.

I learned more than he told me. I saw in the faces of all who came to see him how greatly he was loved by the men and women who worked with him.

"His only protection is the love and admiration of the people," Erika told me. "I think the government would have had him arrested long since if they were not afraid of his popularity. I believe they have been afraid to risk a violent popular reaction."

"He will not stop his work. And, Erika, I can't even ask him to."

"I know. Perhaps he is wiser than we are, Karl. But every day when I come to this house I am frightened that I may not find him here."

It was nearly a week after my return that Johann burst into the parsonage one night with three or four young men accompanying him. Erika and her uncle, Werner Menz, were spending the evening with us.

"There's a rumor that the Nazis have planted a bomb in the church!" he cried. We all jumped to our feet and my father began to crack out orders.

"Every man to the church! On the run! Hedwig, phone the men of the parish at once. Erika, you will remain here with my wife."

We dashed out of the wide front door, leaving it swinging behind us and raced under the chill spring stars to the square where the still stone building stood. Johann, who was the fastest sprinter, was the first up the steps and ran to turn on every light in the church. We spread out our thin numbers and began at the far corners of the nave, searching every nook and cranny for unfamiliar objects. I turned sick with panic as I looked at the vast stretch of the beautiful old edifice. There were so many places where a deadly package might be hidden. We searched under pews and in corners. We hunted in the shadows behind the marble statues. We explored the altar and the cupboards where the sacramental vessels were kept. Within ten minutes other men arrived to join us, Colonel Beck and Rudolph, Herr Schenk and nearly twenty others. We burrowed in every corner of the basement, the church council rooms, the sacristy, the tower, and the crannies beneath the stairs.

I climbed the steps to the high pulpit, and there on the floor stood a battered old traveling bag that I had never seen before.

"I think I've found it!" I shouted, and every man in the church stopped and stared in my direction.

"Get a pail of water," roared Colonel Beck.

"It's too big to go in a pail," I yelled. Then Rudolph and Johann reached me on a dead run up the pulpit steps. Without a word the three of us stooped down and put our hands under the bottom corners of the ancient bag, for we instinctively distrusted the frayed handle.

"Don't tilt it," said Rudolph.

It was unbelievably heavy. Our arms pulled from their sockets as we slowly brought it up to knee height and began the careful descent of the pulpit stairs, carrying it between us. There was not a sound in the vast building as we made our endless way down the center aisle with the menacing object sagging at the ends of our arms. It was too heavy for fast carrying and we were afraid of tripping. I thought that I heard a faint metallic noise from inside it but I was panting too hard to be sure. Colonel Beck sprang to open the doors ahead of us and we were in the vestibule, through the broad front doors, on the church steps, and my heart was beating deafeningly in my ears and my arms were near to breaking.

"Where can we put it down?" gasped Johann, and I heard my mind thinking like some separate thing, "What if we put it down too late? How much time have we?"

"Out in the square," said Rudolph, and we crossed the street and stumbled on with our burden.

"This is far enough. Easy now. For God's sake don't bump it."

We eased it onto the turf.

"Now run like fury," muttered Rudolph, and we turned and ran and with every step I felt my back crawl and I was drenched with sweat. I had not had time, until now, to be afraid.

We reached the church and turned and looked back, panting. The bag sat out on the distant grass, looking very small and singularly non-dangerous. The other men had come out and were gathered on the church steps.

"Herr Schenk," said the colonel, "will you be good enough to go around to the other side of the square and warn any passers-by to keep away. Stay at a good distance yourself." He turned to the rest of us as the schoolmaster trotted off. "There may be another one. Back to work, all of you."

For hours we hunted high and low, going back again and again over the same old ground in fear lest our straining eyes might have missed something on a former round. There were now men stationed at every door of the church to prevent any strangers from entering. Around two o'clock in the morning, when I was exploring the gallery for the third time and some of the older men had gathered with my father in the center of the nave, weary from the long search, there came a crashing explosion from the square outside. The whole church trembled. The heavily gilded chandeliers above my head swung and creaked on their chains and shadows waved up and down along the walls. I forgot to breathe, I was listening so intently for the sound of a detonation to come from somewhere within the church. But nothing more happened. The building had been saved.

The sense of relief and of triumph released all of our tongues. We came pouring down into the nave from all corners of the church and everybody was talking and shouting at once. Men caught each others' hands and pumped them up and down, but their faces were grave and exhausted.

Herr Schenk came hurrying in from the square where he had been on guard. He had been knocked flat on the grass by the explosion, but he had not been injured.

"We must set a watch over the church for the rest of the night," said the colonel. "In fact, the building must be guarded constantly from now on."

Ten men at once volunteered to keep vigil until morning, and my father was determined to stay with them.

"No. That is one thing we shall not allow," Colonel Beck insisted. "You must save your strength, my friend, for the things that no one else can do for you. Home now, and get some sleep."

The watchers turned to the colonel, who began to assign their places, when the church doors opened and my mother and Erika came hurrying in with fear-ridden faces. When my mother caught sight of my father, standing weary but safe in the midst of the group of men, she burst into tears.

Erika had halted at the vestibule doors and stood tottering on her feet with a faint, relieved smile on her lips, but her face was dead white. I ran to her and caught her elbows, and she looked so near fainting that I drew her with me out into the fresh air on the church steps, holding her warm, trembling little body against me and patting her shoulder the way you pat a child.

"We heard the explosion," she whispered into my coat lapel, and I realized that she and my mother must have sat up all night, waiting for the terrible sound that had at last come to their ears. "I wanted to be here all the time," she said, looking up at me.

A glowing pride in her courage filled me, and something else, something that had long been growing within me beneath the grief and struggle of our haunted years. I saw how much she had come to fill my life, that she was more than dear to me, that everything I had done or might do would be empty without her, and with all the pent-up hunger of our years of sorrow, I bent and kissed her.

"I am going to keep you with me from now on."

"Yes," she said quite simply, and our eyes met and shared the wonder that lifts two people out of their loneliness and into the heady sweetness and strength of being one. In the chill and starry night I made a vow in my heart to shield and protect her as long as I should live.

There was not a line in the newspapers about the explosion or the search that had been made to save the church, but the whole town was boiling with the news the next day. Tremendous agitation and unrest seized the people because of the Nazis' bold attempt to destroy the Dom, and the following Sunday five successive services were held, so huge were the crowds that were drawn out. My father gave from the pulpit a quiet and literal account of the night's happenings, but he fed no fuel to the latent resentment of the people.

"Physical threats are all the government is able to bring against us," he said. "And these are not a threat to faith." And he recited the words from the Gospel of St. Matthew, "Be not afraid of them which kill the body, but are not able to kill the soul."

It was the following Friday morning that I set out early on an errand for my father, carrying a number of bundles of pamphlets to the houses where they were to be hidden until Sunday. I had completed my task by nine o'clock and was returning—I had come within half a block of home, striding briskly along the sidewalk—when I saw the door of our house open and five strange men come out. They piled into a car at the curb and drove away.

Apprehension seized on me. Strangers at the parsonage were an ill omen, and with my heart thumping with the quick dawn of fear, I broke into a run. Old Anna was in the front hall.

"Where is my father?" I demanded, out of breath.

"He is in his study, Herr Karl. Some visitors have just left him."

"Father!" I called, striding to the door of the secretary's room that led into his study. "Father!" There was no answer.

I ran to the study door and flung it open. His big figure lay sprawled unconscious across the rug, with arms outspread, his white hair bloody, and a little puddle of dark blood beneath his chin.

There were dark welts across his face and in two places his scalp was cut open to the bone.

At the hospital my mother and I sat for three hours in the midst of bare white walls and the pervading sharp smell of medicaments, waiting. At last a sober-faced surgeon came to us out of the operating room.

"I can give you very little hope," he said. "The skull has been fractured in two places and there is the complication of that old head injury."

"He got that in the war," said my mother quietly.

All that day, while my father lay in a coma, she was completely calm and still.

"I have been waiting for this for years, Karl, knowing that something would come. If he gets well, I shall have to wait until it happens to him again—or until it happens to you."

Watching her, I learned something of the bitter bravery of women.

CHAPTER
SIXTEEN

My father died without regaining consciousness, at five o'clock on Sunday morning. My mother and I had sat the night through in his hospital room, and watched the gray Sabbath dawn come coldly across the windows and heard his breathing grow hoarser and more uneven until it ceased to sound at all. When the doctor laid the pulseless wrist down on the covers, my mother, who was standing beside the bed, did not move but stood looking down at the still, bandaged head on the pillow. With a little gesture of disbelief she reached out her hand and touched her husband's forehead.

"You are sure?" she said, looking up at the doctor like a child who does not understand. "He is still warm."

I moved over to her and put my arm around her. The life heat would ebb quickly out of him now, but my mind, like hers, rebelled at the untenable fact. I had waited for this death, but I had not really believed that my father could die. I had leaned upon his courage for so long, and I did not know how to look forward and see my life going on without him.

When we came back to the empty house I went into his study and found the notes he had prepared earlier in the week for today's sermon. I took them into the living room where Anna was trying to persuade my mother to drink a cup of coffee.

"I have found the notes for his sermon, Mother. I can't put them aside. I am sure I can get permission—I want to preach in his place this morning."

She looked up at me and something close to contentment came into her face.

"I wouldn't have asked you, Karl. And your father, if he had known, would not have asked so much. But I know it is what he would have hoped for."

I went at once to telephone the nearest member of the *Bruederrat,* and secured his ready consent to have me fill my father's pulpit. During the cloudy morning hours I sat in the study and read over again and again the hopeful and tolerant words he had jotted down. And as I read them, feeling my lack of wisdom, my inadequacy to take his place, I suddenly heard as clearly as if they had been spoken to me, the words that I must speak as his requiem. I was filled with a sense of sureness, of deep peace, as if his life and death had taken a tangible form before me and shown me their meaning.

When I entered the sacristy and placed his black robes over my shoulders, I saw with a curious sense of fitness that I had grown to his physical stature, and this seemed to have significance, as if every step of this morning had been prepared long in advance. It was with the same strong serenity in my heart that I entered the pulpit and looked down upon the troubled faces of the great congregation.

"How shall we sing the Lord's song in a strange land?" I cried out the words of the exiles' Psalm, and I saw eyes that I knew turn toward me with apprehension.

"This Germany of ours today has become a strange land in bitter truth." I let the words ring out clearly and with passion. "An exile who looks back to a pleasant and beloved home is in far better case than we. The home we love has altered and become an alien place, not to be recognized, a desolate and strange land while we are still walking its streets and living in its houses. We are exiles in our familiar place. How shall we sing the Lord's song in this strange land?"

Toward the rear of the church I saw one S.S. man turn to another and whisper to him and I realized that I would be held to account for this speaking, but I could not feel any fear.

"I am not the man you expected to see stand before you today. I am not man enough, I am not wise enough to take the place of the man you expected, but I speak in his place today because I am his son—and because he is dead."

A shocked moan escaped from the throats of the congregation, and I saw Colonel Beck's face grow rigid and Herr Schenk's blue lips contort with pain and old Frau Reinsburg's rheumy eyes overflow with sudden tears.

"He died this morning at dawn. Some of you have heard that he had suffered an accident. But that is not true. He died because he continued to speak the Word of God, to sing the Lord's song in this land of persecution. He was murdered. Five men entered his study last Friday morning and beat him about the head so that he died without regaining consciousness.

"He knew that either death or imprisonment waited for him if he continued his work. He was threatened, but he put the threats aside. Two weeks ago, knowing the menace that hung over him, he told me confidently, 'Whatever happens to me, I shall have spent my life well. The truth cannot be defeated.'"

I let my voice drop low. "And yet which of us can look around our nation today and believe that the truth may not be defeated? To be a Christian in Germany in these fearful years is to be an outcast; to speak is to become a victim. On every hand the wounds and the persecutions increase. The lips that speak the word of God are stilled, one by one. Where is our hope? What madman can say that our battle is not lost?"

The eyes of hundreds of men and women hung on my face with tragic intensity. At the rear of the nave I saw the two S.S. men leave their seats and move toward the side aisle nearest the sacristy. I knew with cold clarity as I watched them that this would be both the first and the last time I would be free to speak from a German pulpit, and I turned to the people and cried out with a burning urgency:

"When that word of Love was first spoken, a man died for speaking it. A young man, whose lips were the sole lips on earth to speak the hope of men. He was nailed to a cross, and He died. And over His head there were words of mockery written and His body was marked by the scourge of whips and the nails tore His hands and the life went out of Him. And the rulers of the people laughed and were satisfied that they had destroyed Him and His teaching. And the men who loved Him bowed their heads in despair and groaned that the word and the hope had died with Him.

"But the Word did not die. It rose and flowered through the climbing centuries and lighted an eternal hope in the eyes of men. It became a leaping fire, spreading and blazing in the hearts of the peoples and bringing life out of the fear of death.

"Today an old man has died. He was one of many who have been silenced so that the word they still spoke might be silenced with them. Today the rulers of the people smile with satisfaction, believing that murder and enforced silence can destroy a faith. And today we who loved the man who spoke the truth to us groan in our despair that hope has died with him, that the darkness is closing in on the light, that the sparks we hold in our hands will be brutally crushed out of them and that the Christian hope is dying under the Nazi heel.

"But it is not true." The two secret police stood staring darkly at me from the rear of the side aisle. "The word of Christ was not silenced when only one Voice spoke it. Out of pain and death it drew strength until it was the light of the vast world. Today it lives in our hearts, and there is no tool strong enough in our oppressors' hands to wrest it out. Ours is the faith that grows strong out of weakness, that waxes greater under torture. We who are Christians are not the losers in this fight. Verily, I say unto you, 'We are the victors.'

"The government that has made itself the enemy of God has only physical weapons to use against our faith. Faith is something they cannot lay their hands on. They can crush only arms and legs and skulls—but not minds and spirits." I let my voice ring out with all its strength down the vast nave. "As surely as love and faith are stronger than sticks and stones, as surely as the love of God is stronger than the designs of men, the Nazis have met a force that is stronger than they are. Our strength is not alone of men, and our exile is not forever."

And then I told them quietly, "A man you love has died that

he might show you a light. Now that light rests in your hands. It is the only light in this land, this strange, dark land. Set it then upon a hill, where it cannot be hid."

Looking down into the upturned eyes, I knew by the thing that shone in them that I had not spoken vainly, in the place of the great-hearted man who lay dead. I felt a curious sense of completion, of having written a finish to a part of my life. I felt no trepidation at the knowledge of my impending imprisonment, although I had no slightest doubt that my bold speaking had doomed me to the bleakness of concentration-camp walls for years and perhaps, since this would not be my first arrest in the Church fight, for life. I had reached a peak in my life and I had done what was inevitable, what I knew I must do, and I was filled with satisfaction and with well-being, like a man who reaches a mountain top and contentedly fills his lungs with invigorating air. The belief that had been gathering within me through the tortured years had been put into words. I had spoken everything that was in my heart, if only once, and I was strangely satisfied. I knew that my father would not have been displeased with me.

And then with the thought of my father, the import of his loss finally broke upon me in its full reality. My mind, weary from the nightlong vigil at the hospital and the fervor of my last preaching, suddenly awoke to shock. He was gone. He would not hear. He would not know. And I stood empty and cold. The exultation drained out of me and I was shaken with desolation. Now there seemed no meaning in what I had done. The only reality was that he was gone.

With a shivering automatism I began to read the prayer, and the words sounded hollowly in the air and the responses of the people made a meaningless and monotonous jumble of words, while one thought went droning through my mind: "He is dead."

When the first bars of the hymn sounded from the organ the people surged to their feet with a resolute unity. With the detached half of my consciousness, I could see a fierce will that originated within their minds sweep them and bring them closer together. It was something far deeper than the mob spirit that nowadays set the crowds to "Heil"ing in the streets. This was a free, a voluntary force, and there was an indomitable power in it. With a shout of strength, thousands of voices caught up the words of the old fighting hymn and sent them reverberating against the high vault above them. Every word crashed out with a defiant and sorrowful thunder—

> *"A mighty Fortress is our God*
> *A trusty shield and weapon . . . "*

It is our custom for the minister to retire to the sacristy during the singing of the hymns and I turned in that direction, my emotions exhausted, my heart cold with loss. The triumphant roar of sound beat about me, the battle cry of our fight.

> *"We tremble not, we fear no ill*
> *They cannot overpower us."*

And I knew that the fight would never cease while those words still beat in a single German heart. But I was too numb to rejoice. I was too chilled to feel fear as I came to the sacristy door and saw the black-uniformed Gestapo men striding down the side aisle in my direction, shielded from notice by the standing mass of singers. Slowly I opened the sacristy door and stepped within.

Colonel Beck was there. I had not seen him move out of his pew during the service, but there he was. The moment I entered he seized my arm and pulled me sharply to one side while he snapped the lock of the door behind me.

"Out of those robes, boy. Quick!" he ordered in a staccato whisper, and his hands were already working at the fastenings of my gown.

"But the service isn't over," I protested, still dazed and newly stricken by astonishment at discovering him here.

"You can't go back in there. Come, hurry! One victim in your family is enough for today." He had pulled the robes from me and was pushing me into my coat. "The congregation will say its own benediction. And the more heartily, too, if they can hope you are safe."

He opened the rear door of the sacrity and peered out.

"*Gott sei Dank,*" he muttered. "They haven't got their men around to this door yet. We have a minute—maybe two. Come now. Run!—into the church council rooms and down those back stairs to the basement."

His very violence and decision pulled me along with him. My mind was not working at all. I had a vague feeling that my duty required me to complete the service and I hardly grasped the fact that the colonel was forcing freedom upon me and running an immediate and real danger in snatching me out of the very fingers of the Gestapo. But he was accustomed to being obeyed and the authority in his low-pitched voice was so decisive that I moved under his will rather than my own. We raced on tiptoe through the back rooms of the church and down the dim, twisting staircase that led to the cellar, while the music of the hymn followed us, sounding fainter for every wall we put behing us, and at last stopping entirely.

We drew up in front of a seldom-used basement door that led into the alley behind the church. The colonel turned the key that stood in the rusty lock and the small door creaked open. We stepped into the alley. There was not a person in sight. The colonel locked the door of our escape behind him and put the key in his pocket, and we turned away from the street on which the church faced and walked off without looking backward.

"The S.S. will be trying the sacristy door as soon as you fail to appear after the hymn," he said. "We have only about a two-minute start before they are after us with a vengeance. Walk briskly, but don't try to run here or we'll draw the whole pack down on us."

I began to come awake, to sense the chase that was starting behind us, and for the first time to catch the flavor of freedom floating tantalizingly before me. The alley seemed to stretch interminably ahead of us and our feet to be glued in one spot. My heart was pounding as we reached the street at the end of the alley and turned down it without accelerating our pace.

There at the curb, not fifty feet ahead of us, stood the colonel's car with the engine purring and Rudolph at the wheel. He gave me a quick grin as we piled in and the car moved off. At the same moment we heard a shout from the general direction of the church building. Rudolph swung the car around a corner and for a mile or more we followed a circuitous route in the hope of throwing off any possible pursuers. At length the colonel turned around from looking out the rear window.

"I don't think we were followed," he said with an air of satisfaction.

"That was well timed," said Rudolph, looking grimly exhilarated. "We've got clean away."

"For the present," his father assented. "What do you think, Rudolph? This young fellow wanted to go back and finish the service."

"You've indulged in enough folly for one day, Karl," said Rudolph, but his tone was pleased and I knew he was not rebuking me for speaking so strongly in the church.

"And now we have to consider where to take you," the colonel went on. "The S.S. and any number of Nazi sympathizers in the congregation obviously saw Rudolph and me when we left the church, so you won't be safe at my house. Otherwise I should take you there. But we evolved this plan on the spur of the moment when we saw the Gestapo leave their seats, and it went only far enough to get you away from the church before they laid their hands on you."

"I can still hardly understand how you managed it," I broke in, for through my mental daze was beginning to penetrate an understanding of the courage and quick thinking by which the colonel had saved me.

"I saw that basement door and tried it while your father and I were downstairs during the bomb hunt the other night." The habitual stolidity of his soldier's face was softened by the lines of sudden grief. "We should have set guards to protect the man and let the building go. I shall never forgive the Nazis for his death. Never." I saw his lean jaw set and his eyes darken, and then he jerked his mind back to our immediate concerns.

"Now we can try, belatedly, to save *you*. We must find a place to hide you first of all, my boy."

"But I have to see my mother. I can't leave her alone, now. Not today."

"You have the most thunderingly impractical mind I have ever encountered young man!" shouted the colonel, turning round on me and administering an exasperated thump to the car seat. "Of course you can't go home. The place will be crawling with Gestapo after that sermon of yours. Do you want your mother to see you arrested after you have succeeded in escaping them? There will be a host of her friends with her, never fear. And once I get you safely stowed away, I'll go to see her and let her know how you are. But the sooner we get you off the streets the better—for all of us."

The extremity of my predicament began to dawn on me. I could not go home, and if I went to a hotel I should be picked up immediately. Neither could the colonel safely drive me out of town. The Gestapo would be scouring the city for me and the colonel and Rudolph were in danger as long as I was with them.

"What about some of the church people?" asked Rudolph. "They have hidden a dozen fugitive pastors. And they would be more than eager to offer refuge to Karl. We're not far from the Kellers. Johann and his mother have never come under suspicion and I'm sure he'd be safe there."

"To the Kellers'," directed the colonel with decision, and five minutes later I was installed in an upper bedroom of the big turreted house. The colonel and Rudolph had seen me welcomed and had left at once, reassuring me that I should have news from my mother before night, and Johann had led me upstairs and made me at home.

I had sat for hours trying to accustom myself to the rapid changes the day had brought in my status and in all my plans for the future, when in the early evening Johann came in with news for me. The Gestapo had raided the parsonage within an hour of my escape and had left men stationed there to intercept me if I should attempt to return. My mother knew that I was safe and friends were staying with her, and she had sent me word that her only hope was that I should try to leave Germany. Colonel Beck and Rudolph had begun to lay plans for my escape. The *Bruederrat* knew my whereabouts and in a day or two, when things had quieted down a little, they would arrange to have me moved on to a place where I would be in less immediate danger.

I had only a day or two, then, in which to settle my affairs in Magdeburg, for whatever happened, I would not be able to return to the town where I was known. But I was not willing to leave Germany. I could not abandon my mother, nor did I feel that I could leave Erika behind me. And while I was still free I owed whatever effort I could still make to the cause of my threatened faith.

Johann argued with me with exasperated heat, but I could not see that saving my own skin was sufficient justification for leaving such heavy responsibilities behind me.

"Your future isn't worth a *Pfennig* in this country," he snapped at me. "Even your life isn't safe. You got out of their hands this time by the narrowest sort of squeak. Why should you want to go back and stick your head into the lion's mouth again?"

"My father didn't walk out and leave his job undone, the way you think I should do."

"Your father had vision enough to advise you to leave Germany. I tell you, Karl, you might as well telephone the Gestapo and tell them where you are tonight, as to try to work from hiding in this country. Do you *want* to get yourself arrested again? Did you *like* the taste you once had of the concentration camp?"

"Listen, my lad, I'm just as much afraid of a Nazi prison as I ever was. It's still too good to believe that I'm actually here and free instead of being in a cell tonight. But there are some things that nobody can abandon. As long as I can be of some use here, I have no right to run away. It's as simple as that."

"You're a double-barreled idiot, and we've saved you for nothing," Johann growled. "But it's your own life, my friend. Throw it away if you want to."

I lay awake long into the night, listening to the light patter of rain on the roof outside and tasting the acid cup of the fugitive. I knew I should never sleep again under the roof that had sheltered me from my birth. Every place into which I might fit in the land that was my home had fallen apart, shattered by my own action. I had no desire for martyrdom. I knew a healthy fear and respect for the brutalities of the concentration camps. And yet I was not free to leave.

Late the following afternoon I had a visitor. I got to my feet in surprise when I saw him enter my room, for he was well known to me. He was a member of the *Bruederrat* of the Confessional Church. He had received a message from my mother; he had talked with Colonel Beck; and he had come to advise me to leave Germany.

"I don't feel that I can leave if there is something I still can do," I told him.

"That is just the point," he answered soberly. "I don't say that you should not have preached as you did. Your father was very dear to me, and his loss will be an irreparable one to the Church. Perhaps the people need to hear the cruel truths spoken boldly to them. But it is impossible to speak as you did and be free to speak again. As far as the Church fight is concerned, your usefulness is over."

"Do you think I should have spoken softly and subserviently, as the Nazis wished, with my father lying dead from their clubbing?" I asked him hotly.

"I am not judging you," he replied mildly. "I am only telling you that you have done all you can do for us. There is no further way in which we can use you, and I urge you to save yourself while you have the opportunity."

"You mean there is no work left for me? Not anywhere in Germany?"

"There is nowhere we could use you. I do not believe you realize how thoroughly you have made yourself a wanted man. The moment you appeared you would be arrested. All we can do for you is to protect you and to aid your flight from the country in so far as we are able."

"But that would mean abandoning my faith! I should feel like a deserter who had run away at the very height of the battle."

"My dear young man, you will not further the cause of your faith by choosing to go to prison. You have entered the service of God. And that service does not stop at the borders of Germany. Your mother hopes you will go to America. You can become a minister there, and you will speak the truth there the more surely and clearly because you have fought for the right to speak it here. The truth of God is not destroyed. It stands secure against violence and against the defeats of time. There may yet come a day when you can return to Germany and speak the words of Christ without fear, when this alien belief will have turned bitter on the people's tongues and they will spew it out and return to the older fountain which runs clear and untroubled, waiting for men to come and drink."

I was shaken. My superiors were sending me away from the Church fight. I should have no further part in the struggle that had been the main thread of my life for all the years since I had become a man. The fact that I had made myself useless to it was a wrench to my mind, and I found it hard to accept. For five minutes I sat with my head buried in my hands. In one day, all the ties that had bound me to my homeland had been rived loose. I had long been an alien to the new directions my people were taking; I had fought the new faith that was drawing the allegiance of so many. Today the last bonds were being inexorably cut. Now of a sudden the idea of America, instead of existing as a vague dream in the back of my mind began to loom as a vigorous and immediate possibility. I began to feel the heady lure of escape, to believe that I might taste freedom, I, Karl Hoffmann, who had given up all hope of being free. But the obstacles were not all gone.

"What about my mother? She is alone, and I can't leave her."

"Why not take your mother with you? You have powerful friends who could make the necessary arrangements for her, passport visas and the like. You can meet her, once you are safely across the border, and take her to America with you."

Somehow the idea had never occurred to me. Yet it was true that my mother could in all probability make arrangements quite easily to leave Germany. For me, getting out would be a more difficult matter.

"If she will go," I said finally, and I felt as if I were cutting a cord that bound me to the very earth from which I drew my substance, "I would be a fool not to attempt to escape."

From that moment on, events moved at a whirling pace. It was impossible for my mother to come to see me, for she was being shadowed constantly, but it was arranged for Erika to have an interview with me, bringing a message from my mother and completing all our arrangements for meeting, once we were free of Germany.

When the gentle, fair-faced girl who had grown to be so dear to me came into the Keller's library and walked toward me, smiling, I could hardly speak, so sharp was the thought that this would be the last time I should see her.

"Your mother sends you her love. She is holding up wonderfully, Karl. I think that it has been your decision to leave Germany that has given her new heart. She is making her plans to go to America as serenely as if she were only moving to the next town."

"Erika, my sweet," I stammered, "how can I leave you? If I could only take you with me too! But it would be a sorry marriage I could offer you—an outcast, a hunted man for a husband—and all the hardships of poverty in a land you did not know."

"Did you think I would willingly be left behind, Karl?" she asked me with shy tenderness. "I have talked to your mother and we are going together. If I am a part of your life, now, you are all of mine. You will need me in your new country, and there is nothing left for me in Germany when you have gone. This nation is no longer my home. And I am not afraid of poverty."

We talked for an hour, loath to lose sight of each other even for the few weeks that would be necessary before we could meet again in freedom and security, with a new life opening before us. We talked of my father, and I discovered that she was the only person to whom I could speak without reserve of all his loss had meant to me. And as we spoke of him, out of the love we both bore him, it seemed that we were carrying some of his dauntless spirit with us on our new adventure. We forgot the hazards that might lie in wait; we discounted the difficulties of adjusting ourselves to a strange environment, so intoxicating was the hope that we might be together beyond the reach of the vengeful Nazi power which, until now, had stretched out to overshadow every place we might turn.

Before Erika left we had made all our arrangements. She and my mother would go to Paris and wait there, and I should join them as soon as it was possible for me to make good my flight from Germany. That it might prove impossible I never suggested to her, although I knew how great the danger was that I might be either taken or killed, and that when she walked hopefully out of this room today, it might be the last time I would look upon her face.

Since we were not allowed to take sufficient money with us; Rudolph was to write to Erich Doehr in Chicago and ask him to send what funds he could to the American Express in Paris. For the rest, we could only trust our native wit and courage, believing that the Power we served would not forsake us.

It was on the following day that my father was buried from the Domkirche. At the hour of the service I sat alone in the silent house, separated from my mother and my friends and hearing the words of the service for the dead repeat themselves over and over in my aching mind. Faintly through the open window I heard the bells begin their tolling, and in my heart I said farewell to him. I knew that while they rang their slow lament, the clods of earth were falling on his sealed coffin. And with irrevocable completion they marked for me a last period to the present. The earth that fell to cover him, in my mind was falling upon Germany too. The shining faith that had sustained him I could still cling to, but everything else that was my native country died in my heart with the far-off tolling. I could see that Germany was sinking into a bitter darkness that only blood and torment could expiate, and sadly and finally I put my land behind me.

That night I slipped out of Magdeburg and made my way to a neighboring town, where I entered another hideaway among the people of the Confessional Church. There began a strange journey of zigzags and meanderings from one unfamiliar place to another. I hid in barns and friendly attics, and once in a mansion. I missed a Gestapo raid by minutes. I lost my way at night and lay through the dark in a wheat field. It began to rain and I was soaked to the skin and shivering with cold when in the light of the gray dawn I found a saving signpost that set me on my path again.

At length I reached a dark old house in a little border town which I am not free to name, and there, after three days, the chubby old woman who was concealing me opened my attic door with a smile and ushered in Rudolph. He and his father had decided on this spot as the most promising place for me to make my way across the border, and now he brought me my identification papers and all the information they could garner, a careful map of the terrain below an old mill where I must make my attempt, the stations of the sentries and the time of their rounds, and the obstacles that I must overcome.

He explained everything over to me twice, in the most minute detail, and then he stood up and grasped my hand.

"I must go," he said. "It is not safe for me to stay here too long."

We stood gripping each other's hands but it was very hard to say good-bye. There was too much that we both remembered, and the barrier that would now lie between us would be very high.

"Be sure you choose a dark night," Rudolph muttered the instruction for the third time. "And don't show yourself until you are at least five miles on the other side of the German border."

Our eyes said good-bye.

"I wish I could thank you," I managed to get out. "But you know the things I will remember."

"Good luck," he said tightly. "I—in spite of what lies in front of you here, I wish I were in your shoes." He gave my hand a bone-breaking pressure and said again shortly, "Luck," and turned and went abruptly out the door.

I spent the next day studying my little map until I knew it by heart, and then as evening came on with a drizzle of rain, I burned it and began to make myself ready. I had hopes that the wetness would discourage any too-great zeal on the part of the sentries, and since the night was very black, it offered me good covering.

At midnight I was groping my way by feeling past almost unrecognizable landmarks. The darkness was so intense that it hindered me and made it hard to sense my direction. But there was no one abroad and I thanked the rain for that. Then I was slithering on my stomach through the mud, and stopping and holding my breath to listen, and finally I heard the sentry's sodden tread at a distance. My hand felt the twigs of a small bush and I huddled beside it, while the steps approached until they seemed dangerously close. I shrank against the ground and lay still and the sentry went by a few feet away from me without pausing. I saw a flashlight touch the earth and the raindrops splashing inside the little circle of visibility it made, but it did not turn in my direction and I waited until the sound of feet had faded completely before I began squirming my way forward. There was a hummock that I was sure I recognized from the map, and a brook in the place it should have been, and I lumbered through it thankfully, for nothing could have made me any wetter than I was already and I was sure that I was going right. In a few minutes I was on my hands and feet, scrambling faster but still silently, and there was no sound of alarm out of the night. After a long time I dared to stand up and walk, fixing my eyes on a window light that glimmered far ahead of me. I was sure now that I had missed the sentries on both sides of the line, and I began to stride along through the blackness with my heart breaking into song, for I knew that Germany and all its fear-blackened years lay behind me.

The rattle-bang and untidy bustle of Paris seemed wondrously beautiful to me on the bright spring morning on which I reached it, and I took a taxi through the crowded gaiety of the streets to the hotel where my mother, Erika, and I had planned to meet. At the desk I asked for my mother, and I watched with apprehension as the clerk frowned and shook his head, running his finger down the list of guests.

"We have no Madame Hoffmann from Magdeburg staying

here," he said. "There is a young lady from Magdeburg, but it is another name."

"Mademoiselle Menz?" I asked, hardly knowing what to think and suddenly afraid that something had gone wrong with their part of our plan.

"Mademoiselle Menz is here," he affirmed, smiling and nodding his head as if the discovery of her name was a personal achievement of his own, and not at all to be expected. I sent up my name and in a few minutes I saw Erika step from the elevator and look questioningly around her. I hurried to her and she stopped still, the color coming into her cheeks as she saw me.

"Where is my mother?" I asked her hurriedly. "Her name is not on the register."

Quick tears filled Erika's eyes. "Karl," she said, "she did not come."

"You mean the Nazis prevented it? Something happened?"

She shook her head. 'She changed her mind at the very last minute. She sent a letter for me to give you." She looked up at me appealingly. "I could not persuade her, Karl. I tried to persuade her. But she insisted that I must come alone."

Erika had brought my mother's letter down in her handbag, and we stood together in the bustling lobby while I read it.

"My dear son [it read in part]:

"I am growing to be an old woman, and old trees are not easily uprooted. I need my familiar scenes and the old things around me through which I remember your father and through which he seems closer to me. I will not be troubled here for the remainder of my years, but I am too timid to try a new life any more. Truly, I would rather stay here. You know how many friends there are here to care for me, and that I shall not be alone.

"Only if you and Erika were here and in danger would Germany be unhappy for me. I have allowed myself this little scheme in order to persuade you to go to America, two young people in a safe, young land, which is as it should be. You must forgive me that I made you think I could go with you. My happiness now will only be in knowing that you are safe . . ."

I handed the letter to Erika and she read it after me.

"She never intended to leave at all!" she murmured in astonishment. "That is why I could not move her."

For a moment I thought of trying to go back to Germany to plead with her, to bring her away in spite of her fears, but then I realized that she had seen how I would feel and that she had decided for herself. If she wanted to remain where she could feel close to my father, it would only be cruel to urge her further to come with me. Perhaps when Erika and I were firmly established in America she would come to visit us, and possibly she would find our new home less strange than she had feared. I looked down at Erika. The same thoughts must have been running through her mind, for she said, "If we ask her to come to stay with us for a while, when we have a home, perhaps she will change her mind. It is hard now. Her sorrow is so new."

I pressed her hands, and then there seemed to dawn upon us simultaneously the amazing fact. We were together and we were free. Across the broad Atlantic the future reared its shining towers, and we had left darkness and death behind us.

We were married in Paris as soon as we could arrange the necessary formalities, and then we waited for our turn on the American quota list, and the Bishop of Chichester in England helped us, and so did the Lutheran Church in America. Erich sent us hearty and enthusiastic letters from Chicago (he had supplied all the funds for our first months in Paris). It took us a long time to grow used to speaking aloud without fear and to learn that our neighbors could be trusted. Even now, when we have lived in the United States for three years and are on our way to becoming citizens, even in the country parish where I am a minister, in the midst of my open-faced and generous-hearted neighbors, that caution, that sense of overhanging dread sometimes comes upon us. It is not easy to shake off the Nazi shadow.

But it is not a fear to which we have ever bowed. We have lived under its immediate threat and we know that the forces of God are stronger. We have seen the poisons spread and we have seen the power of faith that lies in simple hearts resist and destroy the poisons. Unquestionably in Germany there were great numbers of people to whom the service of God had become little more than lip service, to whom security and the desire to preserve their silver teapots seemed of first importance. But when the evil force arose and threatened to tear the love of God from their lives, then the teapots became paltry things to cling to. All their freedoms were torn from them, but the freedom to love and serve the Power that made them they would not relinquish. For this one need alone they found they were ready to abandon their safety and their very lives. And that is why they were unconquerable.

The Kingdom of God within became their sure and invincible citadel. It remains so today during a war which unquestionably tugs at their loyalties. In the midst of the war hysteria they still repudiate the pagan gods, the gods of racial pride that seek to narrow their humanity and turn it to perverse and ambitious ends. In their hearts they know the God that made all races with an impartial hand and they remember the love of the tender Christ and the brotherhood He commanded them to show.

I know that the pagan power has not won them. I know that the pagan power can never win, for God waits His hour when the hearts of generous people in the great Christian lands will turn to His strength to gain His victory.

The Nazis often use a phrase, "strength through joy," but I have not seen it written upon Nazi faces. Yet I remember the joyful strength of the faces in the old Domkirche that last Sunday morning when Luther's ancient battle hymn sounded, and there was no fear in those people after years of persecution and the daily menace that inspires fear in minds that doubt. I have seen that same look on thousands of faces, a look that means more than endurance because it is lighted by hope from within. I know that during this war in one of the smaller German cities an Advent service was held at one of the Confessional churches. The government let it be known that to attend this service which held loyalty to God above loyalty to the state came near to treason, yet there were thirty thousand men who thronged to that one service at that one church.

The fight is just beginning. I who have been there know that the battle is not lost. I who have fought without weapons know the sureness of the final victory. But I know also that the victory is God's and not ours. It is not a virtue to enter a war against pagan forces unless in our hearts loyalty to the things that are God's holds the first and only place. To fight for self-preservation is only a cruel human necessity. To fight for the right to show God's love to our fellows is to move with the great tide of Life that He has set in motion.

And from that Love flows the only strength that cannot be conquered. If there are literally millions of men and women in one oppressed and hopeless land across the Atlantic who alone were able to oppose the powers of evil, it was because their strength was not a poor human strength. Their belief was their armor, and helpless as they seemed in the face of an armed and ruthless power, it rendered them invincible. To men who believe like that, strength rises out of weakness and good is created out of evil. That is the power that shone in Niemoeller's face and sent my father walking courageously and surely past the gates of death. How great a resource waits, then, in this vast and beautiful land where men are free to draw their strength from that belief! How great a hope is ours and how great a responsibility, if in the days to come we are to stand before the world, a people who love the Lord our God with all our hearts and our neighbors as ourselves.

I no longer feel the despair I once felt at being forced to leave the fight before it was finished, for the service of God continues for me in this American land. Perhaps it will be permitted me to tell you who have not seen your faith threatened that your faith is your invincibility. God is not mocked. His day of victory is sure to the believing heart.

My wife has told me of the last time she went to church in

Berlin while I was attempting to make my escape from Germany. My mother had gone with her to see her off on her journey and she and Erika had decided to attend the evening service at a church my father had often attended, a beautiful old stone building which stood in the center of a formal park. On their arrival they found the gates of the park closed and guarded by companies of police while thousands of excited people milled about them, crowding the streets. There was a near riot before the crowd could be turned away, so urgent was their determination to enter the church, but when reinforcements of police arrived and they saw their attempts were hopeless, a change came over the people.

They turned back from the gates of the park and all at once it was as if an orderly procession had been formed. There was no wild defiance but neither was there hopelessness or dejection on their faces or in their squared shoulders. They moved down the street like an army marching. All at once a voice began to sing and then another, and suddenly thousands of voices went ringing skyward in the old triumphant battle song that swelled and rang through the streets with their blatant swastikas, a song that rose in a great cry of hope and filled the gathering twilight:

"A mighty Fortress is our God."

That song they are singing yet, and they will sing it until the day of their deliverance, until the people have learned through pain and blood and courage that to live like men they must love like men, until that day when the fragile reins of power shatter in the hands of the powerful, until the day when men of good heart and stout heart throughout the broad earth reach upward for their hope, until they can see their children born in joy and plow their fields and prune their apple trees in thankfulness, until the Power that keeps the weighty scales of human battles smiles upon His children and tips the mighty balance in His hands—until that day.

The End

THE REAL
"KARL HOFFMANN"

(an afterword by Charles Douglas Taylor, son of Kressmann Taylor)

For sixty years the true identity of "Karl Hoffmann" has remained secret, at first to protect his family in Germany from the Nazis, later because interest in his story had faded with the defeat of Hitler, so that neither "Hoffmann" nor Kressmann Taylor ever revealed his identity. In 1996, shortly before her death, my mother told me, "I have always regretted losing touch with Leopold Bernhard." I had never heard that name, so I asked her who he was. She told me he had been the man whose story she had fictionalized as *Until That Day*. I noted the name, and filed it away. Some years later, after her best-seller *Address Unknown* had been translated into French and republished, editors at Editions Autrement expressed an interest in publishing this second of her books and asked what I knew of the real man and his story. Since I knew almost nothing of him, I sought help from the archivists of the Lutheran Church of America, who were able to give me his professional history in the U.S., his last known address, and, the name of his step-daughter, Thelma. Through her came a thread of leads to three surviving friends and associates, all of whom have been most helpful in creating this sketch of Rev. Leopold Bernhard, the real Karl Hoffmann. You will see in the following account that my mother had to fictionalize much in the way of family details, so as to protect the Bernhard family still in Germany in 1942, when this book was first published.

Leopold Wilhelm Bernhard was born June 15, 1915 in Berlin,

Germany, to parents from two old and well-known German families. His mother, Franziska, was a Bokelmann of Lubeck, of an aristocratic line with university educations, MDs, etc. (Thomas Mann's *Buddenbrooks* is her family's story.) His father, Alexander, was an imposing colonel in the German army in the 1st World War, who walked home from France after the armistice bearing his sword and sidearm, which the French officials allowed him to keep because they admired him so. (The father in *Until That Day* was not Leopold's father, but was modeled on his pastor in Berlin, whom he had greatly admired.)

As a child in post-war Germany, Leopold Bernhard was hungry and sickly. Though his family were well-to-do, they could not get enough food, and were always malnourished. Leopold was to suffer most of his life from the effects of this malnutrition and bare-subsistence diet. His step-daughter recalls that even years later, "he would never again eat oatmeal." He lost teeth, had a bowed back and a bad heart valve from rheumatic fever as a boy, later complicated by meningitis, which he contracted in New York in the 1940s. Yet a colleague of later years recalls him as a man of spirit and energy. "During the years we knew him, Leopold was sick, but decidedly not sickly, nor even stooped."

Leopold was educated at Bismarck Gymnasium in Berlin, graduating Mar. 31, 1933 and at the University of Zurich in Switzerland, where he studied under the eminent theologians Karl Barth and Emil Brunner, graduating Oct. 19, 1936. Because Hitler had frozen all ordinations, and because his active resistance to the Nazi takeover of the church had put his life in danger, Leopold was bluntly told by Otto Dibelius, Bishop of Berlin/ Brandenburg, "Get out!" Somehow acquiring a student visa, he arrived in the U.S. in January, 1938 and enrolled later that year in the Post Graduate School of the Lutheran Theological Seminary in Philadelphia. His father and mother came there later for a visit, and he tried to convince them to stay. But they returned to Berlin, then moved during the war to Dresden, where, his father said, "we will be safe; there is nothing there to be bombed." They were killed, along with Leopold's sister, in the fire-bombing of Dresden, Feb. 13, 1945.

Leopold met his future wife Thelma Kauffman in Philadelphia (Erika was a fictional invention). Thelma was a singer with a beautiful voice, who specialized in church music; she was interested in German Lieder, but needed someone to help with the pronunciation, so she called the Lutheran Seminary. They told her, "We have a man, and he really needs the money." The two were instantly attracted to each other and were married in January, 1940, in Philadelphia. They had no children, though she had a daughter, also named Thelma, from a previous marriage whom Leopold adopted and loved as his own.

Leopold had some difficulty being placed in a parish because of the church division—many were in sympathy with Germany and considered any expatriate anti-German. Finally, he was sent to Honterus Lutheran Church in Gary, Indiana, where he was elected pastor in December, 1939, with the subsequent result that he was finally ordained on May 22, 1940 by the Pittsburgh Synod of the United Lutheran Church in America.

At Honterus, he found himself in a bilingual parish containing many Saxon Germans who were in favor of Hitler—so much so that when news of the German invasion of Czechoslovakia was announced in church, there were cheers. One evening, Leopold discovered a group of parish members in the church, showing a film of the German invasion of Poland, cheering, and raising money for Germany. He stopped the projector, ordered everyone to leave, took the money, and later reprimanded the culprits from the pulpit. Shortly thereafter, he was warned by a dying parishioner, who, on his death bed, told him, "You are in great danger of being killed."

Also, Leopold learned that the German embassy, through the powerful Bund and groups of German sympathizers, was hijacking German defectors in the U.S. and secretly returning them to Germany. So he contacted the FBI, was whisked away, and was placed in an obscure parish in a little town in upstate New York.

Through his friend Herbert Klotz, publisher of Eagle Books, Leopold met in great secrecy with author Kressmann Taylor (whose anti-Nazi story *Address Unknown*, had become a nationwide sensation) to tell his story, which, suitably disguised, would be her next book, *Until That Day*. The author's daughter, Helen Kressmann Taylor was eleven at the time. She says,

> "I remember Mother's trips into New York to meet with the man whose story she was writing; I never knew his name. The meetings were arranged by the FBI. She said he was very much afraid. He insisted on meeting at a different place each time, arriving and departing separately. He would not even ride in the same elevator with her."

With unofficial government backing and private financial support, *Until That Day* was slated for the best-seller list, Book-of-the-Month Club, and movie—but all of that was cancelled after the Japanese attack on Pearl Harbor, which made it unnecessary to raise anti-fascist sentiments in America.

In the United States during and even after the war, Leopold vowed never to return to Germany. He told his friends, "It will take Germany 150 years to regain its soul." He became a U.S. citizen, though with some difficulty, as his step-daughter "Thelma Junior" relates:

> "Daddy was sworn in as a U.S. citizen in Jersey City, along with a group of English refugees. But his papers never came through, and he finally hired a lawyer to trace them down. They had been delayed by the judge who had administered the oath. The judge said, 'If I had known he was German, I would not have let him take the oath.'"

In the Lutheran church of the U.S., Leopold soon began to distinguish himself. After Gary, Ind. (1939-1940); he served as a pastor in Cohocton, N.Y. (1940-1942); Jersey City, N.J. (1943-1945); Brooklyn, N.Y. (1945-1951); Baltimore, Md. (1951-1954); New York City (1954-1960); Chicago, IL (in a new mission at Chicago Medical Center) (1960); Columbus, OH, where he worked with Milton Kotler in establishing a first inner-city neighborhood association (1960-1969); Buffalo, N.Y. (1969-1971); then two churches in Washington, D.C.: St. Peter, (1971-1976); and Reformation, where he was appointed assistant pastor to serve the "Public Affairs Sector Ministry" for the Lutheran Church's Division of Mission in North America (something of a liaison between the church and the U.S. government) (1976-1985). He was active on a number of boards, both for the Lutheran church and for ecumenical organizations, and in urban ministry, writing, speaking, and acting on the problems of poverty.

An associate of the later years, Robert Jenson, now a senior scholar at the Center for Theological Inquiry, Princeton, N.J., recalls:

"The aspect of Leopold's ministry that brought me in was his insistence, first, that the church, as a community with money and influence (however great or little), simply is a political actor, whether it will or not; and, second, that the church's decisions about how to use its power must be theological decisions and not merely ethical or prudential. It is, I think, plain that these convictions grew at least in part out of the German church struggle.

"My association with Leopold began when he was a pastor in Washington, D.C. Leopold and Milton Kotler had founded the first parish-based neighborhood organizing movement, out of Leopold's parish in Columbus, Ohio. They were reunited when Milton came to Washington to

head a unit of the Institute for Policy Studies established to
study neighborhood organization. Leopold become involved
and then brought me in. Milton, Leopold and I ran a seminar at Policy Studies for several years, on questions of civil
religion, and generally on the relation between faith and
civil society.

"Leopold was an associate pastor at Reformation Lutheran,
right behind the Capitol. The 'Public Affairs Sector' program was a program for capitol city people—some lowly,
some quite powerful—involving Leopold's direct conversation and counseling on matters of church and state. More
publicly, it was a regular series of lecture/seminars, on topics
such as 'Can there be a moral equivalent of war?' the role of
faith in policy-decision, etc. I was a frequent speaker.

"During our years of association, my wife Blanch and I
acquired a sort of awe before this man: his character, his
unfailing gentlemanly demeanor, his convictions."

Rev. Leopold Bernhard died of kidney failure on March 2,
1985. For several years thereafter, Robert and Blanche Jenson edited
and sorted the vast bulk of Bernard's writings and other papers,
now in the archive-library of the Lutheran Seminary in Gettysburg,
Pennsylvania. His sermons are still studied there, and his influence
continues in many ways, some of them very subtle, but all sure.

The details of this man's life, though interesting and compelling,
can never really reveal his full impact on his time or on succeeding
generations. Informed citizens beget new and better informed
citizens, wise and courageous ministers inspire new and more
capable ministers, so that a single influence spreads in a multitude
of unknown directions, and there is no measuring an end to the
influence of a man like Leopold Bernhard, whose courage and faith

in the face of tyranny compelled his resistance to Nazism and subsequently his new life in the United States, where his influence, perhaps as unseen as his old identity, may live on and expand through many years and many other generations.

From Leopold Bernhard's 1984
UNFINISHED AUTOBIOGRAPHY
saved, typed, and provided by Thelma ("Thelma Junior") Bernhard
Nesbitt, step-daughter of Leopold Bernhard

PREFACE

Why the book is written: As a reminder to myself of God's amazing grace.

When I arrived in America on January 12,1938, I was 23 years old, I had $20 in my pocket, I had completed my required academic studies in theology, and that was all. Today, 46 years later, I remember that I met and was befriended by a number of the spiritual and intellectual giants of the century. I have been close to poor and despised people and to famous and wealthy persons and to some of the movers and shakers of our time. I have served 14 parishes in the U.S., some of them small and insignificant, some of them well known and influential, not only in but beyond my own denomination. I was part of the United Lutheran Church in America for exactly half of its existence and part of the Lutheran Church in America, its successor denomination, from its beginning in 1962.

Mine was a life filled with great surprises, but above all I am filled with a sense of the profoundest gratitude for my experiences.

Chapter 1

BACKGROUND: My Parents, Grandparents, and Forebears

My father had been an Imperial German military officer. After the loss of World War I and the 1918 Revolution, he became a ProKunst for the Hugenberg Concern, the huge cartel which included some of the most influential newspapers and publishing houses, the film industry, the heavy steel and coal industry, and some of the major appliance and weapons industries, the chief German news service, Deutsches Nachricten Bureau (DNB), etc.

My grandfather, Leopold Bernhard, for whom I am named, was the inventor of corrugated iron and of the iron curtain, the curtain which could contain fire which broke out on a theater stage to the stage, and was the sole manufacturer of these curtains and all the Zeppelin halls in the world and of military barracks for the Imperial German Army. He became a very rich man. He was married to Clara Damke, who came from an old Berlin family. She was very intelligent and extremely self-willed; she wrote and published a number of books of children's stories.

My father was the youngest of four children. His oldest brother Ernst was a recluse. His life was devoted to philosophy, about which he published at least one voluminous book. The next brother was Ludwig, who earned 2 doctorates by the age of 22, one in law at the University of Berlin, the other in National Economy at the University of Vienna. He became Associate Professor Extraordinarius of National Economy at the University of Posen—East Prussia. While he was there he joined Alfred Hugenberg in funding the DNB and the Hugenberg Concern. He remained First Vice President of that organization for all his life. At the age of 27, in 1911, Ludwig was called as full professor extraordinarius to the Chair of National Economy at the University of Berlin at the suggestion of the last Kaiser. His coming there became an occasion for some public uproar because some of the older faculty members, among them the other ordinariis in Economics, objected strenuously to Ludwig's appointment at such a young age as full professor at one of the most famous European universities. The affair ended in a duel between Ludwig and a faculty representative. Ludwig remained at the University of Berlin until his death in 1936. During World War I Ludwig served as Adjutant and councilor to General Ludendorf. In that capacity he prepared the land reform legislation for east and west Prussia, which largely terminated the rule of the Junkers. In 1932, General Schleicher invited Ludwig to become his Minister of Education and Culture, but Ludwig refused.

Grandfather Bernhard died in 1907, before my father had met my mother. He had built his huge villa in Berlin in the 1880's. At that time his friend, the theologian Arnold von Harnack built his villa on the right of the Villa Bernhard. The Deb—? Built on his left. (I know that at least the Villa Bernhard still stands where it was built.) It's a big place with about 35 rooms with a large garden, at one end of which grandfather had built a bowling alley.

Until November, 1913, my widowed grandmother and her three sons lived together in their own apartments in the villa. The three sons had been ordered to remain unmarried and to stay with their mother until she died. My father was the only one to disobey that COMMAND. He and my mother married on November 13th, 1913. It was an act which grandmother never forgave. But her anger was not directed against my father or against his four children, but against my mother, who suffered ill treatment and coldness from her mother-in-law until grandmother died in 1938, by which time I was already in the U.S.

Ernst and Ludwig continued to live with their mother until both died, Ernst in 1935 and Ludwig in 1936; grandmother had to bury her two oldest sons.

For reasons unknown to me, the manufacturing business did not survive Germany's defeat in the First World War and its consequences, the 1918 Revolution, and the inflation of the early 1920's. The villa and the factory buildings were the chief remains of a once huge fortune. The villa was grandmother's possession together with the remaining money. The factory and its buildings and installations had been willed to his four children by my grandfather, but the income from the factory went to my grandmother until she died. Income was produced by leasing the factory complex to other manufacturers, an ample income for grandmother's lifestyle.

My liveliest memories of Grandmother are as follows:

1. Christmas Eve
2. December 27th, Grandmother's birthday, celebrated with an annual gathering of what the previous century knew as "the Salon," a glittering assembly of many of Europe's outstanding figures from politics, academia, and the arts.
3. Afternoons at Grandmother's with hot chocolate and fairy tales told by her. I was between 5 and 10 years old.
4. Playing in Grandmother's garden with school friends like the Weiszcieckers. Richard(?) who is now Mayor of Berlin, Friederich who is now the world famous physicist and philosopher.
5. Uncle Ludwig—three instances of personal conversation with me.
6. Ludwig's funeral in the Villa Bernhard. Among the mourners [were] many of his colleagues, former and current students, among whom was also Prince Louis Ferdinand of Hohenzollern, oldest son of the Crown Prince and grandson of the Kaiser. He had taken his doctorate under Ludwig, and Ludwig's intercessions with the Kaiser ended with his permission for the first extended visit of Louis Ferdinand to the U.S.

My father's older sister Johanna had married Herman Kuttner, who was a very famous surgeon and occupied the chair of surgery at the University of Breslau. I found some of his students practicing in the U.S. They proudly showed me their copies of the textbooks on surgery written by Kuttner. Johanna and Herman had three boys and one girl. The youngest, Joachim, became a meteorologist and nuclear scientist. He was brought to the U.S. after Germany's defeat in the group of some 300 nuclear scientists, one of whom was Werner von Braun. For years I knew nothing of Joachim's whereabouts. Actually, I only saw him twice in the U.S. After each of his brief appearances her would disappear again into the most secret places of NASA. His oldest brother, Ludwig, was an architect and became one of the leading "city builders" of Germany after the war.

Herman Kuttner had been a member of the ancient student

fraternity or "Studentenkorps" "Tubinger Schwaben." It consisted of the very select group of students among whom traditionally was, *primus interpares*, the King of Bavaria. Dueling was required activity for all members. This kind of "Korps" produced men with those very visible facial scars which in Germany and for Germans denoted members of the aristocracy and the very upper class. For that reason the church forbade students of theology to join fighting fraternities. The church could not use pastors whose very faces announced pride of class.

My maternal grandfather, Wilhelm Bokelmann, and his two sons, Otto and Karl, were also members of the "Tubinger Schwaben." As "old gentlemen" of the Korps, both Wilhelm Bokelmann and Herman Kuttner used to attend the annual social activities of their Korps and both were accompanied by their wives and daughters. Actually, there were only the Bokelmann girls, Frieda, the oldest of the Bokelmann children, and Franziska Bokelmann, who was a raving beauty, a girl full of spirit, and a fully trained budding pianist. Johanna insisted that her youngest brother, Alexander, had to meet this beautiful, talented young woman. Alexander, the young officer who was quite the eligible bachelor, good looking, wealthy, musical, social lion and ladies' man would in his sister's judgment be interested in Franziska. So in 1910 she persuaded Alexander to join the Kuttners at the festivities at the University of Tubingen. There Franziska and Alexander met. He was impressed with her beauty but rejected the suggestion of his sister to continue to see Franziska in Berlin. She was 17 years younger than he and had none of his sophistication. But when, two years later, they met again, they did fall in love and got married. The wedding was one of the spectacular social events of the 1913 season in Berlin.

Franziska and Alexander are my parents . . .

The Bokelmanns and the Vermehrens:

My maternal grandmother was a Vermehren. Both these families are old aristocratic families. The Vermehrens were one of the leading families of the Free Hanse City of Lubeck. They were of the ruling class already in the year 1000 A.D., when the Hanseatic League was at its height as one of the dominant world powers. The Bokelmanns were landed gentry in the Schleswig-Holstein many centuries ago. They became academicians, physicians and lawyers and servants of the State and Church. Schleswig was and is a border territory in the north of Germany which in the course of the centuries changed hands between Germany and Denmark many times. Wilhelm Bokelmann, my great-great-great-grandfather served as Danish ambassador to the court of Napoleon. The French used to call him "Beau Cel Mann." He married in Paris a girl from a leading French family. Wilhelm Bokelmann, my grandfather, used to say that as a child and a young man he never knew on awakening in the mornings whether he was Danish or German.

Hannah Arendt, in her book *Rachel Varnhagen*, has some very interesting things to say about my great-great-great-grandfather, Wilhelm Bokelmann. The Jewish community of Berlin had urged Hannah Arendt to write about the beautiful Rachel Varnhagen because she had been a well-known, well loved and highly esteemed Jewish lady who had nearly 200 years ago been a respected member of Berlin's most exclusive social set. The Jewish community besought Hannah Arendt to write this book in order to show, as the Berlin Jews told her, "that we were in Germany, even in Berlin society for a long time." Rachel Varnhagen was introduced to and accepted by Berlin society through Wilhelm Bokelmann, my direct ancestor.

In the late 1960's I met Hannah Arendt in Washington. She was so delighted to meet a linear descendant of Wilhelm Bokelmann that she accompanied me to St. John's Church on Lafayette Square to hear Brahm's *Requiem*, cutting short her attendance at Congressional receptions in her honor.

A part of the history of the Bokelmanns was published privately. I have a copy of this booklet and would like to include somewhere in this book one of the anecdotes told there. One Bokelmann was the chaplain to the duke of Schleswig-Holstein. When the Duke returned victoriously from one of his many wars, a Service of Thanksgiving was ordered to be conducted. For the service, the Duke, his family and his officials were present. The chaplain thanked God for the safe return of the Duke and his soldiers and for the victory he had won. Then the chaplain continued, "When we ask ourselves whom did our gracious Duke serve with this war, we must answer, 'the Devil and his grandmother'." At lunch the Duke said to Bokelmann, "Father, that was strong bread this morning in church."

In the last four generations occasional signs of deterioration appeared in some members of the Bokelmann family, something that can be found in many of the very old families. An aunt of my grandfather's suffered from attacks of depression.

They used to call it melancholia. In one of those attacks she committed suicide. My grandfather, who was a physician, hesitated for that reason to get married. While he had received his classical humane training at the famous Gymnasium, the Katherinaeum in Lubeck, he rented a room in the house of Marie Vermehren, who lived with her young children in a big house. Her husband, Jules Vermehren, founder of the first life insurance company in north Germany, had died at the age of 39 of the cholera in Stockholm where he had gone on business. His widow raised her several children by renting rooms and furnishing meals to Katherinaeum students. By the way, she managed to send all her boys to the Katherinaeum and then to the University and all her girls to finishing schools. Her youngest daughter, Hedwig, had a contralto voice of exceptional beauty. She studied at the Conservatory in Berlin and after that was sent by her oldest sister, Emilie, for private study with the famous Viardo Gaicia(?) in Paris. Emilie earned her money as a governess for 20 years in England and for 30 years in America (where she learned to like corn flakes). She returned to Lubek at the turn of the century and lived together with her only unmarried sister, Frieda, in a lovely little house with a wonderful little garden. To my mother's generation and to us, these two remarkable women were simply "Die Tanten" (the Aunts). They played a major role in the lives of my mother, her sister, and her two brothers, and in the lives of my mother's children. In fact, when the first World War was beginning to show signs of obstinate persistence and painful difficulties for Germany, my father closed our house in Berlin and asked "Die Tanten" to take his young wife and her son for the war's duration. "Die Tanten" agreed joyfully. When in 1917 my mother gave birth to a pair of twins, a girl, Maria, and a boy, Dietrich, "Die Tanten" found room for them also. My earliest memories of my parents and of the twins go back to Lubeck.

While a boarder at Maria Vermehren's house, Wilhelm Bokelmann had fallen in love with Hedwig, the youngest of the 11 children. But he was young and naturally had to continue his education and establish himself in his chosen profession before he could think of settling down. He chose as his field, medicine, and as his university, Tubingen. On completion of his training he specialized in gynecology with stress on obstetrics. As a medical student he had to witness the last public execution by beheading. The sight so deeply disturbed him for such a long time that he felt he had inherited melancholia, should not get married, and under no circumstances should have children. He finally opened his practice in Berlin. There he happened to hear Hedwig in a concert. Soon thereafter they were married.

Earliest Memories

I was born in Berlin in Grandfather Bokelmann's hospital for women, with Grandfather himself as the attending physician. It was June 15th, 1915. My father was at the Russian front. He had been wounded in one of the early attacks in the summer of 1914(?). Upon his initial recovery he became military governor of Allenstein in East Prussia. Mother took me there in the fall of 1915. We stayed there for several months until father was ordered to the western front.

My first memory is a walk with my father in Lubeck. I can still see Father's grey pants leg with the red stripe and feel my enormous pride of keeping up with the grand soldier who was my father. I recall being taken in to see the newborn twins for the first time and was told I pressed my forefinger and thumb together and said, "Make dead."

My memory jumps ahead to a grey, cold November evening in 1918. We children were allowed to stay up after our bedtime to greet our father who was to return from the war this day. We saw long columns of soldiers return without music while silent crowds lined the streets. The day wore on but Father did not come. Finally Mother insisted that we children go to bed. And it seemed to me that I had hardly been asleep when a huge figure in full uniform with epaulets and side arms came into the room and Father bent over me. He had returned. Later I learned that Father was one of the few officers who had come home in full uniform with all insignia intact, with pistol and sword only displayed. And Father had come from Li—? through all of Germany, through the midst of revolting soldiers and destructive crowds of laborers.

(*Two pages after this have been torn out.*)
There is no more.
T.

1943

CURRICULUM VITAE

My name is Leopold W. Bernhard. I was born in Berlin, Germany, on June 15, 1915, to Alexander Bernhard, then an officer in the army, and his wife Franziska nee Bokelmann, daughter of Professor Dr. Bokelmann, a very noted physician. My grandfather, Leopold Bernhard, was the owner of great iron factories in Berlin and was an inventor of some repute. He was a confidant of the Kaiser's and the close friend and neighbor of His Excellency the Rev. Dr. Adolf von Harnack whom my grandfather had introduced to the Imperial Court. In Harnack's biography written by his daughter, Agnes von Zahn, it is also noted that my grandfather was a kind and helpful man who provided for many a theological student's education and upkeep. His second son, my father's older brother, Ludwig Bernhard, was Professor of National Economy, Law and Philosophy at the University of Berlin. He was an outstanding figure in German economic and political life. He was a close friend of the Hugenberg's and together they founded the great newspaper trusts, movie industries and a holding company for German "Heavy Industries." My father, who resigned from the army after the last World War, became a director in that company.

My mother's family shows a long line of diplomats and physicians. My mother's oldest brother is chief physician of Robert Koch University Hospital in Berlin and Professor of Medicine at that university. My mother's family is an old, aristocratic Hansa family and can be traced back, always in positions of leadership, to the year 1070.

I went to the Bismarck Gymnasium in Berlin and took my Arbiturium in March, '33. In May '33 I began to study theology at the University of Berlin. Among my teachers there were such excellent men as Sellin, Deizmann, Lietzmann, Seeberg etc. Because of the beginning of the Nazi persecution of the Church I left Berlin to study at the University of Zurich, Switzerland, in October '33 where I finished my theological studies, and on October 19th, 1936, took my final theological examination. I then returned to Germany after the small Lutheran Church of Switzerland had explained to me that they had absorbed as many German pastors as they possibly could. My attempts to come to an agreement with the Church in Germany failed because I refused to sign a written promise that I would preach the Gospel in accordance with Nazi doctrine. I took part in the struggle of the section of the Church which centered around Niemoeller and had many experiences both heartening and disastrous. Then I was advised that my usefulness in the Church-fight was over because I had exposed myself too much and would therefore be put into concentration camp. I attempted to be accepted for service in some Lutheran Church outside of Germany. Finally the Biblical Seminary in New York City offered me a scholarship and I arrived in the United States in January '38. During the summer of '38 I worked as a canvasser for the Board of American Missions and in the fall of '38 I went to the Post Graduate School of the Lutheran Theological Seminary in Philadelphia, where I studied for two semesters. In the summer of '39 I worked for the Refugee Committee of the National Lutheran Council in New York City. In December '39 I was sent to supply Honterus Lutheran Church, Gary Indiana, and was elected pastor there. In January '40 I married Thelma nee Kaufman, a member of Atonement Lutheran Church, Philadelphia, to which church her parents and grandparents had also belonged. On the strength of the call to Honterus I was ordained into the ministry by the Pittsburgh Synod in May '40. In December '40 I accepted the call to Zion Lutheran Church, Cohocton, N.Y. I was pastor there until September '42 when I had to resign my pastorate because of a severe heart ailment. For the treatment of this ailment I came to Port Washington, N.Y. under the care of Dr. Apolant. I underwent a thorough treatment and I am now dismissed by Dr. Apolant as completely cured.

My great desire is to serve again in the Church of our Lord and to use the talents He has entrusted to me to the building of His Holy Church and the glory of his name.

Leopold W. Bernhard

Printed in the United Kingdom
by Lightning Source UK Ltd.
117937UK00001B/172-180